I0600948

CRADLE GIFT

Faerie Legacy Series, Book 2

PATRICIA BOSSANO

WaterBearer Press

CRADLE GIFT

Faerie Legacy Series, Book 2

Copyright © 2013 by Patricia Bossano.

All rights reserved. No part of this book may be used or reproduced by any means, graphic, electronic, or mechanical, including photocopying, recording, taping or by any information storage retrieval system without the written permission of the publisher except in the case of brief quotations embodied in critical articles and reviews.

Published in the United States by WaterBearer Press
Escondido, CA 92030
www.WaterBearerPress.com

Because of the dynamic nature of the Internet, any web addresses or links contained in this book may have changed since publication and may no longer be valid. The views expressed in this work are solely those of the author and do not necessarily reflect the views of the publisher, and the publisher hereby disclaims any responsibility for them.

Cover design and art by Tamra Gerard

Identifiers:
ISBN: 978-0-9994-346-3-5 (hc)
ISBN: 978-0-9994-346-4-2 (sc)
ISBN: 978-0-9994-346-5-9 (e)
Library of Congress Control Number: 2017914939
BISAC: Fiction, Young Adult Fiction: General / Fantasy / Magical Realism / Fairy Tales, Legends & Mythology / Coming of Age / General / Epic / Saga

This is a work of fiction. All of the characters, names, incidents, organizations, and dialogue in this novel are either the products of the author's imagination or are used fictitiously. Any resemblance to actual persons, living or dead, events, or locales is entirely coincidental.

Manufactured in the United States of America

WaterBearer Press Edition: October 2017

Al correo de las brujas y las brujitas.
May we live on and prosper.

ACKNOWLEDGMENTS

Cradle Gift has been a true team effort—I couldn't have done it without this group:

Lynda West Scott, for her infinite patience and generosity, not to mention her competence as a copy, line, and content editor.

My critique group: Christy, Lynda, Michele, Natalie and Drienie; their input was invaluable during the polishing stages of my work.

My parents, Luis and Blanca, for their unconditional and never-ending support.

I am thankful for the love of and for my children, which fuels the desire to bring my literary dreams to fruition.

My sister, Cuqui, for her encouragement during the *Cradle Gift* journey—she's had the patience to read the thing several times.

The constant optimism of my younger sister Silvia and of my beautiful nieces and handsome nephew.

My numerous cousins and the collection of aunts who play no small part of this project; they are the ultimate troop of faeries and I love them all.

All my friends and colleagues, whose confidence in me urges me to ever higher attainment.

And you, the reader—thank you for eagerly awaiting this second installment to *Faery Sight*—even though it is a little behind schedule.

PART I

A Cradle Gift

Fair Fey, for this babe I beseech your favor. Accept this milk—a humble peasant's offer. Bestow upon this child not a curse but fair fortune and all things mild.

But Fair Fey will do as she pleases. She may think, What *fairer fortune than flying with Faery when the moon is full;* where *fairer than where one's desire becomes the setting;* when *fairer than the very hour it pleases Faery?*

Fey takes the child through the veil dividing one world from the next—there the child learns what others cannot yet know, beholds what no human eye has seen, and grasps what has been for times unknown.

Chapter I

From her hiding place behind a jar of cotton swabs, a cloaked figure with luminous, aquamarine eyes peered unblinking at the tag fixed to one of the bassinets in the nursery:

Maité Bottini-Santillán
D&TOB: 21-JUL-1992 3:58 a.m.
Mother: Alba Santillán-Bottini
Father: Sósimo Bottini

Barely two hours old, she thought. Her eyes shifted irritably to the heavyset nurse who continued to fuss over the sleeping babies. *I need only a few minutes.* She bit her lip and transferred the weight of her body to the leg that didn't hurt as bad. She leaned against the coolness of the jar and squinted in the half-light, wishing the nurse would leave at once.

Watched by the luminous eyes, the woman shuffled across the hall to the nurse's station; she picked up a cup of something steaming, brought it close to her face, and took a whiff. However, not until she fell into whispered conversation with the other nurse on duty did the cloaked figure fully come out from behind the jar to better examine her surroundings—a harsh fluorescent strip of light from the hallway cut into the amber glow in the nursery.

Seeming to gather a shape from the shadows, the shrouded figure shifted her height and emerged in human size on the sanitized floor.

She staggered several steps toward the object of her attention, swaying a little. She doubled over with her scraped hands on her knees for support and settled her aching limbs with a series of calming breaths.

Feeling somewhat steady and careful not to disturb the other bassinets, she made her way to the second crib on the third row. She clutched its acrylic edge, overcome with a mixture of relief, exhaustion and excitement. A hoarse sound, like a pained groan, issued from under the frayed hood of the indigo cloak, "This is the one."

With a trembling hand, she touched the baby's smooth forehead. Maité's eyes opened as the woman began to speak.

"*Egun on, Maitagarri*," she whispered. "*Bai*, little one, it has been a long time since I last bestowed a cradle gift." With a grimace, she drew back the hood of her cloak. A mass of disheveled blonde curls streaked with turquoise tumbled down her shoulders, making her quiver with pain. Nevertheless, she smiled as she spoke to the baby.

"But I am here now," she said, trying to ignore the dull pain spreading from the gash on her shoulder to her scraped forearm and wrist. "It is I, Nahia."

She knew full well Maité would not remember or understand this moment for years to come—fifteen, to be precise, as custom dictated.

With her good arm, Nahia reached into the crib and loosened the blanket the nurse had wrapped so tight around the baby. "There. That is much— better," she said, scanning the room as she wiped the beads of sweat from her temple. "Now ... to the point ... my, *Maitagarri*."

Something in the relaxed atmosphere of the nursery shifted, and the smile on Nahia's lips faltered and then tightened. A moan escaped as she lightly pressed her side to soothe the ache there. Nahia's confidence in the energy barrier she'd conjured wavered for a moment.

I couldn't have been followed, she decided, choosing to believe she had time. A faint humming drifted into Nahia's range of hearing, causing her heart to beat double time and her cheeks to flush with dread. She feverishly went over all the details of her recent escape.

"She was unconscious—I made sure!" Nahia insisted even as she searched the room again. Her eyes narrowed, straining in the half-light to make out the source of the hateful sound. She hoped it was a trick of her nerves.

"Time is short," Nahia said, looking down on the infant Maité.

Her wounded arm hung limp and useless. Her breath came in clipped bursts, keeping time with the throbbing slash on her thigh, and she felt certain her ankle was badly sprained, if not broken.

Nahia had fought well, vanquishing the three subordinates the Beautiful One set on her, whose orders were to drag Nahia underground. There they would have demanded Basajaun from Nahia and forced her to resurrect the realm. To have escaped a trap—one set in her own home, no less—was poor consolation now that she knew the truth: the Beautiful One stood poised to usurp Nahia's throne, and over the past decades, the Beautiful One had plotted to destroy Nahia upon her return.

Yes, Nahia had fought well. It wasn't her first victory and would not be her last battle against the greedy Beautiful One.

Nahia shook her head, dismissing the thoughts. "I must not delay," she declared, raising her good arm over the crib so her palm hovered above the baby. The hum started again and became louder. Nahia ignored it. "I will not have time to give you all I intended."

Nahia's eyes darted from one corner of the room to the other as the gift poured out of her. "It will have to be dreams, little one, my *Maitagarri*. Seek the truth in your slumber. Your dreams will take you into the world of others."

Despite the fears assailing her, Nahia uttered the words in a sing-song intonation that filled the room like a choir. Fragrant jasmine petals issued from Nahia's hand as she spoke, falling around Maité and sealing the charm.

Beads of sweat gathered again like dew on Nahia's porcelain brow. "Beware of the—"

The humming became a hiss, closing in around Nahia; she could hear it outside the building, lapping at the walls. She cocked her head to one side, her eyes narrowed into slits. Fear and rage in equal measure overtook her.

Time is up.

Mingled with the unnatural buzz, Nahia detected the virulent laughter she knew so well. *This is the real trap*, she realized at last, and the enormity of the plot appalled her.

Nahia's gaze flitted from the open doorway to the four inky corners of the nursery, and back to Maité in her crib. Still nothing—just the frenzied pounding of her heart in her chest.

"Beware of the Beautiful One," Nahia warned again, ready to depart, but as her eyes took in Maité's small face, she became disoriented by the baby's eerily wide-open and seemingly focused eyes. Maité made a tight fist around Nahia's little finger and clung fast to it.

Overwhelmed with tenderness, Nahia's next words came in rapid bursts. "This is all I can do, *Maitagarri;* they are approaching." She leaned over the crib to kiss the fist, which was strong enough to bind Nahia forever, yet so vulnerable it could be crushed as easily as the jasmine petals surrounding Maité's small form.

Panic set in. "If I brought her to you—" Her words were a guilt-ridden groan.

Nahia pressed her lips into a thin line. "The Beautiful One won't know the truth; I promise you that much. Her ignorance will be her undoing!" She gently lifted the baby's foot and bent down to kiss it, tears of longing gleaming in her eyes.

"*Agur, Maitagarri.* Beware."

Nahia's last words to Maité hung in the air as she shape-shifted. She funneled into herself and now stood a fifth of her former human size. Suspended midair above the crib in the compact size most comfortable to her, Nahia glanced with regret at the baby, aware she was taking too long but hesitating anyway, until a cracking noise broke through the droning hiss.

A horrible laughter drowned everything else, and a surge of adrenaline wiped out Nahia's pain. She gritted her teeth; her energy barrier had been punctured.

"They don't have me yet!" she fumed, as the protective barrier began to deflate around her.

No time to conjure a repair, only escape.

With a swift horizontal shift toward the door, Nahia hastened out of the nursery and passed the nurses' station undetected. She found a partially open window at the end of the hall and squeezed through the narrow gap into the cool air outside. Nahia propelled herself forward with all her might—so eager to escape, she only fleetingly glimpsed a wall of red vapor materializing in front of her.

As Nahia rushed forward, the thick mist stopped her momentum with bone-cracking force. She plummeted like a rag doll toward the concrete sidewalk four stories below.

Nahia twisted in the air and saw the hateful creature, *the Beautiful One*, hovering above the window. The blazing red eyes glared at Nahia's falling body with detached contempt, but the instant their eyes locked, the creature lunged downward, as if pulled by a magnetic force, and Nahia felt herself snatched from the grip of death a fraction of a second before hitting the ground.

Still rattled by the collision with the deceptive vapor, and drifting in and out of consciousness, Nahia caught glimpses of the red locks and the smoldering eyes of her enemy. As they rocketed into the air, the pressure of gravity pounded on her temples.

What has she saved me for? Nahia wondered and then trembled at the possible answer.

"Whatever gift you gave her means nothing. That baby is nothing." The Beautiful One's syrupy voice snaked into Nahia's ear, overwhelming her with loathing and despair. "She will have no power over me. She is no better than her ancestors."

Nahia collected her wits while the redheaded creature appeared to search the sky for a suitable route.

Nahia felt a shift in their direction. *East.*

The Beautiful One let out a haughty laugh but then leaned in close to nuzzle Nahia's neck. Her lips grazed Nahia's ear as she whispered, "Do you realize you are now in my debt?"

Nahia gasped. The effects of the collision seemed to be lifting. She needed to fight, but her limbs wouldn't respond.

"For now, however"—the throaty voice went on while she pried Nahia's mouth open with her fingers—"a little something for the crossing?"

The hated laughter rang in Nahia's ears while the acrid paste smeared into her mouth liquefied on contact.

"No!" Nahia cried, her mouth working clumsily to spit out the potion, but she couldn't help swallowing it and the numbness spread down her throat. Her tongue felt like a stuffed flannel cushion. Very soon her limbs would be immobilized.

Nahia's eyes took on a marble-like appearance as the paste worked through her. Her turquoise-streaked curls flailed in the fierce wind snatching tears of rage from her eyes.

Soon we'll be crossing the ocean. Soon, I'll be trapped underground. How will I keep my promise to Maité?

"Ederne, stop," Nahia murmured feebly, or thought she did. She fought to keep her eyes from closing while the Beautiful One's—Ederne's—laughter clanged in her ears.

Nahia lost the battle against the effects of the strong potion. Ederne's flawless face bathed in moonlight was the last thing Nahia saw before her eyes closed.

The air already smelled of salt.

CHAPTER 2

Fifteen years later.
Bottini-Santillán residence

A flowery scent lingered on Maité's pillow. She breathed it in, weightless in that sparkling place between dreaming and waking.

Jasmine, she thought, relishing the fragrance, which triggered the recall of her dream.

Maité saw the jasmine petals like a nimbus around a baby's head and thought, *Around my head; that baby was me*. She felt the woman's kiss on her foot before the woman took her leave. Then Maité saw her, limp and helpless, in the arms of another, the redheaded creature who had whisked her through the air.

East.

Fear for the woman with the turquoise streaks momentarily overwhelmed Maité, causing her to fully wake.

Most of the dream slipped immediately beyond her conscious reach. The fact that the nursery in her dream smelled exactly like her pillow didn't register.

But it didn't matter; July 21 had dawned.

"I'm fifteen today," she said, stretching on to her back with a pleased grin. It flickered into a frown when she realized her head was at the foot of the bed. How had she come to be so turned around? She tossed her pillow back to its rightful place and tugged at the sheets around her—she'd rolled herself twice in them.

An image flitted into her mind of a pair of scraped hands loosening a baby from a tight blanket, but before Maité could follow the thread back to the dream she'd nearly forgotten, she heard her parents, Sósimo and Alba, already busy packing downstairs.

8

"Happy birthday to me," she sang to the two faeries in their chrome frames on the wall. She imagined they winked at her, and Maité winked back. With one last tug, she freed her legs from the sheets and got out of bed. A quick glance at the clock on her bedside table told her the fun she anticipated was only two hours away.

They'd been planning her birthday celebration at Pineview Reservoir for days. At ten in the morning, Maité, her parents, and the Allens—Verónica and her husband, Michael—plus Emily, Maité's best friend, and Emily's younger brother, Gabriel, would be on the road, hauling two jet skis and four inflatable rafts, plus two buckets full of sand toys, towels, and chairs for everyone.

Maité couldn't imagine a better way to spend her birthday and couldn't wait for the day to begin.

Maité and Emily helped unload the van. They took the last cooler between them and set it down on the sand by their chairs. Maité stood for a moment looking at the sparkling water, convinced all of nature schemed to pull off this perfect day just for her. She took off her long T-shirt and set her squatty chair at the very edge of the water. She wore a white bikini she knew she looked pretty good in. Maité was lean, though rounded in all the right places, and the white bathing suit accentuated her glimmering tan, or her *sepia coloring*, as Emily called it.

Maité's wild mane of dark-blonde hair dangled in a thick braid over the back of her chair, almost touching the sand. Her stormy gray eyes peered at the blue water through white-rimmed sunglasses. It was eighty-seven degrees and she thought the conditions heavenly.

Beside her, Emily, lanky and freckled, thoroughly marinated in SPF70 and wearing a tankini and board shorts, dug her toes into the wet sand.

Maité's lips curved upward, noting her friend's head moving from side to side. Emily's analytical hazel eyes, shaded by a baseball cap, followed the foam football as it passed between two boys waist deep in water. When one of them emerged from a splashy dive for the ball, shaking water off his hair and looking at Maité, Emily muttered, "Showoffs."

"What?" Maité asked, feigning indifference even though she'd also been watching the boys' performance.

Emily let out a snort. "Boys."

"Let's go play ball with the showoffs and cool down," Maité suggested.

Emily pursed her lips but stood at once. Maité laughed, held out her hand, and let Emily pull her out of her chair.

They passed the football back and forth with the boys for a while and then helped Emily's little brother, Gabriel, dig holes in the sand.

When her mother, Alba, pulled cupcakes from the cooler, their group of six, plus the two boys who'd apparently decided Emily was okay even if she threw better than they did—surrounded the picnic table and sang for Maité in a very entertaining jumble of languages: Sósimo in Italian, Alba and Verónica in Spanish, and everyone else in English. When they finished, except for Gabriel, who kept piping up with "and many more on channel four, and a big fat hen on channel ten ..." there was a smattering of applause, even from people beneath neighboring umbrellas. Maité took a bow, punctuating it with a delighted, "Grazie, gracias," and a "thank you."

"I guess this will do—I mean, in place of a *quinceañera* party," Emily said, giving Maité a one-arm hug and touching her cupcake to Maité's as if they were champagne flutes.

"It's great, isn't it?" Maité beamed.

"You should've gone out with Finn," Emily said through a mouthful of frosting.

"If only I were allowed to date, and if only he hadn't gone out of town for the summer," Maité replied, feigning a sadness she didn't feel because she preferred a small circle for special occasions. She treasured the feeling of belonging to a family. And these six people—Alba, Sósimo, Verónica, Michael, Emily, and Gabriel—were her family. They belonged to one another. "Today's perfect!" she said, taking a huge bite of her own cupcake.

"Yeah, cuz you're weird." Emily grinned, thumping Maité on the shoulder.

Chapter 3

That night in bed, Maité let out a contented sigh. Showered and moisturized, her skin still held on to the heat of the day, but the breeze coming through her open window soothed it. Downstairs, Sósimo played his violin.

Maité fell asleep without realizing it, like a reel starting on cue as soon as her eyelids closed, she began to dream.

In her dream state, she recognized the woman with the porcelain face right away, even though she hadn't given her—or the dream of the nursery—a conscious thought all day.

Maité noted that the air smelled of pine, and the sand at her feet felt and looked like sugar.

"Fly with me," the woman said without moving her mouth.

Maité frowned trying to remember the woman's name. When she couldn't think of it she shrugged, stood on tiptoes and stretched her arms over her head.

The woman's eyes sparkled with humor, and tinkling laughter filled Maité's ears. "Not like that!"

How else am I supposed to fly? Maité thought, bristling.

"Like this," the woman instructed. She pressed the palm of her hand on Maité's belly.

A rhythmic pulsation, or a flapping of something large, began in Maité's midsection. In her sleep, she shuddered helplessly as the bizarre flapping tickled, making her feel breathless and light as a feather.

The woman drew her hand away and peered at Maité with impish delight stamped on her face. They were airborne—the ground at least a mile below. Maité shrieked in surprise, waking herself in the process.

Maité stared at the ceiling of her darkened room as her heart settled into a more regular beat. *This was no regular dream,* she thought. A faint, feathery sensation still lingered in her stomach. She laid her hand over it, shuddering a little and feeling like she might laugh. Maité stifled the giggle and shifting her thoughts to the experience itself, she readily identified all she'd seen, heard, felt and smelled. She'd known her own thoughts as well as the thoughts of the woman with the aquamarine eyes. And all of it together gave the dream a feel of reality that puzzled her.

Maité wanted to deny the feeling, to call it all a vivid dream or maybe even a memory, as strange as that sounded, but she kept coming back to the odd sense it hadn't been a dream at all, or a memory. The thought of it being a *jaunt* prowled in tantalizing circles in Maité's mind.

That's crazy! That would mean I left my room—that I was somewhere else, without my body.

Maité shook her head, torn between possibilities. She focused her eyes on the largest plastic star on her ceiling, the one still glowing faintly because she'd turned her light off barely half an hour before.

Could it have been real? she wondered, but before an answer came to her she drifted off to sleep, exhausted from the sun-filled day.

Three weeks later, after many such dreams, Maité awoke with a start, wondering when, if ever, she'd get used to the bizarre sensation that overtook her at the moment of waking. The instant she docked with her body, a guilty feeling hit, as if she'd sneaked away to do something illicit without her parents' knowledge.

"But I was with Mom this time," she muttered.

Although unsure what to think, she realized this was a first because so far, her dreams hadn't included anyone she knew.

Maité flung the covers off. Once again she was upside down on her bed. She shuffled downstairs, pulling her hair into a knot at the top of her head as she went.

Sitting at the kitchen counter, a stricken Maité watched her mother, Alba, sip coffee and listened with increasing distress as her mother recounted her own dream of the night before.

"It was the most beautiful place I have ever seen. Do you remember our trip to Sedona last fall?" her mother asked with a delighted smile.

A thin layer of sweat broke out over Maité's body. Her own dream had been about Sedona, but last night's Sedona hadn't been the desert haven they'd visited.

In the dream Maité shared with her mother, Sedona was on the West Coast.

Wiping her forehead with the back of her hand, Maité remembered her mother raving in their hotel room last fall about a notion that the red rocks and dirt of Sedona would make a striking contrast with a blue ocean.

"Wouldn't such a sight be fabulous?" her mother had exclaimed, completely carried away by her fancy.

In Maité's dream last night, Sedona became just that, and she had joined her mother there. But now, listening to her recite back the conversation they'd had as they walked barefoot on the red sand, admiring the red rocks ablaze in the setting sun, it seemed more than Maité could handle.

"What is it, amor?" Alba asked.

Maité started, "Um, nothing, Mom." She shoveled a spoonful of cereal in her mouth to hide her confusion.

Her mother continued recounting every detail of the vivid dream, "Does it sound crazy? It was so real, I tell you, I wouldn't have been surprised to find sand on my feet when I woke up this morning."

Maité held her breath, dreading what was to come—*for sure, Mom saw the third person in my dream*—and her stomach churned.

"I loved being there with you, sweet girl, and I was so disappointed when it ended," she mused.

Maité blinked several times as her mother continued. "I think that boy coming out of the water made me wake up."

This was it. Yes. The boy also woke Maité, cutting the dream short.

"I couldn't tell who he was because of the sun behind him, but the sight of an intruder upset me and woke me..." Alba's voice trailed off.

Maité squirmed in her seat. She hadn't seen the boy's face either, but that didn't matter. She knew him: Finn. Her face turned a deep shade of red.

"Are you all right?" her mother asked, putting a hand on her daughter's shoulder. Maité took another spoonful of cereal, nodding tensely.

While Alba turned to rinse her coffee cup in the sink, Maité made up her mind to confide in no one, *ever*, about the true nature of her dreams. Who knew what kind of situations might crop up in her nightly alter-life? If they were to involve Finn, she absolutely did not want her mother as a witness. Better to let her believe these were only dreams, an excess of subconscious images making beautiful movies through the night, rather than the shared astral flights Maité now had every reason to suspect they were.

Besides, Maité felt certain her mother wouldn't call this *normal*. A vision of her own head stuck full of electrodes, tracking brainwaves, popped into her mind. *Not happening*, Maité thought fearfully. *I'm not crazy.*

In her bed that night, Maité bit her lip at a sudden realization: she dreaded but also looked forward to falling asleep.

Resolutely, she poured over her dreams again, hoping to define their nature once and for all. The memory of the visit in the hospital nursery seemed incomplete at best; all that remained of it was the lady with the luminous eyes who'd been Maité's regular companion in the evenings following. Somewhere in the back of her mind, there was also the chilling, throaty voice full of menace in a nursery filled with innocent infants.

Maité figured there had to be a connection between the first dream and how her experiences changed afterward. She believed the lady had a lot to do with her dreams becoming like trips out of her body.

To that, Maité added a new feature: she'd been able to break into her mother's adventure last night. This made her wonder if she'd be able to get into anyone's dreams at will. It would be worth a try to bring Finn, fully and three-dimensionally, into even one of her jaunts, but so far she could never make out more than an indistinct shape, usually against a shimmering horizon.

Maité continued to turn the new ability over in her mind but got nowhere, although as she drifted off to sleep, two words swirled in her head: gift and weapon.

CHAPTER 4

First Day of High School

"Freshman year, M. You ready for this?" Emily asked, absorbed in pulling the frayed laces of her dirty sneakers. With a frustrated "humph," she tucked a torn piece of lace in the pocket of her khaki shorts.

Leaving her shoe untied, Emily looked at Maité, who had yet to reply. "Well?"

"As ready as you are, I guess." Maité sighed, glancing at her new surroundings. In the early morning, a slight breeze made the temperature pleasant, although by noon it would be sweltering—August in Ogden couldn't be otherwise. Maité wrestled with the nervous flutters in her belly.

Soon the bell would ring, and they'd be entering the austere building of Our Lady of Grace Catholic High School, where a whole new era would unfold.

Somehow, none of it seemed real—Maité had a gut feeling high school would be a short-lived experience, and it colored the blue-sky morning in forbidding tones as she held tight to the guilty secret of her dreams. Hadn't her mother said bad dreams must be told so they wouldn't come true?

But they've all been good dreams. I don't need to tell, she thought.

Hordes of kids went through the front doors and into the halls lined with lockers.

Emily, looking boyish and gangly, tapped her foot impatiently, and Maité wished it were possible to sneak some of Emily's confidence and contentment, because she could feel herself growing queasier as the start of day drew nearer. More than ever, she sensed a storm brewing.

"Well, so do you feel older?" Emily insisted. "More mature?"

"I haven't been fifteen for a month yet, Em. How can I feel older? And I'll tell you what—I'm stressed about my driving test."

"Puh-leez! It's only multiple choice. You'll do fine," Emily assured her, accompanying her remark with a hearty clap on the back.

Maité grinned. "Still, I wish we could take it together. I'd feel better. You know, my mom said if I want to, I can wait until your birthday in September."

"Gasp, M! Don't be such a wimp!"

Maité chuckled at Emily's diligent execution of the orders given to her: Verónica had instructed Emily to stop rolling her eyes, to quit gasping loudly, and in general to refrain from the extravagant expressions she made a bad habit of. Now Emily *said* them rather than *did* them.

"You can totally do this. Noah said it's a piece of cake. Takes ten minutes, tops. He's had his permit for a week now," Emily declared.

The bell rang. Maité shuddered but picked up her heavy school bag and followed Emily behind a few stragglers. They milled through the crowded hallways, where other students slammed locker doors and slung equally heavy bags over their shoulders on their way to first period.

"Sigh! This week should be a breeze—nothing but introductions and class rules," Emily, who'd memorized the orientation pamphlet they'd received in the mail, remarked.

They entered the sunny biology lab and picked a long table in the back of the room with two stools tucked under it. A microscope with its accompanying Petri dish stood on the table, gleaming in the sunlight.

"First day and already we have a substitute teacher," Emily commented. She read every piece of news published on the Our Lady of Grace website. "Do we know who she is?"

"Not a clue," Maité said, hanging her book bag on the hook fixed at one end of their table. Emily did the same.

"Please take your seats," barked a businesslike voice belonging to the man who marched into the room. He headed straight for the teacher's desk. Those who were still fiddling with their bags or visiting with friends quickly shuffled to their tables. Eighteen pairs of eyes shifted expectantly to the short man who had yet to look at them, seemingly entranced with rifling through the pile of papers he'd pulled from his leather briefcase.

He wore a crisp white shirt and gray trousers. His shoes looked like they'd been shined that morning. The wire-rimmed glasses, sitting perfectly straight on the bridge of his nose, gave his clean-shaven face an air of precision. He held up a single sheet of paper, and without looking at the students, he began a brisk roll call.

"Cody Aames."

"Here."

"Carissa Adams."

"Here."

"Emily Allen."

"Yup."

The teacher's eyes behind the wire-rimmed glasses flickered toward Emily.

Maité pressed her lips tight and whispered out of the corner of her mouth. "You've just been cataloged."

Emily shrugged.

Eventually, the teacher arrived at "Matey Botany."

A series of muffled snorts from the other seven tables greeted the fumble, and the teacher again peered at them. With a patient grunt, Maité raised her hand. She wished her parents had named her Mary, or Julie—anything that didn't require constant spelling and phonetic maneuvers—but being the daughter of Spanish and Italian emigrants, a simple name seemed too much to ask for.

The teacher nodded. "Yes."

Maité stood up, gave a quick tug on her white polo shirt, and smoothed her plaid skirt.

"You tell him, M," Emily whispered at her side.

"It's pronounced My-teh, Boh-tee-nee, sir," she said politely.

"Thank you, Miss *Bow-Teeny*," he replied efficiently.

Maité didn't have to look to know Emily was rolling her eyes.

With all eighteen students present for first-period biology, the teacher returned the list to his briefcase and walked to the center of the room with his hands clasped behind his back. He eyed them sharply for a few seconds, as if trying to spot troublemakers and slackers. Everyone sat up straighter, and although Maité didn't dare look at Emily, she could picture the defiant expression that had surely fixed itself on Emily's face.

He paced slowly as he spoke in a businesslike manner, "Your teacher, Ms. Carlson, asked for a two-week leave," he explained. "But I was informed this morning that because of personal circumstances, she won't be returning after all. Although I was on a sabbatical, I have agreed to take her place for the duration of the school year."

Maité and Emily looked quizzically at each other, as did the students at the other tables. It was too soon to make out whether this was good or bad news.

"My name is Mr. Marx."

Out of the corner of her mouth, Emily wondered, "Any relation to Karl?"

Maité bit her lip to keep from grinning.

"I plan to teach you something you wouldn't normally tackle until your junior or senior year, but as I happen to hold a master's degree on this subject, you are privileged to gain the knowledge now."

The students exchanged more puzzled glances, this time not just between partners but between tables as well.

"So," Mr. Marx barked. Maité flinched, along with half the class. "Genetics."

"Gasp!" Emily let out a strangled whisper as her fingers grasped the edge of the table. "I love Karl—I mean Mr. Marx," she said fervently.

Maité stole a glance toward her friend. Emily's hazel eyes danced with excitement. She loved science—genetics in particular.

First-period biology was a success.

At the end of those fifty minutes, their heads were filled with fascinating new words such as *eukaryote cells, chromosomal aberrations, alleles,* and an entire host of terms holding the answers to life in their meaning. Or so Mr. Marx had implied while Emily squeezed Maité's hand excitedly for the twentieth time.

Maité sensed this subject *did* hold an enormous truth but hoped to grasp it as a whole, rather than break it down into nano-parts, as Emily surely intended to do. When the bell rang, the students returned the sample slides to their storage cases and headed out with furtive glances toward the genetics giant they'd spent nearly an hour with. Their murmurs of "See you tomorrow, Mr. Marx," were said in earnest as they filed out of the lab and into the hall.

Maité left the room looking amused. Thanks to Mr. Marx, she now saw herself as a genetic composite, a quivering collection of cells—like the ones on the slide—in constant motion and eternal interaction with one another, each answering to that miraculous command center called the brain, which dictated how a cell's energy should be spent.

"Oh! Heads-up about Mason," Emily said when they were barely two feet out the door. "Now that you're fifteen, he'll be hounding you for a date. He's been waiting since sixth grade, you know."

"See you in English lit, *matey*," Lorenzo Sanchez teased as he squeezed between Maité and Emily on his way out.

"Roll my eyes. You're so hilarious!" Emily called after him, shaking her head, but when he only waved back and winked, she turned to Maité and scolded her. "Already attracting the attention of sophomores, are you?"

Maité *did* roll her eyes dismissively at Lorenzo's back. "We compared schedules a couple of days ago when my parents had them over for dinner, but the question here is, why oh why, did you have to tell Mason my parents' rules about dating?"

"Hey! The boy's my neighbor. He, like all people, hates to wallow in ignorance, and if I have it in my power to shine a beacon of knowledge, however trivial it might be, then I will."

"Well, I'll thank you to shine beacons of your own knowledge next time, not mine, you lunatic!" Maité said in mock outrage. "And get going or we'll both be late."

"See you later," Emily called back, already being swallowed by the grind of students on their way to second period.

CHAPTER 5

Maité hurried down the long hallway to her next class, eyes focused on the worn carpet, hoping not to run into Mason anytime soon.

"Mason," she muttered, dreading the awkwardness of having to turn him down, or even worse, being too chicken to reject him and actually ending up on a date with him. Maité cringed at the thought of Mason's hopeful glances. How she wished they were from somebody else.

Now if Finn Hayes asked her out, that would be an entirely different proposition. Maité had been looking forward to her fifteenth birthday, nursing a secret hope that Finn would notice her. She'd never spoken to him, but she had seen him every Sunday at church since he and his family moved to Ogden the year before. But Finn was a junior, and juniors didn't generally notice freshmen. To make matters worse, Finn always had a thick ring of admirers orbiting him wherever he went. And the bottom line was, even if he did notice Maité, her father would never allow her to date someone older.

"Hey, you."

Startled, Maité looked up at Finn. She was already at the door of her next class, and Ms. Simmons's voice came from inside. "Please take your seats."

But Maité stood paralyzed, foolishly noticing how thick Finn's eyelashes were. "Uh …"

"I'll talk to you after class, okay?" Finn whispered as he brushed past her to a seat three rows behind the only other empty chair.

"Young lady, are you supposed to be here?" Ms. Simmons asked when Maité lingered at the door.

Flustered, Maité replied, "Yes, ma'am." She took the empty seat and unclenched her arms from around her books, which she'd been holding to her chest. She set them down on the desk and took a deep breath, trying to quiet her heart.

While Ms. Simmons rattled off her introduction to world civilizations, Maité could do nothing but imagine Finn's eyes fixed on her back.

He's three seats behind me, she kept thinking with a flutter through her midsection. Maité hoped her hair lay smooth rather than frizzy, in case he was looking at it.

When the bell rang, Maité took her time gathering her books before casually casting her eyes in Finn's direction. Three giggling satellites blocked Maité's line of sight. As much as she wanted to linger and give Finn every opportunity to talk to her, an impulse inside her, the one that often stirred up her pride, made her shove her pencil case in her bag and leave the room without a backward glance.

Had Maité looked, she would have seen Finn crane anxiously over Sienna Barnes's blonde head and sag in powerless disappointment when she, Maité, walked out the door.

During fifth-period geometry, Maité and Emily met up again, but Mr. Randolph's class was hardly the place to discuss Finn's possible intentions. The white board was covered in lines, angles, and letters—all of it entirely too intimidating; it commanded every bit of their attention.

"I saw Finn," Maité managed to say while worksheets were handed out, and she promised to spill the details during lunch.

After geometry, they hurried to their lockers and exchanged their books for bagged lunches. Their mothers seemed to be the only ones in the entire school who weren't fans of a lunch account. They sidled through the crowded hallway and reached the sunny courtyard while almost everyone else headed to the air-conditioned cafeteria.

All four sections of the school building converged onto the large flagstone courtyard, at the center of which stood a koi pond with a statue of the Virgin Mary, arms outstretched in welcome, on a pedestal fitted with spouts. Maité and Emily sat on the wide brick lip of the pond and began going through the contents of their lunch bags. The Koi were no more than orange blobs drifting lazily in the murky water, now and then disappearing beneath the waxy green leaves of lilies. Water trickled soothingly from the four spouts at Mary's feet.

Maité swapped her pear for Emily's banana and her Oreo cookies for Emily's shortbread. Through a mouthful of peanut butter and jelly, Maité said, "I almost had a heart attack when I saw him standing there. He actually said, 'Hey, you' to me." She swallowed.

Emily focused on stacking her crackers with cheese and round pieces of turkey. "'Hey, you'? That's it?" She glanced up from her six-tiered cracker tower. "That almost gave you a heart attack?"

"Well, then he said he'd talk to me after class," Maité added, looking embarrassed.

"Roll my eyes! And what did he say after class?"

"I left without talking to him."

"Geez, M, why?"

Maité defended herself. "He was surrounded."

"He always is. He's always gonna be surrounded. I mean, my goshness, he's only the hottest guy in the state!"

"I couldn't just stand there pointlessly, waiting like an idiot for his guard to clear, could I? Or worse, try to break through the ranks of—of swoony, twittering girly girls!"

"So you guys didn't talk at all after class?"

"Nuh-uh," Maité said, her mouth full of peanut butter again.

"This is the lamest situation ever!" Emily said looking aghast.

"Thanks a lot."

"Sigh. But I guess the day isn't over yet."

"Finn's too polite for his own good. He can't ever walk away from them, it's so annoying. It happens even at church." Maité tore open the package of shortbread cookies.

"The guy is shy, and girls take advantage of that," Emily commented matter-of-factly. "Specially that Sienna Barnes; she's a snake."

"Still, if he wanted to say something to me, he should do it, don't you think?"

"Sure do! The boy is a spineless worm."

"I wouldn't go that far. He just needs to be a little more assertive," Maité shrugged.

"Right. A couple of sessions of Rudeness 101 with Milo ought to take care of him." Emily laughed, and Maité joined her. "Or," Emily went on, "*you* could talk to *him*."

Maité sobered at this. She pictured millions of smoldering *blush* cells racing to her cheeks. "And say what?"

"Duh! How about, 'What did you want to talk about earlier?'"

Seventh and eighth periods crept by in the stuffy classrooms. The sun beat down on the building, seeming bent on baking them. The portable air conditioners did nothing to cool the rooms, and Maité found herself longing for September and its cooler temperatures. The notes in her book grew less legible as the close of day approached. She felt certain a headache was on the way and rubbed her forehead to ease the tension. She couldn't stop thinking about Finn. She turned over several openers in her mind until at last she narrowed them down to two: *Hi, Finn,* or *Hey, Finn.*

Maité had almost made up her mind to stop by his locker, which was right outside her eighth-period art classroom and take charge, as Emily suggested. What could be easier? Yes. She'd take the initiative. She'd talk to him.

The bell rang, and Maité's resolve steeled. She snapped her notebook shut and put away the ceramic horse that was to be her art project for the first quarter.

Out of the corner of her eye, she saw Finn. A shiver went up her back. He was already there, and it seemed he was looking in her direction.

Could he be waiting for me?

She drew in her breath and felt her face heat up. *Here I go.* Where in her brain did the command to blush come from? She needed to disable it.

She started across the hall, her gray eyes fixed on Finn's blue ones. He swiped his hair away from his handsome face in one smooth movement, and a flicker of a grin lit up his expression.

He does *want to talk to me.* Maité started to say, "Hi, Finn," just as a squealing someone torpedoed into her, shoving her off course.

"Ooooh, Finn! You won't believe what happened!"

Never mind what *had* happened, all Maité saw as she straightened up from her near crash into the row of lockers lining the wall was the back of Sienna's blonde head as she threw her arms around Finn's neck.

This time, Maité saw him crane over Sienna's head with a regretful expression on his face.

She tramped away to her own locker feeling disappointed and bitterly annoyed at his helplessness. She pictured herself grabbing a handful of Sienna's hair in her fist and laying her flat on her back.

"And then what?" she muttered. "It would be my turn to talk to him?"

The very thought of having to fight for a turn to talk to a boy made her cringe. "Not happening. No way."

Outside, after Maité relayed the fiasco, Emily patted her on the back but didn't get a chance to say much.

"Hey, girls!" Mason said, hailing them jovially. His face was covered ear to ear in pimples, and Maité felt certain it must hurt him to even smile. But Mason looked ecstatic to at last have caught up with her.

Maité wanted to crawl underground as she gave him her best deadpan look. "Hi," she said, barely opening her lips.

"So I was wondering …" he began. Emily elbowed Maité significantly. "Would you like to go to the movies with me on Friday night?" He beamed, undaunted by Emily's presence or Maité's cold reception. In fact, he appeared unaccountably confident.

Maité squirmed, catching a flash of his brace-covered teeth strung with rubber bands as he waited for her response. A piece of whatever he'd had for lunch still lurked there.

"Um, well …" Maité fumbled for words to excuse herself from the unendurable. "I can't. I, um, I'm not allowed to date."

"Naw-uh! You turned fifteen this summer. You're allowed now," Mason argued though his eyes flickered toward Emily for confirmation. He clearly didn't want to doubt the virtue of his informant.

"Yeah, I know that was the original plan, but my dad changed his mind a couple of weeks ago …" Emily elbowed her again, but Maité was on a roll and plowed ahead. Besides, she still felt miffed over Emily having told Mason about her dating rules. "He said fifteen is too young, and now he doesn't want me dating until I'm sixteen."

"That's too bad!" Finn said. He'd come up behind Maité and must have heard the entire story meant for Mason, and Mason only. Finn slapped Mason on the back with a grin. "Tough break, my friend."

Mason looked stunned; his lip had caught on his braces midsmile, so he appeared to be snarling.

Crestfallen over Finn hearing her lie, Maité sagged and Emily commiserated by squeezing her arm.

"Can you talk some sense into your dad?" Mason implored with desperate hope.

Maité smiled in spite of herself at the expression on his face, but Finn's presence made her feel uneasy. Both boys looked at her expectantly, and Maité wanted to die, or at least vaporize whatever brain cells made her say her dad had changed the rule. *What was I thinking?*

"No such luck," Emily piped up when Maité didn't respond. "Your best bet is to wait 'til next summer." And with that, she turned toward the line of cars waiting to pick up students. "Look, my mom's here," she said, dragging Maité away.

Mason waved forlornly at Maité as she turned to follow Emily, but Finn caught her by the wrist. She whirled around and gazed into his eyes, surprised.

"I'm sorry about earlier," he said, giving her a resigned look.

"It's okay," she assured him before he let her go.

"I'll catch up with you tomorrow," Finn called after her and she nodded.

Maité made a fist around her wrist where he'd touched her, it felt tingly still. She got into the backseat of Verónica's car and stared at Finn, who stood watching her and looking vulnerable without his ever-present giggling entourage. She hoped to convey to him in one glance that the "new" sixteen-year-old rule had been a lie—that she'd love to go out with him—to the movies, to dinner, bowling even!

He did mean to ask me out, she kept thinking, and she wanted to kick herself for not being more assertive and honest with Mason. *I'm an idiot!*

She waved sadly, and Finn raised his hand in response as Verónica's car pulled out of the parking lot.

Emily's overexcited chatter about surprise genetics already drowned out any other sound in the car. Maité pictured a cluster of *stupid cells* saluting the brain and tripping over themselves to carry out the order to blurt out idiocies. She felt beyond angry with herself.

"What a silly thing to have said, mi amor," her mother said, when, after much prodding over her daughter's funny attitude, Maité finally told her the details. "And now you've put yourself in a position where you'll have to admit you lied or wait until your next birthday to go out with this boy."

"Oh, it's just as well, Mom," Maité grumbled, stretching her arms over the kitchen table and putting her forehead to the tiled surface. "He's a junior. It's not like Dad would let me go out with him anyway."

"A junior, huh?" her mother said as she smoothed her daughter's hair. Maité turned her head and looked sideways as her mother went on. "Dad would say no to dates with juniors or seniors, it's true, but this, Finn, is it?" Maité nodded. "He could come over for dinner sometime, or go with us to the movies, you know?"

Maité raised her head, smelling hope in the air. "Really?"

Alba smiled in that disarming way of hers, which Maité's father proclaimed would hold him spellbound and blissfully married even in the afterlife. "Sure, mi amor, I don't see why not. That way we can get to know him and ..."

The kitchen door flew open, and in came her father, Sósimo. "And how are my beautiful ladies, eh?"

Alba stood up to kiss her husband, and Maité sat up straight, hoping to give no hint of her agitation over the possibility opened up by her mother. Her mind rolled rapidly with thoughts of Finn having dinner with her in this very kitchen.

That would be great! Mom will smooth it over with Dad, and I'll get to see Finn away from his fawning fans. I'll get him all to myself. Then a sobering thought occurred to her. *Will Finn mind? Finn—soccer-team captain. Finn— "hottest boy in the state," as Emily puts it. Will he think it's ridiculous? Dinner with a boring little girl like me?* Maité's fantasies faltered.

"What's going on?" her father asked, looking suspiciously from his wife to his daughter.

Alba flashed Maité a nearly imperceptible wink. "We're plotting," she said with an engaging smile, "We don't want to cook, so we're plotting."

"Ah! You want my famous risotto with clams. Is that your plot?"

"I thought we might go out, since your daughter has survived her first day in high school."

"Ah, *bella figlia*! So you have." He hugged and kissed Maité. "We go out then!"

"Actually, Dad, your cooking sounds way better," Maité said, hugging him back.

CHAPTER 6

Maité lay in bed that night listening to her parents on their way to their room, laughing quietly over one of the many things that made them happy. She smiled too, looking at the glowing stars on her ceiling.

"I'll dream about Finn tonight," she whispered, closing her eyes and wishing wholeheartedly to see him. She clung to the thought that maybe when he grabbed her wrist, something had been triggered. Though the effect of their physical and visual contact circuited between them with synaptic speed, Maité felt it had been enough to establish a connection. *It has to*, she thought feverishly. She convinced herself his touch was the required catalyst to gain access to Finn and couldn't wait to get started.

Sleep caught Maité off-guard. While still worried about Finn, her breathing grew rhythmic, and beneath her lids, her eyes began to swivel in haste.

She found herself on the bleachers, staring at the perfectly tended soccer field at Our Lady of Grace. A shirtless Finn, standing in the penalty zone with his back to her, gleamed with sweat. He was surrounded by half a dozen of his teammates. Practice was over. One of them jerked his chin up toward where she sat, and Finn turned to look. He started toward her, grabbing his crumpled t-shirt on the way and pulling it over his head. Maité wished he hadn't.

Not a single groupie hovered. In a flicker, Maité realized it was because she was dreaming, and so was he. She quickly put the thought out of her mind; she wasn't about to lose this dream. She had hours and hours to spend with him, if only she stayed asleep.

Finn waved and motioned for her to meet him halfway.

Maité commanded her dream self, "Get up and walk over to him."

"So I finally get to talk to you," Finn said, standing so close Maité could see the hair wet with sweat stuck to his neck and forehead. His damp shirt clung to his torso.

"And without your fan club," she teased.

He laughed sheepishly. "So here's the thing …"

Maité braced herself. Staying asleep would be tough through this one. She felt breathless and on the verge of waking with excitement.

"I had a lot of trouble in Spanish last year, and I can't have it mess with soccer. If my grades drop my parents will make me quit the team."

Maité thought the ground beneath her shook a little. Had she heard right? That had to be the strangest, most unromantic opener anyone ever used.

Maybe he's nervous.

But Finn kept talking, "Anyway, my mom told me you guys speak Spanish, you know, you and your mom? That your mom is even a translator and interpreter."

Maité nodded, even though she couldn't believe what she heard. She felt glad her tendency to blush at the slightest discomfort or confrontation didn't exist in her dreams. In fact, if she could see her dream self now, she might even look a little pale.

Finn continued, oblivious to her turmoil. "I figured this year I'm going to start strong with Spanish and keep it up to the end."

Maité stared at him disbelieving. Finn spoke like he was laying out the strategy for a soccer match. Not a trace of nonacademic interest showed on his face, not a flash of attraction toward her, not a glimmer of romantic intentions hidden in his words.

This really is about saving soccer. Her shoulders sagged. Emily would understand and relate, but Maité couldn't fathom how blind she'd been.

"I did this to myself!" she groaned.

"Did what?" Finn asked.

"Oh, nothing, not a thing!"

"So what do you think?"

"About what?"

"About getting together maybe once a week? You know, to go over whatever we've covered in Spanish?"

She wanted to just shove past him and leave him on his own to resolve his stupid soccer problem. But she also wanted to kiss him, so much.

This is a dream. The thought flashed into her mind. Not a gift or a weapon: a tool.

Her heart thumped in her chest, threatening to wake her, but before that could happen, Maité grabbed his face in both hands and pulled him to her. She tasted the salt on his lips, and she was so into the luscious moment that all chances of waking disappeared.

But Finn didn't close his eyes. He didn't respond at all, he just waited for her to finish, as if this was the type of nuisance he was accustomed to putting up with. Maité's grip slackened.

How many girls have done this to him? The idea jarred her painfully. She'd sunk to the level of his fan club. She'd taken a kiss from him—one he didn't mean or even want to give, all to gratify her own feelings.

Where is my dignity? She almost woke herself with humiliation. She let go of him with a sigh and walked away.

"So is that a yes or a no?" he called after her.

Maité let out a resigned humph. She turned and took a couple of steps toward him. "I like your one-track mind, Finn Hayes," she said, thumping him on his chest with mock displeasure. "Ask me again when you wake up."

Maité opened her eyes and glanced at the clock on her night table: 3:30 a.m. She rolled onto her stomach and stifled a groan in her pillow, beating it with her fist for good measure.

"Do I want to tutor the boy?" Her face grew hot in the dark. She was glad that to Finn, the whole thing had been only a dream. He'd never know that, like one of those giggling satellites she deplored, she'd taken a kiss from him.

"I'm no groupie! But I did get my kiss." She smirked in spite of her shame and then frowned. "I won't ever do that again."

She finally relaxed enough to get some sleep. Her last thoughts before dozing off were of being fresh-faced the next day when Finn talked to her.

"I'll be his tutor, for crying out loud!"

Finn did talk to her the next day. Maité studied his face as he spoke and felt relief when she couldn't detect even a hint that he remembered the dream, and in the end, she agreed to tutor him.

Emily took on the job of assistant with her usual gusto and proved to be quite innovative. During their entire freshman year, Maité met with Finn once a week in her kitchen, much to Sienna Barnes's displeasure. Maité's parents got to know him very well and liked him a great deal.

By the end of the school year, Maité had made an older brother of him, and Finn relished the role to the point of being annoying. Maité lost track of how many boys he discouraged from pursuing her. The more she wanted to strangle him for it, the more her father seemed to appreciate him.

Lulling Maité into a false sense of security, sophomore year came without any storms breaking. She and Emily now had their driver's licenses and carpooled in an old four-wheel drive Jeep Wrangler they'd bought with their savings.

Finn graduated with the highest marks in his class in Spanish, but his passion for soccer earned him his scholarship to the University of Utah. He was brilliant at it.

"You'll be playing for Real Salt Lake in no time," Maité told him as she and Emily watched him pack for a short summer trip with his parents.

At her side, Emily nodded. "Remember, I was the one who thought of combining Spanish reviews with penalty kicks."

"Couldn't have done it without you," Finn replied with a grin and a smack to Emily's shoulder.

Maité laughed, remembering the thousands of times she and Emily guarded the goalposts while firing verbs at him. Finn had six soccer balls lined up along the penalty line, and he kicked one for each conjugation. In no time, he effortlessly conjugated any regular or irregular verb flung at him. And his kicks, even with two girls scrambling to block them, hit the back of the net with mind-blowing precision. With Finn playing forward, that was a deadly skill they'd helped him hone.

"I'm gonna miss you at school next year," Maité told him, and Emily nodded briskly at her side.

"I won't be far. Besides, I'm still gonna screen your dates." Finn winked, and Maité caught the raised brow he gave Emily.

"You're turning informant?" Maité exclaimed indignantly, glaring at Emily.

"It's for your own good." Emily shrugged and Finn laughed.

"Then you're forcing me to be sneaky about it," Maité warned them. "I might just have to get on a plane and fly across the world to find me an unsanctioned date!"

A sense of having sealed her fate with those words overwhelmed her, instantly quelling her good humor.

CHAPTER 7

San Sebastián, Spain

A sleek black limousine, a one-of-a-kind Lamborghini, idled on the street in front of the chic Martín Berasategui Restaurant, just after noon in early June.

People strolled by in the sunshine, ogling the magnificent vehicle, which sported the front end of the 2003 Gallardo model. They craned their necks with undisguised curiosity, hoping for a glimpse of its occupant through the tinted windows. The public knew Eva must be inside.

Eva, the astoundingly magnetic new face for the sports-car manufacturer, was one of their own, a Basque, and they were immensely proud of her.

It seemed she'd come out of nowhere just that spring, and had taken the Parisian runways by storm. Rumor had it that looking at twenty-seven-year old Eva through the lens of a camera was the only way to survive the confounding effect of her beauty. A mere sighting of the woman resulted in immediate and well publicized riots; everyone wanted to touch her, to glimpse her up close, to catch a single syllable she uttered. They longed to experience the corporeal touch of her voice, throaty and lingering, something that bred bliss in those lucky enough to be within earshot. To see the red, cascading waves of hair, the fiery glance, the legs—oh, the legs! The full red lips!

Men all over the globe seemed struck dumb by Eva. The last pictorial on GQ, of her on the hood of the Reventón roadster wearing little more than her long hair, had men and boys of all ages forswearing their birthright for her to so much as breathe in their direction.

In the cool interior of the limousine, Eva held a cell phone to her ear while lazily twisting a lock of her hair between her fingers.

"Do you see him?" the solicitous male voice at the other end of the wireless call asked. It was Eva's agent, Sergio, known in fashion circles as Gio.

Having decided she needed someone to "handle" her, Eva contacted Gio out of the blue one afternoon. Being as gay as they come, Gio was the ideal

31

person to do Eva's bidding; she simply had no use for a man who became inarticulate at the sight of her. Gio jumped for joy when she contacted him. Of course he accepted straight away; who wouldn't want to be Eva's agent?

"No, he hasn't arrived yet," Eva replied, inspecting the black and white photo of a very good-looking man in his early sixties, on the leather seat beside her. *Older, but very well preserved.*

"From what I've learned of him these past couple of days," Gio said, "he's the punctual sort."

Eva took a deep breath. Her eyelids closed momentarily as she focused on her next move. When she opened her eyes again, her pupils fastened on the man himself. He stood on the steps leading up to the restaurant entrance. Stately and charismatic, he exuded wealth.

"Yes, Gio," Eva said in her trademark languorous voice. "I see him now."

"Happy hunting, gorgeous."

Mr. Fernando Gonzaga had no clue what was about to hit him.

In a matter of days, pictures of Eva on the arm of her older but irrefutably well-bred and handsome beau were splashed on the covers of every high-profile European fashion magazine. Irate young men across the planet resented the man's good fortune. Speculations abounded regarding Eva's true intentions in choosing such an ill-matched partner, mostly because of his age, but Eva seemed to have eyes only for him. The buzz was that while on a weekend escapade to Monaco, within a week after their first meeting, he'd asked for her hand in marriage, but Eva had refused him. Hope kindled in the hearts of her male fans as this bit of gossip spread like wildfire. Mr. Gonzaga, however, held fast to his trophy.

Gio let slip to the press that Eva imposed a condition upon her acceptance: a prewedding gift—a formidable token of Mr. Gonzaga's devotion. Her fans splattered the social media with their hopes that she'd asked for something he couldn't give and he'd have no choice but to give her back to them.

In a nest of down pillows, caressed by the Mediterranean breeze wafting in from the villa's terrace, Eva voiced her request to him in syrupy, throaty murmurs, putting the ball in his court.

"That land belongs to my late wife's family," Mr. Gonzaga confessed, bitterly helpless to grant this goddess her single wish. "I cannot dispose of it. Only my daughter has a right to it."

Eva stared at him, her eyes ablaze.

Unbeknownst to Mr. Gonzaga, Eva's mind leapt ahead to the disposal of this newly revealed obstacle: his daughter.

CHAPTER 8

At one o'clock in the morning, five weeks into summer vacation, Maité tossed and turned under the influence of a very vivid dream. As if launched from her pillow, she sprang to a sitting position, a scream wedged in her esophagus. Her nightshirt stuck to her trembling body. Her ears rang, and the bad dream fizzled out of her consciousness, leaving her anxious and disoriented. As she fumbled to free herself from the tangled sheets, she wondered at the indistinct surroundings. Everything felt off; even the window was on the wrong side of her bed.

"What is this place?"

A creaking noise in the quiet room—one not caused by her—made her jerk with a surge of bewildered fear. She saw another bed with someone in it.

Emily, Maité thought relieved, the nightmare completely forgotten for the moment.

The digital numbers on the clock between the beds read 1:23.

Rubbing her eyes, she stumbled out of Emily's room, her footsteps muffled by the thick carpet on her way to the bathroom. A series of subconscious flashes arranged themselves in her mind to dispel her grogginess.

I'm staying with Aunt Verónica. I'm sharing Em's room until Mom and Dad come back from their anniversary trip ...

Her mind organized thoughts and events neatly, though at a sleepy pace. The house seemed too quiet. Her throat felt dry, and she wanted a drink of water before heading back to bed. As she closed the bathroom door and flipped on the light switch, her eyes were struck by a billion shiny explosions. Blinking, she looked in the mirror at her disheveled ponytail and puffy eyes, and ran the faucet while her brain continued itemizing.

Mom and Dad will arrive tomorrow afternoon—they're flying back from Guadeloupe—

A choking gasp reached the top of her throat but went no further. Cold water ran over her fingers, which she closed into fists as the horrifying dream speared her mind with monstrous intensity. She groped for the hands she felt certain were squeezing her heart, but there were none.

Oh my God! A knotted string of wails pressed at her tonsils but could not get through.

Mom! Dad! Maité's legs quaked, refusing to hold her up. She bent over the sink to support herself, breathing in ragged spurts while the nightmare garishly played itself out.

Let it be just a nightmare! A harmless nightmare. She repeated the words, hoping to make it so by just thinking it. *Only a wicked, awful dream.*

"Dulce Virgencita, cúbrenos con tu manto ..."

Her mother's prayer had drawn Maité from the safety of Verónica's home while she slept, and at once Maité found herself inside a small space filled with clattering noise. She splayed her arms for balance until she found a flat surface to support herself. The boxlike space dipped with dispiriting groans, like riding an old roller coaster and knowing the rails would soon disappear beneath the cart.

"Mom, Dad," she said, but her voice came out broken, like bad radio reception. So was her body for that matter; she seemed to flicker between solid and mist.

Sósimo had one arm around Alba's shoulder, while the other cradled his wife's head against his chest. Maité stared at them, perplexed, and then at what she could make out of her surroundings. She realized she was inside a very small airplane.

The rickety machine dropped fifty feet, and Maité screamed, but no sound came out of her mouth. The pilot's greasy brow flickered into view with every flash of lightning outside. She could see the control dashboard with all its switches and dials. The pilot kept pounding on it as if he were giving it CPR. "Work!" he ordered. "Work! *Work!*"

The needles on the dials fluttered pointlessly.

"Damn you! Mayday! Mayday!" the pilot growled, while Alba's lips moved in a silent prayer that buzzed in Maité's ears in spite of the noise around her.

Bolt after bolt of lightning eerily illuminated the sheets of rain outside. Maité cleared her throat and tried to speak but couldn't. Her arms hurt from the strain of keeping herself steady.

"Figlia! Ti amo, figlia!" Sósimo called in desperate surprise over the pilot's angry maydays. Alba raised her head and stopped chanting. Their wild, unbelieving eyes fell on their daughter.

"Maité!" Alba shrieked.

Though still confused, Maité understood what was about to happen. She focused her panic-stricken eyes on her parents. "Mom! Dad!" Her voice didn't break this time.

"I love you, Maité. You must be strong, little girl!" Alba shouted through the din. "Don't be afraid for us, mi amor!"

"I won't ever forget you!" Sósimo added hoarsely, his eyes glazing, as if transported by the sight of his daughter miraculously inside the cabin.

"This thing is gonna split down the middle!" Maité screamed, trying to brace herself more securely in the shaking compartment. "Where are the parachutes? We have to get out of here!" she cried in desperation, but even as she said it, Maité knew it was hopeless.

"It's too late, my love. Please, *please* always remember how much we love you!" Alba pleaded.

Lightning lit up the cabin in blood-red flashes, allowing Maité precious seconds to see the anxious, shaky smile on her father's face. Her mother looked frightened, though reconciled to her fate, as tears welled in her eyes. Sósimo's brawny arms wrapped around Alba again.

"Maité, it will be over soon," he said, his voice shaking with emotion as much as with the rough jostling of the doomed craft.

"I'm sorry, folks," the pilot said to her parents, oblivious to Maité's presence. "We're going down."

"What?" Maité's said. "What does he mean? We're supposed to go see the Redwoods next week, remember?" Her eyes darted from one point in the cabin to another.

Why am I thinking of Redwoods? We're gonna crash! She reached out frantically but almost tumbled to the floor when she let go and had to brace herself again, "Mom, Dad! Wait!"

The plane pitched downward; Maité fell against the narrow divider between the passenger cabin and the cockpit and could no longer move. Her mother and father were almost above her, dangling by their seatbelts. "Mom! Dad!" Maité shrieked, "why is everything red in here?"

A pair of strong hands pulled Maité off the wall and pinned her arms to her sides while shoving her toward the exit of the plane. She fought back. All was chaos. How had the greasy pilot managed to get a hold of her? He'd do better to remain at the controls.

Why the hell isn't he trying to land this rattling toolbox with wings?

Maité glared at the pilot and was shocked to see him still in his seat in the crammed cockpit, where he should be. She twisted as best she could to see who held her. She saw a mane of shoulder-length brown hair and a pair of startled amber eyes looking at her with undisguised fear.

Who are you?

Another violent flash of red light and her gaze jerked back to her parents. She wanted to go to them, but the powerful arms held her tighter. They were not the pilot's arms; she knew that now, but she had no time to consider whose they might be. The faltering grumble of the engine coughed away its last seconds.

"Why *is* everything red?" Alba asked, seeming to notice the unnatural light inside and outside the aircraft for the first time. Then her eyes fixed on the man holding Maité, and she screamed, "Maité, *despierta*! Wake up!"

Through the small window of the plane, Maité got a slanted eyeful of the crest of a huge, frothy wave rising to swallow them.

Maité had done as her mother said. She'd woken and left her parents an instant before the plane crashed into the sea.

Now, bent over the porcelain sink, Maité let the water carry her tears down the drain. Her heart hammered in her painfully constricted chest.

CHAPTER 9

The door to the bathroom creaked open, and Maité jumped. "Em!"

"Sorry, didn't know you were …" Emily yawned. "You okay?" She frowned, cocking her head to one side to take a good look at Maité.

Maité averted her eyes and shut off the water, doubting herself for a moment. Perhaps it had been nothing more than a bad dream.

"Geez! What happened? Are you crying?"

It wasn't a dream—I was there.

"My mom and dad are dead." Maité gulped, trying to stifle her emotions. Terror erupted inside her, more horrifying than what she'd felt on the doomed plane, because now she knew. Now there were repercussions to face. The painful knot in her throat grew bigger.

"Gasp, M, what are you talking about? Did someone call?"

"They're dead! I saw it!" her stomach convulsed, trying to let out the horrible scream doing circles inside her.

Emily grabbed her by her nightshirt. "Breathe, M, breathe!"

It seemed like a simple enough command, but Maité couldn't control her spasms any better than she could stop a lightning bolt. She tried to stand erect and draw breath.

Emily kept talking. "That can't be true. You've just had a nightmare; everyone has nightmares, especially when you eat all that Mexican food before bed. How many tamales did you have anyway?"

"That's not it!" Maité cried, turning away from her friend and sitting on the edge of the tub close to the toilet. She felt on the verge of being sick. "I saw what happened in my dream." She swallowed the saliva pooling in her mouth. "They were on a small plane, in a storm. The pilot said they were going down."

Emily shook her head and paced the bathroom as best as she could in the small space. "M, you know that can't be real. It has to be only a dream, a really ugly, awful—"

"I'm gonna wake Aunt V." Maité rose from the edge of the tub and reached for the door, but it opened without her touching it.

"What's going on?" Verónica whispered, making Maité and Emily jump in spite of her quiet voice. "I thought I heard arguing …" she said, looking from one to the other.

"Aunt V," Maité began, but choked on the rest of her words, shaking.

"Maité, mi amor, what's the matter?" Verónica pulled Maité into her arms at once.

Mi amor, Maité thought, *that's just what Mom said, right before …*

"We have to call their hotel," she cried, breaking away from Verónica's embrace to look at her worried face.

"Why? What's happened? Are you all right?"

"She's had a really bad dream, Mom," Emily offered.

"What was it, Maité? What did you dream?" Verónica urged, her voice full of concern as she brushed Maité's hair away from her face.

Between ragged sobs, Maité relived the dream for them, squirming under the horrified looks that Emily and Verónica gave her as they listened to the gory details.

"Stop it, Em!" Maité pleaded, "You're looking at me as if *I* made it happen!"

"But we don't know it's happened, sweetie," Verónica soothed.

Emily looked away, her eyes full of tears too. "I'm sorry, M, I didn't mean to. It's just so …"

"That's why we have to call. I have to know." Maité sobbed. "It wasn't a dream," she insisted. She knew Verónica was rubbing her arms, but Maité couldn't feel it.

Verónica looked around the cramped bathroom as if looking for the right thing to say or do. "Okay," she said at length, "Let's go downstairs and make the call."

"Thank you." Maité gulped again.

"Controllers lost contact with the plane a few hours ago, but when the storm dies down, they'll start a search," Verónica said, hanging up after two calls to the hotels in Guadeloupe and then in the Virgin Islands.

Maité gave a disconsolate nod, the same as she'd done while listening to Verónica's phone conversations where the details of her parents' last actions were laid out.

On the day of Alba and Sósimo's return, their scheduled flight to the Virgin Islands had been cancelled due to a local strike. Then a sudden storm hit, and the concierge at the hotel in Guadeloupe reminded them that if they didn't get to the Virgin Islands, they'd miss their connection to Ft. Lauderdale.

The concierge had referred them to Oliver García, the owner of a small island hopper, who was at the moment in the lobby discussing transportation of forgotten luggage from Guadeloupe to the Virgin Islands.

In spite of the menacing clouds and strong winds stirring outside, Alba and Sósimo thanked the concierge and went with their new pilot, Ollie, to the airport.

In his dirty baseball cap, grimy tank top, and frayed cargo shorts, Ollie explained rather indifferently that the storm was headed south, and that the worst of it had already passed. "We're good to go," he had assured them.

Sósimo paid Ollie, and around midnight, he and Alba, along with three forgotten suitcases, boarded the rickety twin-engine craft that looked like a beat-up trailer with wings and a bad paint job.

They never reached the Virgin Islands.

Coldness had stolen over Maité as her fears were confirmed. *There was a storm. It was no dream.* On the other side of Verónica's tight embrace, Emily cried as well.

"C'mon, girls, c'mon." Verónica led them back to Emily's room, where the girls sat on the bed on either side of her. Verónica shakily smoothed their hair, kissed their wet cheeks, and offered tissues. "The airport authorities will keep us posted. We shouldn't jump to conclusions," Verónica tried to reassure Maité.

Maité shook her head miserably, but still she clung to Verónica's words as if to a life raft.

Having switched to the other bed, with her head on the pillow, Emily stared bleary eyed at Maité until she fell asleep.

Maité coiled on the bed, and although her eyes were open and fixed on a spot on the wall, she was far from being conscious. Through the wreckage of her emotions, she drifted deep inside herself, oblivious to Verónica's hand smoothing the loose strands of hair or her soft fingers wiping the tears that kept falling from Maité's eyes.

"I'm here for you," Verónica whispered. "I will take care of you; you can count on that."

Maité could not make herself respond; she felt only the sting of brand-new tears burning her face before they soaked into the pillow.

Reddish sunlight streamed through the half-closed shutters, marking the beginning of a new day, yet to Maité it was the end of life as she knew it. She closed her eyes.

CHAPTER 10

Maité stumbled downstairs some time near noon, feeling drained and hollow inside. Her stomach made grumbling, hungry noises, but the thought of food revolted her. She passed the study on her way to the kitchen. Maité saw Verónica in there, looking out the window and apparently deep in thought. She chose not to disturb her.

Maité poured herself some water. She drank it down, thinking all she'd accomplished by it would be to replenish her supply of tears. Her eyes were swollen and bloodshot. She decided to go back to bed.

"Hello," Maité said croakily as she passed the study again.

At the sound of Maité's voice, Verónica turned around abruptly. She shot a cautious glance toward her but did not answer. She had the phone to her ear. *"Hablaremos más tarde. Maité está conmigo ahora y yo cuidaré de ella."*

Maité mouthed, "Sorry," and changed her mind about returning to bed. She went into the family room instead, wondering if she'd heard correctly. *Who could she be talking to about me, in Spanish?*

"Hey, M," Emily mumbled, still in her pajamas and taking a seat next to Maité. Emily's eyes had swollen to slits, and she looked positively scrawny in her flannel shorts and tank top.

Maité heard Verónica replace the phone in its cradle, and her stomach tightened wondering again why her name had been mentioned.

Verónica came into the family room with a cup of coffee in her hand. "Hey, girls," she said looking from Maité to Emily with concern in her eyes.

Maité nodded, anxious to ask the question buzzing in her mind.

Emily said, "Hi, Mom." Then, to Maité she whispered, "What's goin' on?"

"I don't know."

Verónica kissed their foreheads before sitting in her rocking chair. She set her cup on the table next to her, saying nothing.

Emily rubbed her eyes with one hand and asked through a yawn, "Any news?"

Maité tried to breathe evenly, but something in Verónica's shifting glances made her feel uneasy. *Something's not right.* She inched to the edge of the couch as if the backrest had sprouted needles. *I really don't see how things could get worse,* Maité reasoned, but Verónica wore such an upset look that she just had to find out.

"Aunt V., I'm sorry, but I thought I heard you say my name on the phone just now …"

Nothing could have prepared her for Verónica's reply.

Verónica's eyes swam in tears all of a sudden and with a guilt Maité had never heard in Verónica's voice, she heard her say, "Um, I was talking to your grandfather."

"What?" Maité gasped.

Emily groped for Maité's hand and found it.

"Your mother never told you about him," Verónica quickly apologized.

Blood rushed from Maité's face, and the familiar racing of her heart took over in her chest and temples. *I'm going to have a heart attack,* she thought as she squeezed Emily's hand. "What do you mean, my grandfather?"

"He's your mother's father, Fernando Gonzaga." Verónica wrung her fingers anxiously.

"Huh?" Emily looked disbelieving at her mother and then turned to stare at Maité. "You don't have any grandparents, do you?"

Maité opened her mouth but didn't know what to say. Of course she had grandparents, but she'd always thought they were dead, all of them.

"She does," Verónica said. "Actually, just one now. No other family, just him," Verónica said, looking wretched.

"No way! Aunt Alba never said anything about a grandfather," Emily argued. "You never said anything about it either. What's going on?"

Maité stared. Entirely too many thoughts went through her mind. *Fernando Gonzaga?* What was her mother thinking, not telling her she had a living grandfather? *Gonzaga.* And suddenly, on the day after her parents' accident, here he was. *Why?* Certain there had to be more surprises, she pressed Verónica, almost angrily, with questions. "What did he want? How did he know to call here? Did you call him?"

A shadow darkened Verónica's face. "I did have his number—and I had to tell him about your mother's disappearance, didn't I? Wouldn't you agree he had to be told?"

Maité looked at her, confused for a moment. "Well, yeah, if she's his daughter, sure …" She trailed off, distracted by the way Verónica continued wringing her fingers. "How can it be, Aunt V? I always thought my mom's parents were dead." Maité couldn't recall her mother ever saying her father was dead, but there had been hints in that direction. "Why wouldn't she tell me?"

"Alba said she would one day talk to you about him, about what happened—I never thought …" Verónica paused and frowned as if trying to collect her thoughts.

Maité sat on the edge of the couch. "Well, what *did* he say?"

"I swear to you, I had no way of knowing what his reaction would be. Never in a million years could I have guessed."

Beside Maité, Emily glowered at her mother. "Is he coming out here or something?"

"No, sweetie. For now he's asked me to keep him informed of everything."

Wondering why Verónica wouldn't look at her, Maité pressed on. "And what else?"

Emily drummed her fingers, waiting for her mother to answer.

"He wants you to go to Spain and live with him," Verónica blurted, and her hands flew to her mouth to stifle a sob.

Verónica said it so fast Maité felt like someone had pulled an old Band-Aid from a raw scrape. Her head spinning, she slumped back on the couch.

Emily sprang up and began walking the length of the family room, back and forth. "Are you crazy? We don't even know if Maité's parents are dead. They could be floating in the ocean somewhere!" Emily raged. "Nobody can make M go anywhere. Not only does she *not* want to go live in Spain, but whoever heard of making someone go live with a complete stranger? In a strange country, no less! How do we even know if he's really her grandfather? He doesn't even have the same last name as Aunt Alba. No! Absolutely *not*. This won't happen, it simply won't—it's ridiculous. It's out of the question. It's—"

Unable to make heads or tails of what had been said; Maité listened in mute astonishment to Emily's ravings. Her eyes followed the lanky shape of her friend, although not really seeing her. *I need to get my head around this, I have to. I need to know why Mom …*

All of a sudden Maité's thoughts froze in her brain. Her ears popped and in that instant a sensory thickness overwhelmed her, covering her like a heavy blanket. Her skin felt dense, like her lips and cheeks felt after getting Novocain at the dentist, except this was all over her body. Soft lips grazed her earlobes. Maité shuddered. Someone's breath, warm yet distant, injected sighing sounds straight into her head.

Maitagarri …

She distinctly heard these exotic four syllables. Head-to-toe goose bumps sprang up on her body. She felt her nerve endings trying unsuccessfully to poke through the new thickness of her skin. *Maitagarri*. The intonation made her think of someone smiling.

Maité felt disoriented because everything had gone quiet, as if she'd been suddenly shut up in a padded cell. All sounds outside of her had been blocked. Fear clutched her heart; she didn't understand what was happening. Only the hint of a peaceful reassurance in that word she didn't even understand kept her from going over the edge of sanity.

Emily continued to rant and pace furiously, while Verónica feigned to listen. But Maité could hear nothing, nor did she want to.

Nothing except the whisper: *Maitagarri*.

She glimpsed, in a sunny somewhere, a smile quivering on yielding lips as the echo of the word warmed her all over. It was just a single word, but it seemed to convey a great deal of mostly good sensations.

Where have I heard that word before? I know I have …

The tingling heat in her ears gradually went away. Maité thought she might even be able to move again if she chose. Though rattled by the invasion of her body, she had to admit it had been a *very* good feeling—so frighteningly personal and so deep within her—but still a pleasant sensation. She tried to shrug it off by focusing on the shrill words coming from Emily—Maité could hear her again—but it was useless.

Then her eyes met Verónica's curious stare. *She must've noticed I spaced out*, she thought, alarmed, and looked away. *Aunt V didn't hear it. She doesn't know I'm hearing voices in my head. Could I be going crazy?*

But for a few precious seconds, that voice, that sensation—whatever it had been—dragged her out of her shock and pain and into an alternate reality. If only for a few moments, Maité experienced something besides the intense despair of the hours before, and for that alone, she chose to treasure the secret feeling; however briefly, it had kindled an unexpected hope in her heart, a hope that defied reason.

CHAPTER II

Three days after Alba and Sósimo's plane went down and Mr. Gonzaga staked his claim on Maité, the local authorities in the Virgin Islands ended their search with only a torn life jacket found two miles from the last known coordinates. The winds had been so strong, and the swells as violent as if it had been the middle of hurricane season, there was simply no hope of locating the wreckage, much less recovering bodies. Such was the official report Maité received.

At the table, over a barely touched dinner, Maité digested the fact she was now an orphaned minor, and nothing could keep her grandfather from uprooting her. He was her next of kin and therefore responsible for her. She glanced at Verónica and Michael, who looked at her with glum expressions. Their eyes spoke of a loss as devastating as Maité's.

Her mother and Verónica had been like sisters—together since grade school. As young adults, they'd traveled together from Spain to the United States and made lives for themselves in a new country. They had vowed to be each other's family until they were parted by death—at a ripe old age in a nursing home. From the moment Maité learned to speak, Verónica had been Aunt V, just as Alba was Aunt Alba to Emily and Gabriel. But technically they weren't blood related, so "Aunt V" would have no legal claim to Maité.

Michael Allen had now lost his best friend and partner in the architectural firm of Bottini & Allen. Creating the firm had been her father's goal in leaving Italy after the death of his mother, and he singled Michael out as his future partner. The two men completed their architectural degrees on the East Coast, where they'd met. Shortly after graduation, Sósimo, feverish with excitement over the construction boom in the west, convinced them all that their future rested at the foot of the Wasatch Mountains in Utah.

From across the table, Maité saw Michael's eyes fill with tears, and she wondered if he was recalling those times—maybe he pictured the small car crammed with belongings of the two newlywed couples, heading west. Maité had heard the story often and had seen the 8 mm reels countless times.

Verónica squeezed her husband's hand. Maité looked away, refusing to witness even that small gesture of love, resenting her own parents for not being here. She stared out the window, hating the summer sun still shining outside. She thought it should stop.

Across from her, Emily poured more milk for Gabriel, which he drank in silence.

Maité knew there would be traditional burial rituals to uphold, even without her parents' bodies to be anointed, or for the blessings to be pronounced over them.

It dawned on her she had been nursing a morbid hope to see them one last time. Even if they were dead, she wanted to see them again. Her eyes gleamed with hot tears.

In the morning, a week after the horrible nightmare where she witnessed her parents' last moments, Maité got out of bed and ambled down to the kitchen. She sat at the table and nibbled blankly at a piece of toast while Emily, who'd recovered her appetite if not her spirits, diligently worked on an enormous cinnamon roll dripping with icing, four greasy sausage links, and scrambled eggs coated with melted cheddar. She periodically washed down a bite with gulps of milk, which reminded Maité that she too should have some fluids.

She sipped a little water. How her friend's lean body could hold so much food was nothing short of baffling. "The secret is in the metabolism," Emily once told Maité, clicking her tongue and winking at her. That day seemed a lifetime ago, but the memory of it put a small smile on Maité's lips, the first in days.

Maité crumpled her napkin with the uneaten half of her toast hiding in it, and threw it in the trash. She refilled her glass with water and headed upstairs to take a shower.

Verónica caught Maité in the hall and gave her a tight hug.

There is no escaping what happens today, Maité thought, leaning her head on Verónica's shoulder. Two empty coffins were scheduled to be buried, and she'd have to accept her parents were really dead. She melted into Verónica's maternal embrace, even though it wrung out more despairing sobs. Her body shook in silence, and her throat ached from the choked emotions she couldn't express. Today, her parents would be symbolically placed underground, out of her reach forever.

Overcoming the pain seemed an impossible feat.

Maité took a long shower, crying the entire time. Her tears felt hotter on her cheeks than the water pelting her body, but it barely registered. She seemed to be in a perpetual state of inward reflection, compounded by increasing flights of fancy.

At one point, a vision of her mother asleep in her father's arms assaulted her. They were leaning against what looked like a tree trunk. A tender breeze blew Alba's hair over her cheek, obscuring Maité's view of her mother's sleeping features, but she saw her parents breathing restfully in unison.

Are you in heaven? Maité wondered, resting her forehead on the cool tile as water poured over her.

Unwilling to wear black on the outside as well as the inside, Maité dressed in a white shirt and a gray tube skirt that made her look even taller. She combed her dark-blonde hair and tied it into a loose ponytail. She inspected her face in the mirror: though exhausted and pale, the summer sunshine on her skin made a striking contrast with her stormy-gray eyes.

"You make me think of faeries when I look at you," her father had told her often. "You are my faery princess."

Tears smarted in Maité's eyes. She didn't want to look in the mirror anymore.

The sun shined with its summer strength high in the blue sky. People poured into St. Bartholomew Catholic Church and filed somberly into the pews. Maité and Emily sat at the front with the rest of the Allens.

The satin-lined coffins stood in front of the altar. They were empty except for Alba's wedding dress and the tuxedo Sósimo insisted on buying for what had been a very intimate wedding ceremony years before. Maité and Verónica agreed those would be fitting articles of clothing to bury in their stead.

Life as someone's child had ended for Maité. As she squeezed Emily's hand, a surge of fear welled up inside her, prompting Maité to lean closer to her friend. Emily returned a comforting smile and put her arm around Maité's shoulders.

During the summer, Emily usually wore a baseball cap, shorts, and a tank top, but on this day she wore a black skirt. Her beat-up sneakers had been replaced with black sandals, and she wore a charcoal silk blouse, surely from Verónica's closet. She'd brushed and braided her hair. Her face was clean, and her scrutinizing, hazel eyes showed only the slightest sign of tears.

Somehow, the sight of such a changed Emily, even if it was for this one day, added another layer of understanding to Maité's reality. She found her heart ached in new, unknown places.

The service acknowledging the lives of her parents was short but eloquent. Then came the solemn procession of mourners moving slowly past the coffins to pay their last respects—so many of her classmates had come, including Finn.

He gave Maité a stricken look, and she felt him tremble when he hugged her. She patted him on the back, and he kissed her cheek, seemingly lost for words. She gave him a watery smile before he went to Emily.

Maité turned politely to the next person in the long line, finding no comfort in the process. Although she knew everyone meant well, Maité wanted it to be over. The old maxim of "misery loves company" didn't feel true today. She didn't want to be hugged, or looked at with pity, or to feel better. Her stomach growled, and she wished she'd eaten more than toast for breakfast. Dizziness struck her in waves.

Finally, with the coffins securely inside the hearse, Maité and the Allens led the procession to the cemetery. The four-mile stretch between Saint Bartholomew's and The Good Shepherd Memorial Park took a full half-hour.

Inside the limo provided by the mortuary for the family, Maité's anxiety built like a nasty black cloud in the blue sky. *When will this day be over?* She fidgeted on the seat next to Emily.

They reached the cemetery. It took nearly half an hour for everyone to crowd around the graveside. Maité wanted to cry out in helpless irritation. The priest pronounced the required blessings for the repose of her parents' souls and said some final words of consolation for the benefit of the orphan. Maité could hardly see or hear anymore.

The sun beat down on her head, and the gusty summer heat overpowered her as she shifted her weight from one leg to the other. Loose strands of hair tickled her cheeks, and she heard herself breathing while her temples pulsed to the rhythm of her heart.

Her ears popped.

Maité glanced around drowsily; wispy lavender swayed in the hot breeze, but she couldn't smell it. A vase with flowers toppled over at the grave next to them. No one paid attention. The eerie thickness of skin took her over again, sealing her off from the outside world.

Everything before her eyes turned into silvery dots. In a sequence of surreal moments, she saw the lid of her mother's casket spring open. Alba rose—not like a zombie might do in a horror movie, but as if she'd been napping in her bed. She smiled radiantly at Maité.

Holy cow! I'm so losing it!

Maité stared at the vision of the open coffin. She knew it was closed, she knew there was nothing in there but the white wedding dress, yet tremors ran up and down her legs and spine.

I need to sit ...

She felt sluggish, and her skin seemed to have gained two inches in thickness. All sounds grew dim around her, and then a male voice whispered, *"Maitagarri."*

Maité shuddered. No one was near enough to have whispered to her. No one.

She no longer felt the summer heat. She tried to focus on the fading vision of her mother, asking her for an explanation, but Alba merely winked at her daughter's confusion.

And in an instant, the hot breath in Maité's ear disappeared, as did the sight of her mother.

Where is dad? she wondered, feeling lost, alone, defeated—about to break down.

In a daze, Maité watched the coffins being lowered into the ground. She thought she heard the quiet pulleys operating. The long stems of lavender blew horizontally. Her hair flapped over her face; she wanted to brush it away but couldn't will even a finger to move. The priest said something about *life everlasting.* The echo of his words seemed to magnify a looming panic attack. She breathed faster.

Yes, I'm going to lose it now. Maité's limbs still felt heavy. Even if she tried, she wouldn't be able to make her body respond. "I feel sick," she groaned.

Emily dropped the fistful of dirt she intended to throw over the caskets and lurched toward Maité. The priest dropped his prayer book and started toward her. The last thing Maité remembered was the feel of Emily's and Verónica's arms catching her before her limp body collapsed.

Consciousness came by degrees. Maité dreamt in between. With her eyes closed, she strained to hold on to the silhouette of her parents walking hand in hand on a long stretch of beach. *Warm and salty,* she thought.

Somewhere in her mind, she knew she'd made it back to the house. Emily's voice and the slight creaking noise of the gliding chair in the air-conditioned family room reached Maité's ears, drawing her away from the small piece of heaven her parents walked on.

Good-bye, she thought. They didn't turn to look at her.

"It was just way too hot out there," Emily remarked.

"I know, and it's no wonder with everything that's happened," Verónica whispered, smoothing Maité hair. Then, with a note of irritation in her voice, she said to Emily, "The chair won't take off flying, you know."

Emily must've really had that chair going, Maité thought, beginning to feel more alert.

"Sorry," Emily said, and the creaking noise stopped at once.

Verónica changed the wet cloth on Maité's forehead. Maité's eyelids fluttered.

"You look so much better now, my darling," Verónica said with a smile.

Maité did not feel better. She wanted to wake up from the nightmare, but reality didn't seem much better.

Maitagarri.

She thought of telling Emily and Verónica about the strange voice but decided against it. *They'll think I'm nuts.* Maité rolled on to her side and drew her knees to her chest. *I am nuts!*

"There, you're coming back. It's nice and cool here," Verónica said soothingly.

Maité sniffled.

"What is it, sweetie?"

"Just now, I mean at the cemetery, I thought I saw my mom, you know?" Maité said, deciding to spare them the entire vision of Alba sitting up and getting out of the coffin.

"Oh, sweetheart, this has been such a trying day." Verónica paused and wiped the tears welling in her eyes. "But it's good for you to think about your mom and dad as they were, full of life, full of love for you."

Cruelly, Maité's brain flashed to an image of her parents' panicked faces before the crash. "Yes, Aunt V," she said dully.

Verónica went on. "You should think about San Sebastián too. It's a beautiful city, and—"

From the glider, Emily kicked off backward and then stopped the forward motion, catching Verónica's eye. "Yeah M, maybe it won't be all that bad. You wait and see."

"San Sebastián?" Maité propped herself up on one elbow, sniffling and wiping her tears though her insides tightened—she missed her parents so much.

"Yes, that's the name of the city you'll be going to. Didn't you know?"

"No," Maité stammered, distressed by her own apathy at not having bothered to find out about her destination.

"Oh! It's gorgeous there. You'll love it," Verónica exclaimed, sounding infinitely glad to have a distraction to offer Maité.

Emily glided moderately on the chair. "What's it like?"

Maité sat up on the couch.

"Where to begin? Oh! I have pictures! Wait right here." Verónica raced up the stairs, and a couple of minutes later, she returned with a box full of postcards and photographs. She emptied them on to the table in front of the girls.

Emily's eyes lit up flashing a postcard to Maité. "It's on the beach?" She moaned looking at the surfboards jetting off the crests of blue waves.

Maité's curiosity got the better of her. She inched to the edge of the couch to see the spread on the table. All this time, her destination had seemed like a big, black hole, but now, as she looked over the pictures in front of her, things began to color with new meaning.

"Look at this one!" Emily gushed. "And oh! You have to check this out!" She put more and more pictures in front of Maité.

"It's beautiful," Maité murmured.

Verónica beamed. "It sure is."

Maité turned over the postcard she held in her hand and read out loud: "*Bahía de la Concha.*" The shell-shaped beach was too lovely; it looked fake, like it had been airbrushed.

Verónica peered over her shoulder to see what held Maité's interest and whispered, "Your grandfather's house overlooks that bay."

Verónica's words made a shiver creep up Maité's back. Her eyes drank in the sunlit postcard paradise, and for the space of a heartbeat, Maité saw herself on a wind-blown slope overlooking that very scene.

A hesitant smile played on her lips; somehow she felt she had really breathed the warm and salty air of that faraway coast just then.

That evening, Fernando Gonzaga made a third phone call to inform Verónica that Maité's electronic ticket awaited her at the airline counter. He did not ask to speak to Maité but stated someone would be at the airport in San Sebastián to pick her up in two days' time.

Verónica hung up the phone and repeated the conversation to Maité. "He's a very important man, and a busy one," she stammered. "He cares about you, I'm sure, but I think he may be away on business now."

Maité shrugged as if it didn't matter, but it hurt that her grandfather gave her such little importance. Her only living relative was snubbing her.

I can snub him right back, she thought. *Heck, I could do way more than snub him. I could irritate him enough to make him wish he'd never sent for me.*

"It's all right, Aunt V," she said calmly. "It doesn't make any difference to me whether I see him at the airport—or *ever*, for that matter."

"I'm so sorry, sweetie. I think it's going to be tough on you over there."

"I don't think so," Maité replied. "I think I might make it tougher on him. He'll be sorry he sent for me."

"Attagirl!" Emily clapped Maité's back.

"And besides, it'll only be one year, because after I turn eighteen, I'll come back to my parents' house."

"That's right, sweetie," Verónica hastened to add. "Their house will be in your name then."

Upstairs in Emily's room, Maité brooded over the miserable state of her affairs. She had never felt as powerless as she did now. Her mother and father had died and taken with them her home, her plans, her ambitions, and even her identity.

Who'll give me their opinion about college? Who'll point out options when choices get confusing? Who'll tell me without hesitation when I make a mistake? Who will I belong to? And who will belong to me?

Maité sighed in frustration, resisting the urge to grab fistfuls of hair and pull them right out of her head. Instead, she rubbed her eyes and entire face as if she itched miserably. "What am I going to do?" she grunted into her own hands. She pressed hard on her eyelids until she saw nothing but shiny dots. When she opened them she spotted the violin her father had taught her to play, calling to her from a corner of Emily's room and looking forlorn. Something quickened within her.

Maité picked up her violin and played it for the first time since the death of her parents. The stirring notes of Mozart's "Voi Che Sapete" from *The Marriage of Figaro* enveloped her like sweet perfume. It was her parents' favorite.

It felt strange to once again hold the instrument she'd played every day since her sixth birthday, but Maité's expression relaxed as she played, her eyes closed, her chin gently pressed against the varnished wood. In her head flashed visions of a powerfully built handsome man twirling a beautiful young woman. He smiled at the dome of trees above him and then beamed at his partner. Maité wondered how her parents could look so different in her imagination.

The notion that the people she played for may not be her parents eluded her completely.

Maité knew the music would likely be heard throughout the house, but she felt okay with that. She wanted to share with the Allens the hopeful feeling it gave her, like a hug from her father.

CHAPTER 12

Headed for the Airport

Misery struck Maité in rolling swells when she woke that morning, and as the hours piled on, the tide of hopelessness threatened to drown her. She could not find a reason to go on; nothing could satisfy her. Nothing could replace the only comfort she wanted, which was simply for her parents to be alive.

Emily's words of a few days ago—*It's not going to be all that bad*—bounced pointlessly in Maité's skull like a rubber ball. She wished she could believe it.

While Verónica drove, Maité fretted in the passenger seat. In fewer than thirty-five minutes they would arrive at Salt Lake City International Airport. Already the lines anchoring her to home were strained. Soon they would snap, and she would hurtle into the unknown.

"I'll e-mail you every two hours, and you'd better answer me and let me know how you're doing," Emily called from the backseat, hooking herself up to a set of ear buds and checking all the various applications and accessories she'd installed the night before on Sósimo's laptop, which Maité was taking with her. "I've loaded a few e-mail addresses in your directory, and mine is there of course, so remember—every two hours."

"Okay," Maité said, doubting she'd have the energy to reply to every message Emily planned to send.

As if sensing Maité's turmoil, Verónica broke the silence in a tentative voice, "You know, your mother and I were best friends since grade school ..."

Maité couldn't bring herself to look up. *What do I care?* she thought bitterly. *That just means you knew her longer than I did.*

It was all starting again; tears felt like acid on the tender rims of her eyes. Maité wanted to scream and rage at the cruelty of it all. She felt like a corked bottle ready to blow, and the helplessness she detected in Verónica's tone as she spoke about the past, sent her over the edge.

Something inside Maité snapped and her eyes widened with fear. "Don't you realize?" she shrieked, "I'll never see Mom and Dad again. Ever! And that can't be! I don't know what to do. *What do I do?* I just want ..."

What Maité wanted was impossible. She covered her face with her hands and bawled.

Verónica pulled off to the shoulder of the highway. Emily ripped the ear buds from the sides of her head and reached for Maité's shoulder, the only part of her she could reasonably reach with her seatbelt still on. "You'll be okay, M, you will," Emily cried, sounding like a wounded dog.

Maité angrily wiped her tears and found her words again. "I want to hug them—I want to kiss them. But I can't, I'll never be able to do that again. And I'm scared out of my mind! What am I going to do in Spain? What? *What?*"

Emily awkwardly hugged the seat and her friend in it. "M, stop it. Please!"

"I can't. They have to come back *today*," Maité sobbed, admitting at last that she couldn't accept the idea of her parents being dead. Day after day, the reality of it hammered her, breaking her heart into tiny pieces, but still she couldn't believe it.

Verónica raced out of the car and came around to Maité's side. She opened the door and drew Maité to her into a desperate embrace.

"Look at me, Maité," Verónica said, seeming to have a sudden inspiration.

Maité obeyed, although she couldn't stop sobbing.

"Listen to me, angel." Verónica smiled cautiously through her own tears. "You'll discover your mother in San Sebastián."

Maité heard the words but didn't want to understand. Her chest heaved while Emily's fingers pinched her clavicles painfully. If Emily thought this was a soothing rub, Maité didn't agree.

"Maité," Verónica continued, "you'll be in the same house she lived in for most of her life, and you'll find her there."

Maité looked at Verónica through the kaleidoscope of her tears and began to internalize the words. The thought of "discovering" her mother—whatever that meant—gave her a feeble consolation. To know who her mother had been in San Sebastián before she came to America and married her Italian prince caught Maité's fancy, and it was a start. Sniffling, she laid her head on Verónica's shoulder, slowly processing the new idea.

Verónica cradled Maité's head against her breast and kissed her hair. "One day at a time, sweetie," she said, rubbing her back encouragingly. "One moment at a time, if you need to."

Maité sat up straight, letting curiosity about her mother's story take over. She dabbed her eyes with the tissue Emily handed her.

She took a deep breath and said, "Okay, Aunt V." After a couple of trailing sobs, Maité asked, "What exactly happened between my mom and her dad?"

"It's a complex story," Verónica began. "I guess the biggest problem was that Alba and her father were so much alike, temperament-wise, you know?"

"Do you mean *Grandfather* is kind of stubborn like Mom?"

Verónica laughed a little. "That would be an understatement—I would say your grandpa is really stubborn, and your mom was only *kind* of stubborn."

"So what was their big fight about?" Emily wedged herself between the front seats to hear better. "Did it have to do with you and Aunt Alba coming over here?"

Maité perked up a bit and Verónica directed her answer to her. "The fight wasn't because Alba and I came to America. The big fight was because your mother met Sósimo three months after arriving in New York. He was studying architecture there, and your mother fell head over heels in love with him, which obviously led to her decision not to return to Spain after the twelve-month break Mr. Gonzaga agreed to let her have."

"Gasp, Mom. What do you mean he let her have a break?" Emily interjected, sounding scandalized by the implications. If Maité hadn't felt so drained, she might have made the remark herself.

"Angel, Alba's father had very definite ideas as to what she should do with her life."

"So my mom's original plan was to take a break in New York and then go back to Spain?" Maité asked.

"More or less," Verónica continued. "Of course, your grandfather was beside himself with rage at the thought of Alba choosing someone he hadn't handpicked for her. You see, he'd found someone he thought ideal for Alba back home, an Emilio Córdoba, if I remember correctly. Alba had agreed to marry him, but only if she could have a year to herself. One year to experience life before submitting to her father's will."

"Geez! Drama! And he bought that? That she would come back in twelve months? Duh!" Emily said.

"When your grandfather heard about Sósimo, he thought Alba had lost her mind. Sósimo had to be a 'good for nothing, swindling, Italian piece of trash,' and your mother could certainly do better than that," Verónica said.

"He said that about my dad?" Maité asked, feeling instant hate toward her grandfather.

"With those exact words," Verónica replied. "But your mother was truly in love, and she'd already made up her mind. And you know how your mom was when she got an idea in her head."

Maité smiled appreciatively. She knew only too well what that was like.

"Mr. Gonzaga hoped Alba would come around in time, but after a couple of months of nothing but arguing back and forth, each defending his or her point of view, your mom received a letter from him saying he'd remove her from his will unless she gave up her ridiculous notion of marrying that 'vagabond fortune hunter.'"

Maité's breast swelled indignantly as she listened to Verónica. The whole story sounded like something out of a soap opera. She couldn't fathom what kind of man would think her father was a "vagabond fortune hunter." To Maité, her father had always been a prince, her mother's prince.

"So what did she do?" Maité urged Verónica to continue.

"Alba sent a letter back to your grandfather."

"What did it say?" Emily demanded.

"Actually, it was more a note than a letter. It said, 'You'll need this at some point, I am sure.' And Alba stapled a copy of her marriage certificate to that note. The certificate was dated the same day it was postmarked, but worse, it also showed that Alba had renounced her father's name of Gonzaga, and opted for her mother's, Santillán."

"Ah! So that explains the last name thing. I'd wondered why Mom didn't have the same last name as him," Maité remarked.

Emily let out an awed "Wow."

Verónica nodded. "Wow is right. Their wedding day was crazy; we ran around like lunatics trying to get a name-change form, and then the blood tests and the marriage license. We did it all the same day so your mom could have the pleasure of mailing the certificate after the ceremony—her way of spitting on Mr. Gonzaga's threats."

"Wow!" Emily repeated.

Verónica nodded again, but when she spoke, her voice sounded regretful. "It was also Alba's farewell to Spain. You see, she was so heartbroken by her father's blind refusal and denial of her that she decided then and there she was done with him."

"Why was he so snooty about my mom marrying my dad? Was it that my dad had nothing? Was he not good enough?"

"Mr. Gonzaga is very well off, and no one argues that he's a man rich in heritage. I think that's the source of his never-ending pride. Your ancestors on your mother's side have been well-known members of high society for generations in San Sebastián. So to your grandfather, a high social standing is everything. Can you imagine what it meant to someone like him, that his one and only daughter married an Italian swindler rather than a well-bred Spaniard?"

Maité's nose wrinkled at this. "Why did he think my father was a swindler?"

"Oh, it was all nonsense on your grandfather's part. He'd never met Sósimo and never cared to. He only knew that Sósimo was poor and came from a no-name family. From there, it was easy for him to conclude Sósimo manipulated the mind of his only daughter. He imagined letters pouring in from Alba, asking for money. He told Alba as much, but it only convinced her how dead wrong her father was about Sósimo," Verónica said distantly.

"And?" Emily shook the back of the seat.

Verónica went on. "I've never met such a hardworking man as your dad, Maité. What drive! No matter how desperate things got later on, the smile on Sósimo's face never faded. He always believed things would work out. If your mom was head over heels for him, he was even worse. He even got thrown in jail once for serenading your mother and disturbing the peace." She laughed.

Maité gave her a watery grin. She felt sure if her dad had disturbed the peace it was because of the late hour—never because of a bad voice. As far as Maité was concerned, Andrea Bocelli had nothing on her dad when it came to singing.

"Actually, he serenaded both of us, since your mom and I still lived together," Verónica said. "Your mother and I emptied our savings to bail him out. We'd saved up $500 to put a down payment on a little apartment instead of the bedroom we shared at an inn."

"You guys shared a room at an inn?" Maité exclaimed. "She never told me that."

"That's probably because she didn't want you getting the wrong idea. Nowadays it wouldn't be the best place for a couple of young girls to be." Verónica gave Emily a sideways glance.

"And then what happened?" Emily said, hurrying her mother along.

"That was about it." Verónica shrugged. "Alba and Sósimo's wild romance was contagious. You couldn't help but be happy if you were anywhere near them.

"Soon after they were married, on one of the many afternoons I visited her, your dad came home from work with a friend tagging along. Sósimo danced into the room with a handful of geraniums he'd picked from the planter outside their building. He kissed your mother"—Verónica lightly touched Maité's cheek—"and then he turned to me and said, 'I brought you a husband,' just like that. I'll tell you, my face went through at least seven shades of red. I wanted to crawl under the table." Verónica shook her head.

"But when I looked at the 'future husband' Sósimo brought for me—someone from one of his drafting classes—something in his eyes told me Sósimo's announcement had been quite pleasing to him as well."

"That was Dad, right?" Emily asked.

Verónica frowned in mock outrage. "Of course! But to get back to Maité's grandfather—according to him, Sósimo's financial situation would be a constant struggle for Alba, and the bottom line was that Mr. Gonzaga would rather have seen your mom married to someone already established, both socially and financially."

"I can't even picture that," Emily remarked. "How can people be so weird about status and money?"

"You're lucky, Maité," Verónica declared. "You grew up in a household where people stood up for themselves and where the measure of their character is based on their capacity to love and their ability to dream. Don't ever forget that, sweetie, no matter where you go or what happens to you, okay?"

The ability to dream, Maité repeated inwardly. "I won't, Aunt Verónica."

CHAPTER 13

Maité felt puffy-eyed but composed as Verónica went back around to the driver's seat and started the car. She put her seatbelt back on and closed her eyes for a moment while Verónica pulled off the shoulder where they'd been parked.

A long string of images of Alba's life in Spain filled Maité's mind and acted like a soothing balm to her wounds. Reluctantly, she began rebuilding the emotional shell that had kept breaking over and over in the past days. *Maybe this time it'll stay in one piece.*

Her mother had had a life in San Sebastián, a life Maité knew nothing about. But she would discover it.

Verónica parked the car in the covered structure across from the terminal, and they unloaded the car in silence. They checked Maité's bag at the airline counter and with only the violin and laptop as carry-on, they walked slowly down the deserted hall toward the security check point. As there was no line and they were early, they decided to wait together a few more minutes.

They made light conversation, which Maité kept up with although her head swam with all the information Verónica had given her minutes before.

Emily busied herself with last-minute adjustments to the laptop's setup, while on Maité's other side, Verónica sighed. She thought it sounded like a brooding sigh; maybe Verónica worried about what would become of her best friend's daughter, alone in San Sebastián, with a grandfather whom she'd never met, and nothing but the memory of her parents to sustain her. Maité caught Verónica's eye and nodded. *I worry about the same thing*, she thought.

"I should go," Maité said gesturing toward the twenty-some passengers queued for the security check.

"Okay, sweetie." Verónica said giving her a tight hug and a kiss.

"Watch yourself." Emily advised, rocking Maité side to side with a hug of her own.

"Will do." Maité sniffed, surprised to find herself increasingly anxious to get on the plane. *Better sooner than later*, Alba always said.

"Have a safe flight!" Verónica called after her. "Remember to call us when you get there."

"Mom! She's gonna e-mail me!" Maité heard Emily correct Verónica.

She waved one last time after the security check and headed to the gate.

In single file with the other passengers, Maité squeezed along the narrow aisle of the airplane, lugging the violin and laptop. She mulled over the fact she was on her way to another country. Two more airplanes and a new life would begin.

Her heart thumped in her chest. When she found her seat, she slumped down in it, feeling stifled because the air conditioning wasn't working yet.

At length, they were cleared for take-off.

The engine roared beneath her, and she felt sucked into the backrest of her seat. Maité had a fleeting sense of dread; she strained to hold down the swell of panic boiling in her stomach. She would not close her eyes because she knew she'd see images of the last plane she'd been on. *That flight didn't turn out well at all.* She gripped the armrests on either side while she repeated the prayer her mother taught her. *Sweet Virgin Mary, cloak us with your shroud, take us where we're bound, and through our journey keep us safe and sound.*

She chanted the words, feeling hot tears spill down her cheeks, knowing her Mom had said the very same prayer seconds before she died, although she'd said it in Spanish.

The plane leveled off; feeling somewhat clear-headed, Maité recalled the particulars of her mother's one-year plan. She thought some of the finer points were very similar to the plan she formulated for herself—Maité intended to return to America on her eighteenth birthday.

Grandfather snubbed Mom as well, she thought, *but Grandfather couldn't stop her from doing what she wanted,* Maité reflected with a hint of amusement, and felt inspired by her mother's resolve.

Maité sighed and closed the window shade, which diminished the daylight glare only slightly. Her body ached with exhaustion, and although her eyes were focused on an indifferent spot ahead, she saw nothing. Eventually, her circling thoughts put her in a trance.

The familiar thickness settled over her. Her ears popped, and she worked her jaw to dispel the pressure, but it didn't go away. Instead, the husky male voice invaded her senses as before, just as it had the morning at her parents' graves. Not having the energy or the desire to break the spell, Maité surrendered and dared to consider what the voice said.

Maitagarri, you are brave.

A certain joy seemed hidden in the short sentence, which made her recall her mother's bright smile the moment she sat up in her coffin—as carefree as one would sit on a park bench. The memory of her mother's radiant smile was the last thing Maité saw before she nodded off to a light sleep, lulled by the voice.

Maitagarri, come to me ...

"I'm on my way," she mumbled as her head lolled to one side.

Maité dreamt about her mother. She helped Alba out of the coffin and they walked arm in arm out of the cemetery. Upon crossing through the iron gates of The Good Shepherd Memorial Park, things that should have been there, like Monroe Boulevard and the vacant field of Weber Applied Technology Center, faded. Instead, she and her mother were in the midst of a deep-green alpine forest. The air was thick with the scent of pine and fertile earth, but there was also the hint of a fresh sweetness Maité could not place.

"It's the flowers from the citrus trees," Alba told her, and then crushed two small white petals between her fingers, taking in their scent. "Isn't it odd? I wouldn't have thought citrus trees grew up here."

"Where is *up* here, Mom?"

"I'm not sure. But look at this place," she said as their glances drifted over the Himalayan thicket they seemed to be in. "If not for the citrus trees, I'd say we were at a really high elevation."

"Mom, is this heaven?"

"No, it's not, angelfish. It's a dream."

"I miss you so much, Mom!"

"I know. But you'll be fine; I know you will."

Maitagarri, sighed the trees, and mother and daughter wondered at the voice. They looked around but saw no one.

Maitagarri, you'll be arriving soon. The voice encircled and caressed them lovingly.

"It's that guy again," Maité said, thinking of the smiling voice she'd been hearing in her head.

"I know. I guess you'd better find out who he is and what he wants," Alba said with a cryptic smile on her sunlit face.

"Do you know who he is?"

Alba looked around again. "No. But I think we're in Spain."

The muffled sound of the snack cart making its way up the aisle grew louder, until it bumped her seat, breaking through Maité's shallow sleep. When she opened her eyes, the dream receded so far back in her subconscious that she had not the faintest recollection of it.

She fluffed the tiny airline pillow and breathed in deeply, puzzled by a flowery scent she couldn't quite place. She buried her whole face in the pillow and breathed in again, delighted in the elusive aroma. She wondered if perhaps it was nothing more than her shampoo. But she knew better.

She felt calm and contented even as her mind went down the tired string of events that had put her on this plane, except this time, the sting of tears did not come, and the choking lump did not make its way to the top of her throat. She exhaled in relief.

Part II

Welcome to the world of Faery!

Did you deceive yourself? Did you think it necessary to travel by air, sea, or land?

Not into the world of Faery.

One need only close their eyes to see it. One need only travel sideways into sound. Believe! Never shall paradox be as evident as it is in the dimension faery inhabits.

Faery can wave away the gossamer that divides us, and then take our hand and pull us through. What treats await, should faery beckon!

Only then shall we feast our eyes in a shower of light, or rest under a blanket of star-studded darkness. The fair dimension encompasses a good for every bad, and a renewing respite for every electrifying thrill—

May faery beckon!

CHAPTER 14

Wandering through the crowded corridors at Chicago's O'Hare Airport, Maité felt a surge of energy coursing through her tired body. The hordes of businesspeople and tourists rushing or strolling past Maité infected her with a sense of purpose. Tragedy notwithstanding, she acknowledged the first glimpse into an adventure unlike anything she'd experienced. Perhaps it was because of sheer exhaustion borne of constant despair, or maybe it was a little of Emily's influence coming through. Whatever the case, Maité smiled as the lure of the unknown began working its spell on her.

When the boarding call came over the speaker, Maité's heart knocked loudly in her chest.

This is it.

She picked up her violin and laptop and stood in line with all the homeward-bound Spaniards. Maité glanced around surreptitiously. Fragments of conversations in Spanish reached her ears, and she was pleased to detect her mother's accent in the fluid dialogs.

One more connection, and I'll be there, she thought as she took her seat. *Madrid and then San Sebastián.*

Once in the air, to pass the time, Maité followed suit with a couple of her fellow passengers by firing up the laptop. She poured over the screenshots Emily had printed as PDFs for her. She read about San Sebastián and the Basque country until her eyes hurt and she was full as a tick, as Emily might say.

Stretching her arms over her head, and twisting as best she could to relieve her back, Maité realized she'd been flying for more than four hours. She felt encouraged and alert. After dinner, however, the thought of it being close to one o'clock in the morning back at home made her fall into an instant stupor.

People began raising their window shades, and daylight flooded in from every direction. Through bloodshot eyes, Maité spied the drink cart at the back of the plane and realized she'd missed the meal. She felt certain her sleep had been light, but it had obviously been deep enough to miss the entire food and drink shuffle.

The voice of the pilot came over the intercom making her jump out of her tired skin, but he informed them they would be arriving in Madrid within the hour.

The layover at Madrid's Barajas Airport was only three hours, during which she had to clear customs, go through immigration, and recheck her bag.

"Bathroom will have to wait," Maité muttered as she raced to catch a shuttle from the international to the domestic terminal.

Maité clutched the stitch in her side as she approached an available counter. She checked her suitcase and answered the questions the airline representative asked at the gate. Then she marched down a flight of steps and into another jetway connected to the smaller craft that would take her to San Sebastián.

Breathless and hot, Maité boarded the plane, stowed her violin case overhead and fell into her assigned seat. She carefully placed the laptop on the empty seat next to her and rubbed her eyes. "I need a bed!"

The pilot announced a twenty-minute delay, and Maité let out a dispirited groan. She closed her eyes, which gave her instant relief from the strain of a restless night. Her ears popped and she knew it was the voice coming back to her.

Laister ikusiko dugu elkar, Maitagarri …

Already she felt as if a heavy blanket were being tucked in around her. Her limbs tingled pleasantly.

"What on earth are you saying?" Maité yawned. She thought she heard an answer, but she couldn't react. She'd turned to mush inside her thick skin, welcoming the complete helplessness she felt. She allowed herself to be drawn into a world where everything was conveyed to her in glimpses.

A picture is worth a thousand words, she thought—or was told, *more so when one can smell it and feel it.*

In the reddish darkness beneath her eyelids, the sensation of relief from daylight felt marvelous. The dreamy notion that the plane had lifted off the ground overcame Maité, but in radical contrast with that vague idea, an acute awareness struck her; this was more than just the airplane taking to the sky. It was something altogether different but she didn't understand it; her mind offered explanations that didn't make sense. Only as she dropped off to sleep did her brain make one last suggestion: overlapping realities.

Yeah, that makes sense, Maité thought.

Her body flew through the air inside an airplane, but she had parted with both her body and the plane.

A pair of deep-brown eyes laughed at her, yet there was no mockery or malice in them, only the thrill of making contact. A flash of dark hair and tanned skin, he leaned against a thick tree trunk with tortuous creases etched in its bark.

The sharp scent of pine and dark soil assaulted her; she filled her lungs with it. Then came the blinding sunlight glistening on the surface of a huge lake. Her pupils contracted to the diameter of a pinprick, even beneath her eyelids. She glimpsed straight white teeth in the flash of his smile. She felt sugary sand at her feet.

"*Maitagarri*," the man said.

Maité couldn't get a straight look at him, and she thought if she so much as rubbed her eyes, this astral leap would come to an end. She didn't want that. Here at last was the man who'd been calling to her.

He pointed to the edge of the water, and she followed where he directed. A single palm tree stood there, so out of place among all the pines. Two people slumbered beneath it.

Mom? Dad?

"*Laister ikusiko dugu elkar, Maitagarri,*" he whispered in her ear again.

"'I'll be seeing you soon'? Is that what you're saying to me? How soon is 'soon'?"

Maité startled herself awake with the realization that she understood his message in spite of the language, but she didn't hear his answer. Her head jerked toward the other two seats in her row. Empty.

"You were talking in your sleep," a passing flight attendant said, much to Maité's alarm.

"What did I say?"

"Nothing too revealing." She winked. "Something about a lake and that you'll see it soon."

"Hmmm." Maité glanced out the tiny window, her heart racing. "That thing down there is no lake," she said recalling the map Emily had PDFd for her. "The Cantabrian, right?"

"That is correct."

She was descending upon her destination.

Through the small oval window Maité saw strips of land and harbors like long fingers on the water. Fishing boats bobbed, and sailboats glided on the bay as if in a tub of greenish-blue oil. She got her first glimpse of the Old Town of Fuenterrabía with its ancient cathedral rising from a sea of terracotta rooftops near the old town square. The newer part of town extended from its perimeter, covering a landscape that long ago must have been as green as the distant hills.

The reality was more exciting than the color images Emily had gathered for her, and all of a sudden, she couldn't wait to get off the plane and see it all with her own eyes, even her grandfather.

CHAPTER 15

Madrid, Spain

From the terrace of an exclusive restaurant in Madrid, Mr. Gonzaga surveyed the enormous courtyard of the Museo del Prado sprawling before him. His brow creased into a scowl.

My granddaughter arrives in San Sebastián today.

He gripped the banister tightly and muttered under his breath, "It would have been proper for me to receive her." At once the sparring between him and his conscience erupted again. "Going was not a necessity," he told himself. "Not by any means. The child doesn't even know me. What difference will it make who picks her up at the airport?" he said, echoing Eva's conclusions, which had been voiced at least three times during their latest *petite-escapade.*

Mr. Gonzaga had again yielded to her sense. Or was it her will? He didn't know which and it didn't matter, he couldn't resist either one. He was aware of this and thought it a natural symptom of being in love, but sometimes, when they were apart, Mr. Gonzaga had the disturbing sense of being handled.

The languid interest with which Eva did it maddened him yet drove him to new heights in his quest to impress her. It also plunged him into the vile depths of his human nature where groveling didn't make him recoil. He told himself that for passion, for love such as this, all was justified.

Still, her mother—my daughter—*has died.* The weak voice of reason persisted on this point and Mr. Gonzaga bowed his head. A defeated grumble issued from him, but the sparring session would not be prolonged. Eva would see to that. It seemed all he had to do was think of her name, *Eva,* and there she was; a voluptuous genii, ready to grant his every wish, to satisfy his most secret cravings. Irresistible.

His neck stiffened, and his thoughts quieted as he detected the light steps of his companion returning to him.

"Is not Madrid a most enchanting city?" A throaty voice coiled itself into his ear, igniting a searing heat that made every square millimeter of his body wake with desire. A pair of slender arms slipped under his and embraced him. He felt every curve of Eva's body pressed against his back.

His recent monologue, his guilt, his concern, his doubts all vanished. Mr. Gonzaga exhaled and tilted his head to one side, pressing closer to Eva's face. Her breath smelled sweet. The heat of her words smoldered inside him still, and her hands stroked his chest over his starched shirt.

He closed his eyes feeling Eva all around him. "Can anything be enchanting after one has seen you?" he asked hoarsely. He pulled her around to face him and kissed her rather roughly; she did not complain.

He saw Eva's dark eyes drift over his shoulder toward the magnificent building of El Prado, but only for a moment. Mr. Gonzaga thought it calculated sensuality the way her fingers grazed his cheek and then grasped his neck. Eva both thrilled and enslaved him. The touch from her flesh electrified him and he was lost.

Even as his mouth covered hers, he felt her lips curl upward. "Oh, yes," she sighed through the pressure of his mouth. He moaned in return, coherent enough to think they would have to get to their hotel, and soon.

Through half-closed eyelids he saw Eva close her eyes as if surrendering to him.

I am not subservient, he thought, momentarily relieved of the doubts that plagued him.

CHAPTER 16

The aircraft touched down safely in San Sebastián at 3:31 in the afternoon, and taxied leisurely to the terminal. There were no jetways here, only a flight of stairs wheeled over to the door of the plane after it stopped.

Maité gathered her things and stepped out into the thick, salty air. It struck her as something evocative and ancient yet wondrously fresh. It had the smell of a home centuries old—a home called earth, coast, and mountain—and she couldn't help feeling a little smug; it was hers to discover.

She walked down the stairs and followed the other passengers across the tarmac to the small terminal, which consisted of two gates, a modest café doubling as a gift shop, and, as far as she could tell, only three check-in counters.

There were no baggage claim carousels, but Maité found her suitcase stacked against a wall in a section chained off and marked with the words CUSTOMS—ADUANAS—INMIGRAZIO. Following the lead of the other passengers, Maité dragged her bag out of the customs area, wondering if at some point someone would ask to see her baggage claim ticket, her passport, or search her suitcase. No one did.

There were no wheeled carts on which to load her things. Feeling hot and sweaty from the brief walk into the terminal, Maité stood surrounded by her belongings, watching the people who had flown in with her disperse. No one waited for her; no one held a sign with her name on it.

Maité dragged her things into the bathroom and emerged a few minutes later, feeling somewhat refreshed. She started worrying about how to get to her grandfather's house.

I suppose I can take a cab. I do have his address.

Standing in the deserted corridor, she glanced toward the coffee shop with its unattended register; only one customer sat at a table hiding behind his newspaper.

71

"He didn't send anyone to get me after all," Maité said under her breath and draped the strap of the laptop case across her chest so she could haul her bag and violin. Her neck ached.

Outside, the merciless sun beat down on her head. Shading her eyes with her hand, she looked up and down the street, hoping to hail a cab. Nothing.

Crud! I'm probably supposed to call for a cab. Duh! Feeling foolish, she dragged her things back into the air-conditioned terminal to the nearest payphone. Once there, she realized she had no Euros and the phone didn't take US currency.

Wiping the sweat off her brow, she eyed the coffee shop's one customer and wondered if he might give her a dollar's worth of coins. Maybe he'd even call a cab for her. Maité had started toward him when she spotted a man entering the airport. He looked directly at her, as she was the only other person in the empty hallway, and made haste to reach her.

"Uh oh," she muttered, watching the man stride assertively toward her. He looked irritated. *Who in his right mind would wear a suit in this heat?* she thought. *Maybe that's why he looks so cranky,* yet she thought him an attractive older man.

Having reached her, the man gave a forced smile that didn't reach his eyes, nor did it soften his stern voice. "Miss Maité Gonzaga?" he inquired in slightly accented English.

"Maité Bottini-Santillán," Maité corrected him, realizing at once she must have sounded defensive. Nevertheless, she shook the hand he offered her and smiled awkwardly.

"Of course, my apologies," he said. "I had to park the car because you were not outside, but I will go back for it now while you get your things close to the door, yes?"

"Yes. Yes, sorry, I will." Maité gathered that somehow, she'd already transgressed. "I didn't know who to expect, and I wasn't sure if someone would be coming to get me. It was so hot outside, I—"

"Fine, fine," he said dismissively and started toward the exit. "I will be back in a few moments."

"Who are you?" she called after him.

The man stopped. He turned on his heel and came back to where Maité stood shuffling her feet. "I am so sorry, Miss," he said, with a frank smile this time, evidently ashamed that his irritation made him forget his manners. His eyes kept darting from one spot to another, never quite settling on her. "My name is Emilio Córdoba," he said, bowing tensely. "I am a good friend of your grandfather's." He cleared his throat. "I am also curator of the Art History Museum in San Sebastián."

Maité nodded, feeling a little nervous because she'd been as brusque with him as he'd been with her. "Thank you, Mr. Córdoba," she stammered. "For coming to get me."

He glanced toward the door, and not looking certain as to what else he should say, Mr. Córdoba cleared his throat again and gave her a guilty look. "Miss Bottini, I am most … I was very sorry indeed to hear about Alba." His eyes flickered to her face for the briefest of seconds, and Maité felt the sincerity of his words. "I will bring the car around in just a few moments."

As she watched him walk into the heat, she mouthed his name. "Emilio Córdoba."

Córdoba. This was the intended suitor for her mother!

He's nothing compared to my dad, she thought, quickly going back on her initial conclusion that though stern, Mr. Córdoba was attractive.

She stood just inside the air-conditioned terminal until she saw Mr. Córdoba pull up in a silver sedan. In his shirtsleeves now, he opened the trunk. She pulled the suitcase, which seemed to be getting heavier with every effort she made to move it. This accounted for the dull ache she felt between her shoulder blades.

The terminal doors slid open, and the early afternoon heat rose from the sidewalk like shimmering plumes of clear vapor. In no time at all, she felt sticky again. Mr. Córdoba loaded her suitcase and violin into the trunk, and she slipped the laptop next to them. He then came around and held the car door open for her.

"Are you feeling all right?" he asked, clearing his throat but not quite looking at her.

"Oh, I'm fine, really. I'm just tired. And it's so hot." Maité warily eyed the leather interior of the vehicle.

"Ah, yes, well." He closed her door and trotted back to the driver side. He started the engine, and at once the vents spewed hot air at them. From the speakers came the voice of a radio announcer saying something in Spanish about a park concert series.

"It will not be a long drive," he promised and then turned up the volume.

Maité gathered there would be no conversation and she stared at him, trying to make up her mind as to whether she should thwart his efforts to avoid her. Knowing he'd been intended for her mother somehow made Maité want to provoke him. There was no doubt he was refusing to look at her.

Let it pass, she thought and wondered instead if the reason he avoided her eyes was simply because she reminded him of Alba. *Why, after so many years would he still feel tense about my mom?*

Mr. Córdoba had his seatbelt on now.

"Did you ever meet my mother, sir?" she blurted, knowing full well he had to have met her.

Mr. Córdoba checked the rear-view mirror, turned off the emergency lights, and turned his blinker on. "A long time ago, yes," he replied, focusing on his driving.

Maité wished she hadn't said anything. His short answer sounded bitter, and she didn't want to think about what his regrets might be.

The radio announcer stopped babbling, and a piano and violin sonata began as they merged into sparse traffic. Maité distracted herself with one of her favorite exercises, putting her life to music. *Leave it to the violin to fix my first glimpses of the Basque Country forever in my head.*

The air conditioning at last began to cool, and in less than half an hour they entered the city of San Sebastián. Tall apartment buildings lined the highway, and Maité amused herself looking at the clean clothes hung out to dry from every other balcony. She didn't see any blue jeans on the lines. Mr. Córdoba exited on a ramp marked "Amara" and drove west, away from the laundry.

He broke the silence to call her attention to the Urumea River. His tone was dry, and his words were scarce. Maité thought his attempt at conversation seemed more out of obligation than a sincere desire to draw her interest. She wondered if he held a grudge over Alba's refusal to marry him. That would certainly explain his unsociable behavior toward her. It also placed him in a distressing position, she realized, to be carting around the daughter of the woman who refused him.

He can stew in his own discomfort, Maité thought as he turned the volume up again. She glanced at the water flowing lazily alongside the road and was visited by a desire to jump in and cool off. Her day-old clothes were getting to her, but that would have to wait.

Maité gaped at the lofty architecture on the opposite side of the river. Gone were the apartment buildings. Now everything looked regal and ancient. Stucco and plaster curlicues decked every edge, corner, and rain gutter of the grand mansions sprawling the length of the street. They all had gated fences and wide staircases leading up to their main entrances.

How Dad would've loved these buildings, she sniffed.

Maité marveled at the thick vegetation sprouting around these structures and in no time, she made up her mind as to what gave the buildings their unique appearance: it was the lively greenery and dazzling splash of color from the mounds of bougainvillea and geraniums everywhere.

They approached two enormous pillars on either side of the avenue. A large copper plaque on the pillar closest to Maité read "PUENTE SANTA CATALINA." They crossed an old bridge, with the wide Urumea River rushing beneath them, and upon exiting on the other side Maité's eyes were inexplicably drawn to the only battered-down building she'd seen on the entire block. It stuck out like jeans and a T-shirt among evening gowns.

Having followed her gaze, Mr. Córdoba turned down the volume again, and without taking his eyes from the car ahead of him, he said, "Mansión María Celeste."

That meant nothing to Maité. "Sorry?"

"Mansión María Celeste," he repeated. "It belongs to your grandfather."

"The house has a name?" Maité retorted, looking at the grand building in astonishment.

Mr. Córdoba gave a brief, seemingly accidental chuckle and nodded without looking at her.

Moss sprouted from every gap between the foundation slabs of the María Celeste. The overgrown shrubs and ferns, together with the overall decaying state of the mansion, made the adjacent buildings look as if they turned their noses up at it. This made Maité uncomfortable for reasons she couldn't explain. A surge of irrational protectiveness overtook her and Maité told herself that in spite of its current state, this ruin of a mansion could once again be the grand estate it had once been. All it needed was a little attention.

Her eyes roved over every inch of the neglected façade and then crept up its walls, imagining restored masonry and fresh paint.

And the glass ...

Someone ducked out of sight behind one of the windows on the third floor of the María Celeste. Maité shuddered. "Does anyone live there?" she asked, shaken.

"No, Miss. The house has been empty for years," he replied.

"Why?" Maité stared up at the window with its grimy glass. She saw no one there now.

"I don't believe anyone was interested in refurbishing it after the fire." He glanced at the house, which bore no discernible traces of fire damage. "The owners of the Victoria Eugenia Theater," Mr. Córdoba said, pointing to the elegant building flanking her grandfather's ramshackle one, "have repeatedly offered to buy this property from your grandfather."

Maité did not like the sound of that. Dilapidated as it was, the María Celeste was the embodiment of possibility. During the brief period it took for the stoplight to change, the house sucked her into visions of massive reconstruction. She felt unaccountably possessive of it, and had Mr. Córdoba been a warmer person, she would have imposed and asked him to stop, to tell her about the fire, and explain why exactly no one wanted to fix up the place. But Mr. Córdoba drove on, and Maité kept her eye on the María Celeste until it faded from view.

Thin clouds began to roll inland—a *marine layer*, Emily would call it.

Mr. Córdoba made a left turn away from the river, onto a wide street called Alameda del Boulevard. He drove between towering buildings, which housed businesses as well as residences, and then, quite unexpectedly, the buildings parted to reveal the sea, gleaming in the sunshine like a pool of jade.

Maité gave a start and gripped the hot dashboard, trying to get as close as she could to the astonishing vision just outside the windshield. She took in the spectacular site of the Bahía de la Concha and registered various conflicting reactions within her. The splendor of it humbled her—made her feel like the luckiest person alive to be seeing it. It made her jealous to think others had been enjoying this while she didn't even know it existed, and it made her ache with desire to make it her own and be part of it forever.

Bahía de la Concha was a perfect seashell, just as its name implied. The postcard Verónica had shown her, which seemed a lifetime ago, did not begin to do it justice. Maité would've liked nothing better than for Emily to be at her side, right now, so they could properly gush over the sight. Still, she could not repress a smile of delight; the reality of the bay was beyond any airbrush magic in print. She beamed at Mr. Córdoba, and he gave her a curt nod and a half-smile to show he agreed and understood.

The strip bustled with people on their afternoon break. Shops were closed, restaurants were open, and businesspeople, women, children, and tourists alike hurried about or strolled on the paved promenade overlooking the white sands and the beckoning water.

The tamarindo trees, with their flat-as-a-pancake canopies, looked like green parasols lining the walkways, just as she had seen them in print. They provided shade for anyone who cared to sit on the benches beneath them.

Once again, Maité could scarcely contain the urge to leap from the car and plunge into the water and let the waves pelt her clean. She also wanted to be jostled by the hordes of people soaking up the salty sunshine outside and to feel the fine white sand beneath her feet.

But all too soon, Mr. Córdoba made another left turn, away from the miraculous sight, and they began winding up a steep hill, dense with shrubbery and tall trees on either side. In a matter of seconds, all traces of the paradise-like beach below were gone as they traveled uphill in dappled sunlight.

CHAPTER 17

Santillán Manor, San Sebastián

The massive wrought-iron gate stood open. Half of an S emblazoned on each side of the gate would make the letter whole when it closed.

S for Santillán, Maité thought, and a little tremor of satisfaction coursed through her. *Mom gave up her father's name for this one.* How could someone as proud as she imagined Mr. Gonzaga to be live in a place boasting the Santillán name rather than his own?

Mr. Córdoba drove the sedan past the gate and onto the gravel road beyond it.

"Is this my grandfather's property?"

"It is."

The tall trees lining the path beyond the gate put Maité in mind of a winding green tunnel; the canopy was so thick she couldn't see the sky above, nor could she see what might be at the end of the road. But after one last turn, the house made its appearance—sudden and out of nowhere, with its staggering height and massive construction, like a monstrous eruption of dark stone. The manor consisted of two hexagon-shaped towers, partially covered by ivy, and a middle section that connected them. Maité thought it looked like a fortress.

Judging by the windows carved at intervals into the massive stone, each tower appeared to be three stories high, and the center portion, though not as tall as the towers, had two rows of windows above the main entrance. She thought it splendid.

Mr. Córdoba took the circular driveway around a tiled fountain. He stopped the car at the base of the wide staircase leading up to the front door, which were two massive planks of solid oak. Each had a square porthole with ornate iron grills.

The engine stopped, and Maité's whole body sagged a little, as if the motor of the car had kept her going too.

"I'm beat," she sighed to herself.

Mr. Córdoba came around and held the car door open for her. She stepped out and stood facing her grandfather's house, feeling an ache, a deep-rooted yearning she couldn't describe. She made a silent wish, something along the lines of figuring out who she should become, now that she was on her own. The gravel shifted under her tired feet with a dry crunch.

Her eyes were drawn to a window on one of the towers. Flimsy fabric flapped in and out of it, blown by the breeze like flickering violet tongues from a mouth made of stone.

She raised her eyes to the now-overcast heavens. The sight of the ominous clouds moving inland didn't oppress her or fill her with a sense of foreboding. Instead, Maité breathed in slowly, as if revelations clung to every bit of air entering her lungs. She savored the scent of eucalyptus and salt, and her heart caught in her throat at the sight of the Cantabrian far below, shimmering in dark and light shades of turquoise.

Maité fancied herself rising with the water, swelling with the bewitching rhythm only a large body of water can muster, and she wanted to cry, to raise her arms toward heaven and declare she belonged here; she had returned and would never leave again. But she held it all in, baffled by the intensity of her feelings, and wondered how in the world she could feel such things when she hadn't even known this place existed. It had to mean something, didn't it?

"Thank you, Mr. Córdoba," she stammered, realizing he'd already unloaded her things from the trunk, and she hadn't offered to help.

"You are welcome," he replied as he wiped his forehead with a handkerchief. "I will see you later this evening."

"You'll be back for—" Before Maité could finish her question, a high-pitched scream made her wince. Mr. Cordoba locked eyes with her and arched his brows knowingly. Maité wheeled around to see where the sound came from.

A heavyset woman, almost as tall as Maité, came thundering out of the house wiping her hands on the white apron covering her light-blue uniform. All the while the woman squealed like an ambulance. "*Ay! ya llegó, mi niña!*" she screeched over and over until she was so close it made Maité's tired brain rattle inside her head.

She was scooped right off the ground and crushed into the woman's very ample bosom. Maité had no time to protest or even catch the breath being squeezed out of her. When the woman finally put her back on the ground, Maité realized Mr. Cordoba had disappeared, car and all.

"I didn't get a chance …"

"It is *soooooo* good you are here, mi niña!" The woman clamped her pudgy arm around Maité's waist and marched her toward the house. "I just cannot believe it, mi niña, that you are here!" With her free hand, she pinched Maité's cheek while her approving eyes inspected every inch of Maité's face.

Maité gaped at the plump, flushed-with-excitement face of this complete stranger who kept cuddling her forcefully. While the woman prattled and ogled, Maité wondered if her ribs were intact, and whether she'd get a chance to say anything, for the woman gushed incessantly, like a busted fire hydrant.

"*Mi niña, mi niña,* come this way! *Ay. Pero qué bonita estás,*" she babbled on. "*Mi nombre es Soledad,* but you call me Sole, okay? I take care of the house for your *abuelo.*"

"Um, my name is Maité." She managed to squeeze the words in when Soledad took a quick breath.

"*Sí, sí. Claro!* I just have to hug you again, mi niña!" Without waiting for so much as a nod, Soledad crushed Maité in yet another tight embrace. "*Ay!* And when I heard about your mamá!" now Soledad bawled, "my little Alba! She is gone!" Soledad gave her own face a broad wipe with her apron and went back to crushing Maité in her arms. "How I loved your mamá!"

It was impossible to refuse or escape Soledad, so Maité gave in to her warmth with a mixture of apprehension and longing. One way or another, it felt good to be welcomed. It felt good to be hugged by arms that had—very likely—hugged her mother too.

"*Lo siento mucho* that your *abuelo* won't be here to meet you," she said, shaking her head as she dragged Maité into the manor's cavernous foyer.

"What?" Maité spurted, fixing her eyes on Soledad. This was a new revelation. Only vaguely did she register the grandeur of her surroundings.

"Sí, mi niña," Soledad said with a sniff, "he won't be back until, how you say, *Sábado*? Saturday!"

"That's three days! But why?" Maité realized only now how curious she'd been to meet her grandfather, and her disappointment at not finding him upon arrival was acute. So what if he wasn't at the airport?—she had been sure she would meet him at the house, tonight.

"Ah, *porque* he had to go on a trip with the lady, you know, the one I don't like?"

"What lady?" Maité's head swam. Even with her low expectations of her grandfather, Maité thought a prolonged absence was downright offensive, as if he was going out of his way to avoid her.

"A lady. *Vaya!* I don't really think she's a lady," Soledad huffed, "But a—a woman—who has been coming to see him mucho. She is trouble for him, I think." She clucked her tongue in disapproval.

"Sole! What are you talking about? What woman?"

"Ay! You called me Sole!" Soledad gave her a one-armed squeeze that made Maité's eyeballs wobble in their sockets. "*Perdóname, niña!* Is too much for you, you just arrived. *Lo siento, lo siento!*" Soledad apologized and bear-hugged Maité some more, apparently to make up for loading her with too much information so soon. "You don't worry, okay?" Soledad said, bending Maité down to her like a long-stemmed daisy and planting a big kiss on her forehead.

"I show you the house and your room. You look so tired!" Soledad went on. "We get your things later." She led Maité across the foyer and up a huge, zigzagging staircase lined with windows, from which she could see thick foliage outside, swaying in the breeze.

Maité wrestled with her confusion. Her grandfather wasn't home; he was out with some woman who was obviously more important to him than the arrival of his orphaned granddaughter. Certainly not what she'd expected. This man wouldn't be attempting to win her over, as she had secretly imagined.

Soledad's prattling diminished considerably while they climbed the three flights of stairs. Evidently, she needed all the air she could get and did a lot of panting and grunting at every step, which left Maité to her turbulent thoughts.

At the top of the stairs, Soledad gave one last grunt of relief and said, "Going downstairs is better." She wiped the sweat off her face with a corner of her apron. Maité smiled politely and glanced over the rail. They were on the third floor, and the foyer was indeed a long way down.

I'm not interested in him either—I'll show him, she couldn't help thinking.

Soledad breathed deeply and made whistling noises while gripping the banister. They were in an airy rectangular landing with two doors at opposite ends, which she imagined led to the towers on either side. "I don't come upstairs too much, but you are young, so you go up and down these stairs to me, okay? Okay, *aquí estamos!*" She pulled Maité to their right.

With a satisfied smile Soledad opened the solid panel door and gestured for Maité to enter. This was the room whose windows Maité had seen from the driveway; it was decorated in shades of purple and white.

Two tall windows stood on either side of a set of French doors leading to the room's private balcony. The windows were hung with delicate lavender gossamer, ballooning out in the breeze in soothing waves, like the green sea beyond. A four-poster bed covered in immaculate white bedding and loaded with pillows was the centerpiece, and the sight of it transported Maité into thoughts of a long-awaited nap.

Or a coma.

A heavy armoire stood open and ready for her things, and opposite the French doors, she saw a sparkling clean bathroom. She thought again about how much she needed to shower, and suddenly she wanted nothing more than for Soledad to leave her alone. Maité wanted to explore her new room and collect her thoughts.

Mercifully, Soledad appeared to have read her mind. "I go finish the dinner now, and Plinio will bring your things *en un momento*. Plinio works here too. He is very nice. You take a shower and sleep, and then I come call you to eat, sí?"

Yes, shower and sleep. Maité sighed. Soledad took this as a sign that she needed another hug. This time Maité giggled and hugged her back.

Soledad closed the door on her way out, and the room became blissfully quiet.

Well, Grandfather—I'm not interested either, she thought and then became distracted by the distant sound of the surf far below and the muffled rumbling of cars along the promenade.

Maité opened the French doors and walked onto the narrow balcony and into the dwindling warmth of the afternoon. Columns of sunshine broke through the clouds and sparkled on the water. The place felt like a dream.

No, not dreaming, Maitagarri, came the caressing voice in her ear. The numbing began to take over. Maité shuddered, wondering if she'd imagined it or if there really was someone speaking to her. Could there be a ghost or a spirit traveling with her?

The voice wasn't her father's; she knew that. Yet whoever he was, he certainly seemed aware of where she was and what was happening to her at all times, like an invisible witness to everything Maité thought or did. She experienced no fear with the voice, nor did she feel concern for her sanity any longer. As irrational as it seemed that a disembodied voice had made contact with her, it didn't disturb her anymore. In fact, she embraced it, although she could not honestly make out whether it was to satisfy her curiosity or to indulge in the thick sensuality she experienced with each contact.

On the balcony, the breeze blew soft and warm. She supported her weight on the banister, trying not to lose herself in the luxurious heaviness prompting her to dream.

Her eyes came to rest on a mass of shrubby earth protruding from the sparkling bay. She remembered seeing postcards of it and recalled with a little effort it was the island of Santa Clara. *Yes,* said the voice, and the feeling began to dispel, as if he'd at last gotten her to look at what he wanted.

She noted the dome-like shape of the islet beneath its thick vegetation and thought its roundness peculiar, like it had been made that way on purpose. That seemed odd enough to Maité, but there was more; the island appeared suspiciously deserted. Not one of the small sailboats glided near it or docked on its shore. The scattered fishermen in their canoes seemed intent in keeping a safe distance.

Why?

Maité looked on from her balcony, feeling drawn to the small island. She appraised the distance from the beach and wondered if she could swim out to it. But before she could come to any conclusion about whether or not she had the stamina for such a feat, she came back to her current need of a shower. Without further delay, she dragged herself into the bathroom and let the water run.

Clean towels and toiletries had been set out for her, as well as a robe hanging from a hook behind the door. She undressed and stepped into the hot shower. She noticed a sweet fragrance mingling with the steam but couldn't believe bathroom cleaners in Spain smelled so good. It had to be the water. Half an hour later, and most reluctantly, she shut it off. By then she'd grown accustomed to the flowery scent wafting in the air and figured the house must have its own aromatic spring. It felt wonderful to be clean again. She put on the robe and wrapped the towel around her head like a turban.

She heard a faint knock at her door. When Maité opened it, she found herself face to face with an upsettingly disfigured old man who appeared to be on the verge of snarling. A pair of coarse trousers and a wrinkled linen shirt hung from him, giving him a vague resemblance to a scarecrow.

Grandfather? she thought in confusion. *This can't be him ...*

She choked down a panicky gasp as she glimpsed her suitcase, quickly remembering Soledad had said something about a man bringing up her luggage.

She cleared her throat to hide the uncomfortable feeling overwhelming her. She couldn't be sure, but she had a feeling the man was shocked at the sight of her. She wondered if perhaps he considered her robe and headdress completely inappropriate. Or perhaps he was simply angry she was here.

"I'm sorry," she stammered shuffling her feet, which she noticed made steamy auras on the polished wood floor. She wondered if it would stain as she pulled the robe's collar higher to cover more of her neck, "I didn't have my bags, so, um, I couldn't get dressed."

He averted his gaze, ignoring her words. He slung the laptop bag over his bony shoulder and lifted the suitcase and violin with ease. He limped past her into the room without excusing himself or asking permission. He hastened to place everything by the armoire then walked toward the door, still avoiding her eyes—in fact, ignoring her altogether, as if he hadn't seen her in the first place. He was almost out the door when he stopped abruptly.

He appeared to deliberate a few moments, his withered hand clasping the door frame, and then he fixed her with a crooked glance from his squinty eyes and blurted, "I have seen you before." With this puzzling declaration lingering in Maité's ears, he turned on his heel and headed for the stairs.

Maité didn't know what to make of his unnerving statement. Could her mother have sent pictures to her grandfather? She started quickly after him, "You have seen me?"

He turned back and Maité paused, worried. His hunched-over body made his movements deliberate in a frightening way. He cocked his head to the side so one eye looked like a slit, while the other bulged almost entirely out of its wrinkled socket. Startled, Maité took a step back.

His voice was more of a bark when he said, "My name is Plinio."

Disconcerted, Maité stared at him for a moment wondering if his mind, like his face, wasn't quite there. "Um, yes, nice to meet—"

He cut her off. "You are welcome." The man obviously had a knack for making disconnected remarks, for she was certain no form of thanks had come out of her mouth. Or maybe he was having a conversation with someone inside his head, and Maité heard only his side of it. Now there was a thought. Maybe he, like her, had a secret, mental correspondent.

That's whack.

Plinio began hobbling down the stairs, and Maité, having forfeited the question she wanted to ask, *Where has he seen me?* watched his awkward descent with a mixture of pity and terror. He clearly didn't want her enquiring further, but why then would he assert such a thing as having seen her before and then just leave it at that?

Creepy.

CHAPTER 18

Still mulling over Plinio's attitude, Maité went back in her room, thinking she might have time for a short nap before dinner.

Better not, she thought. *If my head hits that pillow, I won't wake up for a week.*

"Boy! Sole sure was off on that one," she muttered, remembering Soledad's description of Plinio as *nice.* His ailments aside, Maité found him abrupt and rude. "He has no manners," she told her reflection in the mirror as she angrily unraveled the towel from her head and began combing her wet hair. "'Nice' my butt! He seems more like an escaped convict." When she finished combing, she pulled her suitcase onto a chair and rummaged through it until she found something comfortable to wear.

Still absorbed in her thoughts, Maité left the room, eyes downcast as she went down the stairs. She reached the second floor landing and, spotting a pair of worn boots out of the corner of her eye, she gave an involuntary jerk, realizing in a blink they were attached to someone's legs. Someone stood there like a statue of a hunchback.

A scream gurgled in the back of her throat, but it came out like a short yelp as her eyes searched Plinio's face. He looked at her through his squinty eye while a malignant smirk spread across his disfigured face. He seemed pleased to have caught her off guard.

"Why are you just standing there?" she demanded, angry at having been spooked and incensed by the disturbing expression on his face.

"I have something for you." His voice was like a deep grumble issuing from his chest.

"What?"

"You will see." He cut her off again with that malevolent sneer of his, which further disfigured his withered face.

"I'm *not* interested!" she glowered at him and held his gaze, and she then purposely turned her back and continued down the stairs. "What is wrong with that guy?" she muttered, careful not to look back, because she knew he was still on the landing, leering at her. She could feel it.

Where does he get off creeping around like that and making pointless comments?

Maité felt beyond any fear of him because his insolence put her past all patience, but still, she hoped he didn't hang out inside the house too much.

She reached the bottom of the stairs and found herself opposite the front door in the receiving hall. Two impressive portico-like archways faced each other, centered lengthwise along the foyer. Swords and shields hung on the walls on either side of the porticos, and massive ceramic pots with leafy fichus trees gave the otherwise cold entrance hall a welcoming look. She looked from side to side, wondering which of the two archways would lead her to the kitchen.

From her left, Maité heard the muffled sound of dishes clinking, so she set out in that direction. She found Soledad in the kitchen, bustling about putting dinner together. The smell of fish among the layers of spice filling the air roused her appetite at once.

Here, like in her room, Maité found the well-crafted French doors, except this pair opened to a lush garden complete with tomato vines, herbs, and a delightfully green forest. The kitchen had no ocean view, but the cool darkness beneath the trees and the well-tended rows of bushy plants made the sight serene and inviting.

"*¡Aquí estás, mi niña!*" Soledad squealed, hurrying over to her and wiping her hands on her apron before scooping Maité into a hug. "You smell so pretty, and you look so nice!" she gushed. "You remind me so much of your mamá." Soledad shook her head.

"Thank you, Sole. What are you making?" Maité asked, trying not to break down as she'd been doing so often in the past few days.

"Mr. Córdoba is coming to dinner, he will be here *a las nueve*, and he likes the fish—do you like the fish?"

"Yes, I do," Maité said politely, hoping it wouldn't be some bizarre local recipe. She dismissed the unsettling visions of a bug-eyed catfish, whiskers and all, surrounded in parsley and staring at her from a silver platter.

"*¡Bueno, bueno!*" Soledad smiled, whirling back toward the stove.

"Why is Mr. Córdoba coming if my grandfather isn't here?"

"Your *abuelo* told him to. He didn't want you to feel all alone."

"How thoughtful of him," Maité said snidely, more to herself than to Soledad. "I wish he—"

"I know, I know."

"What will I talk to Mr. Córdoba about? He hardly said anything in the car on the way here."

"*Sí—qué lástima*—he is a very quiet man, but he is bringing his son with him, and maybe you can talk with him?" Soledad grinned hopefully.

"Great. Dinner with two complete strangers." Maité sighed, wishing dinner time was earlier in Spain so she could be in bed in an hour rather than just starting the night. "And what's the deal with that Plinio guy? How can you say he's nice?" No sooner had she uttered the words than she realized Plinio was standing at the kitchen door. Maité jumped; he'd followed her in.

"Plinio!" Soledad scolded him. "What are you doing there? And don't be smiling like that! You are going to scare *niña* Maité!" Soledad shook the wooden spoon at him, and to Maité's complete surprise, Plinio's scarred face rearranged itself into a sober expression, which accompanied by the sheepish shuffling of his feet and the nervous turning of his straw hat in his hands, made him appear vulnerable and chastised.

Plinio lowered his eyes to the floor, which gave Maité a few moments to compose herself from the shock.

"Go, go!" Soledad shooed him away. Plinio submissively opened the French doors and disappeared into the mini forest outside. "Come, niña, help me take these dishes to the dining room."

Maité followed Soledad through a narrow swinging door leading into a hidden service passageway. Sconces lined the way, and she imagined in years past that torches must have burned in them, but now they were merely decorative. Through another swinging door, they entered a huge dining hall.

Fine lace covered an enormous mahogany table partially set for a meal. The silverware sparkled under the light of the ornate chandelier above their heads. Soledad began deftly arranging the three place settings. It seemed to Maité there were way too many knives, forks and spoons—not to mention cups. Each setting had three different glass sizes. Maité felt something heavy and cold settle in her belly as visions of her fumbles through the elegant dinner party tortured her.

The delicate china clinked while Soledad layered one dish over another. Maité felt underdressed, and not only that, but she was unprepared, incapable of handling this type of affair. She'd pictured a quick meal in the kitchen with Soledad and Mr. Córdoba, but now she felt foolish for not having foreseen the reality. This is what Verónica meant by "social standing and breeding."

In her grandfather's world, there was the right and the wrong sort of people, and Maité was beginning to feel like the wrong sort. She took in the large room, feeling more and more oppressed by its sumptuousness. She longed for the casual warmth of the kitchen counter back at home, where she and her parents ate their meals most of the time.

The high ceilings encased in their massive wood carvings seemed to stare their disapproval of her. The tall windows stretching from floor to ceiling mocked her with the breezy freedom beyond while holding her captive.

The mural on the wall opposite the windows had no doubt been commissioned for this room. Maité couldn't recall ever seeing anything so rich in detail. This was no swap-meet bargain, nor was it a mass-produced lithograph. It was a depiction in sepia of San Sebastián's Bahía de la Concha.

As it must've looked more than a hundred years ago, she conjectured somberly.

She counted twelve high-back leather chairs around the table and tried to measure the massive stone fireplace, which took up the entire wall opposite the passageway. Everything about this room intimidated her. The fact that soon, two very stiff Spaniards would be expecting her to play hostess didn't ease her mind at all.

"*¿Qué pasa,* mi niña?" Soledad cooed, holding a delicate porcelain dish midway to the table, "are you feeling bad?"

"Oh. No, no!" Maité stammered, trying to arrange her expression into something less sickly looking. "Should I change my clothes or something?" She spoke in a nonchalant tone, hoping to hide her fears of being found inadequate.

"*¡Ay,* mi niña!" Soledad laughed. "You can dress in paper bags, and you will be beautiful anyway!"

"So I shouldn't change?" Maité hesitated, wondering if she should at least do something about her still-damp hair. "I know Mr. Córdoba will show up wearing a three-piece suit, and his son will probably be wearing the same."

"No, no, you are fine. Don't worry, mi niña. Is only dinner!" Soledad replied, setting the last plate on the table.

Maité wasn't convinced; she looked down at her jeans and cotton shirt. *Flip flops, for crying out loud!* Sitting at such a table dressed as she was would certainly offend Mr. Córdoba and his son.

"I'm running upstairs to change," she said ready to sprint, but the sound of chimes interrupted her; Maité whirled toward Soledad, who smiled benignly as she fussed over the napkin on the last place setting,

"They are here, mi niña, come with me to the door."

Maité's feet seemed glued to the floor, but Soledad swept past her, snagging her with one flabby arm and dragging her out of the dining hall, not through the service passageway, but through the portico and back to the foyer.

It was after nine o'clock and Maité felt dead on her feet from exhaustion. Also, she dreaded the look of disdain and disapproval she'd surely see in Mr.

Córdoba's eyes. Slouching, she followed Soledad and stood silent by one of the fichus plants. Soledad straightened her apron and patted the sides of her hair, tucking a few stragglers behind her ears. Maité backed a little closer to the wall wishing she could excuse herself from the whole thing.

Through the beveled glass panels and ornate iron of the front doors, Maité could distinguish two figures on the other side. Both wore dark clothes.

They'd better not be wearing tuxedos, she thought in a panic.

In the midst of her turmoil, her ears popped. The voice came heatedly into her head, taking her completely by surprise. *Remember, you are mine,* Maitagarri.

Her gasp went unnoticed because Soledad had opened the door and was already welcoming Mr. Córdoba and his son in her jolly manner.

All of Maité's senses shifted inward, tucked neatly under the heavy blanket of her thickened skin. There was nothing but that delicious shiver brought on by the voice. His hot breath on her neck and ears coursed up and down her spine and to the very tips of her toes. The warmth—*good God,* had she actually felt someone's lips grazing the line of her jaw?

All she could make out were two indistinct male silhouettes in front of her. Mr. Córdoba kept speaking, but all Maité heard were polite fragments. "… see you again, I trust you … a chance to rest …"

You are mine.

Maité fought to place herself back in the moment, but it was hard when her ears seemed packed with cotton balls and her limbs felt so heavy she could hardly move.

Maité gradually became aware of Soledad's chubby fingers squeezing her elbow. Floundering, she cast her eyes on Soledad's inquiring face, and that simple gesture seemed to break the trance.

At once Mr. Córdoba's voice reached her more clearly. "…indeed such a long trip … difficult circumstance," she heard him say. "I was so sorry to hear what happened to your parents …"

Remember, you are mine, said the voice again, and Maité shivered visibly but forced herself to remember who the man in front of her was and why he was there.

Maité offered her hand as a greeting, and he took it, but instead of shaking it, Mr. Córdoba pulled her toward him and kissed first one side of her face and then the other. She felt no more than a light pressure on either side. She still seemed to have five layers of flesh, though they were thinning.

Air kisses. That's how people greet one another here, she reasoned distractedly.

It felt awkward, especially after the way Mr. Córdoba behaved during the ride from the airport. His polite kisses couldn't help having a cooling effect, quite opposite to the lingering sensations left by the assaults of her disembodied companion, although the intensity of the last contact with the voice had rattled Maité to the core; never before had she become so disoriented, and she didn't like that.

Mine, the voice again echoed through her.

"—meet my son, David," Mr. Córdoba continued, and Maité strained to listen.

My Maitagarri, the voice declared.

Mr. Córdoba's son. Maité withdrew her hand and extended it mechanically toward the young man. When her gaze shifted to this new acquaintance, all disorientation and thickness of skin lifted entirely. There was no voice, there was no warm breath on her neck, and there were no shivers, only a young man standing before her, his green eyes twinkling with interest.

David looked like something out of a fashion catalog, although not clad in a tuxedo. *Flip-flops*, Maité thought again, and shuffled her feet. When he spoke, his deep baritone set her to imagining him whispering to her, somewhere where they were all alone. He took the hand she offered and she flinched in confusion, like he'd caught her thinking impure thoughts, which she had.

His laughing eyes stayed on her. "It is a pleasure to meet you, Miss Bottini," he said. Like his father had done, he drew her toward him and kissed her right cheek, and then her left. Maité's heart fluttered.

She struggled with the ups and downs of her body. She'd gone from a state of near paralysis with the voice of one man, straight to tachycardia at the sight of another in fewer than two minutes! Meanwhile, Soledad looked like a windmill, swinging her arms in great big circles in her efforts to get the two men to pass the threshold and into the house.

David motioned for Maité to go ahead. She followed Soledad, who guided them into the sitting room through the archway on their right. Panic-stricken, Maité realized she had not uttered a single word in the past five minutes. She hadn't responded to either man's greeting, and she hadn't attempted any kind of conversation, although things were said where it would have been appropriate for her to comment. Mortified and at a loss for a way to rectify her blunder, she turned crimson when David motioned for her to sit.

David sat on the chair next to hers while Maité's eyes remained fixed on an indifferent spot on the rug. Soledad babbled away to Mr. Córdoba, and before retiring to the kitchen she informed them that dinner would be served in half an hour.

In the uncomfortable silence following Soledad's departure, Maité thought of her mother and felt more out of place than ever, aware that her mother would have known exactly what to do at such a moment, and resenting the fact that she wasn't here to save her.

But I'm my mother's daughter, she told herself firmly, realizing there were, in fact, some etiquette basics embedded in her; she just needed to make a little effort and venture beyond her shyness.

She sat up straight at once and raised her eyes to Mr. Córdoba, who bounced on the balls of his feet, bearing a complacent smile as he inspected his surroundings with interest. Maité's expression relaxed, and with a voice that sounded fresh to her own ears, she heard herself say, "I would like to offer you something to drink." She hoped she sounded confident. "But I don't know where anything is …"

"You are too kind," Mr. Córdoba interjected. "And of course, you have only just arrived. If you will permit me, I will show you where your grandfather keeps a cabinet. I am sure we will find something suitable to drink prior to dinner there, yes?"

Maité nodded, relieved, and stood up with Mr. Córdoba to go find the cabinet. David stood up as well. When she looked at him, his expression seemed to flash encouragement.

She averted her gaze, not knowing what to make of him. His eyes were so expressive, so penetrating, but she couldn't bring herself to look at him long enough to decipher what he sought. She stared at the floor again, and in doing so, she noticed David's designer shoes and expensive-looking trousers.

I should've changed my clothes. Maité let out a miserable grunt but regretted it at once; she knew the two men heard it, and it humiliated her that they pretended they hadn't.

Maité's inner turmoil gave way to awe as she followed Mr. Córdoba into the library. She hadn't been in there yet, and she gaped open-mouthed at the grandeur of this new room. There where shelves filled with leather-bound volumes, and very important-looking tomes lined every inch of the walls. The room appeared to be made of books!

Maité looked around at the velvet-upholstered chairs arranged before yet another massive fireplace. Several paintings hung on the walls, and she made a mental note to study them more closely; a handful appeared to be portraits of family members.

The windows were hung with heavy draperies in a deep shade of red, parted and tied with golden ropes. Beyond them, Maité could see the restful courtyard.

"Allow me to be the host this once," Mr. Córdoba said. "Would you care for a glass of wine?"

"Oh no, not for me, thank you," Maité said. "I'd just like some water, please." She added the latter, feeling it was wrong not to have accepted the wine. But she was nowhere near twenty-one, and the few times her parents allowed her a sip of it, she hadn't liked it anyway.

"I'll have some water also," David put in. "Come sit here, Miss Bottini." He motioned toward a piece of furniture too small to be a sofa and too big to be a single chair, clearly intending to share it with her.

Maité felt herself burning and was silently thankful for the dim lighting in the room. "Please call me Maité," she managed to say. She didn't dare look at David; she didn't want to see his teasing eyes. "I can't get used to being treated so formally." She felt immature making such an admission, but there it was.

"Of course. Things are so casual in America," David remarked.

She was gratified not to detect even the slightest trace of scorn in his deep voice. Maité relaxed her hands, which had been balled into fists.

"So, Maité, there will be no need for us to be so formal. We can get on with being friends, no?"

Her name sounded delicious coming from his mouth. "That would be nice," she assented, already regaining some degree of composure. Feeling a little braver, Maité sneaked a darting glance toward him. He sat very close to her, but he was listening to his father at the moment.

What a perfect profile, she thought, and when it seemed like he would look at her again, she turned the other way.

"Here we are," Mr. Córdoba said, handing her a napkin and a heavy crystal goblet filled with water. David took his as well. Mr. Córdoba held aloft his glass filled with red wine and gravely declared, "Welcome to San Sebastián, Miss Bottini. We are happy to have you here."

Maité smiled, raising her water as Mr. Córdoba had done. David clinked his glass to hers, and looking into her eyes, he leaned closer and said, "Thank you for coming to San Sebastián."

No way! Her eyes grew round with surprise. *He's flirting with me!* The realization felt like a spray of something toasty in her belly. A disbelieving grin appeared on her face.

After half an hour in the library with the two men, Maité's blushing attacks calmed a bit. She'd also stolen longer glimpses at David and was at a loss to find a flaw in him. He was too handsome for words, and she couldn't help feeling greedy for him; she wished they were alone, but then she didn't know what she'd say or do if they ever were.

Through dinner, Mr. Córdoba kept up the conversation almost entirely on his own, which left Maité free to sort out her nerves and confusion and to duck David's direct glances—it seemed he couldn't keep his eyes off her. Maité's belly fluttered reminding her vaguely of the first time she'd been shown how to fly in her dreams. And like that time, Maité put her hand over her stomach, wondering about the similarities between the two sensations.

By the time Soledad brought dessert and coffee, Maité had learned Mr. Córdoba was not only curator of the museum but her grandfather's financial advisor and executor of the Santillán estate. He was Mr. Gonzaga's right-hand man.

"Pardon me," Maité murmured, for she had a nagging question she thought Mr. Córdoba would be able to answer. "Why do you call it the Santillán estate? Shouldn't it be Gonzaga?"

David, who had attentively fixed her with his eyes while she posed her question, now leaned back in his chair and looked expectantly at his father.

Mr. Córdoba cleared his throat. "Yes, of course."

The clearing of his throat and the "of course" seemed his way of beginning his sentences. Maité figured it was probably an exercise to remind him that people didn't share his considerable knowledge, which, in her case, was perfectly true.

He set down his coffee and continued. "It has been so for many decades. Sometime in the mid-eighteen hundreds, there was a consolidation of two rather large properties through the marriage of Celeste Santillán to Etienne St. Michel. You might say that is where the affluence of the family began, but it was not until 1916 that legal documents were drafted. In them, Santillán was the name used when referring to the family's holdings."

Maité nodded. Clearly, someone with the name of Gonzaga wasn't allowed to own something labeled with another's name. But she dared not press for confirmation; she didn't want to appear completely ignorant of legal issues, even if she was.

Mr. Córdoba went on. "The family owned several large estates throughout the Basque country, and their investments have always been sound. Today, the Santillán estate consists of three parts: the María Celeste by the river, which you saw earlier on our way from the airport," he reminded her, "worth its size in gold because of its location; then there is the manor we're now in—equally valuable; and the vast lands at the base of the western Pyrenees. These three properties are the patrimonial estate of Santillán, which confers the solid social standing and financial stability its holders enjoy."

All had been fine and good for years, Maité heard him say, but then a woman came into Mr. Gonzaga's life—the woman Maité's grandfather was with on this very night and who, for reasons known only to herself, wanted the land in the Pyrenees. Mr. Córdoba's eyebrows arched significantly as he spoke of this woman, but his meaning was lost on Maité. She had no way of grasping the seriousness of the circumstances, unaware as she was of the events leading to the current state of things.

Mr. Córdoba sighed and looked away, which she took to mean, "Why do I bother explaining things to this child?" She felt a prickle of injured pride and berated herself for being so distracted by David's nearness and for having missed a crucial piece of information from this man, who obviously meant to include her in her grandfather's affairs.

Maité resolved to make up for her negligence straightaway, but Mr. Córdoba shook his head and cleared his throat again. "Miss Bottini, I am most sorry to have troubled you with this information, and I hope you will forgive me."

Maité didn't like the condescending tone he'd assumed. Something had gone amiss. "There is nothing to forgive," she stammered, giving David a helpless look and trying not to wonder about the mix of empathy and mirth she saw in his eyes.

David came to the rescue and said with a diplomatic, pleasant voice, "Your grandfather will not be returning for a few days. I'm sure you'd like to rest and get your bearings tomorrow, but may I call on you the day after and show you our beautiful city? It is my opinion that San Sebastián is the jewel of the Basque country."

Maité acknowledged David's proposition with a tremulous nod, but her eyes went back to Mr. Córdoba, still feeling he'd let slip something important that she'd glimpsed too late—and misunderstood to boot. Maité wished she knew what the secret was.

"It is an excellent idea, Miss Bottini," Mr. Córdoba said. "Allow David to show you around; no sense in your being cooped up here in weather such as we have this time of year." He had returned to the polite, obligatory demeanor that irked her.

Exasperated, Maité wanted to raise some sort of protest but didn't know where to begin. It seemed there was so much she didn't know, she had no choice but to ease up on her own frustration. She made a mental promise to remedy her ignorance, even if, for the time being, they had brought her around to do their will.

"That would be very nice," she said about David's invitation. *And at least,* she thought, *I'm irritated enough not to turn blotchy red.*

Dinner ended, and in a show of good breeding, the two men refused to linger and further impose upon the hospitality of their exhausted hostess.

Back in the foyer, Mr. Córdoba and David looked politely attentive while Soledad talked to them at high volume. She accused them of not coming to the house more often and of looking as if they worked too much. Without drawing breath, Soledad went on to hug David, much in the same manner she'd been hugging Maité since she arrived, almost lifting him off the ground.

"You have stayed away too long, *mi* David, and you keep getting so tall!" she chastised him, and he laughed heartily at that. "Maybe now you come more often," Soledad hinted with a shifty glance toward Maité.

Maité shuddered at the thought.

Mr. Córdoba kissed Maité again. *Three times for good-bye*, she thought as she turned her head this way and that. He wished her a good night, and she uttered a timid, "You too." David's lips lingered close to her ear after his third kiss.

"So long then," he said. His eyes swept over her whole face as he withdrew. Her legs trembled. How would she survive an entire day with him?

"*Hasta mañana*, sorry, *pasado mañana*," she corrected herself, and he gave her a winning smile.

"Yes, day after tomorrow," he nodded.

Soledad put one arm around Maité, giving her a hearty squeeze while waving with the other. "That was not so bad, eh?"

Maité shook her head, staring after David. *Not too bad at all*.

CHAPTER 19

After less than half an hour of Soledad's whirling chit-chat, everything was sorted in Maité's new room; all her clothes were unpacked, folded, and deposited in drawers or hung in the armoire across from her bed. Her violin stood in a corner of the room where Soledad promised to put a stand for it. "I will find one in the attic, sí?"

"Thank you, Sole," Maité said, giving her a kiss goodnight and receiving one last hug in return.

Maité closed the bedroom door, shaking her head because she could still hear Soledad's groans as she made her way down the three flights of stairs. She heaved a tired sigh as she looked at her new space and grinned when David's face popped into her thoughts. "Nope, it wasn't bad at all," she whispered, but a nervous flutter darted across her midsection at the prospect of seeing him again. What would she do? What would she say? *I'd better come up with something!*

But that something was forgotten as soon as she saw the laptop on the night table beside her bed. Sick with guilt, Maité booted up and found more than *forty* new messages waiting for her. "Em!" she moaned in despair, "how could I have spaced you out!"

She'd been so overwhelmed with the particulars of the arrival, and then so immersed in the presence of the two men she hadn't spared a thought to anything else.

But now, reality came crashing back in cold waves: the recollection of why she was here, and what she'd left behind gave Maité a sort of spiritual nausea she felt she deserved. Why did she allow herself to become so engrossed in this house? *It's just a building.* And in David? *He's just a guy!* How could she have forgotten her parents were dead? Nothing, absolutely nothing should have taken her mind off that. *How could I!*

As if telling her to lighten up, Alba's laughter filled Maité's mind all of a sudden, reminding her of a day long ago. "You're such a faery, little girl," her mother had said, and when eleven-year-old Maité looked puzzled, she explained about the transient nature of the faery in the book they'd been reading. She said the feelings of faery were only skin deep.

"Faeries have a hard time focusing on anything but what is happening at the moment," Alba had explained.

"But I'm not a faery," Maité said now, swatting away the memories. "So I have no excuse." With a groan, she scanned through the numerous and increasingly desperate messages from her best friend.

"Hey, M, by now I'm sure you've landed, so I'll give you a couple of hours to get to your grandfather's house, get settled, and let me know how it all went. Love, Em."

Ten messages later: "Hey M, did you get stuck in customs? I hope everything is okay. We should have reviewed that Basque language, you know? At least some basic phrases! Where are you??? Love, Em."

Then the messages seemed to pour in at ten-minute intervals.

"M? My mom says you're probably exhausted and that the last thing on your mind is sending me an e-mail. Is that it? Worried about you, Em."

"Cuss words, M, I'VE HAD IT! Oh no! I just thought of something. What if someone stole your laptop and you're not getting any of these messages? Or what if you were attacked and you're lying in a gutter somewhere, with your fingers crushed so badly you can't even type a message? M? Even more worried about you, Em."

The messages grew more frantic and increasingly far-fetched. Had she not felt so guilty, Maité would have laughed at Emily's nonsense.

She clicked open the last message: "I don't care what my mom says. I'm calling you right now!"

Maité barely had time to check what time the message had been sent when she heard the phone ringing downstairs. She ran out of her room and craned over the railing; within a couple moments, she saw Soledad's face looking up at her.

"It's for you, mi niña. It's your friend Emilia," she called up, looking relieved not to have to take on the stairs.

Maité raced down and snatched the cordless phone from Soledad's plump hand. "Thank you!" she said breathlessly.

Soledad pinched Maité's cheek and made cooing noises at her before heading back to the kitchen.

Maité put the phone to her ear and grinned at what she heard "—Spanish and all, but it's E-mi-ly, not *Emilia* okay?"

"Hey, Em."

"Where have you been? And why didn't you answer my messages? I thought you died or something, and now I find out—through some woman who keeps calling me *Emilia*—you've been pleasantly dining while I was on the verge of puking because I was so sick over what might've happened to you!" Emily drew a quick breath before continuing, but Maité jumped on the opportunity.

"I'm sorry, I'm soooooo sorry! I mean it. I really do, Em, and I have no excuse. I got so distracted with … well, things are not at all what I expected and I don't—"

"What's your grandfather like? My mom said she doesn't remember him being bad-looking. Is he old and cranky? Distinguished and interesting? What?"

"That's one of the things I didn't expect—I haven't even met my grandfather."

"What?"

"He wasn't here when I arrived, and he won't be here for a few more days," Maité said, hoping to sound breezy.

"He snubbed you?"

Maité felt the sting; that had been her feeling all along, but to hear it out loud made it even more painful. "Yeah, well," she began, a defensive note in her voice. "He's trying to sell some property out in the mountains, and this woman he's been seeing is interested in buying—"

"So he's out with a girlfriend rather than being home for you? After your mom just died? She was his only child! And he's out with some woman who, on top of everything, wants to buy off a chunk of your birthright?"

Tears smarted in Maité's eyes. Emily's biting words summarized the entire evening in a light that, harsh as it was, couldn't help but illuminate the truth taking shape in her own mind. There had been insinuations made by Mr. Córdoba about the property, significant glances exchanged at the mention of the prospective buyer—*How could I be such an idiot?*—and even Soledad had told her about the woman her grandfather was seeing, a woman she didn't like, a woman who was "not a lady."

How can Emily see this from ten thousand miles away, in fewer than five minutes, when like a total fool I sat there for three hours not putting two and two together?

Through Emily's rattling, Maité's thoughts spiraled into determination. "Emily!" she cried out. "First of all, I don't feel snubbed by my grandfather at all—I don't know him, and I really don't even care about getting to know him," Maité lied. "Second, I've been told that business and status come first to him, so it's no surprise he's looking out for himself. And third …" She gulped, wishing she could say this last thing without her voice quivering, for it was the most hurtful, "If he's out with a woman in that—you know—for romantic reasons, then that just makes me even more certain he's a selfish old man, and that he won't ever forgive my mom for disobeying, or care about her even after she's dead, and that's why I won't ever bother with him!"

"Geez, M! Chill already, will you? It's just that I've been so worried about you. I haven't slept all night, and all of today I've been waiting to hear from you."

"I'm sorry. I'm really sorry, but I got here and there have been so many things to see, and then I found out that the guy who picked me up at the airport was coming to dinner. He showed up with his son, and we had this massive dinner situation—you should've seen all the forks and spoons on the table just for three people! And then there were—"

"Did you say 'son'?" Emily interrupted.

"What?"

"You said son. How old is he? What does he look like?"

Maité's face felt hot. She wasn't prepared to answer questions about David, least of all the kind put to her by Emily. "Um, well, I don't know. He looked like he was nineteen, I don't know, maybe twenty?"

"Yes, and he looks like …"

"He was all right, I suppose," she said in what she hoped was an indifferent tone.

"Just all right?"

"Yeah, just all right."

"If you had to compare him to a movie star, who would you say he looked like? C'mon, c'mon! Details!"

"Emily, stop it. He was just all right, okay?"

"Oh, this is bad, really, really bad!"

"Emily …"

"He must be a real hottie if you don't even want to tell me what he looks like."

Maité could hear laughter in Emily's voice and hated the fact her friend knew her so well. "Oh stop it!" she said irritably. "It's been a long day, and I'm exhausted. I promise I'll e-mail you tomorrow as soon as I wake up and tell you everything that's happened since I got here, okay?"

"Make sure you include a lengthy stat page on the son."

Maité laughed. "I miss you, I really do, and fine, I'll try to give you an accurate description of the son, as you call him. I'll tell you all about Plinio too."

"Oh boy! Who's *Pleeno*?"

"It's Plee-nee-oh, and I'll e-mail you all about it, but I have to go to bed now because I'm falling asleep where I stand."

"All right, take care of yourself. I'll be waiting by my laptop, clicking the refresh button every thirty seconds."

"You're insane! Please kiss your mom and dad for me. And Gabriel too!"

Maité hung up, and with a smile still planted on her face, she headed for the stairs, only to find someone had been watching and listening all along.

Plinio stood semihidden in a dark corner of the foyer. The whites of his crooked eyes gleamed eerily. Maité froze.

By way of an explanation he jerked his chin toward the fixture above, and Maité figured he must've been waiting for her to finish so he could turn off the lights and lock up. Something wheezed and gurgled deep in his throat, and Maité didn't think he looked vulnerable at all right now. Maybe Soledad alone could make him look that way. She didn't dare take her eyes off him, and she gave him a wide berth as she hurried to the stairs.

Maité wanted to take the steps two at a time, but she paced herself, refusing to give Plinio the impression she was scared.

When she reached her room, she immediately locked the door, unable to shake the feeling that if she turned around, Plinio would have somehow materialized inside the room and would be staring at her from behind the curtains. With trembling knees, she turned and swiftly scanned the bedroom. Having confirmed she was alone Maité let exhaustion creep over her and soften the sharp edges of the day's tensions.

Once in bed, with the blankets pulled up under her chin, she let out a deep groan of pleasure as she sank into the thick mattress and pillows. Maité reached over and turned off the lamp. It took a few seconds for her eyes to adjust to the darkness, and then she began to see the room by the coppery glow of the city lights coming through the windows. She so wanted to relax and fall asleep, but something was not right. Something bothered her.

I'm too tired, she reasoned. But the thought didn't ease her into slumber. She thought about Emily and again told herself that first thing in the morning she would make it up to her with a really long e-mail. Maité smiled in the darkness, thinking of her friend, but then her smile froze as a flash of realization struck her.

She had seen it out of the corner of her eye when she reached over to turn off the lamp. She'd glimpsed something on the wall above the bed, something that hadn't been there before. The wall had been bare before Emily's phone call; no crucifix, no nothing. She felt certain of it.

Maité clamped her eyes shut to block out the sinister conviction that something horrible hung on the wall.

I have something for you, Plinio had told her with that evil smirk, and now that something hung above her head.

Maité's mouth felt dry and her chest felt too small for her beating heart. Tears welled in her eyes, but she blinked them away.

"*Remember you are mine, Mait—*" the hot whisper injected itself into her head with ear-popping intensity, and Maité sprang upright.

"Oh stop it! Stop it, please!" she cried through gritted teeth, clamping her hands to her ears, which still felt warm. All of a sudden she felt angry with herself and with the situation. The terror of only a few minutes before disappeared, leaving a feeling of annoyance at the unexpected *everythings* happening to her.

"I don't want to hear it anymore!" she snapped at the invisible intruder. She reached for the lamp, knowing she'd feel bolder with the light on. She tugged on the sturdy chain and the room lit up.

A thousand shiny pinpricks crowded Maité's field of vision. She rubbed her eyes and looked around the room, building up the strength to look behind her once and for all. Her overstimulated mind had conjured possibilities of the shadowy square above her bed as a black hole to another dimension, or the gaping lair of a monster, *for crying out loud!*

When at last it came into focus, the object was just a picture.

Maité relaxed. There didn't seem to be a bloody-tentacled creature— painted or otherwise—grasping for her through the wall. Maité ventured to take a closer look.

It was a portrait in a simple wood frame, which had been hand-painted in a deep forest green. Nothing extraordinary there, but the subject of the canvas was quite remarkable; a likeness of her!

There she was, Maité, beautifully rendered in oils, in the middle of a lush forest. The young woman in the painting stood at the edge of a pond, about to dip her foot in the illuminated pool. Her features were lit up by the glow from the pond, but the trees around her had been left in a spooky darkness, broken only by the large points of light Maité couldn't explain. They shined on every tree, though only on scattered branches.

Maybe they're supposed to be overgrown fireflies.

Maité studied what she thought was her own face in the portrait and noticed the eyes weren't gray but amber, like the color of honey. That's when she realized the girl wasn't her at all; it was someone else.

"How could it have been me?" she said out loud, dispelling the last of her confusion. "It's silly. Nobody knows me here, so why would they have a picture of me?" But still she knelt on her pillows and got close enough to smell the dust on the canvas. She saw three strange symbols on the right hand corner of the painting, arranged in a sort of triangle where the signature of the artist should have been, followed by 1844.

She heard Plinio's words again, as clearly as if he were standing next to her: *I have seen you before.* She gave an involuntary jerk. She knew what he meant now; the resemblance was remarkable. But who was the woman in the portrait?

Curiosity over the identity of her twin overwhelmed her so much she no longer cared how the portrait got to her room in the first place; she speculated freely but came up with nothing.

Eventually her body and brain shut down from total exhaustion. She didn't even turn off the light. *She has to be a relative*, was her last thought.

CHAPTER 20

Maité opened her eyes and registered the sunlight warming her pillow. It took her a few seconds to realize this meant it was early afternoon. She'd slept for fifteen hours!

She smiled at her surroundings and stretched her limbs, relishing the lazy pleasure of it—until she caught sight of the portrait above her bed. The incident of the night before came back to her—the fear she'd felt and the realization that the woman in the portrait, who looked like her twin, had to be a long-lost relative.

Kneeling on her pillows, Maité inspected the woman's face, but a sharp beep stopped her. "Oh shoot!" Maité scrambled off the bed and plugged the laptop in to charge the dead battery. She couldn't believe she'd slept so long; for sure there would be another long string of e-mails from Emily.

Leaving the laptop to charge, Maité walked to the landing outside her room and peered down the three flights of stairs. When no sound or movement greeted her, she decided to ascertain if she'd been left alone.

Downstairs in the foyer she found a note from Soledad and read the Spanglish scribbles with a grin—tired of waiting for her to wake, Soledad had gone for groceries.

Maité went into the kitchen and returned to her room with a glass of milk, a banana and a pear. In keeping to the promise she'd made, she typed a horrendously long message recounting everything that happened after she got off the airplane in San Sebastián. When she arrived at the part about David, she pursed her lips and typed, "Yes, he's hot." She laughed out loud, imagining Emily's reaction.

Maité took a long shower and dressed before checking her messages. She thought for sure Emily would check her e-mail every fifteen minutes, so it surprised her to find no replies.

She's probably rereading the whole thing to Aunt V, Maité thought with a chuckle.

Eyeing the violin, she picked it up before stepping out on the balcony. Pressing her chin against it, she began to play, her gaze drifting over the green Cantabrian below and settling on the island of Santa Clara.

Maité closed her eyes and swayed with the music, while in her head, Santa Clara became flat instead of round. She imagined it covered in sugary white sand in place of the green shrubs she knew grew wild there. She saw palm trees too—their fronds blowing sideways in the balmy breeze.

Unbidden, a couple waltzed into Maité's musings and turned gracefully to the music from her violin. Maité's eyes popped open in surprise.

The bow and violin hung at her sides while she stared at the shrubby island—the couple pixelated out of her thoughts, yet she felt certain she'd seen them before, even played for them in another dream.

Soledad's loud, "Mi niña, ya estoy de regreso," reached Maité from downstairs. She set the violin on its stand and stole one last glance at the island: it just sat there, covered in bushes. She skipped downstairs and helped Soledad put away the groceries, all the while talking about Alba.

Soledad shared a hundred tidbits with Maité, like where Alba used to sit at the kitchen table—the same spot Maité had chosen; Alba's favorite foods and how she loved tomatoes from the garden, with nothing but red onions and a splash of lime juice—same as Maité.

She loved hearing those things about her mother and became so engrossed in listening she thought she could see a young Alba moving about the kitchen. She forgot the painting and the questions she wanted to ask.

By the time they finished organizing things, it was close to nine thirty. Maité opted for a cup of tea and toast, plus the scrambled eggs Soledad pushed on her in place of the full-blown dinner.

By ten o'clock Maité could hear her bed calling again, and she gave Soledad a hug. As she climbed the stairs to the third floor, she promised herself that tomorrow she would be done with jetlag. Tomorrow David would be coming for her.

True to form, Maité got out of bed by eight o'clock in the morning. She took a quick shower before going down for breakfast, once again pleasantly struck by the flower-scented water springing from her showerhead. *I'll have to tell Em about that*, she thought happily and then, to her reflection in the mirror she added, "Yay for me, I adjusted to the time zone!"

Dressed in a long cotton skirt, a tee and a pair of leather sandals tied with ribbons at her ankles, she headed for the kitchen.

"Mi niña! Buenos días! Did you sleep good?" Soledad scooped her into her arms, rocking her violently side to side as she spoke.

"Yes I did, thank you," Maité replied.

"*Ven, ven,* mi niña; breakfast is ready for you, see?"

The kitchen table was crammed with food as if half a dozen people were expected. "I can't eat all that!" Maité said, horrified.

"You just eat what you can. You sit right here." Soledad pulled out Alba's chair for Maité and patted its back invitingly.

She sat and took a banana from the fruit bowl while Soledad poured a cup of coffee for herself and came to sit across from her. Maité surveyed the table trying to decide what she'd have after the fruit, but the sudden appearance of Plinio just outside the French doors made her jump.

His crooked shape filled the entire frame. The nasty, conspiring smirk on his face made her realize they shared the secret of the painting in her room, and Plinio seemed to be looking for her reaction.

Soledad clutched her breast, startled by Maité's reaction, and turned to see what had caused it. Upon spying Plinio she scolded him shrilly, "Why are you standing there like that? I told you not to smile because you scare people when you do that!"

Plinio's face rearranged itself into a chastised look, which suited him a great deal better than the smirk. He took off his hat in a hurry and twisted it in his hands; he moved forward, like he might come into the kitchen, but stopped short to give Soledad an inquiring look.

"*Y bien?*" Soledad said with her hands on her hips. "Come in here already."

He came in and set his hat on the counter. He poured himself a cup of coffee and drank it in silence.

"Plinio had a stroke a few months ago, mi niña," Soledad explained while sipping her own coffee. "And he can't move one whole side of his face, so if he smiles, he looks mean."

Maité looked from him to Soledad. Things were making a little more sense now; perhaps Plinio was a nice man after all.

"Maybe you can tell me," Maité said to Plinio politely, though not quite ready to be friends, "about the portrait that appeared in my room?"

Soledad looked from Plinio to Maité. "What picture?"

"A picture of a lady."

"What lady?" Soledad asked, clearly distressed at something going on in her household she didn't know about.

"It is her picture," Plinio said jerking his chin toward Maité. He cleared away the peculiar rattle in his voice with another thick cough.

"What you mean *her* picture?" Soledad's eyes popped, affronted now.

Maité broke in. "The day I arrived Plinio told me he'd seen me before, and that he had something to show me," she explained, avoiding the now embarrassing drama and terror she'd felt during the original experience. "It turned out to be a portrait of a lady who looks a lot like me. Actually, *I* look a lot like her." Maité added the last bit, recalling the blurry date on the bottom corner of the painting.

"Plinio, what picture you give to her?" Soledad demanded.

He coughed again. "The picture that woman wanted to take," he explained, grabbing the hat from the counter and slapping it on the side of his leg as if to dust if off.

Now it was Maité's turn to be confused. "What woman?"

"The painting that was donated?" Soledad exclaimed, ignoring Maité's question.

"I hid it," Plinio confessed.

"Ah, sí." Soledad clicked her tongue knowingly. "The one Mr. Gonzaga was so upset you couldn't find, and she was so mad!"

"Sole—what woman?" Maité asked again.

Plinio continued in confession mode; he obviously felt bad about what he'd done. Though what it was he had done, Maité had no clue.

"I hid it because it was a family picture."

"You were right to hide it," Soledad said. "Who she think she is? *Serpiente!* Wanting paintings from the family of other people."

"What woman?!"

Soledad turned a commiserating eye toward Maité. *"Ay.* Remember, mi niña? The woman I told you about, the one who wants to get your *abuelo?"*

Maité nodded and then shook her head, realizing she didn't know. "She wants to get my abuelo? What do you mean 'get' him? Who is she?"

"Her name is Eva, mi niña," Soledad replied patiently. At the sound of that name, something quickened in Maité. "She is very young and much too famous for your abuelo, but very nice looking, mucho, mucho red hair." Soledad fanned her fingers down her own broad shoulders and over her ample bosom to illustrate Eva's flowing long hair.

"Beautiful? With lots of red hair? And famous?" *Holy cow*, Maité thought. "Oh my God, Sole! You don't mean *the* Eva; the supermodel?"

"The very one!" Soledad nodded emphatically. "Don't ask me what she wants with your *abuelo;* he is too old for her. Maybe because Mr. Gonzaga is very handsome man, and he lives very well, maybe this woman ..."

Maité put her elbows on the table and held her head between her hands. "My grandfather is dating the famous supermodel Eva? She has to be at least twenty years younger than him," Maité cried out, remembering the magazine the boys at school had been passing around with an article about Eva—the woman was naked on the hood of a car, covered in nothing but her own red hair! *Emily is going to blow a gasket when she hears this.*

"What in the world does she want with him?" Maité demanded, outraged.

"She says she loves your abuelo." Soledad shook her head like she didn't believe there could be love between them. "But Mr. Gonzaga is handsome, and he is a gentleman. A woman like her maybe *nunca* knew a charming man like him!"

Even if Soledad didn't consider Eva the right companion for Mr. Gonzaga, Maité could hear the pride Soledad felt over his conquest. Maité didn't agree.

"But why would she want that painting?" Maité asked.

"*Dios sabrá*! God knows why she want it. She saw it one time, at the old house next to the theater, and she told your abuelo to clean up that house—to donate the old things. And when your abuelo sent Plinio to pick up things, she says she remembers that one picture. She says she want it."

Plinio interrupted; apparently Soledad was leaving out too many details. "She came to the María Celeste when I was there and says, 'Put this one aside, because I want it,'" Plinio quoted Eva, wagging one of his crooked fingers at a vacant spot in the kitchen. "I told her she had to ask Mr. Gonzaga, but she didn't like that."

Soledad let out a derisive snort next to Maité as Plinio went on. "She hissed like a snake and told me to bring the picture here to Mr. Gonzaga because he already knew about it."

"Ah, *bandido*! Tell us what you do after," Soledad urged excitedly.

"I took the picture down from the wall and hid it so I could pick it up the next week, see? Then I wrapped another painting in brown paper and I put the rest in the truck, and went to the Cruz Roja, because Mr. Gonzaga said this donation was for them. Then I came to the house." He finished with that crooked smile of his, but somehow it wasn't as frightening anymore, and knowing the cause of it took away whatever remaining anxiety Maité may have had.

"Why you, bandido, you never told me this!" Soledad put in, breathlessly looking from Plinio to Maité in disbelief. "And the lady in the painting looks like mi niña Maité?"

"Go on, Plinio, what happened next?" Maité asked, nodding and squeezing Soledad's pudgy hand, urging her to keep quiet.

"When I came here to the house, she was already here."

"I remember that day. She was so mad!" Soledad said gleefully.

"Mr. Gonzaga asked for the painting. So I went to get the one wrapped in brown paper and gave it to him together with the receipt I got from the Cruz Roja for the others. She was smiling the whole time with that smile—you know the one I mean—the one that is not a smile?"

"I know the smile! Ay yes! I know that one." Soledad nodded wisely.

Maité looked from Soledad to Plinio, her eyes wide. "And then what happened?"

"She took the package and took the paper off. When she saw it was not the right one, I could tell she wanted to scream, but she did not, because Mr. Gonzaga was there."

"Ay! That *bruja*!" Soledad said through gritted teeth, her hands balled up into fists.

"She cried to Mr. Gonzaga and told him it wasn't the right painting. She told him I did it on purpose, but when he asked me what happened, I just told him I was sure that was the one she pointed to."

"Bandido! Bandido!" Soledad gushed, pulling Maité to her and giving her a hearty squeeze, carried away with excitement.

Maité saw satisfaction glimmering in Plinio's squinty eye as he went on. "Mr. Gonzaga said it would be no problem. He said, 'Go back to the María Celeste and fetch the right picture,' but then I told him I already dropped everything off at the Cruz Roja."

"Ay, ay! That is when she screamed." Soledad all but bounced on her chair. "I remember. I can hear her still!" she squealed, cupping her hand like a shell to her ear.

Plinio went on. "I told Mr. Gonzaga I was really sorry, because the day I went to the Cruz Roja was the day the truck went to the big center in Madrid, and the truck left right after I helped them load the things."

Soledad burst out laughing. Maité joined in with a dazed smile, amused by a vision of how frustrated Eva must have been through Plinio's apparent comedy of errors. But what in the world did that woman want with the portrait of someone else's relative?

In the meantime, Soledad had worked herself up into such a fit of laughter that her entire frame jiggled, making her look like a huge mound of Jell-O with an apron. The sight made Maité laugh out loud, which made Soledad positively howl with laughter while reaching for a napkin to wipe the tears streaming down her cheeks.

Plinio stood by the door with his hat still clamped in his hand. He too kept wiping his eyes with the back of his hand as he shook with laughter.

"Ay, Plinio! I can't remember when I laughed so hard!" Soledad said, jiggling giggles still escaping her.

When they finally sobered up, amidst sighs and moans on Soledad's part, Maité asked, "So we don't know why Eva wanted the painting, but do we know who the woman in the painting is? Is she a relative?"

"Eat your breakfast, and I tell you what your mamá said about it," Soledad promised.

Maité picked at her food while she listened to the mixture of English and Spanish coming out of Soledad's mouth, which she didn't have any trouble understanding.

Soledad had been nineteen when Alba's mother died, leaving Mr. Gonzaga a most unhappy widower who didn't know how to care for his two-year-old daughter.

Soledad had recently started housekeeping for the Santillán family, and like her mother before her, Soledad made it her life's work, because the pay was unparalleled, the responsibility was minimal, and everyone answered to her—even Mr. Gonzaga—Soledad bragged.

Raising little Alba had been Soledad's passion and her reward. She did it with a firm hand and all the love a child could want, thus earning Alba's trust and devotion.

"That is why your mamá wrote to me every month," Soledad sniffed.

At that, the fork Maité held dropped with a clatter. Soledad quickly grabbed her hand and gave it a squeeze.

Her mother corresponded all those years with Soledad? While letting her daughter, Maité, grow up in complete ignorance of this other life.

"But one day, your abuelo said he was going to sell the María Celeste, and he hired some men to fix the house," Soledad went on, and Maité gulped down her resentment with some orange juice.

Having nothing better to do that summer, Alba had gone to the María Celeste every morning to watch the workers. With her overactive imagination, the María Celeste quickly became her palace. Every afternoon Alba came home to Soledad, exploding with ideas about the house. She wanted to live in it, she wanted to fix it, she wanted to make it live again, and she begged her father not to sell it, but he would not listen.

On one of those warm summer days, while the crew repaired the plaster statuettes perched on the outside corners of the third floor, Alba found a portrait rolled up in an old storage area. The woman in the painting intrigued her enough to make her bring it home. Alba showed it to her father, renewing her plea for him to keep the house. She argued that, like that painting, there were many treasures there.

"The house itself is a treasure," she assured him, and all those treasures belonged to the family. Could he really sell it all, or give it away? But Mr. Gonzaga didn't want to hear any of it and told her not to meddle.

Soledad had hugged Alba tight, smoothed her hair, and dried her tears as Alba confessed she didn't want to part with her palace, but how could she convince her father?

"My Alba cast her spell when she was only twelve," Soledad said, and the particular choice of words impressed Maité deeply. "I was right next to her when she did it," Soledad said, clucking her tongue.

Alba's eyes swam with tears and her voice quivered with emotion, but she had stood her ground and demanded her father stop the sale of the property. But Mr. Gonzaga waited until it appeared his daughter had finished, and then he asked her to leave, for he had work to do.

"But her little face got all hard," said Soledad squeezing Maité's hands in hers. "And she got really mad when she said to your abuelo, 'The María Celeste lives and breathes like a human; it talks to me. And like a human, it has blood, and that blood is what runs through our veins. You will not sell it.'"

Maité almost forgot to breathe as she listened. *That was the spell.* Could a child inherit her mother's obsession? she wondered—like eye color or height? Maité had seen the María Celeste only briefly, but she knew how it made her feel: unaccountably possessive.

"You will not sell it," Maité murmured but Soledad was on a roll, and only Plinio seemed to have caught what she said. They exchanged a quick glance—it seemed to Maité he approved.

Alba took the painting and decided to build a frame for it. It was Plinio who helped her cut the wood and fit the pieces, but she sanded it down herself and then painted it. She took it back to the unsold María Celeste and it hung there for years.

"Sí, mi niña." Soledad nodded significantly. "Your abuelo got tired of paying to maintain the house—it was months and months and the house wasn't selling!"

Plants and weeds grew faster at the María Celeste than on any other property, and even the paint seemed to rust quicker than on the neighboring buildings. In an ominous voice, Plinio chimed in with the news that the María Celeste soon got the reputation of being cursed. Unaccountably, prospective buyers lost interest, and no amount of schmoosing could bring them around to the excitement that made them inquire about it in the first place. Some house hunters couldn't wait to be shown the property, yet as soon as the rusted iron-gate swung open, something came over them, and they couldn't be persuaded to take more than a few steps onto the flagstone path leading to the front door.

Delighted, Alba ran an inventory of the María Celeste. She sorted the relics and set up a pile for donations, mostly ancient frocks and moth-eaten dresses, a few dozen books with yellowed, brittle pages, and random pieces of furniture fit for furnace fuel at best. Other things she considered treasures, and those she hauled up to the large hall on the third floor of the María Celeste.

"My Alba was going to live on the third floor one day," Soledad mused. "She told me that a lot of times."

Maité couldn't wait to really see the house, to go inside. She remembered that on her way from the airport, she thought she saw someone looking out one of the windows of the María Celeste—*was it on the third floor?*

"It was up there she found a book," Soledad said. "The writer was a lady called Xiomara, and when my Alba read it she found out the woman in the painting was called Celeste and they were her family."

"You mean Xiomara and Celeste?"

"Sí, mi niña."

Alba continued to go to the María Celeste every week and came home to Soledad, her head filled with fantasies, saying that even the walls spoke to her.

Soledad worried about Alba's obsession, but she couldn't bring herself to even suggest she stay away from the María Celeste.

As it turned out, Alba left her father's house only a few years later—never to return.

In a rage over the disappointment caused him by his daughter, namely her marriage to Sósimo, Mr. Gonzaga vowed he would be rid of the things Alba cherished most.

When Soledad learned about Mr. Gonzaga's decision, she quickly told Plinio to empty the third floor, where Alba had kept her true treasures. She couldn't bear the thought of losing everything that had made Alba's life happy for so many years.

Plinio gathered everything and brought it to the attic of the manor where Alba had already placed some things she wanted to have more at hand. The portraits on the main floor of the María Celeste, including the one Alba had framed, had to stay behind, because Mr. Gonzaga was familiar with them, and Soledad and Plinio didn't want to take the chance he'd miss something.

Maité had taken a total of two bites of toast, and her scrambled eggs were cold.

"And so all the things my mom ..." She cleared her throat, her voice sounding alien to her own ears—particularly the word "Mom," as if it had been removed from her vocabulary. She'd been vividly picturing Alba as a young girl, and the sudden linking of the girl to "Mom" made a painful knot at the top of Maité's throat.

She swallowed it and tried again. "So all the things my ... *mom* accumulated, they're in this house now?"

"Sí, mi niña. In the attic." Soledad seemed to brim with anticipation for Maité.

"So I can—"

"Plinio will show you!"

Maité jumped up, clapping her hands like a little girl. "Thank you so much!" she breathed into Soledad's pudgy cheek, where she placed a loud kiss. "I really mean it!"

"Ay, mi niña! You go—go play with my Alba's things." Soledad sighed, wiping tears from her eyes with a napkin.

Maité followed Plinio out of the kitchen, overwhelmed with emotion that these two people had had the presence of mind to safeguard her mother's treasures so she could see them today, touch them, lose herself in her mother's childhood.

CHAPTER 21

Carrying a stepstool, Maité followed Plinio to the third floor, wishing he could walk faster.

After what seemed an eternity, they stood in front of the table with the big mirror on the wall. Just as Soledad had said, the trap door was in the ceiling above this table. Plinio scooted it off to the side, and Maité helped him take down the mirror and lean it against the wall. He climbed on the stool and unlatched the trap door. A rope ladder with wooden rungs tumbled down in front of him and he turned to Maité with his not-so-frightful-anymore smirk, gesturing for her to climb.

"Thank you, Plinio," she murmured, giving him a quick hug and taking hold of the ladder. Up into her mother's past she climbed, vaguely aware of Plinio limping back down the stairs.

Maité's head poked through the opening. The attic looked no bigger than about fifteen by twenty feet; four walls and a slanted ceiling with a skylight in the middle made up the simple room. A million dust particles swirled in the cube of sunlight coming from above.

Maité pulled herself all the way up and stood, hands on her hips, eyeing everything with a contented expression on her face. She moved about the space, running her fingers over the forgotten dusty books on the shelves. Her eyes caressed the ancient leather trunks lining the back wall and the richly crafted frames of the faded paintings hanging on the other two walls. A satin dress pinned to a dressmaker's dummy had a string of pearls draped over the bust, and Maité touched them too, knowing her mother might have placed them there. These were the things her mother had rescued from the María Celeste.

Maité's journey into the lives of her ancestors began, with all its smells, and its yellowing letters and books, its disintegrating lace and perfumed revelations.

The thought of the woman in the portrait crept into Maité's mind; she had to find her ancestor's journal. *What was her name?*

She sorted through books, mostly novels, which she figured her relatives enjoyed. Had her mother read them? A great many were in a language she didn't understand or even recognize, while others were in Spanish.

She didn't find the journal on any of the shelves, so she approached the three large trunks next. Their rusty locks were difficult to dislodge, but she managed the first one and completely lost track of time sorting through the contents. She was so absorbed in her rummaging she didn't realize someone had climbed up the ladder and was staring at her from the entry. When her eyes fell on the intruding shape, she choked down a gasp.

"David," she croaked and cleared her throat, wondering why he wore such a strange look of fascination. He appeared frozen in time, supporting himself with his elbows on the attic floor. Maité's brow creased as the seconds ticked on without any movement on David's part. Was she hallucinating? "Hi," she said.

David blinked, and Maité wondered what she must look like to him. She'd pinned her hair in a knot on top of her head, her hands were covered in dust, and her clothes were no better.

I'm a wreck! She yanked out the pencil holding her hair up and smoothed it down. In doing so, she pulled out a stringy chunk of spider web stuck to it, and cringed at the thought that her hair must look like she'd swept the floor with it.

"Hello," David said. "Sole told me where you were."

Maité tried to smile but couldn't; she wanted to say something, but nothing came to mind. She stood up, slapping the dust off her clothes and feeling a prickly, tingle in her legs. She wasn't sure if David was the cause, or if her legs had fallen asleep.

He finished coming up into the attic and pulled something white out of the back pocket of his jeans.

Good grief, who carries handkerchiefs in this day and age? He came toward the trunks, where she stood like a statue. He put one hand on her shoulder and with his handkerchief, wiped something off her cheek and then showed it to her with a smile.

Maité's heart fluttered as she looked at a black smudge on the white cloth. She remembered the greasy residue on the lock and had a sudden vision of what her face might look like. She wiped it off, realizing much too late that her fingers had more of the grease residue and that she was making it worse.

David laughed. "Here, let me take care of it," he offered, unfolding his handkerchief and again holding her by one shoulder as if she were a toddler. "There you are," he said, stepping back and leaving a warm spot on her shoulder where his hand had been.

"Thank you," she stammered. Reaching for a rag she'd glimpsed on one of the shelves, she wiped her hands compulsively.

"We were going to see the city today," he reproached her.

Maité's heart sank. She'd forgotten all about their date. "I'm so sorry; I don't know what to say," she sputtered, still rubbing her hands with the rag.

"This looks like fun," he said and made a whistling noise as he glanced over the spilt contents of the trunk. "Have you found what you're looking for?"

"What? How did you? What?"

"Well, judging by the mess you have here, I assume you're looking for something."

"I, um, well …"

"Can I help you?" he asked with a smile that softened her all over.

"Um, sure. Okay," she stammered, wondering if she would survive this experience. Her heart went from beating too fast to not beating at all.

"So what is it you are looking for?" He sat in front of the second trunk and opened it without any resistance from the lock.

Maité relaxed a little and took her place on the floor next to him. Before she knew it, she was telling him about the portrait in her room, the story she'd heard at breakfast, and the journal that would reveal the identity of the woman in the portrait. He listened without interrupting, and when she finished, he heaved a good-natured sigh. "Better get started then."

Soledad left a lunch tray on the landing, which David retrieved and they ate hungrily, exchanging their impressions of the uninteresting contents in the second trunk. It was crammed with books, water colors done by children, and an enormous tablecloth with sixteen matching napkins covered in cross-stitched landscapes.

It seemed to be only a few minutes later when Soledad appeared again, this time with dinner. Time had gone by so fast. The third trunk had been emptied, its contents examined and repacked, but they'd had no luck finding the journal.

Not until they finished dinner in the attic and sat looking around in quiet disappointment did Maité notice the painting of a Spartan fortress overlooking a beautiful valley. The painting itself was not remarkable, per se, but it hung crooked on the wall above the trunk that doubled as their table. They'd knocked it askew while moving things around, revealing something like a crack in the wall. Maité stood up to inspect the signature on the painting. It was faded, but Maité made out the name: Xiomara.

"This is the same person!" she cried out.

"You mean the person who wrote the journal?"

"Yes, that's her!"

They stood up and set the painting on the floor between them. Maité and David looked at the clean rectangle of plaster left behind and smiled at each another, not because of the clean spot, but because of what it revealed: a concealed niche carved into the wall. It was about a foot square and had two ring handles, which Maité pulled toward her. The plaster lid came right off. In their excitement to see the contents, they peeked into it at the same time and knocked each other's heads. "Ouch!" They laughed.

"You first," David said, rubbing his forehead.

Maité reached in and pulled out the only thing inside: a leather attaché case with the initials A. G. engraved between two buckles. She placed it on the trunk and looked up at David.

"A. G.—Alba Gonzaga. This was my mother's," she said, her voice filled with emotion. She felt certain the last person to have touched it had to have been Alba. She ran her fingers reverently over the smooth leather and closed her eyes, feeling her mother's presence all around her.

Her ears popped all of a sudden, and the familiar tingly warmth enveloped her hands, while somewhere near her neck, the stealthy someone murmured, *Maitagarri ...*

She opened her eyes and found David looking at her, his hands covering hers, and for a moment, she wondered if somehow, his was the voice whispering in her ear.

No, was the instant response, *You are mine, Maitagarri ...*

Well, that takes care of that, she thought, pleased that the voice inside her head and David were not one and the same. A smile curled at the corners of her mouth.

"Let's see what's in here," David said.

Maité undid the corroded buckles. She lifted the leather flap, and her heart skipped a beat.

"It's the journal, isn't it?"

"It is," she said in breathless anticipation, pulling out a stack of pages bound with string. "This is quite a book. And take a look at this." She held up a single piece of parchment that wasn't part of the binding.

"It looks like a family tree. It goes back almost two hundred years," David said, running his fingers over the dates on the old document. But Maité's eyes were fixed on the annotations, which she knew had been made by her mother, for she recognized her impeccable handwriting.

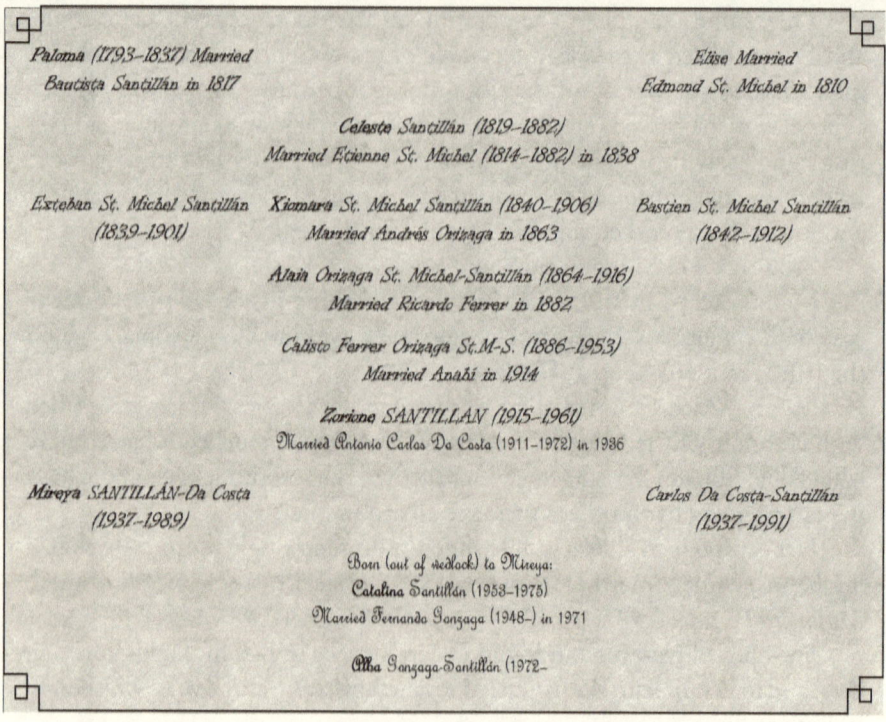

Paloma (1793–1837) Married
Bautista Santillán in 1817

Elise Married
Edmond St. Michel in 1810

Celeste Santillán (1819–1882)
Married Etienne St. Michel (1814–1882) in 1838

Esteban St. Michel Santillán
(1839–1901)

Xiomara St. Michel Santillán (1840–1906)
Married Andrés Orizaga in 1863

Bastien St. Michel Santillán
(1842–1912)

Alain Orizaga St. Michel-Santillán (1864–1916)
Married Ricardo Ferrer in 1882

Calisto Ferrer Orizaga St.M-S. (1886–1953)
Married Anahí in 1914

Zariona SANTILLAN (1915–1961)
Married Antonio Carlos Da Costa (1911–1972) in 1936

Mireya SANTILLAN-Da Costa
(1937–1989)

Carlos Da Costa-Santillán
(1937–1991)

Born (out of wedlock) to Mireya:
Catalina Santillán (1953–1975)
Married Fernando Gonzaga (1948–) in 1971

Alba Gonzaga-Santillán (1972–

"My mother wrote this," she told David, drawing his attention toward the more recent ballpoint writing, which brought the family tree up-to-date from the late 1700s to Alba's birth.

As if reading her mind, David pulled a pen out of his breast pocket and handed it to her. She mouthed a thank you and in her best print, emulating the format of the previous entries, she made a note of her father's name next to Alba's. She wrote the year in which Sósimo had been born, then the year of their deaths, and suddenly she was overcome with the significance of the moment.

Maité couldn't fight back the tears. From the depths of her soul tumbled out her resentment at being abandoned, and she cried again for the loss of her parents, for the loneliness and confusion she was submerged in, and for the constant fear she felt at the prospect of having to go on, alone.

David scooted next to her on the floor, and without saying a word, he put his arms around her. She buried her face in his shoulder, and he rocked her in silence until she breathed evenly again. Maité looked up at him through watery eyes.

"Thank you," she said in a squeak of a voice.

"You're welcome." His eyes gleamed as he said it and Maité felt a closeness to him that had nothing to do with the fact his arm was still around her shoulders.

Beneath her parents' names, with a trembling hand, Maité wrote her own name, followed by the year in which she'd been born. She and David gazed at the updated page, and she spilled a few more tears over the comfort she felt at finding herself among the branches of this family tree she hadn't even known existed.

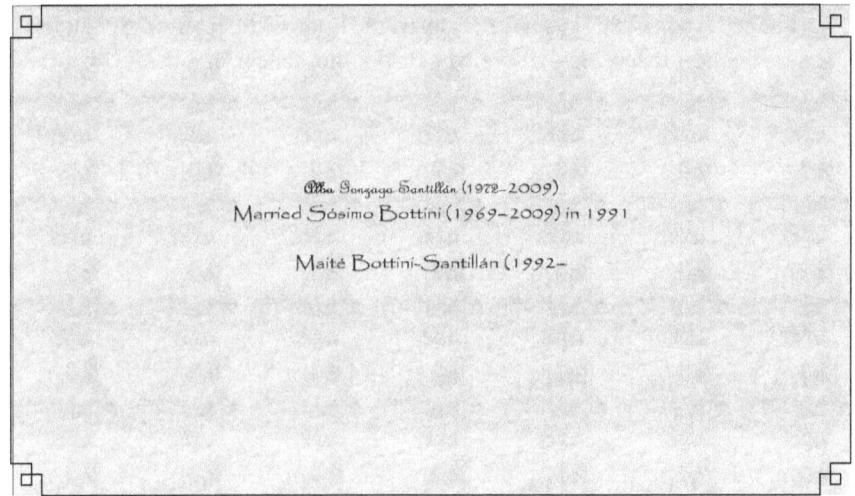

Alba Gonzaga Santillán (1972–2009)
Married Sósimo Bottini (1969–2009) in 1991

Maité Bottini-Santillán (1992–

In the quiet that followed, Maité and David heard the distant chiming of the clock in the foyer three stories below. They counted: eleven o'clock.

"I must go," he said in a sleepy voice. "I have been here the entire day …"

Maité felt a pang of guilt as he helped her to her feet. He'd squandered his entire day on her. She knew her eyes and nose were swollen, and she was sure her face was a blotchy, tear-stained mess. *One of these days, he'll be shocked to see that I actually have normal skin tone*, she thought miserably.

"Thank you for keeping me company and for going through this stuff with me," she said, tucking her hair behind her ears.

"It really was a pleasure."

Maité wanted to protest; he couldn't possibly have enjoyed himself, but something in the way he looked at her said he wasn't just being polite—she felt all toasty and pleased inside.

"Could you take me to the María Celeste?" she blurted. *Oh, my God! Ultimate rudeness. As if he's at my beck and call!*

David's eyes twinkled at her upturned face, and he kissed her on the forehead.

Maité looked at him through saucer-like eyes. The kiss, although chaste, had been so spontaneous, and it happened so fast, her mind didn't even register it until it was over. Then disappointment set in. She was so certain he'd flirted with her before, yet now he treated her in an almost brotherly fashion. Then it occurred to her David may be acting his part. *His dad probably asked him to entertain the little orphan girl, and being the good son, that must be what he is doing …*

The sensation of his kiss slipped away. He looked at her through laughing green eyes and tucked her disheveled hair behind her ears again. "Of course," he said.

I'm definitely just a little girl to him, and I look so gross. Covered in spider webs and hinge grease … Her old friends, the blushing cells, rushed to her face.

David lifted her chin toward him, setting off a delicious thrill and making her doubt the inner diatribe of seconds before.

"Should I pick you up tomorrow at around ten thirty?" he asked.

Maité nodded. His fingers still held her chin up, keeping her hopeful to the last second that he might kiss her. He didn't.

"All right, ten thirty it is, and we'll go to the María Celeste," David said.

He hung the painting back on the wall while Maité put the manuscript and parchment with the family tree back in Alba's attaché case.

"After you," he said, motioning toward the trapdoor.

Once downstairs, she walked him to the front door, still stupefied by her inability to read people. It was Finn all over again. At this point, she just wanted to get to the door and say good night without any further silly exchanges.

She turned to face him, and even in the shadowy foyer, she could tell he was smiling. She let out a short spurt of a laugh. *Oh my God, here I go again. At least Soledad didn't leave the lights on.*

Click! The lights went on.

"David, mi niño! Don't fall down the steps!" Soledad came, jostling her rotund frame out of the kitchen. "I finished with the dishes and I hear you talking, and I thought, *necesito encender las luces!*"

The late-night breeze cooled Maité's face, and she felt some semblance of ease.

"Thank you, Soledad," David said amiably. "I'll be back tomorrow morning to take Maité to the María Celeste."

"*Ay, qué bueno.* You come for breakfast then."

"Yes, please come for breakfast," Maité joined in the invitation. She kissed David good night and thanked him again for his help. Clutching her mother's briefcase to her chest, and with Soledad's hefty arm clamped around her waist, she watched him disappear into the darkness.

CHAPTER 22

Alone in her room, Maité showered and brushed her hair and teeth. She pulled a long T-shirt over her head and then propped herself on pillows at the foot of the bed so the portrait on the wall opposite was in plain sight whenever she raised her eyes.

Maité became engrossed by the uncanny similarities between the woman in the painting, whom she now knew as Celeste, and herself. *She's my grandmother to the seventh power*, she thought, amused. Maité focused her attention on the quality of the painting; everything in it seemed poised to move at any moment. The sparkling orbs hidden in the dark trees, and their reflection on the still water of the pond, gave the painting a mesmerizing depth—Maité believed she could see Celeste's breast rising and falling with each breath; the surface of the water ripple by an unseen breeze; the lights among the swaying branches twinkle mischievously.

Magic!

Maité's hand idly caressed the smooth leather attaché beside her. Then, remembering it was close to midnight and that she intended to do a lot of reading, she heaved a sigh and removed the thick manuscript from the bag. She fanned the pages, trying to estimate how long it would take her to read them. It was all in Spanish, which would most likely slow her down. The author hadn't numbered the pages, but she guessed there were about three hundred. Judging by the blots of ink on various pages, Maité could tell the whole thing had been written with a real fountain pen.

She glanced at the parchment containing the family tree and did the math in her head; Xiomara had been sixteen years old, same as Maité, when she completed the manuscript. They'd be the same age for a couple more days, as Maité would be seventeen soon. She scanned the pages admiring Xiomara's exquisite calligraphy and stopped at the dedication:

To my mother, Celeste;
From your loving daughter,
Xiomara
1856

She turned the page and found the next contained nothing but a title in bold print: Faery Sight. Something in Maité's belly quivered and filled her with a sense of apprehension, but also with a deep excitement at the mere sight of the delicately printed words. She glanced at the portrait and sighed.

Faery.

She turned the page, and her eyes fell on a paragraph written in a hand that wasn't Xiomara's.

> *To read beyond this page*
> *Is to agree to complete and utter secrecy.*
> *You are the only person these pages were written for.*
> *We ask you now for proof, before you proceed.*
> *Bear in mind identities are hallowed—*
> *Thus the names contained herein*
> *Have the power to extinguish life, or, at the very least,*
> *Wreak misery on every instant of your existence.*

Not only were these words written in a hand other than Xiomara's, the page they were on was a different shade and texture of paper than the others. In fact, the page wasn't paper at all; it felt more like cloth or maybe …

"Vellum," Maité said, remembering the word she was looking for and wondering what type of animal skin it might be. But that question didn't need an answer; she could tell the vellum had been inserted years later, which made the paragraph she'd just read a great deal more interesting.

Grasping the page between her thumb and index finger, she translated the Spanish words in her head as she reread them. Her eyes wandered to the ceiling as she pondered what such a warning might mean.

The page, or something on it, pricked her finger. "Ouch!" she gasped, sucking on her thumb. A speck of blood stained the vellum, but even as she stared at it, worried she'd ruined the precious document, the blood became absorbed and was clean within seconds.

Maité inspected her thumb; it was red from sucking on it but otherwise okay and with no puncture marks or cut. She ran her finger over the surface of the thick page thinking that if vellum was animal skin, then the porous surface could somehow explain the blood disappearing so completely. And the actual pricking of her thumb—maybe the pear-like spines of the vellum hadn't been shaved clean off. *Could be*, she thought.

With a shrug, Maité flipped the vellum and began reading. The minutes stretched into hours without her feeling it. The words Xiomara had written so many years ago transported her into the lives of people whose names were at the top of her family tree. Maité consulted the genealogy record over and over as she read.

Five blissful hours later, she emerged from the magical past. The sun would soon come up, but she felt not even a grainy ache in her eyes from lack of sleep. The places Xiomara described crowded Maité's head: Santillán and St. Michel, where Celeste and Etienne lived. Handi Park, which was the seat of Oihana—the faery queen. Other faery names like: Nahia, the faery princess; handsome Amets; playful Sendoa and scornful Ederne, mingled with terms and concepts such as Potions, Spells, Faery Glamour, and Evil.

Maité could barely contain her fascination; she wanted to leap out of bed and race to those mountains. *My great-great* (she didn't know how many greats would be appropriate) *-grandmother Paloma, while pregnant, was cursed by the witch Arantxa and banished to a place where she was expected to die. The witch Arantxa, in the meantime, impersonated Paloma and gave birth to her own child back in the great citadel of Santillán. But Paloma didn't die as Arantxa planned. Paloma found a new, enchanted life with a troop of faeries. There, the faery queen, Oihana, softened the curse so Paloma didn't suffer the indignity of looking like the horrible Arantxa every day. Paloma had her baby and named her Celeste, and I look like Celeste's twin.*

Maité massaged her temples and ran her fingers through her hair. "Unbelievable." She didn't need to close her eyes to see the world Xiomara had brought to life. It was so clear to her, like looking through a window at the solstice celebrations in the realm of Faery. She could see her ancestors bathing in ponds, playing games with gorgeous male faeries, sleeping out of doors, learning to fly, cooking up potions, learning about glamour and enchantments. And then, Celeste met Etienne, and she fell in love with him. But the faery princess, Nahia, condemned her for that. Paloma's death, however, rallied Celeste and Etienne and the faery troop, because at last, a way had been found to expose Arantxa's treachery.

"Faeries on every page," Maité said with a sigh. But was it merely a faery tale? Was it Xiomara's imagination? After all, she was only a girl of sixteen when she wrote it. Was she just entertaining herself and her mother? Were Celeste and her mother, Paloma, really exiled by an evil sorceress? Did they really commune with a band of faeries? *Faeries!*

Holding the manuscript to her breast, Maité walked out to the balcony. She gazed at the dark mound of Santa Clara Island rising from the water, and pondered the fresh details of the fantastic tale Xiomara had spun. She thought she saw a minute light flickering in the distance between the darkened trees covering the island, but it vanished swiftly, and she couldn't spot it again. She wondered if there were people there, perhaps kids up to mischief before the day began.

Or maybe it's a faery.

Maité smiled, pressing the manuscript tighter to her breast. "Do I believe it?" She let the question hang in the air and thought more about what she'd read.

Maité returned to her bed before the sun broke over the horizon. The word yes escaped her lips as she fell asleep with the manuscript safely under her pillow. She gave in to magical dreams of Paloma in her hour of peril and of Celeste's final redemption—her return to the human world—with her prince at her side, to begin a new life. A life that, in time, gave birth to Alba, and then to her.

In her dreams, Maité knew the story wasn't myth, that it was entirely true. Maité suspected her mother believed Xiomara too, yet Alba had given up this truth and the adventure to track it down, for love and for her life in America. But she, Maité, would not.

In Maité's dream, the flickering light she'd glimpsed on Santa Clara Island catapulted itself toward her room and exploded into shards of light, allowing her the momentary sight of porcelain skin and the pleading aquamarine eyes of a very familiar woman whose face was framed by golden ringlets streaked with turquoise.

You must find me!

CHAPTER 23

The sunlit room seemed to wish Maité a good morning when she opened her eyes. The woman's plea receded from her mind as she felt the lump under her pillow. All her discoveries came back to her in a rush. She stretched and turned lazily on her bed. She wanted to see the portrait again, so she knelt on the fluffy pillows to study the fluorescent dots on the branches. Some even had their reflection caught on the surface of the rippling water.

Maité imagined herself in the peaceful scene depicted by the artist, and then wondered what it would be like to have someone paint her portrait—brushstroke after brushstroke—until her face and body came to life the way this woman on the canvas seemed to live and breathe. She sighed and touched Celeste's face with her fingers.

What do you want to tell me?

Maité ran her finger down the length of Celeste's body to where her dainty foot was perpetually poised over the water, and what she saw startled her.

She saw the sparkling reflection of one of the diamond-shaped lights in the trees, which from a distance appeared to be no more than that, but now, inches away, Maité could distinctly see the reflection included a tiny yet perfect face. It also had arms, a body, and legs that disappeared into the bright aura around her. Maité searched the tree behind Celeste, trying to find the orb that would make such a reflection, and there the girl was, in even more detail, though still shrouded in her bright sea-green aura. She appeared to have yellow ringlets framing her perfect porcelain face. Turquoise highlights streaked her hair, and she stared quizzically at Maité, who gasped as a surge of palpitations galloped through her chest.

She scanned the other branches, and sure enough, different faces were cloaked in their own light, about a dozen of them. Maité's mind raced with all sorts of questions. Did the artist make up these faces? What did they mean? Was it just to add a touch of magic to the scene? Was the picture painted to honor the book she'd read? But no, the portrait was dated 1844, so it had to be the other way around. The book had to have been written based on the painting. The thought disappointed Maité. She so wanted to believe Xiomara's story, but somehow in the light of day, it seemed childish to even entertain the idea of magic and faeries.

She slumped on the bed, wanting to cry, yet feeling silly about it. Then her dream came back with dizzying swiftness.

You have to find me, said the voice, and then there was the face—the aquamarine eyes and the smooth porcelain skin. Maité bolted upright and stared at the painting, determined to confirm the crazy notion that overtook her.

The sea-green aura ... there you are. Yes, it's you! I dreamt of you! Maité let herself fall back on the bed. *What does this mean? Who are you?*

She became conscious of the all-too-familiar calling as it approached from the realm of fantasy. The delicious weight settled upon her, pressing her deep into her bed.

Maitagarri ... Maitagarri ...

She fought the dizzying sensation; certain she had finally recognized the word. She'd seen letters similarly arranged in the volumes she'd scanned the day before in the attic—not the word itself, but perhaps it was the same language? The thickness of skin lifted, and Maité sprang out of bed. She raced downstairs to the kitchen, where Soledad was busy preparing breakfast.

"Buenos días, mi niña!" Soledad greeted her happily. "David will be here soon."

"Good morning, Sole—good Lord! That's right, David!" Maité kissed Soledad on the cheek. "Do we have a dictionary?"

"Dictionary? Yes, *diccionario*, in Spanish or Basque?"

"You have one in Basque? Perfect!"

"You come with me."

Maité followed Soledad into the library. The enormity of the room and its infinite contents impressed themselves upon her again, except this morning it daunted her to think how difficult it would be to find any one book in this place. But Soledad knew just where to look: in the desk drawer.

Maité grabbed the new paperback dictionary from Soledad and tore through the pages until she found the *Ms. Ma ... Mai ... Mait ...* and there it was. *Maitagarri.*

"Soledad, do you read Basque? What does it say?" Maité asked, tapping the word as she passed the book back to Soledad, who frowned at the definition, clearly trying to convert the words into Spanish first and then English.

"Fantasy person, girl person with power—she can tell future, this girl." Soledad clucked her tongue, displeased with her translation. "You wait—here is this one," Soledad beamed reaching for another paperback and handing it to Maité. "This one is Basque to English diccionario."

Maité could scarcely contain herself as she read, "'Maitagarri: faery—mythical being of folklore and romance, usually having diminutive human form and possessing magic powers—goddess of fate."

And there it was, in black and white. Now she knew someone believed her to be a "Maitagarri." And this someone had been calling her and continued to hound her.

For what? Maité wondered.

"Why, mi niña? What is this about?"

"I don't know, Soledad, I don't know." Excited, though mostly puzzled, Maité felt flattered and proud at the thought of being considered a mythical creature, especially if she was pictured as one of those luminous beauties in the painting. *Way flattering.*

Part III

Have you heard tell of mortals being abducted into Faeryland? Indeed.

Beware the eyes! Beware the sing-song voice—for should you gaze into their eyes, and be caressed by their voice, you will be gone from us in but an instant. All will know Faery's enchantment has touched you. It will be evident in your bewildered gape and in the hazy shadow of your smile.

Yet do not ignore or disrespect. Indeed.

Beware the Unseelie Court!

Through narrowed eyes and finely tuned ears, take stock of the terrific force of creatures seemingly of this world. Hold tight to your truths! Lest you become lost in the swoon of secrets whispered, through smiling lips, in the quiet of your heart.

Have you the courage to fly with Faery? Brace yourself!
'Tis not for the faint-hearted.

CHAPTER 24

Maité went back to her room. She needed to shower and get dressed to be ready when David arrived because immediately after breakfast, he'd take her to the María Celeste. A shudder of excitement ran up and down her back at the thought of it. After last night's reading, and the brief but immensely fruitful research in the library that morning, Maité felt thrilled, though a little uneasy over what was to come. She memorized the definition of *Maitagarri*, and the more she mulled it over, the more confused she became. Was her secret correspondent misled himself, or was he misleading her?

Maité's entire life had been sprinkled with that word—faery—or at least with the idea of it. Ever since she could remember, Maité had been her father's faery princess, her room had been a faeryland done up in murals of sleepy forests, which her mother had painted for her. Now she knew why—Alba had been trying to recreate the María Celeste for her daughter. Birthday faeries and autumn faeries guarded her window, and every night back at home, Maité had fallen asleep gazing at the starry ceiling above her bed.

When she turned thirteen, Maité chose to have the murals painted over with a more mature set of stripes in gold, tangerine and fuchsia and the ceiling lost some of its celestial quality. In came the candles and the incense, the beads and pouf chairs. But Maité could not part with the faeries; not all the way. So until the day she left for Spain, modern-day, stylized faeries in chrome frames adorned the walls of her old room.

Where are those pictures? Probably already sold at a garage sale ... no, in storage, more likely, if I know Aunt V.

Could Xiomara have been telling the truth? Maité didn't think it was a coincidence that her mother sprinkled her childhood with so many faery-related things. "Maybe it was just Mom's way of bringing the María Celeste to America," she decided, glancing at the painting above her bed before going into the bathroom. It pleased and frightened her to see how much like Celeste she appeared, and for a fleeting moment, Maité considered the possibility of reincarnation. *Am I Celeste returned?* She waived the notion away at once, hearing Emily's dismissive snort and comment in her head: *One chance is all we get.*

As she shampooed her hair, Maité pictured her mother's life like a long, knotted cord that Alba had spun over the years. She had started with a single thread in this very manor house, unwittingly tethering herself to this part of her life. And now, Maité had picked up that same thread and followed it back to Spain, to confront the past and figure out what her future would be.

But what is the past? There are faeries in a portrait, a book telling me of the experiences my ancestors Celeste and Paloma had with real faeries. Let's not forget the voice in my head—it's been calling me a faery for almost two weeks.

And the latest in a mess of bewildering knots on that cord; the creature with the porcelain face and the aquamarine eyes, the one she'd dreamt about, the one she needed to find.

Can she really be Nahia, the daughter of the faery queen in Xiomara's book? The description certainly matched.

Maité came out of the shower loving the flowery scent that clung to her skin. Her thoughts were of Celeste and Paloma bathing in their pond. She promptly recalled a passage from the book where they proceeded to the primping rituals in the hall of glamour built by Celeste, Nahia, and Sendoa, "And Amets."

Her head swam with vivid images of her family history—or at least Xiomara's version of it.

Although her mind was fixated on faeries, she managed to put some thought into what she wore that day. She had advance notice of David coming, so there was no excuse to be caught off guard. Being adequately dressed might give her added confidence and perhaps even help her avoid blushing outbreaks. *Just be chill, M,* she heard Emily's voice in her head. "Right."

Maité combed her long hair away from her face and worked it into a thick braid, which she pulled over one shoulder. She liked her reflection in the mirror; her sepia coloring contrasted nicely with her gray eyes.

The laptop's reflection caught in the bottom corner of the mirror, making her insides squirm with guilt. Maité rolled her eyes while turning to the forgotten machine as if it had been shrilling at her. She propped it open and felt wretched at the sight of some twenty messages waiting for her from her best friend.

"Oh, Em!" Maité began typing straight away. "You'll never forgive me!" She couldn't make up excuses, not to Emily. She wrote exactly what she'd been occupied with and typed it exactly as it came out of her head, confessing at last, though not in extensive detail, about the voice she'd been hearing since her parents' funeral, all the while hoping the revelation would soften her friend's wrath about being ignored. *Maybe she'll think I'm crazy and pity me and forgive me.*

She typed nonstop for twenty minutes, not bothering to keep things in sequence—about the journal, the painting—*and oh!*—the family tree, of the definition she'd memorized. *Can't forget that.* The dream about the woman with the porcelain face, and the fact that Maité was on her way to the María Celeste a few moments after she pressed the send button. That she would walk in Alba's footsteps the entire afternoon, and how much she was looking forward to it went without saying.

She finished with, *Tell Aunt V she was right—I am discovering my mom here.* ☺

Looking over her message, she realized there were no paragraph breaks in the text. It had all come out in one long string, with barely any commas or periods, but there was no time for editing now; David had probably arrived already. She signed it *Luv u always, M,* and pressed the send button, laughing at what Emily's reaction would be to all she was dumping on her.

That will keep her entertained for a few hours, she thought as she floated downstairs, drawn by David's rich, baritone voice coming from the foyer.

Maité's face didn't change colors at all when his lips lingered on her cheek—twice for hello—nor did she feel faint when he smiled and grazed her face with the back of his hand, telling her she looked "clean." His laughing eyes were filled with good humor. She gave him a mock frown in response.

They ate in the kitchen, and her forehead, cheeks, neck, and whatever could be seen of her skin remained a neutral shade in spite of David's scrying glances and knee-buckling smiles. Soledad bustled about the two of them, refilling glasses, offering them second helpings, and hovering over David—wooden spoon in hand—poised to comment on their conversation.

When they finished their meal, Soledad adamantly refused to let them assist beyond clearing the table, but Maité and David delayed their departure nevertheless to talk to Soledad until she finished washing dishes.

It was close to noon when at last they left the manor.

The hot, humid air outside entered thickly into Maité's lungs; she squinted in the bright sunlight. The Cantabrian sparkled green at the foot of the hill; Maité realized she hadn't been out of doors for two whole days. She took a deep breath, which David seemed to understand, again as if he'd been reading her thoughts all along. He flashed his best smile, the one that made a long dimple down his cheek as he helped her into his car.

Maité tried to suppress the thrill she felt at the prospect of being in David's company. His casual manner captivated her; he exuded a confidence that contrasted with the awkwardness she felt in his presence.

But, hey, I lived through breakfast without a single blotch, she congratulated herself.

"How old are you anyway?" she blurted as soon as he got in the car and couldn't help cringing at her randomness. *Whatever,* she thought, angry with herself. *I'm probably already red from the heat inside this Dutch oven with wheels!*

David started the engine and the air conditioning, which wouldn't do much for at least five minutes.

"How old do you think I am?" was his playful response.

"I don't know. Twenty?" she said, trying to avoid his face.

"Twenty-two," he said with a satisfied grin.

He's six years older than me—no, only five 'cuz I'll be seventeen tomorrow.

"And do you go to school?" she asked, suddenly despairing about the fact that for the first time in her life, no one would make a big deal of her birthday, or even acknowledge it.

"I'm on summer break now, but yes, I go to … are you all right?" he asked, fixing her with a worried glance.

"Huh?"

"Are you all right? You look upset."

"Oh, sorry, yes, I'm fine. But what were you saying? You go to school where?"

"I attend the Universidad de Deusto. We can drive by it on the way back from the María Celeste, if you like. It's not far from there."

She nodded. "What do you study?"

"My major is in biomedical science."

"Biomedical science? What do you hope to be?"

"I like research."

The thought of him in a lab coat, buried in books and computers, did not agree with Maité's fantasies. "It doesn't suit you," she remarked without thinking.

David frowned. "What do *you* think suits me?"

Maité felt herself flush. *Now what am I going say? Oh I know, I'll tell him that I see him as Tarzan. I'll be his Jane, and we'll have jungle babies and live on bananas. What an idiot I am.*

"I, um, I don't know. A doctor?" she said, feeling immature—David had seen her write her birth date on the family tree, and she felt certain he was thinking about their age difference.

They were stopped at a traffic light at the bottom of the winding road below the manor.

"And you have one more year of secondary school, right?"

"Two, actually." Maité's cheeks burned. She hated being so much younger than him. She looked out the window at the Cantabrian ahead, wondering if David was only following his father's orders—make sure she was entertained, as she was the daughter of a big client. Maité didn't like the idea. *I'm just a job, and David probably has the hottest girlfriend ever.*

Maité pressed her forehead to the window. David had kissed her forehead, like a dad kisses his daughter, like Sósimo had kissed her a million times. She suddenly wanted nothing more than to escape the confinement of the small car. He couldn't be interested in her.

Five years apart. He won't even look at me that way.

"So you'll be a junior, right?" David continued.

"Yes," she said curtly, and wished she could come up with something else to talk about. She felt tongue-tied around him; she only wanted to know if he felt any attraction toward her.

Duh! Ask him, would be Emily's recommendation, but Maité couldn't formulate the question in her head, much less say it.

The light changed, and David steered the car to the left, onto Paseo de la Concha.

The promenade along the bay bustled with people enjoying the breezy afternoon warmth or lingering around the colorful kiosks scattered throughout. In the water, surfers bobbed up and down on their boards, waiting to catch the next wave; small boats with their swollen sails glided merrily near the shore. Thousands of umbrellas dotted the scorching white sand, shading mothers and children as well as the elderly, while the rebels, with their glistening oiled bodies, sprawled on bright, colored mats, reveled in the sun.

David maneuvered the car away from the coast and took them inland. To their left, the Urumea River flowed lazily toward the sea, and Maité admired the classic architecture to her right, glad to have a reason to look away so he wouldn't notice her heightened color. At least the air conditioner blew cool air now.

In a few minutes, they reached the María Celeste, but David had to circle the area several times before they found a place to park. He finally settled on a spot two blocks away.

It felt good to be out of the car and stretch her legs. David walked beside her, pointing out different buildings and giving her brief accounts of their purpose, which endeared him to her tremendously. Before they got out of the car, Maité had made up her mind to be safe and say as little as possible. So with him doing all the talking, Maité allowed herself an "oh" or an "ah, yes" where appropriate while enjoying the rich depth of his voice and his charming accent. She decided he must have learned English in Britain—and a little late in life too—because he hadn't lost the Spanish inflection.

"So two more years of high school?" he asked again, momentarily breaking from his role as tour guide. "Have you given thought to your higher education?"

It seemed odd to think of something as real as a college education when so many outlandish things had happened to her in such a short period—she hadn't realized how out of the sphere of normal she felt until David's simple question. She thought for a moment about the plans she'd made with her parents.

When an answer at last came to her, she said, "I wanted to be an architect, like my dad." She blinked away the tears welling in her eyes at the recollection. "I was going to be the third partner in the architectural firm of Bottini & Allen—one day." She wondered where all of those scraps of paper and napkins were, where she and her father scribbled plans for their dream home. *Mom probably threw them out.* She'd always nagged them about leaving trash all over the house. "Until those scribbles are actual blueprints, I don't want to see any of it on my counters," Alba had insisted. The memory of her mother's feistiness passed like a shadow over Maité's face, but then her expression relaxed as David spoke.

"You wanted to be an architect?" David had stopped to look at her, forcing people to sidle around them. "Not anymore?"

"I don't know what I want to do," she admitted. Maité wanted to turn away but forced herself to face him and think her position through rather than dissolve into tears. "I thought I knew … up until, you know … until my parents died, and then everything changed."

Maité felt relieved to have said the words; David now knew how lost she felt. She didn't care if she appeared weak or immature. She searched his face for traces of mockery, maybe for a look of condescension in his eyes—after all, she was a little girl to him, not even out of high school, while he was almost done with college. But there was no such look.

David's brow creased, giving his face an expression of hesitation that puzzled her. His smile faded. "You know," he said, looking away as if hiding something, "My mother died when I was eleven, and I still haven't managed to deal with that. Neither has my father, for that matter."

"I had no idea. I'm so sorry," she said, dazed by this confession. In an instant, a single-minded interest in his circumstances replaced her self-pity.

He smiled uncomfortably. With a brisk motion of his hand, he wiped something from his eye and then hooked his thumbs in the belt loops on his jeans. "It was a car accident," he explained. "A truck ran a red light and hit my parents' car on the passenger side. My mother died, but my father lived," he said simply, trying to sound casual, though Maité could tell the crux of his feelings on the incident had to be *but my father lived.*

David raised his eyes toward the tops of the buildings as he spoke, then down to the trees in their planters, and then up to the sky—clearly anywhere but Maité's expectant face. "I think he blames himself," David said of his father, balling his hands into fists, but then he exhaled, and with a nonchalant shake of his head, he added, "I never learned the details of what really happened. I know it was an accident, but I think somehow I blamed him too." At this, he looked into Maité's eyes, which by now were swimming in tears.

The urge to comfort him, to protect him, was unbearable. The sight of her watery eyes seemed to distress him further. David plunged his fists deep into his pockets, and his gaze dropped to the ground. She could see him working his jaw almost angrily as if he regretted having clued her in to that part of his life. She blinked, and her tears spilled, but she wiped them off before he could see.

"I have never seen eyes like yours," he said in a transparent effort to break the somberness of the moment. "They remind me of thunderstorms."

Maité couldn't think of a thing to say to this—she sniffed and watched him standing there, his hands stuffed in his pockets, rocking back and forth on the balls of his feet—looking unnervingly handsome. She wanted to hug him, and she wanted him to hug her back. She wanted to kiss him and make the sadness go away from his eyes—how had he been hiding that all along? That his mother died, that he felt guilty about blaming his father? She hadn't noticed it before, but now that he'd shown it to her, she could see nothing but sorrow seeping out of him.

"We're almost the—" he began, but she didn't let him finish.

Maité stepped toward him, her heart fluttering, and pressed her mouth to his. His eyes opened wide, letting her know he couldn't believe what was happening. She couldn't bring herself to stop; kissing him was too wonderful. David gave in to her. He closed his eyes and put his arms around her.

This is no brotherly kiss! This is not Finn. And this is not how someone would kiss a little girl, either!

Maité felt so ecstatic, she wanted to laugh out loud. She'd never been kissed this way before.

Oh please, she heard Emily say. Save it for someone who'll buy that crap, M! Who's kissing who here? Again, she had that wonderful urge to laugh; Emily was right. She felt her heart would explode with pleasure; she closed her eyes again and surrendered to the strength of David's arms enfolding her and to the beating of her heart in her ears.

David lifted Maité off the ground and made a half-turn with her in his arms. She threw her head back and laughed. And at this moment of moments the hot whisper came into her ears and directly to her brain.

Maitagarri.

Her flesh grew heavy, like someone had poured a rubber coating on her. Could David feel her turn to lead in his arms? *No.*

You are mine …

But Maité held her breath; she wanted the voice to stop. Nothing should interfere with this kiss. *Not now.*

There was silence for a brief moment. She strained to hear the voice again, but nothing came.

I stopped him! Maité congratulated herself, but her triumph was bittersweet. Was the silence a reproach? She couldn't deny she'd heard a hint of resentment in the whispered plea.

She felt a slight breeze touching her skin as the thickness began to lift. She felt only David now, nuzzling her neck, and a very subtle awareness of his aftershave.

Hmmm.

Gradually, the voices of people walking past them on the sidewalk swept into her range of hearing, and she caught their furtive glances and smiles.

Maité searched David's green eyes. The sadness had disappeared, or had been sucked back to its hiding place deep in his heart.

Mission accomplished, she thought with pleasure, the lingering warmth of their kiss still on her lips.

"I was trying to say …" he said, his eyes laughing. She returned a satisfied smile, holding him as tightly as he held her. "We're almost there, see?"

Maité followed the direction he pointed, and there was the María Celeste, rising like an enchanted ruin from a nest of brick and greenery.

Chapter 25

Maité and David crossed the street and walked alongside the six-foot tall brick wall. They arrived at a break in the fence, where a rusted iron door with the letters MC soldered like a shield on it blocked their entrance to the back of the property.

David uncoiled the chain, which fortunately had no lock. He unlatched the gate and forced it open, leaving a quadrant engraved on the packed dirt beneath it.

"Doesn't look like there's much traffic through here," Maité commented.

"Only those who didn't bring a key to the front door," David replied, shoving the gate back to a closed position.

"So this is the ultimate keyless entry then." Maité laughed.

They stepped into a dense jungle of citrus trees and shrubs. The thick scent of the white blossoms seemed to be locked in the cool shadows beneath the branches. Maité's brows knitted wondering if the trees should be flowering midsummer. She had no clue about the timelines for orange harvest, but she was sure most everything flowered in the spring in this latitude.

Women in her family definitely had a thing for this particular type of plant. Their fondness dated back to the days of Paloma and Celeste, when the trees supposedly flowered year-round in the realm of faery. *Can faery magic reach all the way downtown?* Maité wondered, plucking a cluster of white flowers and breathing in the scent.

"Who knew we'd need a machete?" Maité said, grinning as she followed David's lead toward the house. She caught herself before smashing into his back when, having reached a flagstone courtyard, he stopped abruptly.

Wide-eyed with wonder, Maité grasped David's hand as she took in every detail.

Thick, green moss swelled between the pavers. Heat rose in a quivering haze from the sun-beaten stone. A couple of trees lay like corpses between them and the house; whether they'd rotted or been torn apart by wind, Maité couldn't tell.

Wiping her forehead with the back of her hand, and wishing she'd thought to bring some water, Maité squinted at the building and counted five large and very murky windows on either side of the back door. Something like a memory stirred within her, or perhaps a dream. Even the back door of the mansion, seemed to be a portal to a world she couldn't wait to discover. She glanced at David. "Should we?"

He nodded and motioned for her to go ahead. They sidestepped the fallen trees up to the door in silence, Maité looking almost reverent at the sight of the open door.

"Do you suppose someone tried to break in?" Maité asked.

"It doesn't look like it's been forced," David observed. "But I will go first, just in case."

"My hero," she teased, and he made a slight bow before stepping inside. She followed. Just beyond the threshold, she stopped and stared at their surroundings, not really conscious of the door creaking to a close behind them. "Wow."

"I agree," said David.

This was the biggest mudroom Maité had ever seen, equipped with lots of shelves and hooks for jackets, hats, and umbrellas.

Maité passed this area and into what looked like an indoor avenue lined with pillars. David seemed as enthralled by the sight as she was. They drifted in opposite directions but hadn't gone more than twelve feet when the sound of laughter reached their ears. Maité froze.

Something very familiar—in a horrific sort of way—rang in that laugh, making it hollow and forbidding. While she looked intently at the staircase where the voices came from, she heard David walk up behind her.

Is the house haunted? But no, the door had been open. "Is it trespassers? Should we kick them out?" she whispered.

"I don't think it's an intruder." David held onto her elbow. She knew he meant to stop her should she venture too far.

A woman appeared at the top of the stairs, clad in the most scandalous shade of orange. She wore a full-skirted dress, which looked like it had a fan constantly blowing beneath it, as it ballooned out at intervals to reveal the woman's shapely, spike-heeled legs. A mess of wavy red hair tumbled loose over her shoulders and framed a disturbingly perfect face, although at the moment, it was partially turned from Maité. The woman was busy nuzzling and cooing to a man grinning peculiarly at her side.

He was older, but there could be no doubt he'd aged with grace. His salt-and-pepper hair suited him very well, and in spite of his juvenile smile, he had a strong jaw and a determined look accentuating his good looks.

"That is Mr. Gonzaga," David whispered in Maité's ear, startling her.

For a moment she looked bewildered at the man, and then David's words clicked. She was looking at her grandfather!

"And that must be Eva," Maité whispered back, unable to hold back a little flutter of excitement; after all, Eva was a celebrity. When had Maité ever been this close to anyone famous? *Never.*

Eva clung to Mr. Gonzaga, laughing and kissing his neck below the ear. "Wouldn't this be just delightful, Fernando?" she simpered in a throaty voice, and her comment echoed in the empty grand hall, loud enough for Maité and David to hear.

The contented grin on Mr. Gonzaga's face irritated Maité.

"Do you not see us here, my darling?" Eva said, ungluing herself from him in a flurry of extended arms and bouncing tresses while she gazed covetously at her surroundings. Her eyes fell on Maité and David; she teetered on her heels, surprised.

Eva's sudden stop seemed to awaken Mr. Gonzaga from his trance, and he too glared at Maité. Then a spark of recognition gleamed in his eyes. He cleared his throat and started down the massive staircase. He appeared all business now, the awkward grin gone.

Eva stood still for a moment, but the initial shock wore off in a flash, and she too sprang into action. She caught up with Mr. Gonzaga and coiled her arm around his, so that when they arrived at the foot of the stairs, they stood side by side. His look was haughty and in control—hers, dangerous.

David eased his grip on Maité's elbow.

So this is Grandpa, Maité thought, her eyes darting from him to Eva; the woman's unblinking glare unnerved her. *And this is Eva, who wants lots of land and now this house!*

As Maité approached them with David at her side, she observed a remarkable change come over Mr. Gonzaga's face; it softened, but not with the grandfatherly feelings she would have expected. Rather it was curiosity, a sort of wonder at the sight of her. As for the woman's contemptuous glare, Maité couldn't help but feel Eva recognized her, or at the very least found her to be an unwelcome presence. This notion too was unsettling.

Maité caught a most elusive, very pleasant scent of aftershave as she halted in front of her grandfather. Eva's eyes narrowed and her nostrils flared indignantly, as if she could hear Maité's reflections and felt insulted by them, but Maité refused to be distracted.

By all accounts, Mr. Gonzaga couldn't fail to make an impression; he stood taller than six feet, and the marks of age on his skin punctuated his appeal with the wisdom that must accompany experience. Yet it surprised Maité to find traces of vulnerability in his black eyes.

Eva clung to Mr. Gonzaga's arm even tighter and nuzzled his neck, as if challenging Maité, who more than ever, refused to acknowledge Eva.

Instinctively, Maité knew she was better off with the least amount of contact with the woman. After almost a whole year of having the kind of dreams she'd been having, Maité wondered if a connection would be established when she locked eyes with someone else's, especially such eyes as Eva's. Maité didn't want Eva in her dreams.

Eva withdrew from Mr. Gonzaga's neck, and Maité saw the fleeting vulnerability in his eyes evaporate.

She sucked it right out of him!

"You are my grandfather?" Maité asked with as much censure as she could charge into her voice. She hated that this man, a relative of hers, should be a sucker for a woman like Eva. She couldn't make out what bothered her most—that he was so much older than Eva, or that Eva was so sticky.

"Yes. I am your grandfather, and I am not dead as my daughter had you believe all these years."

Maité noted bitterness in his voice; it made her feel as if she were something unpleasant Alba's death had forced him to take on.

"Is it not true that you weren't aware of my existence until just a few days ago?" he asked.

Eva, with her head resting on Mr. Gonzaga's shoulder, smirked.

"You say that as if it were my fault," Maité replied, avoiding Eva's eyes. Mr. Gonzaga dismissed her comment.

"I have no idea why you're loitering here. I imagine a degree of curiosity is the reason, maybe even a childish fancy." He spoke in an all-business manner, but Maité sensed they were both thinking of Alba's obsession from years ago. "So go ahead with David. I'm certain he'll answer questions to your satisfaction, but I beg you not to linger or remove anything from this property."

Maité winced at his remark. It was a distasteful insinuation, in all probability meant to injure her father; hadn't Verónica said her grandfather thought Sósimo a loser, swindler? Also, it hadn't escaped her that Eva had again exerted the slightest pressure on her grandfather's arm, as if prompting him to make the unfeeling statement.

To confirm her suspicions, Mr. Gonzaga put his arm around Eva's waist and added, "I will be gone for a few more days, during which you'll familiarize yourself with the city. When I return, we will discuss your education. There too David should be able to address any preliminary concerns you may have."

This was too much for Maité. Her eyes flashed angrily at her grandfather. "Mr. Gonzaga," she said, feeling her mother's influence all around her. "If I had a choice, I wouldn't be here, so don't talk to me as if you're doing me a favor. I know what you thought of my father, so I'm not surprised you'd feel the same way about me. I don't need any reminders about whose property this is." Her voice shook only a little. It still angered her that anyone could think ill of her Dad. *Italian swindler, my butt.*

Maité hoped with all her heart that she reminded Mr. Gonzaga of his dead daughter. She loved her father and if she didn't defend him then who would? Maité felt certain Alba would've been proud.

"My father was a great man. He, my Mom, and I already talked about my education, and they provided for it too. There's no need for you to hurry back. Stay gone for as long as you like. In fact, stay away until I turn eighteen. I'll be happy to forget we ever met."

Mr. Gonzaga stared at her stupefied. He seemed on the verge of saying something but nothing came out.

The sight of Eva still clinging sappily to his arm further inflamed Maité's temper. "What are you smirking about?" she barked, and Eva raised her head languidly to look on Maité. "Since you seem to be calling the shots, make sure you keep him gone for the next year!"

A red ring blazed round Eva's pupils for only a fraction of a second, but it was enough for Maité to shrink back in alarm. *What the heck was that?* Her confidence wavered.

At that moment, Mr. Gonzaga managed to find his words, and he reprimanded Maité. "That is quite enough, young lady. I'll not have you disrespect Eva or me, is that clear?"

"Really," Eva said as if she were appalled.

Out of the corner of her eye, Maité caught a satisfied sneer spreading over Eva's face—gloating over being Mr. Gonzaga's favorite. Maité's blood boiled. Throwing caution to the wind, she turned her eyes fully on Eva, risking a visual connection that might have consequences.

Let Eva show up in my dreams, Maité thought recklessly, and the sudden image of past tutoring sessions combined with soccer practice popped into her mind. Eva's head was the ball and Maité, instead of Finn, practiced penalty shots.

But then, the unexpected happened.

Someone peeked at Maité over Eva's shoulder. The figure had a pair of large, aquamarine eyes, a face framed in golden ringlets streaked with turquoise, and a delicate finger over its red lips, asking Maité to be quiet.

Her shock was so obvious, the orange bundle of fabric and hair that was Eva had to steal a glance behind herself to confirm no one was there. Apparently, Eva saw nothing.

Shaken, Maité decided to comply with the brief apparition's request for silence. She contented herself with casting one last scathing glare at Eva before turning back to her grandfather.

The look on Mr. Gonzaga's face showed his wrath would be a thing to behold, and Maité had gone out of her way to rouse it. *Too late to take it back. I don't want to anyway.*

"I wish I could say it was a pleasure meeting you, Mr. Gonzaga, but I was taught not to lie," Maité said. With that she turned so abruptly, David had to jump out of the way to avoid colliding with her.

"Good day, Mr. Gonzaga. Miss Eva." David said, and then he was at Maité's side.

CHAPTER 26

Maité stormed out of the María Celeste and into the sunlit courtyard. She stalked across the pavers. David cut in front of her unobtrusively to once again swing branches out of her way as they trekked through the tangled vegetation to the back gate. She was angry at her grandfather—how could he let Eva manipulate him that way? How could he approve of someone so hostile?

The recollection of Eva's sneering face, alternating between sulky and boasting, only increased Maité's anger. And the topper was that because of Eva, Maité hadn't been able to get past the entryway of the María Celeste! She hadn't been able to explore the mansion, or look for her mother's footsteps as she'd planned.

Maité trembled with rage and had half a mind to swivel on her heel and head back in there, but no, the woman with the streaked ringlets had said no.

"Please take me back to the manor," she said shakily, tears of outrage gleaming in her eyes.

"Of course," David replied without turning to look at her, his attention fully on the branches.

Maité followed close behind in silence. She couldn't think of anything to say. Her thoughts were in turmoil, and she wanted nothing more than to be alone. Things were not at all what she imagined they would be. What was more, she felt herself becoming someone she never thought she'd be. The intense anger she felt toward her grandfather made it evident she'd expected to find an ally in him. After all, the same blood ran through their veins. But hadn't she insisted to Verónica and Emily that she didn't care about him?

So why should it matter how he treated me?

Of course it was plain to her now that Mr. Gonzaga didn't see her as family. He preferred Eva to his own granddaughter.

Apparently, my mom's disobedience is something he won't soon forget, she thought bitterly. "But then why the heck did he bring me here?"

"I beg your pardon?" David stopped at this and turned to look at her. The crazy jungle hemmed them in.

"What? No, it's nothing; just talking to myself," she muttered, eyeing the mangrove-like surroundings as if she didn't know where they were. "I'm sorry, David, it's just … that woman—she's something else, isn't she?"

David nodded. "I'm sorry you didn't get to see the whole house." He plucked a couple of dried leaves from the top of her head.

"The whole house? I didn't even get past the hallway, oooh! She makes me so—so—I don't like her!"

David chuckled and resumed his job of parting branches like saloon doors. "Go ahead, vent your spleen and be comforted. Except for your grandfather, we all have the exact same reaction to her."

They arrived at the gate at last. David dragged it open and allowed her to pass before closing it again. They walked back to the car, picking twigs and leaves off each other's hair and clothes.

They drove in silence in the stifling heat of the car. The splendor of the world outside the window seemed dull and alien to Maité who started worrying she may have done wrong.

"She really got you riled," he observed tentatively.

Maité jerked her head toward him. *Does he think I was rude and harsh?*

"I don't know what got into me," she admitted.

"Don't be too hard on yourself; she does have a way about her that makes people feel threatened," he said. "Most everyone agrees she's using your grandfather for her own purposes."

"Most everyone? Who doesn't feel that way?"

"Your grandfather, for one. Eva seems to have wiped away his common sense, and he follows her lead as if she's the only person worthy of his trust," David said in uncharacteristic heated tones.

"What exactly is she after?"

"It is a delicate matter, and it involves you more than you think."

"How?"

"The Santillán estate belongs—strictly speaking—to a designated female bearing the name of Santillán, specifically to a descendent of Celeste Santillán. At least that's how the holographic will was written decades ago."

"A holographic will?"

"A reference to it, in the estates' dossiers," David explained.

Maité shook her head. "I'm lost."

"The actual holographic will has been misplaced, but the reference to it has been upheld for years. Your grandfather is trying to get around it now that Eva is pressing for large portions of the estate."

"Hang on a minute." Maité thought about this rapidly. "So this means that—"

"That the estate can pass only to a female of the line of Celeste Santillán."

Celeste is the heroine of Faery Sight. It all starts with her. She's at the top of the family tree, and ... "It ends with me ..."

David nodded. "After the death of your mother, you became the only living female descendant of Celeste, but while you're a minor, your grandfather is your legal guardian, and he may act on your behalf."

The color rose to Maité's face with an angry blast of heat. She bit her lip, unable to find a way to fight this. How could she even hope to prevail upon her grandfather to delay his decision? Emily would certainly recommend a lawsuit.

"Title transfers are being drawn up for two of your grandfather's properties. The one we were in just now, plus a great deal of land up in the Pyrenees. The land is worth a fortune, and the María Celeste is prime real estate, so there is no doubt in anyone's mind why Eva would want them. What no one can figure out is how she managed to convince your grandfather to part with them. The land and real estate have been part of the Santillán legacy for centuries. So it's shocking, to say the least, that he would transfer the title to her."

"Transfer? You mean he's not even selling it to her?"

"No, he's not. It seems she agreed to marry him if he signs over the deeds to her. If money is to change hands, my father hasn't been informed of it. This is why it's such a delicate situation. You see, this is the first time the legacy has been threatened. I'm afraid there are no provisos for the female heiress being a minor."

Maité's jaw dropped. Things were bad indeed. Mr. Córdoba had tried to broach the subject, and she hadn't picked up on it.

Poor Soledad. She must not know, or she would have said something.

"Some people think if they marry, the property will still be in the family, and it won't make a difference who's on the deed, but others—like my father— fear Eva has no intention of marrying him, because she keeps insisting the paperwork be signed prior to the wedding. Why your grandfather can't see through her scheme is beyond anyone's understanding."

"So what's stopping him from signing everything over? Why hasn't it been done already?"

"Originally, Mr. Gonzaga delayed it because he would have had to get your mother's signature to effect the transfer, but with things being what they are ..." David paused uncomfortably, and Maité encouraged him with a nod. "He can now act on your behalf, without further delay."

Mutinous thoughts flashed through Maité's mind, and she suddenly saw herself having a conflict similar to the one Alba had with Mr. Gonzaga over the María Celeste and the land. But fighting would be pointless. As a minor, Maité's desires carried no weight.

"So Eva will have what she wants," Maité said. "But what does she want it for? It can't be just money. She's gotta be a bijillionaire."

"Your guess is as good as mine."

They were cruising Paseo de la Concha once again; soon they would be back at the manor house.

Seeming to float on the green water, the island of Santa Clara drew Maité's attention away from her thoughts and toward the crowded beach and promenade. The island looked like an enormous turtle that had been asleep for centuries and wouldn't wake no matter what level of activity went on around it.

Come and find me.

Maité rested her head against the window, and although the inside of the car was cool now, she felt the heat outside through the glass.

But what do I do first, find her or figure out what Eva wants with the land and with the María Celeste? And how can I stop my grandfather from giving them to her?

David slipped the car noisily into second gear to take on the steep climb to Santillán manor. Maité closed her eyes and wiped away rebellious tears from her cheeks. Gravel crunched under the rolling tires; her head rocked slightly against the hot glass while the car wound up the trail.

David's hand closed over hers, and she returned the pressure. *Thank you*, she thought. Her hand tingled where they touched; their fingers were laced, and she tightened them a little to thank him for his positive influence. Whether David returned the sentiment with a similar expression, Maité had no idea.

Her mind slipped sideways into visions of another time. She recognized David right away in a young boy she saw, sitting alone on a heavily varnished bench, inside an empty cathedral. His green eyes were fixed on the candlelit altar, at the foot of which stood an ornate coffin covered in flowers. A hand, bearing several deep scrapes, squeezed the boy's shoulder, but David didn't react until Mr. Córdoba, in a haggard voice, told him it was time to leave.

David looked up at his father with an expression in his eyes that Maité never imagined could have been there—it was hate; it was blame; it seemed to say, "It should have been you." And he may as well have said the words, for Mr. Córdoba appeared to understand. He recoiled; his brow creased, and his shoulders dropped as if vanquished by the young boy.

"Don't you think I would have died instead, if I had the choice?" The strain of defeat marked Mr. Córdoba's voice, and as she took in his tortured expression, Maité was visited by a desire to comfort him, at least pat Mr. Córdoba on the back—maybe David would.

The boy David bowed his head. His hands lay limp on his lap, and she saw tears spilling onto his black trousers. Now her heart ached for the little boy; she so wanted to put her arms around him, but he'd risen from his seat and looked at his father with a much-altered expression, which Maité recognized as horror and remorse that his father had seen through him.

"I know, son. I know," Mr. Córdoba said, giving David a bracing one-armed hug. He then grabbed him by the shoulders, his bandaged left hand exerting as much pressure as the other. He looked at his son square in the eyes with such a penetrating glance that David looked alarmed.

"That I gave your mother more than a moment's doubt with my foolishness is the cross I must bear the rest of my life. But I must get this off my chest!" he exclaimed with an almost deranged flash in his eyes, while beseeching his eleven-year-old son to hear his confession. "I thought I loved Alba, you see, and like a resentful child, I sulked over the loss of her, not caring that my attitude was hurtful to my dearest Catalina, and now that she is dead, I see her devotion crept into every corner of my soul, and I know without a doubt it was only her—your mother—whom I loved and will always love. Such a fool I was!"

Mr. Córdoba was almost shaking David at the height of his own guilt. When his son didn't react, his shoulders sagged in defeat.

"Who is Alba?" the boy David asked blankly.

Mr. Córdoba released his son's shoulders and straightened up; the question had brought him back to his senses. "She is no one. And I have said my piece," was his brisk reply.

David only stared at his father, conjecturing who knew what around the name *Alba*.

Maité watched them leave the church, Mr. Córdoba resolute in spite of the slight limp he still nursed from the accident, and little David seeming to bear a huge weight on his shoulders.

Fewer than five minutes had elapsed in the car, and they were already on the manor's circular driveway, but to Maité, it felt like she'd left the world for at least three hours. She opened her eyes and looked at David, who'd released her hand and stopped the car at the foot of the steps leading to the front doors. She could almost see the eleven-year-old boy in the features of the manly face before her now.

"Do you know who Alba was?" she ventured quietly. David's shocked reaction made it clear he hadn't realized Maité was privy to his recollection.

"She was your mother," he replied, giving her a cautious glance.

Maité nodded. "My grandfather wanted her to marry your dad."

David grimaced. He clearly hadn't known that part.

"I didn't know either, until recently," she admitted, hating to see his confusion but feeling certain his father's words of that day might at last make sense to him. Whether it would help or hinder his forgiveness, Maité could not tell.

Seconds stretched into minutes, during which neither one said a word. Maité wanted to repair whatever damage this revelation might have inflicted on David, but she could think of nothing further to say. She let the silence lengthen, and then David clasped her hand again and brought it to his lips. He kissed it and voiced the conclusion he'd been mulling over in silence.

"Had Mr. Gonzaga succeeded in marrying Alba to my father, you would not be here today," he declared.

Though flustered, Maité replied, "Or we would be brother and sister."

"That would *not* be good," he said with a furtive smile.

She pursed her lips and shook her head.

"Perhaps Mr. Gonzaga is contemplating an arranged marriage for his granddaughter?" David hinted with a saucy smirk that made her heart race.

"And what would you think about that?" she asked.

"It would be redundant if the arrangement were with me; destiny has already taken care of it," he said, kissing her.

Maité yielded. *He thinks he's my destiny. He* is *my destiny.*

With the air conditioning turned off, the car quickly became an oven, so Maité let herself out. She felt giddy over David's words, yet her mind returned to the information he'd given her about the Santillán estate, and she didn't know what to make of the fierce emotions this knowledge triggered inside her.

Maité heard David close the car door and then gravel crunching underfoot as he came around behind her. She climbed up the steps to the double doors thinking, *The María Celeste is mine, and so is the land in the Pyrenees where Celeste and Etienne lived.* It dawned on her the strong reaction was because therein lived her family's history—her legacy. *They're mine, and I'll keep them,* she decided, and even the thought of her grandfather's rejection couldn't dispel it.

David put his arms around her waist and turned Maité to face him. "Is everything okay?"

She hugged him, her glance drifting over his shoulder toward Santa Clara. "Yes."

Clouds moved rapidly across the sky; if not for David's arms, she might lose her balance just looking up at them. A reckless gust of wind swooped up the hillside to where they stood, carrying with it a soft scent that vanished as quickly as it struck her. Above, the clouds parted to reveal two orbs of blue sky, oddly tinted in green like the Cantabrian below, and for an instant, Maité thought they were that woman's aquamarine eyes again, only they loomed over her as if she were a mere figurine in the titanic stage where her life was being sorted out.

The clouds swirled fiercely overhead, her arms tightened around David and she smiled, knowing that her only choice was to trust the images and messages she received, confident she'd be able to distinguish between the good and the bad when the time came.

She let go of David and looked at him, "It's all good. Definitely."

Maité kissed him.

CHAPTER 27

Their early return seemed to catch Soledad by surprise, but she recovered quickly and looked ecstatic to have them back in her kitchen, where she could mollycoddle them to her heart's content. Despite their objections, she threw together a quick snack, which she placed on the table along with a frosty pitcher filled with lemonade, and two glasses.

At the sight of the improvised spread, Maité realized she was hungry after all. David pulled out a chair for her, hurried to get to his own, and they sat down to devour the cheese and cold cuts.

"So, what's going on?" Maité asked setting down her glass and eyeing Soledad slantways. She'd been bustling around anxiously emitting fitful giggles every so often but not saying much, very unlike Soledad. As if that wasn't suspicious enough, Soledad seemed to be avoiding Maité's eyes. Even the constant petting and pinching of Maité's cheeks whenever she swept by seemed strained. When Soledad didn't respond, Maité insisted, dodging another pinch—her cheeks were starting to smart—"Something's up, Sole. What is it?"

Whatever Soledad was trying to hold in would no longer keep. She exploded into that contagious laugh of hers and pretty soon David grinned too while Maité shook her head. "What? What is it?"

"I'm so happy, mi niña!" Soledad blurted, dabbing at her eyes with the corner of her apron.

"About what?"

"You will see. It is a *sorpresa*. You will see!" Soledad rested her pudgy hand on the countertop, taking a deep breath to compose herself, but again launched into a long shriek, making Maité jump. "Aaaaay mi niiiiiiñaaaaaa!"

Maité clutched her chest, glaring at Soledad, while David shrugged. Then a well-known voice came from behind.

"Listen, lady, you just have to stop being so loud. You're gonna give someone a heart attack!"

Maité couldn't believe her ears. She didn't want to turn around for fear she might be hearing things, after all, that seemed to be the trend with her these days. But the sight of Soledad jiggling with laughter was oh, so reassuring.

Maité turned around, and there stood lanky Emily by the kitchen door with a towel wrapped around her head, wearing very short shorts, a skimpy tube top, and canvas shoes. She was shaking her head at Soledad, who wasn't even bothering to wipe her tears with her apron.

Maité leapt from her chair. Emily was really there, with that smirk on her face Maité knew so well, the one that said *I got you good!* She hurtled herself at Emily. It felt so good to hug her, to see a familiar face.

"I couldn't let you spend your birthday all by yourself, could I?" Emily asked, patting Maité's back.

"I had no idea you were—"

"Yeah, well, M, if you'd check your e-mail, you'd have a clue. But you probably didn't even notice I hadn't answered. I mean, after the load you dumped on me this morning, for me not to answer? Hello?"

David cleared his throat, and Maité turned abruptly toward him. "Oh, I'm so sorry," she stammered. "Emily, this is David."

Emily gave Maité a shifty sideways glance as David kissed one side of her face and then the other. "Very good to meet you," she said, grabbing his hand and shaking it vigorously, as if the air kissing exercise hadn't counted as a greeting in her book.

With an indulgent smile, David pulled up a chair for Emily, and the three of them sat. Soledad split her petting and random hugging between Maité and Emily while she refreshed the spread on the table.

Emily began quizzing David straightaway, this was standard procedure, so Maité didn't interrupt, and in the process, she found out new things about him. Like the fact he had a small sailboat, which he took out every weekend during the summer, and that the type of research that interested him most was genetics. Maité shifted uncomfortably on her chair.

How does Emily do that?

David looked thoroughly entertained. He laughed in his good-natured way, and Maité felt a prickle of jealousy. She had a sudden fear he might find Emily infinitely more interesting than her. They now had genetics in common, and the thought of them sharing such a big thing worried her.

She tried to look naturally at Emily, who kept discussing all the things Maité should have had the imagination to talk about with David. *But he's my destiny,* she remembered suddenly and managed to relax, just as he said,

"There are a few things I need to look into at work."

"Oh no!" Maité protested putting her hand on his and ignoring Emily's raised brow.

"You come to dinner tonight?" Soledad asked him while drying a pot with a dish towel.

"Yes, do." Maité joined in the invitation.

"It would be my pleasure," David replied, getting up to leave. "I'll be back at nine."

"Well, I'll have to have a snack before then," Emily said under her breath to Maité.

"I know—dinner is at your bedtime over here," Maité sympathized.

After seeing David to the door and waving good-bye, Emily detonated. "OMG! M, 'hottie' doesn't even begin to cover it! And I can't believe you're already holding hands with him." Emily wagged an accusing finger at Maité. "Have you seen his eyes? And I'll bet under that shirt there's one ripped—"

Maité guided the chattering Emily back into the house. Emily was having the same reaction to David she'd had—and who could blame her? Maité continued slowly toward the stairs, listening as Emily rambled on.

"—can already tell he's one of those polite types, but you're gonna have to give him a break and let me at him—"

"What?"

"You know, so I can talk to him?"

"What do you mean, give him a break?"

"Chillax, M, I just told you. He's definitely the polite type. I could tell he was humoring me—probably 'cuz I just got here and all—but it's obvious he wants to be hanging on your every word." Emily stopped and cocked her head to one side to study Maité.

"What?"

"I see what you mean about the blushing," Emily commented in forensic tones.

Maité let out a disgruntled sigh.

Emily shrugged. "So anyway, the boy's smitten, and all I'm sayin's you gotta cut him loose, at least for half an hour, so I can quiz him on that project he's working on. The one about the funky gene?"

Maité nodded. If Emily had noticed it, then David must be smitten, as she put it. "I'll see what I can do," Maité promised and then, jutting her chin toward the three flights of stairs, she said, "Race ya!"

"It's not fair! You started before me!"

In no time, Emily was referring to Eva as the "gold digger" and didn't seem to care much for details of Eva's affair with Maité's grandfather. Glad to drop the subject as well, Maité moved on to the things that really excited her. They *ooed* and *aahd* over the portrait, and they looked over the parchment containing the family tree, which Maité had extracted very carefully from its place inside the cover of the manuscript and placed on top of the bed to be examined at their leisure.

Maité dazzled and increased her friend's anticipation by translating excerpts from Xiomara's manuscript, which Emily refused to read for herself until "I'm fully rested and can give it the time it will require."

They stood side by side on Maité's private balcony with their arms interlocked and their hair flapping in the wind, looking at the island of Santa Clara. Maité poured over that portion of her story, namely the light she thought she'd seen, and the woman with the porcelain face who needed to be found. She told Emily she suspected Santa Clara was the place to look for her.

It felt good to have someone to confide in.

"Gasp, M, leave you on your own for less than a week, and you drop yourself into another dimension," Emily said, thumping her on the shoulder.

"You're the only person who would see it that way. Almost everyone else would think I've lost it." Maité laughed.

"Yeah well, it could turn out it's no mysterious dimension at all—it could be you're just good-ole crazy," Emily suggested as she pulled Maité back into the room. "But if we're going to figure this out, I think we need to tackle this in an organized way."

"Oh no!" Maité rolled her eyes anticipating a full-blown, strategized plan of action.

"I'm serious. It's the only way. Otherwise you'll feel like you're not getting anywhere. You don't even know what a blessing it is I'm here," Emily said.

"I do know," Maité said, hugging her friend. "I do too know!"

"So let's get to work!"

"What do you mean? What are we going to do?"

"We'll start with a summary of the facts. You know—the stuff we know. Then we'll do a flowchart." Emily ran a comb through her hair.

"A what?"

"A flowchart. To map out the steps we need to take to get you sane again."

"Or back to a normal dimension," Maité teased.

"Yes, well, I'm only here for two weeks, and I'd really like to have this project done before I leave."

"Yes, ma'am!"

It was close to seven in the evening when they started, and time flew, with Emily putting question after question to Maité and interjecting eagerly as more details were revealed.

As nine o'clock approached, Maité took a quick shower and dressed for dinner while Emily sat on the bed, putting data neatly into text boxes on her laptop.

Dinner turned out to be a toned-down affair, as Mr. Córdoba had decided to join David.

Maité mourned the loss of opportunities to hold David's hand, because she felt self-conscious under Mr. Córdoba's scrutinizing eye. She could tell Emily was a little tense too; she wasn't eating with her usual gusto.

Emily was predictably worn out from her journey, so as soon as David and his father left (Emily again allowed them to kiss her, but then insisted on shaking hands), Maité and Emily said their buenas noches to a grinning Soledad and a severe-looking Plinio. Then, hand in hand, they walked up the stairs, where, after making sure her dear guest had everything she needed, Maité retired to her own room.

CHAPTER 28

Mr. Gonzaga and Eva left the María Celeste shortly after Maité and David. Eva thought it best to distract Mr. Gonzaga from the first encounter with his granddaughter—that arrogant little mortal. She took him to the Martín Bersategui Restaurant, where they first met, and they had a couple of drinks. It was after eight when they left the restaurant and headed to Eva's apartment a few blocks away.

The couple enjoyed a romp on her large bed and then drank a bottle of wine while watching the sun sink into the Cantabrian.

Mr. Gonzaga now sat leisurely on a sofa in her sumptuous suite with a view of the *Bahía de la Concha*. He looked satisfied.

From the threshold of her boudoir, with nothing on but her hair to cover her naked flesh, Eva heard him on the phone. She watched him with a mixture of contempt and irritation, pondering the fact he was not as easily controlled as she had estimated.

Mr. Gonzaga gave her an arched smile when he noticed her. He seemed to mistake the intensity of her gaze for lingering desire, which suited Eva just fine. Just in case though, she arranged her face into a seductive pout before he could conjecture otherwise. She blew him a kiss.

"First class, of course," he said into the phone, turning his attention back to the agent on the other end of the line. Eva closed her bedroom door, leaving him to finalize their travel arrangements for their trip to Paris.

She walked into her lavish bathroom and closed that door as well. She took the precaution of locking this one. Eva ran her fingers over the smooth granite countertop, cluttered with bejeweled boxes and crystal bottles filled with colorful oils and expensive perfumes. She raised her eyes to the vast mirror over her dressing table and took in her reflection; she judged it splendid and indulged in a few moments' admiration of her shapely charms.

Had someone been watching, they would've thought Eva simply vanished, but she had only adopted a more compact size of about ten inches in height.

She now stood, barefoot, on the counter's granite surface and again stared at herself in the mirror, her nude body appealingly set off by sparkling bottles. With a languid, well-practiced motion of her fingers and wrist, she pulled her red tresses over her exposed breasts.

But the gray eyes of the girl, Maité, blinked in Eva's mind, and the rim of her own irises flashed red in the mirror.

"That brat looks a great deal like her idiot ancestor Celeste," she said, her mouth twisting into a snarl. "So much for Amets ... he's useless to me now; I can't trust him." She tiptoed among the crystals, all the while eyeing every part of her sinuous self in the looking glass.

"But I'll need to hurry my plan; this Maité can cause me unnecessary troubles, and already Fernando breaks away from me too frequently—oh that I could exert my full powers while at wretched human height!" She cried angrily, her circumstances as fresh in her mind as the day she breached full time into the world of humans. Not twenty-four hours passed before Eva found that shape-shifting and sustaining her increased size consumed a great deal of energy. As if that wasn't bad enough, it also made her ability to enchant humans into submission barely a third of what she was accustomed to.

On the upside, Eva still had her innate allure. Her fame and the reaction her eager fans experienced at the sight of her were largely due to her natural endowments and the raw sensuality she exuded, which spoke to men in particular, drawing them to her as if she were a magnet, with very few exceptions. So with Gio's help, Eva's career—her cover—had been secured without any exertion on her part, which was a good thing, as there was precious little energy to be squandered on anyone but her object: Fernando Gonzaga.

"I mustn't underestimate this girl," Eva said, staring at her own reflection through narrowed eyes. "Perhaps her mother wasn't the true obstacle."

The door handle to the bathroom jiggled, and Eva whipped her head around toward it; she quickly unlocked it, already at human height, disposed to receive Mr. Gonzaga, perhaps into the bathtub. She aimed to have the sought-out documents prepared and signed while in Paris—away from Maité.

CHAPTER 29

Exhausted, Maité sank into her bed at eleven o'clock that night.

This has been a good day, she thought, allowing herself a relaxing stretch. The confrontation with her grandfather had left her mind with Emily's arrival.

Sleep came over her as swiftly as ever. Her thoughts seemed to drift toward the woman with the aquamarine eyes who had asked her to be silent, except somehow the images continued from there. Suddenly, the memory became a dream, new and different.

After casting a meaningful smile meant for Maité, the woman with the turquoise-streaked curls turned away and began climbing the wide staircase at the María Celeste; the three other people there didn't take notice of her. Mr. Gonzaga said something about needing to take a few things from the mansion, to which Eva replied she already had them boxed and ready to be loaded into the horse-drawn carriage waiting on the drive. David said the approval process for removing things from the estate was quite time-consuming and nothing could be taken just yet.

Maité inched away from the group and couldn't hear Eva's response. She followed the woman up the stairs. No one seemed to care or notice she'd wandered off.

Maité hastened to keep up, but her legs moved sluggishly and she felt out of breath. She could only see the hem of the woman's robe at every turn, which kept her in constant dread of losing her. Maité's heart raced wondering what she'd find at the top of the stairs and soon lost track of the number of stories they'd climbed. Was it five? Somewhere in her conscious mind, Maité knew the María Celeste was only a three-story building and this perplexed her.

At the next landing, a huge crack in one of the walls revealed the blue sky. When she leaned out, Maité saw clouds above and fog so thick below she couldn't make out the street or even the jungle surrounding the mansion. She reeled on wobbly legs. The air seemed thin, but the hem of the woman's robe disappeared behind a set of double doors opposite Maité, prompting her to go on.

She followed the faint sound of cloth sweeping the wooden floor, and when crossing a threshold, she found herself on the shore of a lake sparkling in the moonlight. They were no longer inside a building. *Or is this what's hidden on the top floor?*

A slight breeze cooled Maité's face, and the sand at her feet felt cold and wet. *Where'd my shoes go?* Her eyes were drawn to the other side of the lake where the blonde woman stood. She seemed to say something, but Maité couldn't make it out.

Water lapped at her calves and then swirled around her thighs as she moved further in, wanting to reach the woman or at least catch her words. Maité began to swim. *What are you saying?* Her arms ached and her breathing became strained. She rolled over on her back to rest, and water quickly filled her ears—nothing but open sky where the roof of the María Celeste should have been.

Stars twinkled merrily at Maité, but then a throaty voice broke through the soothing rhythm of her breathing. It came from several directions at once, mocking and disorienting her. She recognized it.

No you don't … Maité jerked herself to a standing position but found no bottom to stand on; she began to sink.

No!

She kicked frantically toward the shore, but the water felt thicker somehow—either that or her body became denser, harder to command. Maité's thrashing feet brushed something under water that made her recoil in panic. She squinted at the gathering darkness, wrenching herself this way and that, trying to see what had slithered by her.

Something dark emerged from the water only a few feet away. It made a terrible sucking noise as it moved. Maité swam frantically in the opposite direction but couldn't escape; no sooner would she decide on one course than she found herself pawing the water toward the dripping apparition. Peals of laughter rang in her ears, confusing her even more. A wintry cold claw caught her ankle and began to drag her down. Maité thrashed for a few agonizing seconds and then she was underwater. Her lungs ached, and her thighs cramped from the exertion—they seemed to have turned to lead.

Maité opened her eyes in the watery darkness and found Eva's merciless face almost touching her own. She yelled but only a gurgle came out. Eva's tresses were like clots of red cotton candy suspended around her beautiful, demonic face. She heard Eva's triumphant laughter; the piercing sound of it went straight into Maité's head. She knew it was because she had to be dead—well, almost dead.

She foolishly screamed out the last of her air, her eyes bulged, her throat tightened. Her hands and feet went numb.

The secret male voice, which had been her companion for several days now, whispered in her head.

This is your dream, Maitagarri ... you can do what you will with it. Even die. If that is what you wish.

Maité's ears were about to implode; she knew there was wisdom in the words whispered to her, but she could not process it. Cold, wet darkness—that was all she could feel and see.

Die, if that is what you wish.

She looked up. The surface of the mucky pond seemed leagues above her.

Well, is it? Do I want to die?

"No!" Maité screamed again; the huge effort seemed to squeeze oxygen out of her at a cellular level causing her excruciating pain.

This is my dream! Maité thought desperately, remembering "The Exquisite World of Dreams" workshop she'd attended with her mother a lifetime ago. *I'll do whatever I want with it!* Conscious enough to know it was a dream, but still asleep enough to continue dreaming on her own terms, Maité drew a lungful of water through her nose, and it miraculously relieved her aching chest and clouded brain. The pain in her thighs vanished, her constricted chest opened, and her throbbing head felt lighter.

Feeling revived, Maité's fear alchemized into sharp rage, and she imagined a single self-guided spear, which she hurled with a mighty effort toward Eva. "I'm not dying with you in my head!" she growled, and although the sounds came out of her as if through a pillow, they were a very clear thought in her head.

Eva dodged Maité's energy spear and shot to the surface. Maité gave chase, her arms digging her way out of the depths, but when she broke through and opened her eyes to look around, Eva was gone, and she'd taken the darkness with her.

Nothing but lavender sheers swelled in the breeze. Morning brightness filled Maité's room.

CHAPTER 30

The dream disappeared as Maité's door flew open and in came Emily, still in her shorts and camisole, feet bare and hair pulled on top of her head in a ragged knot.

"Oh good, you're awake! Happy birthday!"

"Thanks, Em. I'm so glad you're here," Maité replied, overwhelmed with gratitude for her friend's presence.

"Now take a look at what I've put together," Emily said, waving two pieces of paper in the air and hopping on to the bed.

"Good morning," Maité said, scooting over to make room; her legs felt sore under the blankets.

"Ditto. But look," Emily said, putting a sheet of paper, crammed full with what looked like a schedule, in front of Maité's face.

"You did this last night? I thought you were exhausted," Maité said, scanning the paper in disbelief.

"I did it this morning. Did you know the sun comes up at like six in the morning on my side of the house? And straight onto my pillow? Why didn't I get the west-facing room?" Emily complained, looking around at Maité's bright though sunless room.

Maité laughed, eyeing the timelines Emily had scribbled on both sides of the paper; she had even put a title on it: Project Maitagarri. Phase I. Below it were things such as borrow boat to go to Santa Clara, go back to the María Celeste and do a walkthrough, read entire manuscript by Xiomara. Ask David to take us to the mountains. Try to call out to the voices. See if Eva is on a city directory. Lunch.

"See this one?" Emily asked proudly, pointing to the entry that read "Take apart the showerhead and see where the smell comes from." "It's just so you know I didn't forget anything."

"I see. You've been busy, but what happened to the flowcharts?"

"This was better. I opted for timelines because we have nothing but action items right now, so a flowchart didn't make sense—and besides, I didn't bring a regular mouse. It takes forever to do flowcharts with that silly button thing on the laptop," she said gazing smugly at her work.

"I think you have stuff in here I hadn't even thought about."

"What hadn't you thought about?"

"For instance—lunch. What's that about?" Maité teased.

"Before we even get into that, let's deal with breakfast. I'm starving!" Taking the pages from Maité and grabbing her by the elbow, Emily pulled her off the bed.

They made their way down the stairs, still in their pajamas, and into the kitchen where Soledad waited with a table covered in plates and silverware, plus a pitcher filled with orange juice, steaming coffee, hot bread, and fresh fruit.

"*Feliz cumpleaños,* mi niña! Happy birthday!" Soledad cried as soon as she spotted Maité—the accompanying whirling hug left Maité unsteady on her feet.

As soon as they sat, Soledad brought over a large frying pan with sizzling sausage and an omelet, which she cut in half with a spatula and gave to each girl along with a generous helping of sausage. They ate Soledad's good food until they were thankful for the elastic waistbands on their pajama bottoms, and after helping Soledad with the dishes, they headed upstairs.

Back in her room, showered and dressed, Maité stood in front of the mirror braiding her hair when Emily came in.

"I see what you mean," Emily said. "I smelled your shower all the way from the hall."

"Thank you! That means I'm not crazy."

"That's just one item on the list; I wouldn't confirm your sanity based on that alone," Emily retorted with a wink. "Are you about ready?"

"Yup."

"Okay, we'll start with the book. Since you've already read it, I'll catch up. If you don't mind, I want to read it on your bed so I can look at the picture whenever I need to—is that okay?"

"Yes, ma'am!" Maité saluted her.

"We can look at the showerhead later. Maybe we can even ask Plano—"

"*Plinio*—"

"Whatever—to help us."

"All right, that sounds good, and while you're reading *Faery Sight*, I'll put the family tree into the computer, so we can have a carrying copy of it. I'd hate to lose or tear the original. I almost want to frame it."

"Right."

"Right." Maité walked over to her nightstand, pulled out the book from the drawer, and handed it to Emily.

"Talk to me in four hours," Emily said, already sounding distant while she made herself comfortable on Maité's bed with her notebook, pencil, and two apples close at hand.

Maité watched her for a moment before she extracted the delicate parchment from the dresser. It felt good to have someone on the inside, knowing all she knew and helping her sort it out. She placed the family tree on the table by the window and brought her laptop over. But before Maité could begin transcribing, a frustrated grunt made her turn around. "What is it?"

Emily scowled at Maité from her place on the bed. She looked both suspicious and resentful; Maité had never seen those expressions in Emily's eyes, not directed at her, anyway. "Em? What is it?"

"I'll tell you what," Emily lashed out, "this stupid piece of paper bit me three times. I'm gonna need a transfusion if it keeps it up. It's like it doesn't want me to read beyond this stupid first page!"

Aghast, Maité raced over to the bed and pulled the book toward her. She saw three specks of Emily's blood at different stages of being absorbed into the vellum. "The same thing happened to me, but what do you mean it doesn't want you to read?"

"I mean I can't read a word of this!" Emily seethed while shuffling the thick pages.

Even as Emily fanned the papers, words jumped out at Maité, words she recognized, yet Emily insisted, "Nothing—this is nothing but one long scribble. They're not even letters!"

How could this be? Maité had thought nothing of it when it happened to her—she figured it had been a paper cut or something, and then she went on to read the rest of the book, which was perfectly legible to her!

"Em, I can see the letters just fine. Look right here." Maité stuck her hand between two pages and urged Emily to look. "You can't recognize this word? It says 'Celeste.' Can't you at least make out the letters?"

"That's what I'm telling you!" Emily cried, looking embarrassed by her failure. "It's a bunch of squiggles to me, some short, some long. They're nothing but meaningless wavy lines."

Perplexed, Maité stared at Emily, wondering if maybe she was joking, but the scowl on Emily's face said otherwise—Maité could almost hear that analytical brain whirring inside Emily's head, scrambling for an explanation. Why had she been able to get past the vellum and read everything after it, when Emily couldn't?

"I wonder if you have to be related to this Xiomara chick," Emily suggested, "to be able to read the dang thing."

Maité pondered this, trying to get her head around a new piece of evidence. "You're sure you're not messing with me?"

"Are *you* messing with *me*?" Emily snapped.

"Why would I?" Maité returned helplessly, scanning the pages that to her were crowded with identifiable text.

"So now what?" Emily looked stumped.

"How should I know? Could this be a charm, or a spell of some sort?"

Emily gave her a weak nod, and Maité noticed something akin to fear stamped on her freckled face. Fear of something Emily couldn't rationalize. *Magic.*

"How about if I go over these chapters with you?" Maité suggested helpfully and in a hurry to move past this bewildering moment. She didn't want to lose Emily's determination and encouragement over this, and it was certain she would if she allowed her any more time to dwell on it. *Better keep her moving.* "We'll go chapter by chapter, so you'll have a general idea of what's in here."

"Fine," Emily said dryly frowning at the thick book, as if she'd been slighted by it.

"Emily?"

"What?"

"Before we go on"—Maité paused, not knowing how to say what she'd suddenly began to worry about. If she was to relay the contents of this book to someone who couldn't read it for herself, then she thought it best to at least have a verbal promise.

"Yeah?"

"I don't want anyone wreaking misery on every instant of my existence," Maité said, sheepishly running her finger over the vellum, where all traces of Emily's blood were gone.

"Oh. Okay," Emily replied, biting her lip as she pulled the book toward her. Careful not to touch it, she made her promise. "I agree to complete and utter secrecy—because the identities of the people in this book are hallowed."

"Thank you, Em." Maité beamed and eagerly launched into the highlights of the tale. She smiled every time a quizzical humph escaped her audience of one, or when Emily let out a grunt or a sigh. Sometimes Emily gazed at the portrait above the bed or ran her finger over the top of the family tree, where the names of the founders of the Santillán clan were printed in exquisite calligraphy. What Emily didn't do was interrupt Maité's narrative, not even once, although she grew visibly disappointed as the stack of pages waiting to be read shrank.

"And so these are your ancestors." Emily sighed a couple of hours later, placing the family tree within the pages of the book. Her resentment over not being allowed to read the thing herself seemed to be forgotten.

"Yup." Maité beamed.

"And do you think it's all true?"

Maité thought Emily's question curled at the end with a little tail of challenge. She dropped her gaze to the book on the bed and closed it, unable to answer. She couldn't say *Yes, I believe every word of it*, because if she did, Emily might frown on it and conclude Maité had lost her marbles. "We'd better get to work putting the family tree into the computer," she said evasively.

Whether Emily took the hint, or the thought of tackling a straightforward task excited her, Maité didn't know. It was enough Emily didn't pursue the question and dived right into Maité's genealogy instead.

As she read off the dates and names for Emily, Maité felt she knew the main players intimately and imagined faces to go with each one.

"Next to *Calisto*, it'll be *Anahí*," Maité said, and as she spelled it out for Emily, she became distracted by sudden thoughts of the woman with the turquoise streaked ringlets. *Come and find me* ... but Maité shook her head and read off more names.

"We're done," Emily said groggily half an hour later. She got up from the desk to stretch her back and then sprawled on the bed to stare at the portrait again. "Humph."

"What?" Maité asked, carefully replacing the original family tree within the covers of the book.

"You do look a lot like this Celeste chick."

"I swear, the way you talk, you sound like a guy," Maité said, climbing onto the bed and drawing her knees to her chest. "Celeste's eyes were brown though."

"What is that?" Emily cried, pointing to Maité's ankle, which had been hidden by her pants until then.

Maité looked down and was startled to find a dark bruise around her ankle, as if someone had tied a rope around it and dragged her by it. "I don't know," she said breathlessly, pressing on it and confirming it was indeed tender to the touch. A cold chill raced up and down her back; she could feel adrenaline, like prickling hot spray inside her. "I mean, I do know, but it can't be. Holy cow!"

"What? What is it?"

The nightmare rushed back, and Maité shut her eyes, trying to get a good grip on the thread before answering. When she felt it safely anchored in her mind, she began telling the dream to Emily, who looked at Maité's ankle as if Eva's hand still clung to it.

"OMG, M!"

Maité stared mutely at the dark, purple ring around her ankle. "She actually tried to kill me," Maité muttered.

"But your other boyfriend saved you." Emily smirked.

"Huh?"

"Well, yeah, he told you to live, didn't he?" Emily said helpfully.

"Yeah, I guess—well ..."

"I know, I know, you feel awful 'cuz here he saves your life, even after you've been prancing around with David, totally blowing him off ..."

"Oh, shut up!" Maité retorted, thumping Emily on the shoulder.

"It's the truth though, isn't it? You can't be fooling around with two guys at the same time. You have to make up your mind. Pick one, and let the other one off the hook!"

"Are you even listening to yourself?"

"No." Emily laughed. "I think it's the hunger speaking, so don't pay any attention to me. But just so you know—if I were you, I'd probably do the same thing. You know, try to keep on good terms with both of them until I decide which one suits me best. Of course, if push came to shove, I'd pick they guy I can see, hear and touch."

"You're a nut, Em, and you need to refocus. The thing here is not the two guys; it's this bruise on my ankle!"

"Seriously," Emily said, looking soberly at the bruise, which had already begun to turn yellow in spots, "that woman tried to kill you. If only the boys back home knew the Lamborghini goddess is a conniving, murdering bi—"

"Emily!"

"Well, she is."

"But is it even possible? I mean, it was a dream," Maité cried, fearing Emily might pronounce her crazy or possessed. Neither diagnosis suited Maité because although she didn't admit it, she wanted Emily's earlier words to be the reality—that she, Maité, had broken into another dimension.

"I've read studies on dreams," Emily began, surprising Maité once again with her objectivity. "Your mind can build crazy things around a single idea when you're in dream mode, and it's happened before that people do weird things in their sleep. It's possible you did this to yourself"—she indicated the bruise—"while you slept."

Maité nodded half-heartedly.

"What if you tangled your ankle in the sheets? What if you tightened them yourself, while in your head you thought you were trying to pry off Eva's hands?"

Maité's hopeful conjectures crumbled under Emily's logic. It seemed more reasonable that she'd done it to herself. It was perfectly plausible, more so than Eva having the power to penetrate her mind and her dreams. More so than being saved by the voice of a man who whispered confidence into her and helped her save herself, more so than that man being a faery. And infinitely more so than *her* being part of a century-old magical conflict. Maité flushed pink at her dashed childish ideas.

But what about the warning page in the book? she thought hopefully. How could it be that a perfectly legible narrative to Maité was no more than a long scribble to Emily? All because of a rejected blood sample? Wasn't that magic? Wasn't that proof something, scientifically unheard of in this day and age, was happening?

Good grief! How could Emily discount such a thing? Who ever heard of a piece of paper drawing blood, testing it, and then allowing a person to read its contents based on the results? This was nothing short of magical encryption, in Maité's opinion.

"Mis niñas!" Soledad called from the bottom of the stairs. "Lunch is ready!"

"Bless her," Emily said fervently as she uncurled her legs and got off the bed.

Maité followed, feeling a little better because all was *not* lost. She didn't say so, but she felt certain Emily would come around and have to accept that the answer might be somewhere beyond science. She'd have to give magic its rightful place in the scheme of things.

CHAPTER 31

When Maité related what happened at the María Celeste the day before, Soledad declared herself convinced it had been all Eva's doing.

"She is no woman, that serpiente!" Soledad muttered on her way to the phone, snagging the Cab company card stuck to the refrigerator door as she passed.

My feelings exactly, Maité thought, but she couldn't let Eva take precedence in her thoughts. There were other, more important, things to puzzle over. Even if Emily chose to dismiss the magical qualities of her circumstances, Maité would be open to explaining them from that angle.

Really, who walks around hearing voices in her head? Feeling some guy's breath on her neck at the weirdest moments? Whose dreams are real enough to mark you? "Crazy, psychotic people" was the answer that popped into her head, but she deflected it with another thought: *What if I've broken through the gate of an everyday dimension and slipped into a place where things like time and distance and the limitation of five senses doesn't exist?*

"The taxi will be here in five minutes," Soledad said as she hung up the phone.

"Gracias, Sole," Maité said, and Emily nodded from the kitchen table where they sat finishing their lunch.

With full bellies and excited for their outing, the girls waited by the door until the cab arrived. Soledad waved them off with promises of dinner, and they blew kisses at her from the backseat of the car.

The cab descended the tortuous hill toward Paseo de la Concha, and Maité once again felt exhilarated by the sights. Would she ever get used to the beauty of it all? She didn't think so. Seeing it anew through Emily's eyes only heightened her enjoyment of it. The high-desert scene of Ogden with its crisp vegetation was no more than a hazy memory. In its place were the lush greenery, balmy breezes, and iodized air of San Sebastián.

They paid the cab driver, who dropped them off at the back gate of the María Celeste, and Maité led the way for Emily, as David had done the day before.

"Can you believe this place?" Emily complained as she helped Maité shove branches out of the way.

"Yes, I can," Maité sang, thrilled she'd see the entire place this time.

They arrived at the courtyard abruptly, and the house made its appearance once again; there were the tall windows, the French doors with the broken glass panels leading into the mud room. The damaged stucco on the walls bore rust stains, like markings testifying to the passage of time. Miniscule ferns and thick moss erupted from every crack and crevices, making it look like the mansion might be filled with vegetation as desperate to burst out as Maité was to bust in. Unknown voices seemed to call to her from within.

"You actually like this place?" Emily cringed.

"Are you kidding me? Yes!" Maité laughed.

"I sure hope none of these plants are like poison oak or something. Aaaah, eew! Look at that huge bug—what is that? Yuk, yuk, yuk!" Emily squealed and stomped on a harmless species of spider no bigger than a dime, twisting it underfoot with a vengeance.

"I'll bet you anything the inside of this, this grave"—Emily eyed the María Celeste with what looked like irrational fear—"is completely infested with rats and bats and crawling things!"

Frowning, Maité watched Emily scraping the squashed bug from the bottom of her shoe. Although teetering on the edge of annoyance, Maité couldn't help noticing how out of place Emily appeared in the midst of this ruin and decay.

Emily's idea of roughing it was eating sandwiches on the bleachers of a soccer field. Drop her in an all natural habitat, confront her with nature's crawling little creatures, and suddenly she became a petrified toddler who panicked at the touch of a leaf from a tree or the whistling of the wind.

Emily finally stopped fussing over her shoe and seemed to notice Maité hadn't moved or said anything for a few moments. "What? What!"

"Nothing. Just you," Maité smiled. "Do you want to stay here in the courtyard? You know, just in case the house is crawling with termites the size of cockroaches and bats that could carry off an infant?"

Emily paled.

"Oh, c'mon." Maité smacked her on the shoulder. "I'm just kidding about the bats. But if you want to stay behind, you could reread our schedule and draw up a plan for our visit to Santa Clara." The thought of Emily screeching and ricocheting off the walls in a fright over every chunk of dirt on the floor or every piece of fluff floating about in the María Celeste was simply not what Maité had in mind for her grand, self-guided tour.

"Just give me an hour in there," she urged.

"Oh please. A bug here and there is not going to bother me."

Maité rolled her eyes. "No, but it's going to bother me. Look at you, you're a basket case."

"I'll be fine," Emily said, straightening up. "I want to go in there with you."

"Not if you're going to be whining the whole time—there might be mice."

"Mice?" Emily gulped. "That's fine. I'll be fine."

"Emily?"

"Really. I'll be fine. I'm sure they're more scared of me than I am of them," she said, as if trying to reassure herself.

"All right then." Maité sighed. "Let's go."

"Okay." Emily cleared her throat and followed Maité.

The wooden panels and frame on the French doors were mostly intact, although the glass was nonexistent in some panes. But when Maité tried the handle, she found it locked.

"I suppose Grandpa locked it on his way out yesterday," Maité said dryly. Emily caught her eye, and they laughed at the futile safety precaution. Maité reached through one of the empty panes and turned the lock. She began making a mental list of repairs.

They crossed the mud room and found themselves in the middle of the grand hallway.

Maité's eyes, like Emily's, swept from one corner of the immense space to the other. Maité couldn't tell if Emily was measuring or looking for bugs.

To the left were several closed doors along the hall, and to the right, some fifty feet away, the grand staircase, where she first discovered Mr. Gonzaga and Eva the day before. The staircase was at least fifteen feet wide, and the steps seemed to reach as high as the sky.

The walls and floor in this section were in very good condition compared with the outside of the building.

"This place is amazing," Maité said, hugging herself.

"It's like being inside an airplane hangar," Emily observed openmouthed.

"Em, it's like I can hear it breathing—talking to me," Maité said.

"You're not going to start with your demented symptoms are you?"

"I'm not demented. Can't you hear it?"

"Hear what?"

"Sshh!" Maité whirled toward the staircase with Emily right behind her. Every molecule of air seemed to gather and press on Maité.

Her ears popped, but she could see no one. "It's nothing. I just thought …" Her voice trailed off as she caught something out of the corner of her eye. Her skin felt denser already.

"There," Maité whispered, "at the top of the stairs. Do you see it?" Her voice sounded alien to her, as if she were listening to a recording of herself.

"What?"

"I don't think she's seen us yet," Maité said.

"Who?" Emily breathed down her neck. "*Who* hasn't seen us?"

From where they stood in the middle of the great hallway lined with pillars, Maité saw a woman standing halfway down the staircase, her hand resting on the dusty banister. Framed by the massive architecture, she looked frail and small to Maité.

The specter didn't move, nor did she look at them. It seemed an eternity that Maité stood there staring at the phantom until there was a change.

"Are you done seeing whatever it was you saw?" Emily whimpered.

"Uh oh. Now she's looking at us," Maité replied, unable to hold back a smile. She loved every new revelation, every new turn of her circumstances.

"Who? You're scaring me!"

"Can't you see her? She's right there," Maité said, pointing helpfully toward the stairs.

"Cuss words, M! I see no one."

"Do you even have your eyes open?"

"Duh! Yeah," Emily replied and then added, "well, I opened them just now—for a little bit."

The figure looked distractedly at Maité. She appeared more preoccupied with the decaying condition of the dusty banister than with them. At first Maité thought she was wearing a gown but then realized it was more like a shabby robe, torn and dirty. Her matted hair was in desperate need of a good wash and combing. Her face was pale and sad. Dust clung to her as if she were a forgotten piece of furniture.

"Let's get out of here, let's just …" Emily pleaded.

"Oh, hush. We're not going anywhere. Are you nuts?"

"Maité, this ghost situation is just way too freaky for me! Mice are one thing, but ghosts?"

"Calm down. Ghosts can't hurt you. And besides, you can't even see her."

"I can't see her, but I swear I can feel fingers around my ankles. Are you sure ghosts can't hurt us?"

"I promise. Because actually, what I'm seeing over there"—Maité lifted her chin in the general direction of the stairs—"is no ghost."

"What?"

The woman's voice reached Maité. "Come find me ... "

There was something infinitely sad in her voice; it made Maité want to cry, but the woman turned away. The hem of her rotted robe dragged on the steps and then disappeared around the corner.

"Right. We have to follow her," Maité said, determined to see what it was she'd been told to find.

"What?" Emily asked again.

"She's gone upstairs. We have to follow her. It's just like in my dream."

"Are you crazy? You know what happened in your dream!"

"Yeah, but I seriously doubt there's a lake up there. Besides, you're with me." Maité grinned at Emily. "So if there's a lake, and I start to drown, you'll have to save me."

"Okay, but just in case, don't try to breathe the water, 'cuz I'm pretty sure that wouldn't work in real life."

"Okay."

They reached the first landing, and in front of them stood a broken door. Maité opened it and found a six-foot deep balcony with a curved, wrought-iron banister, which stretched across the entire front of the building, perhaps even around all three remaining faces of the mansion. She closed the battered door, pleased with what she had seen.

Back inside, a rectangular hallway surrounded the stairwell. On one side was the door leading to the balcony. The other three sides bore enormous archways leading to various sections of the second level.

"How cool is this," Emily exclaimed as she ventured through one of the entryways. "It's like a little reading room or something, and it has a balcony too. You can see a river from up here!" She sounded delighted; her anxieties seemingly dispersed.

"That's the Urumea River," Maité pointed out.

"Aren't you quite the tour guide," Emily teased.

They continued up another flight of steps and found what Maité decided was the heart of the house.

This is where my family lived. She longed to get a closer look at this floor. The woman in the shabby robe leaned against a wall, looking distantly at Maité, as if granting permission for them to linger.

They found one bedroom in each of the four corners. So huge were these rooms that they seemed to Maité more like modest apartments, each complete with a bathroom and veranda. The main door of every room opened to the central area shaped like a cross, with the stairwell in the center framed by an ornate banister.

"This has to be like a family room, don't you think?"

"Sure looks that way," Emily said, running her fingers over bookshelves and then plopping herself down on a dusty piano stool. "I wonder what happened to the piano."

Maité looked regretfully at a torn portrait still hanging on the wall. The canvas was slashed, but Maité could see it was a painting of a couple. Their faces were blurred and cracked, but the man wore a tailored suit, and she wore a frilly turquoise gown.

"Check it out," Emily called out. "It's a liquor cabinet, and here's one of those old gramophones with a broken funnel thing!"

Maité touched the fine cherry wood with the tips of her fingers, wiping away some of the dirt and debris covering the massive armoire. Only faintly did she hear Emily's exclamations over whatever she was looking at. Maité walked toward the tall stained-glass windows, and even though she couldn't see out, the effect of the light shining through them was beautiful. In the center of what she called the family room, she sighed as the different shades of light from the stained-glass panels reached her in soft and relaxing waves of color.

"I wonder who in my family tree built this place," Maité said.

"Got me. Maybe we should ask Mr. Córdoba when the María Celeste was built, and we can go from there."

"Good idea." Maité was overcome with the sense of being part of a big family, an ancient family. They shared the same blood, and as she stood there, Maité understood what her mother said to Mr. Gonzaga all those years ago about this house—it too has blood, and that blood is what runs through our veins. The María Celeste was like the genetic imprint of the family.

As Maité made her way back to the stairs, she spotted a broken clay pot sitting on an iron stand near a window. She peeked inside and gasped at the sight of a tiny sprout trying to rise from the small clump of dirt inside. "Emily, look at this!"

"What? Wow," Emily said, gaping at it.

Maité thought the struggle of the frail plant seemed akin to her own. "Whatever kind of plant this is, it sure is a sturdy one," she declared. "I'm taking it with me and I'm gonna help her grow."

The rustling of fabric reached her ears again. "That's our cue." Maité headed for the landing.

"What?" Emily asked.

"Over there," Maité said, pointing to a twisted ladder tucked away in a corner. "It looks like there's a fourth level."

"What, like an attic?" Emily stammered, turning eyes full of misgivings to the corkscrew stairs, "You know, our attic at home has tons of wasps' nests."

"And us without bug spray."

Despite her apprehensions, Emily followed Maité rung after rung to a fourth floor they hadn't figured on. There was no trapdoor like the one at the manor, and when Maité emerged through the ceiling she saw an "under construction" site.

Feeling physically dwarfed by the enormity of it, she remained there for a few moments, her palms resting on the floor, just gazing at the unfinished work and wondering what it was meant to be. Emily—four rungs below—smacked Maité's backside. "Hullo?"

Maité pulled herself up and helped Emily the rest of the way. They walked around in the dust and construction debris, trying to decipher the purpose of this huge space. There were framed column-like structures surrounding what was obviously going to be an indoor pool, judging from the half-completed plumbing. The columns, which seemed to reach all the way to the glass dome ceiling, had all been textured to resemble tree trunks.

"This has to be the biggest bathroom I've ever seen," Emily said flatly.

"I think they wanted it to look like a forest," Maité said, running her fingers over the fissured columns and wondering what it would be like to bathe under the stars in a copse. Maité had no trouble imagining a sumptuous indoor world made to resemble nature in every way. She looked at the little plant she'd rescued and wondered how many more could be planted here to make this space into a grove.

"Makes you think of Paloma bathing in the forest, doesn't it?" Emily remarked off-handedly as she walked the perimeter.

Maité looked up, astonished. She hadn't even thought about it, but it was true—someone may have wanted to recreate Celeste and Paloma's bathing place.

"It's huge," Emily called from across the debris-strewn vastness. "I'm thinking about 150 by, um, by 90 feet," she concluded, satisfied.

The air seemed stuffy because the insulation wasn't very good, and the sun shining through the dirty glass on the windows made it feel hotter in a dusty sort of way. Maité walked to one of the windows and rubbed a spot clean with her hand. Down below, she could see the street lined with parked cars and traffic crawling slowly in both directions. People waited for cabs or buses in designated areas, while others bustled about, looking harried. Her eyes drifted back inside and paused when she saw Spanish scribbles on the wall: *Vidrio Tallado, verde/púrpura.*

"I found some notes here," Maité called to Emily. "They wanted to make these windows out of cut glass. Green and purple." Maité walked the length of the floor excitedly, looking for more annotations, and found that all the windows were to have cut glass, and the majority of them were to be tinted blue, green, purple or pink.

"Oh Emily! I can just see it. It was supposed to be a magical forest in here!" She sighed. "And that's exactly what I'll make of it."

"You'll make what?"

"A forest. The Hall of Glamour."

"Hello? Have you lost your mind completely?"

"I can dream, can't I?" said Maité defensively.

"Okay then, so long as it's just a dream. 'Cuz you know, it sure sounds like your grandpa is trying to give this place away—to your future step-grandmother no less—and she's probably going to turn it into a hotel or something."

Maité tried not to look horrified at Emily's words. She couldn't stand the thought of this place becoming something it was never meant to be. She gave Emily's hand a squeeze but turned so Emily wouldn't see her blink away tears.

"I don't know," Maité said, clearing her throat. "I don't know what I'm thinking anymore, and I don't know what I want to do either." She lied, afraid to lose Emily's confidence if she spoke her heart's true desire. It seemed tragic to be so helpless; to be so dependent on decisions made by her grandfather, who didn't even contemplate the possibility of asking for an opinion.

"I don't think there's anything you can do. Though I know what I want!" Emily went on. "Not to blow off your worries, but it's a beautiful afternoon. I want to go to the beach and think on this stuff! How 'bout we go get a salad or something at one of those places right on the water?"

"Yeah, let's do that," Maité mumbled, holding up the piece of clay with the plant and inspecting it again.

"Are you seriously bringing that twig with you?"

"She's a survivor," Maité said fondly. "And I've decided she'll rise again."

Emily shook her head. "You're crazy."

They left the house as they found it—locked, in spite of all the missing panes of glass. They took a cab to the beach of *Ondarreta*, right below Santillán manor, where they ordered their food at a small restaurant near the water. They sat on stools at a table with a single steel leg buried deep into the ground.

Maité took off her shoes and dug her toes in the cool sand while they ate their salads and drank lemonade. She could see her grandfather's house up on the hill. It looked medieval yet timeless, somehow fitting in this paradise of blue sky. The green Cantabrian sparkled at her and Maité closed her eyes, offering her face to the salty breeze.

Santa Clara rose from the green water in the middle of the bay like a purposeful monument to something, and Maité was caught in the mystery of that heavily wooded protrusion just sitting there. A sudden vision of the island, bursting with light and music, popped into her head. Flashes of color like meteors darted uproariously around it, adding to the festive sight.

"Are you enjoying your salads?" a smiling waiter with a heavy accent asked.

"Yes," Emily answered. Maité nodded, wondering about the flashes of color she'd just seen.

"The entire island," the waiter said, noting the direction of Maité's glance and motioning toward Santa Clara, "is covered with those." He seemed to recognize the droopy plant Maité had placed on the table.

"Really?" Maité gaped.

"Oh yes. They're quite lovely. In the spring they blossom with white, very fragrant flowers."

"What kind of plant is it?" Emily asked.

"Citrus. But it produces flowers, no fruit," the waiter said.

Emily gave Maité a knowing look.

"Really?" Maité couldn't be sure, but it seemed a vision of the blonde woman just flickered over the waiter's shoulder. She squinted in the bright sunlight but saw nothing.

Emily paid the bill. "My treat," she said. "It's your birthday!"

The girls spent the rest of the afternoon jostling their way through crowded sidewalks. They visited the impressive Palacio Miramar and then rode the cable car to the top of Monte Igueldo for spectacular views of La Concha Bay and Ondarreta Beach. The late afternoon wind blew strong at the lookout point.

Gazing through one of the coin-operated telescopes standing in a row, Santa Clara seemed to look back at Maité, deserted and idle, with nothing to offer. Shifting her angle, Maité spotted the place where they had eaten and where the blonde woman had come back to her thoughts. Maité told Emily about her last "hallucination" at the restaurant.

"Humph," Emily said. "Whoever she is, she seems to be getting desperate."

"You think so?"

"It just seems you've been having visions of her way oftener in the past couple of days, more than your verbal-boyfriend guy. Do you think they're a tag team or something?"

"I guess. Maybe. But what do you mean by 'desperate'?"

"How should I know? She keeps asking you to find her." Emily shuddered, probably remembering the eerie experience at the María Celeste. "I wish she'd change her cryptic little message to something more helpful, like, 'Look for me here.'" Emily traced an X in the air as she spoke.

"I don't know what to do."

"Yeah. You keep saying that."

"What?" Maité bristled. "I'm supposed to know exactly what to make of all this stuff that's happening to me? Like I could just have conversations with these people and straighten it all out?"

"Geez, M! You don't have to bite my head off! But as long as you're going to, then I might as well say it—why not?"

"What?"

"Why not?"

"Why not what?"

"Talk to them, M. Next time one of them tries to lay their little invasion-of-privacy routine on you, make them stop and answer some questions. Give it a try, at least."

Emily completely staggered Maité with her practical approach to things. Now that she'd pointed it out, talking to them seemed the obvious thing to do. How could it not have occurred to her to establish two-way communication?

"You're absolutely right," Maité admitted.

"Duh!"

"Next time the voice guy tries to get in my space, I'll start asking questions. No one's coming into my head anymore until I get some answers."

"Of course there's the little stun factor to deal with," Emily pointed out.

"Yes, *that*," Maité conceded grudgingly, wishing she hadn't shared that with Emily. "I'll just have to snap out of it," she promised, sincerely hoping she'd be able to resist the pleasurable encounters. Half the time, Maité was happy to just let the sensations wash over her. But that would have to stop. "I will, Em. I can ignore that part of it." She frowned at Emily's doubtful grin.

"You'd better."

"I wonder," Maité began, her eyes once again drawn to Santa Clara. "Do you suppose anyone lives there?"

"I read a little about it on the Internet and I don't think anyone's allowed, although people used to celebrate feasts there—ages ago—like pagan harvest festivals or something."

They drank an iced tea at the hotel bar at the top of Monte Igueldo and then cruised the small amusement park with its carnival rides and attractions.

They took pictures of things they saw and of each other, and Maité took every opportunity to practice her Spanish by talking to anyone who made eye contact with her. Emily was astounded at how many people actually did.

"Maybe it's 'cuz of the way we look. They feel sorry for us. I don't think there's a single person in this city who owns skate shoes or T-shirts," Emily complained.

"Everybody is just so nice and polite, don't you think?" Maité asked, not caring a thing about the differences in attire that Emily had just pointed out. Everyone seemed to have a piece of advice for them on where to eat and what to see. "They're like the perfect hosts!"

"Uh huh," Emily said as she looked through the coin-operated binoculars and swiveled them as if manning the guns in a World War II plane.

The afternoon sped by. All too quickly, the sun began to plunge behind the Cantabrian.

"Soledad's gonna kill us!" Maité fretted as they rode slowly down the mountain on the cable car. When they reached the bottom, there were no cabs to be hailed.

"We're not that far. Let's just walk to the house," Emily offered.

"I don't think that's such a good idea ..."

"What else are we gonna do? Tell you what—let's start walking, and if we see a cab we'll take it the rest of the way."

"Okay."

The marine layer rolled in and darkness closed in on them faster than Maité would've liked. She didn't recognize anything. "Do you even know where we're going?" Maité said irritably, trying to keep up with Emily's long, confident strides.

"I'm sure this was the street we came down in the cab. So as long as we keep going uphill, we're good," Emily assured her.

"So you don't know where we're going."

"Not exactly. No."

Maité tried not to panic. The streets were dark and deserted; tree branches loomed above them like enormous hands waiting to claw at them. For the life of her, she couldn't remember where the right turn leading to the private gravel road was; she feared they may have passed it already. A cold gust of wind swept a bunch of dried leaves off the street and blew dust into her eyes. She held tight to her little citrus plant, hoping the fragile clump of dirt and roots wouldn't disintegrate and fly away in the wind.

Maitagarri ...

A sweet tenderness spread through Maité. It'd been a long time since she'd heard him like that. In her dreams, his voice came from outside of her, but this was his voice again, inside.

I've missed you. His admission came ardently to the fore without even a mild effort on her part to stop it—perhaps because she had missed him too. When the voice spoke again, she could almost hear a smile.

You are not lost, he told her. Obviously he'd read or heard her fears.

They reached a T on the road. Emily stood there, confounded, looking from right to left.

"Can you smell that?" Maité asked, thrusting her chin up like a dog sniffing. She drew several short whiffs.

"Smell what?" Emily said, putting her nose to her armpit.

"Be serious." Maité laughed. "It smells like my shower. Can't you smell it?"

"Not a thing."

Glad for the darkness hiding her lying face from Emily's eyes, Maité announced they were taking a right. Hadn't she just promised to stop indulging in tingles and shudders? Hadn't she been determined to get answers? But when he'd come just now, all she'd managed was a silly grin that still lingered on her face. She had asked no questions and made no demands, but she sure felt good and toasty inside. *And let's not forget, we'll soon be back at the house, thanks to him.*

"Almost there," Maité panted to Emily.

CHAPTER 32

As they took the last turn on the gravel road, Maité saw light pouring from the downstairs windows of the manor. She clutched the stitch in her side, struggling to keep up with Emily, who'd taken the lead as soon as it became certain they were on the right track. Winded, Maité reached the door a few paces behind her.

"I'm starving!" Emily said, irritably working the brass knocker.

"You're always hungry."

The door opened, and Mr. Gonzaga himself glared ominously at them. Eva stood beside him, looking sulky. "You will let me know where you are at all times, and you'll not be out of this house after dark. Do I make myself clear?"

Maité could only stare in astonishment. Next to her, Emily stood petrified. All thought of food seemed to have left her.

"I had no idea you were here," Maité said flatly, having recovered from the shock of finding her grandfather home. "You said you'd be gone a few more days."

She remembered his insinuations and the specific request from the day before—*Do not remove anything from my property*, he'd said, and Maité put her hand behind her back to hide the plant she had removed from the María Celeste.

Mr. Gonzaga cleared his throat and stepped aside to let them in. Eva moved as one with him. Maité noted his frown became less pronounced as he said in a gruff voice, "I understand it is your birthday."

Eva tightened her grip on his arm and rested her head on his shoulder.

Ah! Maité thought, Soledad must have tracked him down for this. *I wish she hadn't.*

"It is," Maité replied, her glance shifting from her grandfather's face to Eva's arm, clamped tightly to his.

Why does she do that? Maité let out a contemptuous grunt. A red ring smoldered around Eva's pupils.

"Soledad has prepared a special meal for you. David and his father are here to partake."

Maité felt a squeeze on her elbow. It was Emily, but she couldn't acknowledge it. She knew Emily must be as shocked as she was; nothing to do but get the evening going.

Maité walked past her grandfather and Eva into the house, closely followed by Emily.

It was the strangest birthday dinner Maité ever endured. Not even David's diplomacy could ease her. The hate—however unexplained—emanating from Eva felt palpable. Maité could hardly swallow the delicious cake Soledad had baked for her.

Her grandfather, extremely sedate, *or sedated*, Maité thought suspiciously, had eyes only for Eva. Once again, Mr. Córdoba made conversation. The hour it took for the party to come to an end was the longest Maité had spent in the grand dining room.

"My best wishes to you, Miss Bottini," Mr. Córdoba said at last, and Maité felt herself revive at once. It was over.

"Thank you very much," she replied with slight turns of her face to receive the good-bye kisses.

"I'll be by tomorrow morning to pick you up for our sailing excursion," David said.

That was the bonus. The entire hour of clipped, cold dialogue was worth it because a sailing trip had been agreed upon, with Mr. Gonzaga's stamp of approval.

"That'll be so much fun," Maité heard Emily whisper as she shook David's hand awkwardly. Then he kissed her cheeks.

Eva had hardly said a word the entire time. She seemed intent on letting Mr. Gonzaga know she didn't want to be there. She cast her eyes on whomever spoke but held tight to his arm. Maité thought it hateful and found Eva's clinging distasteful.

Only now that everyone was at the front door did Eva speak. "It was so kind of you to join us," she said to the Córdoba men with a slanted look at Maité.

Maité wanted to lunge at her throat. *Who does she think she is, the lady of the house?*

Emily again squeezed her elbow; Maité took a calming breath and exhaled.

Right after Mr. Córdoba and David left, Mr. Gonzaga excused himself to take Eva to her apartment.

At least he's not letting her spend the night, Maité thought with relief.

Maité and Emily helped Soledad with the cleanup. "You're the best, Sole." Maité kissed her as Soledad scrubbed a pan. "Thank you so much." Somehow Maité felt more festive now with everyone gone. Or maybe it was just that Eva was gone, along with her cloud of hate.

While Maité showered she thought about Soledad convincing Mr. Gonzaga to come home—for sure it had been Soledad's doing. Maité decided her grandfather, in spite of Eva, might actually be trying to get better acquainted with her, and the thought appeased her.

Maité smiled at the little plant she'd placed on the shelf above her sink and gave it a few drops of water. "Tomorrow I'll get you a real pot and more soil for you to spread your roots."

She got into bed and fell to thinking about the fourth floor of the María Celeste covered in vegetation and a saltwater pool in the middle.

That night, Maité's dreams were turbulent. She ran on a darkened path through a gnarled mess of branches covered in thorns, blown by a chilling wind. The thorns pierced her skin and forced her toward a steeper, more treacherous path littered with jagged rocks. She had to cling to the rocks and climb around them to advance.

Her progress became tortuous. Strobes of lightning showed her path narrowing upward and disintegrating behind her. She couldn't turn back. On either side of her, erosion did its job at a rate equal to every clumsy step she took. Behind her, Mr. Gonzaga helped it along by working an enormous chisel and hammer to erase the way back. In shirtsleeves, he darted from one side of the path to the other; with each move he dislodged a huge boulder, which plummeted into the black chasm that would soon swallow everything.

Maité knew she had to continue climbing because the hellish path was disappearing from under her.

A blinding bolt of lightning revealed a tunnel where the path ended. But at the mouth of the tunnel, Maité glimpsed Eva watching her like a ravenous cat waiting for its kill. Eva was inescapable.

Yet above the tunnel stood a single palm tree, desolate and out of place in the quarry-like landscape. Its fronds thrashed in the merciless wind. Her mother leaned against the tree, oblivious to the heart-stopping thunder and searing flashes of light. She smiled at her daughter, infusing Maité with hope. Maité didn't have the heart to even hint to her mother that right below her, blocking the path between mother and daughter, waited a menacing creature, raring to attack them both.

Maité awoke to the grayish light of dawn, feeling as sore from the strenuous walk back to the house last night, as from her dream-time exertions. For a moment she enjoyed the warmth and comfort of her bed, but the image of her grandfather, severe and contemptuous, slipped into her thoughts. Her lip curled in disgust, because the vision of him in shirtsleeves, methodically chipping away at her path, overcame her illusory hopes of the night before.

If only he had stayed away longer, like he said he would. She reluctantly got out of bed and found a note someone had slipped under her door.

"Sole says David called and he'll come get us at ten instead of nine. G'night, Em."

Maité grinned. The happiness swelling inside her shoved away the disgruntled feelings caused by her grandfather. She showered and got dressed, swept away by images of what the day might bring: sailing with David in the sun and the wind. Perhaps they could sail to Santa Clara.

Come find me ...

"Where?" Maité whispered as she brushed her hair in front of the mirror, "up in the mountains? Or in—"

Her bedroom door creaked open, and she shook off her daydreaming to find Emily wide awake though disheveled, climbing into her bed. "You already showered?"

"I woke up about an hour ago and couldn't go back to sleep," Maité admitted.

"Boy, that was some birthday party last night, huh?"

"Yes, well." Maité shrugged.

"Let's get breakfast. Can't start the day with an empty tank."

But breakfast was not a satisfying affair. Soledad shooed them out of the kitchen and off to the formal dining room. There they found Mr. Gonzaga sitting at the head of the massive table, looking as displeased as ever; maybe because Eva wasn't there, or maybe because he'd been made to wait for his meal.

Maité stiffened as soon as their eyes locked.

"Good morning," he said as tight-lipped as ever while they took their seats.

Maité's face colored with anger, managing only a curt nod in response. How could she possibly eat anything when the atmosphere around her felt so tense?

"Good morning," Emily said quickly, her eyes glued to the plate in front of her. Maité said nothing.

"It seems you've not been taught manners," her grandfather said without looking at Maité or acknowledging Emily's greeting.

Maité could hear blood rushing in her ears. *He's impossible!*

Soledad came out of the service passageway and set a platter with eggs and bacon on the table, where there was already bread, butter, juice, and coffee. She patted Maité's shoulder as if to calm her.

Maité and Emily served themselves after Mr. Gonzaga got his food, and they ate in silence for a long few minutes.

"David is coming for us at ten," Maité finally said, an uncharacteristic chill in her voice.

Mr. Gonzaga looked up from his cup of coffee but said nothing.

"For sure we'll come back after sunset."

Emily's eyes shifted nervously between the plate in front of her and Maité.

Mr. Gonzaga cocked his head to one side as if trying to detect a note of challenge in her tone. He kept his penetrating gaze on her, but Maité stared right back, refusing to be intimidated.

Mr. Gonzaga cleared his throat. "David is a very good sailor," he declared, and with that, he stood and marched out of the dining room, having barely had two gulps of coffee and a bite of toast.

Maité's brows arched in surprise. Emily sat stunned a few instants longer, and then said, "Holy cow!" She grinned. "At least you're all ready to go. I still gotta get ready!"

While Emily ran upstairs to shower and dress, Maité stayed behind to ask Soledad for David's telephone number. She called to let him know they were pretty much ready and weren't expected back home until after sunset. "But why did you change the time?" she asked.

"I offered to take my father into town for his appointment with Mr. Gonzaga at eleven. They'll be discussing the development of the property in the mountains."

"What development?"

"Mr. Gonzaga's lady friend …" He paused significantly before continuing. "Has grand ideas for the property soon to be hers. Apparently Mr. Gonzaga just received the plans for some sort of resort she intends to build."

Maité was stunned into silence. *That's why he stayed last night. It wasn't because of my birthday at all.*

When she didn't answer, David prompted her from the other end of the line, "Hello?"

"Yes, sorry, I'm here. It's just, I …"

"I know. It's rather shocking. It doesn't seem—"

"David?" Maité interrupted him.

"Yes?"

"I'm sorry, but I really need to see this property. I think there's something up there I need to know about."

"I'm sure we can plan a trip there, maybe over the weekend?" David offered.

"No, it has to be today."

"Today?"

"Yes, today. How far is it from here?" Maité asked urgently. Although she couldn't hear them at the moment, she felt herself goaded by her two dream visitors—the man whose voice she trusted and the woman with the aquamarine eyes—as if this was exactly what she should have done after getting off the plane in San Sebastián.

"Today?" David repeated, a note of incredulity in his voice.

"Yes."

"Okay, well, it's not very far. I don't think it'll take more than a couple of hours to get there. You realize though, that depending on what you want to do once we arrive, we might not make it back before dusk."

"I know, but so what?" Maité wouldn't let a curfew hold her back. Not when a plan was taking such definite shape in her mind.

"I take it that, for all practical purposes, we are still sailing today?" David hinted, and Maité could hear the smile in his voice.

"Yes. Because I don't want my grandfather or Eva to know I've been to see it."

"Okay, but what is it you want to see up there?"

"I'll find out when I get there," she said, but that was a lie. The map Xiomara detailed in her book seemed to be etched in her mind. Maité meant to follow Etienne's footsteps into the Realm of Faery.

"That sounds a bit vague."

"I don't know what else to tell you," Maité apologized. "Other than it bugs me Eva is so determined to get her hands on that property and I want to know why."

"Right, I'll see you at ten then."

"Thank you, David. We'll be waiting."

Santa Clara would have to wait. *It doesn't matter if Emily believes Xiomara. What matters is that I believe it, and I need to see it for myself. I'm not going to let Eva take over the land where the entrance to another dimension lies.*

Chapter 33

When Emily came out of the shower, Maité slapped her, as it were, with the change of plans. Although she wasn't ready to confess to Emily her driving desire yet, the certainty she would discover her dream visitors in the Pyrenees overwhelmed Maité. Also, the unsettling dream of Eva peering at her from a dark cave had awakened Maité to a suspicion that Eva might know about the magical treasure lying at the top of those ridges. The notion festered like an infection in Maité's heart; fear consumed her when she considered Eva might take more from her than just land.

"So we're not sailing today?" Emily asked, pulling the towel off her head and staring at Maité.

"No." Maité straightened the covers on Emily's bed. "I need to check out that piece of land in the Pyrenees. I want to see it before Eva goes through with her plans—before it's changed."

"And are we telling your grandpa what we're doing?"

"Absolutely not."

"You know, I thought it was perfect timing for us to be sailing today so we could cruise to the little island thing." Emily sounded a little cross. "It bugs me to skip stuff."

"Emily, please." Maité didn't want to be lectured on the evils of omitting steps in a process. She wanted to be on the road. "It doesn't matter what order we're doing these things in, so long as we're checking them off. We'll get to Santa Clara another day, but right now the mountains are the place to be."

"It's not like they're gonna turn it into a resort tomorrow, is it?"

"No, but I have the strangest feeling we can't leave this for another day."

"What do you mean?" Emily squinted at Maité. "Did you get a secret message or something?"

"No secret message, just an intense feeling—but move it, move it, move it! David will be here any minute."

"Okay, okay. I'm movin'."

Maité could already distinguish male voices coming from downstairs. "Yikes—David's here already. Hurry up."

"Wait! Go get some hiking boots or something and put 'em in a bag. You can't go to the mountains in sandals," Emily said, rummaging in her own suitcase and pulling out a pair of thick-soled shoes. "I know we'll probably be driving the whole time, but just in case, right?"

Maité stared at her bare toes. The thought of tramping through the woods in flip-flops was ludicrous. *Why can't I ever think of the practical stuff?* "Right, right." She raced to her room and threw a pair of boots into a canvas bag along with a long-sleeved shirt and a couple of energy bars leftover from her flight.

Maité and Emily rushed downstairs, trying to appear composed as they faced Mr. Gonzaga and David.

"So I'll expect you back shortly after sunset," Mr. Gonzaga said, looking at each of them in turn.

Maité nodded. Emily's head sort of bobbed.

"Yes, sir," David said.

"We'll be back in time," Maité added, trying to sound cheerful and believable. She didn't like to lie, and the boots poking her side made her nervous; Grandfather might question the unseemly bulk in her bag. She slung it over her shoulder and with a jerk of her head motioned Emily toward the door.

Emily waved feebly to Mr. Gonzaga and said good-bye to Soledad, taking the basket of goodies she had packed for them.

Once they were safely in David's car, Maité let out a sigh of relief. He shook his head at her and Maité apologized, sounding a little embarrassed. "Sorry about that."

"No worries," David replied.

"Here, I'll take that!" Emily said from the backseat, reaching for the map David pulled out of the glove box. "Where are we going?"

"The property is mostly farmland being rented out," David said. "But there is a striking waterfall I thought we might visit, right after we check out the remnants of the old Santillán citadel."

Maité's heart leapt at the mention. *The old citadel of Santillán—the waterfall!* A giddy sensation swirled in her belly; she'd pictured these locations vividly since first reading the book.

"Let's start at the waterfall," she said, her belly doing a somersault. She put her hand over her stomach and caught her breath. She knew the waterfall hid the secret passage described by Xiomara—Wizard's Pass, she'd called it. *I will follow Etienne's footsteps.*

"The falls it is," David said as he pointed out their destination on the map.

Emily took it from there. She began to talk right away and soon brought the conversation around to her favorite subject: genetics. This was done with only brief pauses in her remarks to navigate through foreign streets and highways as they headed out of town.

She's a human GPS, Maité thought, impressed.

They barely cleared the outskirts of San Sebastián, and already David was discussing his genetic research with total ease. Maité smiled at the passion she detected in his voice when he spoke of his involvement in the discovery of a hidden—or rather, an enhanced—chromosome in human DNA.

Maité kept stealing glances at Emily, dazzled—as ever—by her uncanny ability to extract information from people and draw them out of themselves.

He hasn't been this talkative with me, Maité reflected with mild concern. *But they can share genetics. David and I will share each other.*

Emily directed them onto Highway N1 through Irún and Hondarribia and then told David to head east along the border with France. They drove for about an hour after merging onto Highway N-121 and then proceeded onto a country road, which took them further in, alongside the banks of the Essa River, which was a glorified stream flowing south from the tall Pyrenees.

The copilot duty didn't seem to hinder Emily's fascination with all the data David had gathered. She expressed an earnest desire to review every piece of his catalogued research.

David nodded encouragingly, "There is something to be said for bringing a fresh set of eyes into an old problem," and he launched into a summary of historical accounts and the official findings of his research.

"The Monte Perdido dig started, what—two years ago?" Emily interjected; she was clearly familiar with the subject.

"That's right," David said, and Maité saw the impressed look he gave Emily in the rear-view mirror.

"So what's the crux of your theory? What's your hypothesis?" Emily leaned forward eagerly. "You have one, right?"

"I do." He smiled. "But I'll tell you in a minute. I have a collection of documents I've been reviewing the past couple of months. They're in my briefcase."

"May I?" Emily asked, holding up the case.

"Please do. The green folder."

While Emily extracted the folder, Maité looked out the window at the scattered houses and fenced-in prairies. When she glanced back, Emily was already flipping through David's compilation of some five hundred random DNA case studies, neatly summarized in a dozen pages.

"Whose case studies are these? They're not all from Monte Perdido, are they?" Emily asked, leafing through papers.

"They're from a handful of archeological sites in the region. We use them as reference and as a basis for comparison."

Emily's eyes flicked up and down over the pages with dizzying speed. Maité turned her attention to the scenery again, listening to David.

"We gathered about two hundred and fifty samples from Monte Perdido," he said. "We analyzed them sideways and crossways, and as far as my team and I can tell, the community of Monte Perdido in the 1500s was home to quite a few people who carried this extraordinary human gene." He paused and Maité quickly turned her attention to him. Emily leaned forward expectantly. "It is extraordinary because it includes a superior set of codes. Trouble is, Monte Perdido burned down to a cinder ages ago and apparently, there were no survivors, which means there was no one to pass on the DNA."

"And that's a bummer because if you could isolate or match this gene in present day, you'll be able to bring this brood of superhuman villagers to light?" Emily guessed shrewdly, then added, "OMG and gasp! You're not thinking of duplicating it, are you? Building your own Frankenstein?"

David laughed heartily at this. "Well, now that you've put the idea in my head that might be the thing to do!"

Emily laughed with him.

"There had to have been survivors," Maité argued.

"Maybe, and I'm sure they've been as easy to find as needles in haystacks," Emily retorted.

David gave a curt nod. "Not a single one has been identified so far."

"Don't despair," Emily said, leaning toward David and patting his shoulder.

"I've analyzed thousands of genetic strands from the population in the Huesca valley near the site. I've also branched out to local blood donors in San Sebastián, looking for the marker, but I've come up empty handed every time."

David dropped the car into third gear as they began ascending a narrow and winding two-lane highway with no shoulder and no lines painted on it. All was green and woody on both sides of the road.

"By the way," Maité said, "what exactly does this marker represent, characteristics-wise?"

"I thought you'd ask about that." David grimaced and went on uneasily. "The marker affects brain functions, so if a person were made up entirely with this type of protein strand—at all levels of their genetic configuration—

then theoretically, that person would be able to communicate through telepathy and manipulate their body mass through energy distribution. That person would also use areas of the brain every day that we aren't even aware of."

Maité could hear the discomfort of this admission in his voice, and she understood why. If the evidence of his prized discovery was no more than hair or eye color, that would be one thing, but when he began talking of superhuman behavior, things were bound to get hairy. That kind of belief would put David in the ranks of such nuts as UFO chasers and ghostbusters.

"Do you think this was an alien experiment?" Emily piped up quick as lightning, yet completely serious.

"Believe me, I've considered it. But every time I think I'm convinced extra-terrestrial intervention is the only possible explanation, I manage to come up with one more test and one more reason to review all the data." He shrugged.

"Sigh, David, what are you waiting for? Do mine!" Emily said offering her index finger. "Prick my finger in the name of science! Analyze the heck out of it!"

"Why not?" David laughed. "Do your parents have a clean bill of ancestry? I mean, are they of Spanish descent?"

"I don't honestly know," Emily admitted. "My mom was born in San Sebastián and so were my grandparents, but beyond that, I couldn't tell you. My dad is American, though I think several generations back his family came from England."

Maité listened in silence, thinking about the family tree in her computer. *There's a clean bill of ancestry,* she mused.

"What about you?" David asked, putting his hand over Maité's and startling her out of her thoughts.

"Huh?"

David lifted her index finger suggestively. "Only a few drops," he said.

"Um, yeah. Sure." Maité agreed and gave his hand a squeeze.

"What happens if you find what you're looking for?" Emily cut in. "Do you have to drain the subject of all her blood?"

David shook his head, chuckling.

He turned the car from the paved highway to a small, crooked dirt road. It climbed the steep hills with difficulty; over some sections it couldn't do better than first gear. Other than an occasional wild goat, there was nothing in sight but Alpine greenery.

Their talk of genetics ceased, and Maité and Emily fell to exclaiming over the majestic Pyrenees looming before them. David became the perfect tour guide, announcing they'd entered the property of the Santillán family. Maité couldn't help being impressed. She scanned her surroundings, fancying she recognized some of it from the descriptions given her by Xiomara.

"Geez! Does he own the whole mountain range?" Emily exclaimed.

"Not quite, but there is a fair bit of land, and if he gives it to his lady friend, and she develops the land, she'll be doing what advisors have told your grandfather to do for years."

"Why hasn't he developed it?" Maité wondered out loud.

"His official response has always been that he doesn't wish to spoil the land with ski runs and lifts or fenced trails, but there are those who think he doesn't have the means to finance an enterprise of that magnitude. Others believe he just doesn't want to be bothered."

"But Eva has changed his mind," Maité remarked soberly.

The road became increasingly steeper and full of pot holes. They had to hold on to dashboards, backs of seats, and window jams to keep from being jostled out of their seats. They continued at a snail's pace up the hill until at the summit, the track ended.

"This is entirely too much nature for me," Emily muttered.

David cut the engine, and Maité's body tingled as if her limbs were asleep. It was so still. She grabbed her canvas bag as she got out of the car after Emily and David.

"Now what?" Emily asked, looking around. "Can you believe all this flora? Hopefully there's no fauna to speak of."

"Did you mean to hike around for a bit and see things?" David asked, watching Maité exchange her flip-flops for the socks and boots she'd pulled out of the bag.

"Yes and no," Maité said, tugging at the extra long laces of her boots and wrapping them around each ankle before tying them.

"What's the 'no' part?" Emily asked.

Maité finished with her boots and pulled the thermal shirt over her head before she turned to face them. Emily and David watched her suspiciously while she extracted a piece of paper from her canvas bag. She opened it and flattened it out as best as she could on the hood of the car to show them the map she'd transcribed from Xiomara's book.

"When did you do this?" Emily murmured.

"While you were in the shower." Maité didn't pause over the concern she saw in Emily's eyes as she seemed to realize what Maité was up to. "I marked only the key locations I need to get to this lake," Maité said, tapping the dotted oval marked "Moon Dancer Lake."

Partial comprehension of Maité's intentions seemed to dawn on David too. He eyed the improvised map with an arched brow.

"What?" Maité asked, catching his worried expression.

"The waterfall seems to be placed accurately enough," David remarked pointing at landmarks he recognized. "In terms of its location from the city—the bay of San Sebastián."

"How far is the waterfall from here?" Maité asked eagerly.

"I don't see any trails or signage," Emily observed, and Maité knew for sure her concern was scaling to new heights.

"I'd say a good half hour up that ravine," David replied. "Shall we get started?"

Emily positively panicked. "What kind of bugs are out here?"

"Nothing too awful, and definitely things with fewer teeth than humans," David said with mock sincerity.

"Yeah, but what about legs?"

"Can't ease your mind there," he said earnestly. "We're bound to find a lot of many-legged creatures."

"That's just great!" Emily said, rolling her eyes at David.

Maité carried her canvas bag with nothing more than the map and the energy bars. Emily, on the other hand, lugged the basket Soledad had prepared as if it were a security blanket. "I'm gonna need all the comfort food I can get," she said under her breath.

David offered to take the basket from her, and they set off after Maité, who in the absence of roads or trails switched places with Emily and became the human GPS.

Maité's heart rate increased as they advanced, from the physical exertion as much as from excitement. No longer humbled by the sight of the mountains, she paused for a few moments and smiled encouragingly at Emily and David, who were a few feet behind.

No way am I turning back now, she thought and the thrill of it churned within her again. They would soon reach the waterfall dividing one set of peaks from the next. There was no road access from the other side, as Maité had read in Xiomara's tale, and David had confirmed it; the geology of the land didn't allow it.

They were on the Santillán side of the waterfall. As they progressed deeper into more gnarled territory, Maité felt reassured that this could never be a tourist haven. It was desolate and inhospitable, as it always had been.

And it has to stay like this.

She heard the thunderous roar of the waterfall before she saw it.

They reached a partial summit devoid of tall trees, and Maité was struck dumb by what appeared before her eyes. Several jagged peaks rose unexpectedly to form a misshapen crown of solid rock, with the waterfall as a centerpiece. Maité thought it looked like the stony back of a longhaired woman, whose watery, white mane almost hid the rigid crown atop her head.

They had arrived. The waterfall appeared unapproachable and threatening. Maité whirled around exhilarated, searching for Emily's reaction and laughing out loud. The spray had soaked Emily's hair so it stuck to her head, giving her the piteous look of a half-drowned cat. Her eyes were wild, and her gaping mouth couldn't form words. David appeared to be enjoying the exercise and scenery.

The time had come to reveal her intentions.

Maité's anticipation reached new levels. The flutters in her belly were a permanent vibration holding her on the brink of hilarity. Emily and David closed the short distance separating them. He set the basket down and stretched his back with a groan. Emily remained speechless.

"Now what?" he asked.

"This is where we separate," Maité announced.

David's eyes grew wide with disbelief. "I beg your pardon?"

Emily appeared to come to her senses. "You're crazy!"

Maité ignored her, squinting toward what lay on the other side of the waterfall. "I'll continue from here."

"Wha—how? What do you mean?" Emily sputtered.

"There's something on the other side of these peaks," Maité assured them. "And I need to see it for myself."

"I don't understand," David said. "I truly thought you meant to come up here and get a feel for your ancestral lands, but you're out of your mind if you think you can cross this raging mess of water!"

"Right," Emily added feebly.

"There is a way. Come look!" Maité grabbed David's arm and pulled him toward the edge of the precipice. "Do you see down there?" She pointed at a narrow ledge leading to what looked like the entrance to a passageway behind the white water. The sight of it heightened her conviction.

Wizard's Pass, just like Xiomara said. She felt so exhilarated, she could hardly breathe.

"You're raving mad!" David flared up.

The fluttering in Maité's belly became an outright flapping of something with wings doing circles inside her as if gearing for an explosive escape. Before she could think what might blast out of her, words spilled from her mouth, funneled through her need to get across the passage. David and Emily would not stop her.

"No, David," she said in a tremulous though soothing voice. "This is what I came here to do, and I'm not just talking about today. I mean I came all the way from America to hike this mountain and cross this waterfall." A fierce shudder went through her as she spoke. Her words were true; this was what the secret voice had been guiding her toward.

Maité could see that her words, coupled with the intense gaze she fixed on David, were having a most peculiar effect on him. She put her hand on his shoulder and exerted the slightest pressure. He winced at her touch, as if an electric charge had gone through him.

Maité smiled because it didn't surprise her. The fear she saw in his eyes subsided, evolving into a calmness she knew would lead to his approval and support. Only mildly disconcerting was the thought that the dreamy expression on David's face was remarkably like her grandfather's while Eva had been hanging on his arm at the María Celeste.

"Nothing can possibly happen to me up there," she assured him. "Someone is expecting me, and besides, I have a map. This is how it must be done."

David's eyes twinkled sleepily at her, and she kissed his lips, which further sealed the charm.

Mission accomplished.

Emily made a hiccoughing sound behind David. Maité's diatribe had only partially reached her, and Maité hadn't made physical contact, so the look on Emily's face was of someone not yet convinced.

"Wait just one minute!" Emily protested.

Maité cut her off, holding out her other hand to Emily, which she clasped. "Em, I need you."

The three of them were connected now. "This won't work without your help. I need you and David to stay until I've crossed the waterfall, and then you two will return to the manor. If Grandfather asks where I am, tell him I got seasick and went straight to bed."

"You mean you're not coming home tonight?" Emily's voice already had a distracted quality to it.

Maité shook her head. "No, I'm not." The flapping in her belly intensified. "But David, you'll come get me tomorrow at dawn, won't you?"

David's brow creased a little, but one look from Maité was enough to make him lapse into calmness again.

"It will be all right, Emily," David said. "I'll be here tomorrow to pick her up. I'll bring her back home, and Mr. Gonzaga won't be the wiser."

Emily looked past the roaring waterfall to the other side. "You know I'd go with you if you weren't going into the woods, right?"

"I know you would. But I'll be fine. It's only about three hours' worth of walking, and I have all the directions I need." Maité patted the bag slung on her shoulder, remembering how long it had taken Etienne to get to Celeste two centuries before.

"Let me look at that again," Emily said gruffly, grabbing the map out of the bag. "Let's see then—once you get to the other side of the waterfall, you'll go up the ravine to the hills we can't see from here, and you'll hike to the lake on the other side? I guess it's not too bad."

They exchanged glances, and Maité knew Emily could now see the whole plan. "I take it you're heading east of the lake?" Emily asked tentatively.

Maité winked. "That's right."

I'm going to Paloma and Celeste's pond, to their home of so many years, and if all goes well, to the entrance of Handi Park, the seat of the faery court.

CHAPTER 34

The deafening roar of the waterfall beckoned.

For a brief moment before setting out, Maité pondered how easy it had been to impose her will on Emily and David. Had she managed to make them ignore their better judgment with just words? Maité decided it had been more of a combination of speech, touch, and that giddy feeling, like her stomach had turned into a huge beating heart. She wondered if she'd had the ability all along but felt inclined to believe it had more to do with the place.

From the other side of the waterfall, hidden in a knotted clump of vegetation, a pair of brown eyes fixed on Maité with an intensity that almost pulled her off her feet. Before she could react, the apparition vanished in the spray. She could tell Emily and David hadn't seen it; she'd almost missed it herself.

"Thank you for bringing me up here," she said to David with a searching look to make sure his concerns were well-buried. They were.

He nodded. "I'll be back for you early tomorrow morning." He said this with a distracted air while Emily inched closer to him, placidly admiring her surroundings and munching on an apple.

"It really is beautiful out here—in a wet sort of way—maybe a little too loud," Emily observed. "What a racket the water makes."

Maité giggled. Looking past David, she searched the vegetation across the way. Though she didn't spot the pair of brown eyes again, she knew they waited for her out there. She was about to enter the realm of fluttering giddiness, of things conveyed in glimpses and of dreamlike realities.

Eva, Maité thought again, but she didn't want to dwell on her, besides, the flapping in Maité's belly whirled with renewed vigor, threatening to make her airborne. Every molecule in her body whirred with energy; Maité couldn't wipe the smile off her face. She felt deliciously out of control, wild and able to leap over the waterfall, fly across the forest if she wanted to. She couldn't wait to get started.

Emily rummaged through the food basket again. "Gotta get you something that won't get squished in your bag," she said, pulling out a couple of apples.

Looking somewhat distracted, David held out a tube of lip balm he'd pulled out of his pocket. "It has sunscreen," he said wistfully.

Maité accepted his offering as if it were a most precious charm. *Apollo himself presenting me with a healing balm*, she thought, amused.

A little voice, nothing mystical or secretive, just the voice of her own reason, whispered in Maité's head. *Any way you look at this, it's insane! They shouldn't be giving you apples and Chapstick. They should be tying you to the roof of the car and taking you back home.*

But instead of worrying her, the little voice exhilarated her all the more.

"I think you're ready to go," David said, holding the canvas bag. Its handles were long enough for Maité to wear like a backpack. He helped her put it on.

"I can't believe you're doing this," Emily said half-heartedly.

"I'll see you tomorrow morning," Maité replied, kissing Emily on the cheek.

With Maité between them, they walked over to the edge, and the three of them leaned over the cliff. David pointed out her target: a narrow ledge some fifteen feet below and very close to the torrent.

Maité had a fleeting, disturbing thought that perhaps she was being summoned by some evil force, straight to her death. She remembered Eva's smoldering eyes glowering at her from the mouth of a cave but dismissed the idea. It didn't feel true. She would not stew over it.

"It's best if you turn your back to the water and lower yourself on your belly," David suggested. "Feel with your boot for a solid step before you put your weight on it."

"Do what he says, M," Emily added, betraying only the mildest apprehension.

Maité kissed David and got down to it. Holding herself up with her arms while her feet dangled over the void, Maité winked reassuringly at Emily.

"It's really muddy and slippery, so take your time," David said, getting on his knees, he gave her hand one last squeeze as she began her descent.

Maité heard Emily gasp right before she slipped out of sight.

Maité dropped a good ten feet before one of her boots caught on a knobby root. She heaved a sigh of relief and mustered a smile for Emily's sake. She looked down while her hands held on to whatever branches she could grip. Her destination was about a yard to her right and about five feet below. Her legs began to shake.

"You're doing fine!" David called down to her. "A little to your right."

"Thanks!" Maité grunted and started again, aided by the flapping in her belly, which made her feel buoyant. Her thoughts flashed back to the first time she'd flown with the woman with the turquoise-streaked curls. She thought she heard her again now.

Trust yourself. You can fly if you want to.

"Wish I could," Maité muttered, imagining she looked like a big X on the side of the muddy cliff. She stifled her own laughter at the image while feeling around for solid footing. She was at a near impossible angle to reach the ledge.

Gotta move on. It's not like I can live here like this. Maité slid her right boot, trying to find her next position, but the rock under her left boot gave way. She let out a shocked yelp and fell another three feet, scraping her belly on the brush, roots and dirt as she slid.

"You need to get just a couple feet to the right," David called again, his voice barely audible over the thundering water. Maité wondered if he feared for her, or if whatever she did to his head prevented him from caring at all.

She fervently hoped she hadn't made a huge mistake; maybe what she needed now was a David in full possession of his faculties rather than this pliant version of David who might watch her plummet to her death in a resigned fashion.

"I'll be sure to bring a rope tomorrow!" she heard him say.

Thank you, Maité thought, feeling reassured. Catching Emily's eye, she gave Emily a quick thumbs-up.

Maité's hands were scraped and cut, and her arms were starting to shake. She stretched her leg over to the ledge, and when it felt like solid ground beneath it, she recklessly flung her weight in that direction.

"I made it!" she shrieked, and her heart exploded in her chest as she waved excitedly up to David and Emily.

They were jumping up and down, hugging each another in their excitement. Maité didn't like that at all. The thought of David and Emily driving back together and having all that time alone made her insides squirm. She wasn't used to feeling jealous of Emily, nor so possessive of David, but the sound of the water came to her aid. It obliterated even her jealous thoughts.

The blinding mist turned Emily and David into a blurry vision, and Maité squinted at the water, trying to determine how to cross. As if responding to her, the spray lifted briefly, giving her just enough time to see the distant opening. She again thought of Etienne, more than a hundred years before, tackling the very same crossing, obsessed with seeing the human Celeste.

The reverse was true for Maité—her obsession of a faery sighting overtook her again.

"I'm on my way!" she yelled, waving at her friends and hoping her voice would reach them, but she didn't wait for a response. With her back to the cliff, she began sidling along the slippery ledge. She made her way to the entrance of the passage behind the curtain of water, which would take her to the other side of the waterfall.

Once in the passage, the air became thick, and her vision diminished because of the spray. The opening was so narrow she had to continue walking with her back as close to the wall as the backpack allowed. She became drenched in seconds. The torrent in front of her looked like a frothy white wall; she stretched her hand toward it, but as soon as the tips of her fingers made contact, the water rejected the intrusion. The force of it was immense, like an electrical current biting her. *If I slip, I'll be a mangled carcass at the bottom*, she realized.

Maité focused on the other side, already visible a few yards away, and went on.

She came out feeling ecstatic. She waved at Emily and David one last time. They waved back and appeared to be saying lots of things she didn't have a hope of hearing.

The climb up the ridge on this side of the waterfall was a lot easier than sliding down the other. There were footholds and plenty of protruding vegetation for her to use as rungs. She reached the top and found herself on a gravelly table surrounded by boulders, but Maité knew there was a path beyond this rocky entryway.

She sidestepped the boulders, scanning the sloping hills until she spotted a trail and headed for it, but not without stealing one last glance toward Emily and David. They were mere specks blurred by the mist.

The surge of adrenaline that got Maité through the waterfall soon wore off, and monotony set in. The tedium of the uneven terrain and the abundant brush was broken only by a few members of the rodent family here and there scurrying out of her way. But she found a rhythm and fell into it.

She indulged in vivid reflections as she walked, and in the wake of her steps, a long string of old ideas and plans lay dead as she let go of her past. With each stride, she felt more prepared to embrace whatever came her way. She emptied her mind of prejudice and opened her heart to the unbelievable. The problem was, nothing unbelievable had happened since she crossed the waterfall, not even an encouraging peek at those brown eyes. The realization brought her spirits down a notch as she tramped through one gully after another. She'd been expecting an entirely new realm to materialize out of thin air and felt disappointed when it didn't.

She became aware of her aching feet. Her muddy clothes had dried on her skin, and a swarm of gnats kept her company, whirling two inches from her face. She gave up swatting at them but walked on, in constant dread of inhaling a bug by accident. In and out of ditches, up and down ravines, through and around thick groves she went. Her calves burned; the scratches on her bare legs stung in a maddening way. Thank goodness for long sleeves. The sameness of the grueling advance got to her.

Maité's hands slapped around for the hundredth time at the bugs buzzing in front of her face. She looked at her hands, hoping to see several little corpses flattened on her palms, but instead caught sight of a magnificent pool of crystal water. She had arrived.

Under the blue sky framed with tall evergreens, she saw what had to be the lake Xiomara had described. It was better than Maité imagined.

Struck with wonder, her heart echoed Etienne's reaction of that night long ago when he witnessed the Moon Dancers for the first time. Her aching feet forgotten, Maité resumed walking with renewed strength and with the conviction that not only was she on the right track, but she'd soon find the mystical dimension revealed to her by her ancestor.

To rebuild the bonds with the faery realm, to devote her life to discovering them and knowing them, was a notion that overwhelmed Maité—it was what she'd been unable to confess to Emily.

Maité trudged onto the white sandy shore of Moon Dancer Lake. She walked into the water, boots and all, and scooped some of it in her hands. "Cold!" she gasped in surprise. Hadn't Xiomara said the water of this lake was warm? It was supposed to be kept that way in spite of the altitude through the power of the keeper of the forest. She puzzled about it but scooped more of it and drank it, glad it was cool and soothing to her parched throat.

Having splashed some water on her face, Maité turned her attention to the forest; the remnant of a trail wound its way into the cool shade of the trees, and she headed toward it, still bothered but not deterred by the temperature of the lake. Maybe winter had been longer up here this year.

It didn't take long for Maité to find the small creek trickling into a quiet pond at the foot of a tattered marquee. Thanks to Xiomara, Maité knew exactly where she was at last, although the vegetation surrounding the place didn't have the look of being maintained at all. Hadn't Xiomara talked about flowers in every color of the rainbow—flowers tended by faeries? There was nothing here but tangled greenery. No matter. Maité knew this was the spot; this was where she planned to jump for joy, maybe even do a couple of back-flips, at least a rapturous *yessss* should come out of her mouth.

But before any of those expressions could take shape, the brown eyes she glimpsed from the other side of the waterfall caught her again, except this time they were only a few feet away, and not just the eyes, but a whole godlike male form.

Part IV

I know a bank where the wild thyme blows,
Where oxlips and the nodding violet grows,
Quite over-canopied with luscious woodbine,
With sweet musk-roses and with eglantine.
—William Shakespeare, *A Midsummer Night's Dream*

Chapter 35

He leaned against the weathered trunk of a sycamore tree.

Maité glanced at him, briefly wondering why she could see him. Wouldn't she have to be granted faery sight to actually see a faery?

His dark eyebrows knitted, giving a fierce expression to his otherwise smooth face. His straight dark hair spilled over his muscular shoulders, and Maité's eyes drifted furtively over his flesh, for he wore no shirt. He had his arms folded over his powerful chest and wore what looked like a pair of bronze-colored chinos gathered at the waist with a drawstring. One bare foot was firmly on the ground, and the other rested casually against the sycamore's trunk.

Maité licked her lips and swallowed hard, realizing she too was being examined.

"Maitagarri." His lyrical voice reached her ears.

She waited tensely for the popping sensation she'd grown to expect and for her skin to thicken. But this time, the sound of his voice didn't trigger the inward shudder. Yet this was really him; his was the secret voice pursuing and guiding her these past two weeks.

For the space of a heartbeat, she yearned for the intimacy of his previous calls, but wasn't this so much better? Wouldn't she rather have him as he was now, a corporeal being, not just a disembodied voice?

Every bit of her said, *Oh yes!* She wanted to fling herself at him and put her arms around his neck, but she didn't act on the impulse, afraid it might not be proper—at least not without asking first.

As if having followed her thoughts, he gave her an approving, intensely warm smile that filled Maité with gratitude and relief.

"May I?" she asked, gesturing with her hands for permission to approach. He beamed. Maité walked up to him and kissed him on both cheeks. She thought she heard a short gasp escape him. He smelled of fresh air and mountains, and she loved him.

"You are returned to me," he declared, holding her at arm's length and staring hungrily at her. "I have waited, *Maitagarri*, and now you are here. Say my name; say you are restored to Amets at last!"

Maité's brow creased. *Restored to him? Yes*, she thought, *restored to the legacy of my family*.

"I am here, Amets." Maité laughed gleefully and congratulated herself in secret. Any other person in her situation would've given up or gone straight to denial rather than go the distance, but not Maité. This was her vindication; this was evidence she was *not* insane. She was touching him, listening to him, seeing him, a real, live faery.

Definitely not crazy!

"Come with me," he said, holding his hand out to her. "You'll want to see your mother's home." Maité felt the ground shake at this and took his hand in part to touch him, but most of all to steady herself.

His words unsettled her, like a grating note in a familiar tune.

Amets held her hand tight and led the way along an indistinct depression of undergrowth that might have been a trail in centuries past but was now overgrown with elderberry.

"What do you mean *my* mother's house?" she blurted.

Amets looked at her as if she were teasing. "Where you and Paloma lived of course, until Etienne took you away."

Maité froze. A torrent of thoughts erupted in her head.

He thinks I'm Celeste. Should I tell him I'm not? What if he goes nuts—I think he might already be *nuts!*

"Amets," she began cautiously, but he interrupted her.

"Do you not remember me? What have they done to you?" he pleaded. "Oihana said you would never come back, and that if you did, you would not be the same."

"Oihana?" Maité wondered out loud, and instantly regretted it because her question seemed to have caused him anguish.

Of course, how could I have forgotten.

"Oihana, Nahia's mother. Of course I know who she is," she said tapping her forehead.

This seemed to ease his pain a bit, but Maité could see a hint of suspicion curling in his gaze. He squeezed her hand and pulled on it gently.

Maité tried her best not to appear tense. *I'll just pretend I'm Celeste. I'll tell him I bashed my head or something, and that's why I'm a little off*, she thought, nonplussed over the fact that the first faery she encountered should be mentally unhinged.

"Everyone is so happy you have returned," he assured her.

Maité groaned at his side, and Amets paused to look at her through narrowed eyes. She gave him a half-hearted grin.

"All is well here, you will see," he announced with a satisfied look on his face and continued on his way.

The loud chirping of birds, the scampering of squirrels—and whatever other critters she hadn't noticed before—magically turned back on. It was as if all the noises of the forest stopped when he stopped. Now that he was in motion again, even the sound of trickling water and the branches of the leafy trees swaying in the breeze were loud.

Maité realized she too responded to his motion; she felt awake as never before, physically and mentally.

"I cleaned for you," Amets announced, letting go of her hand to part the gnarled mess of jasmine branches concealing the entrance to a cave. The floor of the dwelling had been patted down so firm it looked like stone. There was a bedstead with a feather mattress covered in silky sheets, unlike anything she had ever seen at a store, although the set looked so weathered and brittle Maité felt certain it would crumble to dust should she so much as touch it. A rustic, wooden table stood off to one side with three chairs arranged opposite one another—just as Xiomara had said.

"And I prepared a meal for you, your favorite!" Amets fetched two bowls and two cups from a shelf. They were made of glass tinted in primary colors. He placed them on the table.

Maité took the makeshift backpack off and set it on the floor. She joined Amets at the table and started popping berries and walnuts into her mouth as quickly as he put them in her bowl. He poured water from a decanter for them.

"I knew you would come back to me," Amets kept saying, as if repeating it would make it more real.

Maité racked her brain for every detail of Xiomara's story regarding Amets. He had figured throughout the manuscript, but his fate hadn't been revealed until the very end.

"That sucks," Emily had said when Maité read that last paragraph to her, for Amets, going against faery wisdom, sacrificed his first kiss to the human Celeste, making her the keeper of his heart. When Celeste died, she took his heart with her, leaving Amets to wander the earth, bearing the curse of a life without love.

He thinks I'm Celeste returned. I wonder what he thinks will happen? Maité wished she knew more about faery lore. *Is there a counter-curse for that first kiss rule? Can it be undone?*

Through the brush blocking the entryway, Maité saw the sky becoming a deeper shade of blue and realized it must be getting close to five.

Amets watched her every move with an expression of immense delight.

CHAPTER 36

Emily could no longer see Maité. She had disappeared up the rocky ravine on the other side, leaving Emily with only a mild discomfort over the thought that she should've stopped her, that Maité shouldn't be alone on that desolate mountain overnight. But it seemed someone had shrink-wrapped her fears and stowed them out of the way. Looking at David, Emily recognized the same detached expression on his face.

When she thought about how much Maité really wanted to do this, she saw herself and David as indulgent parents who had it in their hands to reward their star child for good behavior. And Maité was such a wonderful girl—where was the harm in her hiking for an afternoon? What was so wrong with camping overnight in a pristine forest?

The scale had tipped in Maité's favor. Who was Emily to thwart her efforts when she only wanted to study her family's history? Emily didn't even suspect Maité had reshaped her common sense in order to get what she wanted.

"I'm getting hungry," Emily said.

David nodded and they started back to the car, although not without Emily noticing a couple of hesitant backward glances on his part. "Totally smitten," she muttered.

David drove down the winding, bumpy road, and before they reached the paved highway, they were submerged once again in their discussion of genetics. So as to not interrupt, Emily pointed mutely whenever David needed to turn. He followed her directions without question.

Mealtimes being a major highlight in Emily's day, she navigated them straight to a restaurant she'd spotted the day before while out with Maité. At the thought of her, Emily let out another resigned snort, to which David responded with a meaningful, "I know." Apparently his thoughts, like Emily's, switched back to Maité now and then.

By the time David got them to the restaurant, their now dry clothes emitted a faint moldy smell Emily chose to ignore, engrossed as they were in alleles and digs.

"*Por aquí, por favor*," the hostess said, seeming to disapprove of their appearance. They followed her to a table tucked in the corner, away from other guests, but still elegantly set for two. The hostess dropped a couple of menus on the table and left the new customers without further words of welcome.

Emily and David continued their conversation. They sat down and grabbed the menus but did not browse the contents.

"Let's say this protein strand constitutes all levels of someone's genetic configuration—" David said.

"*Una botella de agua y un vino blanco, por favor*," Emily whispered to the lingering waiter, who'd been poised beside them the last forty seconds. He left in a hurry to get their water and wine order, and Emily turned her attention back to David—the small exchange between her and the waiter had been no more than a speed bump in his monologue.

"I don't know, Emily." David put his hands to his head and ran his fingers through his hair with fanatical passion. "I keep coming to the conclusion that a person would be able to manipulate body mass ... by sheer willpower. Good God, he'd be a shape-shifter!"

"Boy, what my dad wouldn't give for that gene," Emily interjected. "He can't lose half a pound without playing racquetball for a week straight and eating only yogurt three times a day. So what do you mean, anyway, 'manipulate body mass'?"

David shook his head. "Sometimes I don't think I know what I mean."

"Hmmm ... tell you what? Why don't you have a drink." Emily took the glass of wine the polite server had brought and handed it to David. "*Gracias,*" she said to the waiter, and, "drink up," to David.

David stared at the glass in his hand. With a baffled frown, he gazed at his surroundings, apparently unable to recall how he'd gotten there. "Emily, my apologies," he stammered. "I'm very sorry, I should've—what I mean to say is, *I* should be showing you the nice places in this city, but instead you're ... I'm so sorry."

Emily rolled her eyes and chuckled. "Mr. Mad Scientist, it's no biggie. Stop stuttering and stumbling all over yourself already!"

"I get so caught up in my work," he admitted with a sheepish grin.

"Gracias," Emily again said to the waiter busily arranging two tiny plates with butter seashells along with a basket full of sliced bread.

"*¿Vuelvo en un momento para tomar su orden?*" the waiter inquired solicitously.

"*Un momento largo, por favor,*" Emily replied, her chin jutted briskly toward David, and the waiter nodded. "Gracias," she added, knowing he understood her request to wait a long while before he came back for their order.

David gulped half his wine. "I *did* drive us here, didn't I?"

"Roll my eyes, David. We took a cab, don't you remember?" Emily teased, handing him a heavily buttered piece of bread. "Yes—of course you drove us here, but you were mentally absent babbling about DNA."

He laughed at that and said, "When I come to visit you in the United States, I'll be the navigator, and you can be as spaced-out as you wish."

"Deal." She gave him the thumbs up and washed down her mouthful of bread with two gulps of water.

"Thank you, Emily," he said, reaching for another wedge of baguette. "I didn't realize how hungry I was."

"You and me both. What were you saying about the mass manipulation thing? Sounds like politician genes." She buttered another piece of bread for herself.

"The workings of your mind are unique; you know that?"

"Yes, I know, I'm weird," Emily conceded proudly.

"It's manipulation of mass. That protein strand is responsible for specific brain functions—sort of like enhanced telekinesis—and the challenge in finding it lies in how deceptively similar it is to the corresponding protein strand common to humanity."

"I'm lost on this, how can they be so alike they can be overlooked, yet so different that they'd make someone superhuman?"

"It's like this. Here you have butter," he said, cutting half a butter shell and holding it on the tip of the knife. "And here, you have margarine." He pointed to the half still on the plate. "If you don't know which is which, you would eat either one and not think too much about it, but if you taste them one after the other, you would notice a difference in such things as texture, flavor, and so on."

Emily's head bobbed as she chewed her bread. "So unless you're specifically looking for those differences, you wouldn't be able to tell how inferior margarine is to butter."

"Exactly! Those people with the protein strand were few and far between in that isolated community in the 1500s. We've collected a little more than two hundred samples at Monte Perdido, but only 20 percent had this strand. How can that be?"

Emily shrugged. "What if this little allele was peculiar to only one family? Are there census records anywhere dating back to that time?"

David, who'd put his elbows on the table as he listened, suddenly leaned back and stared at her wild-eyed. "Census records," he echoed, and then began to ramble. "Besides the bodies found, there were artifacts that survived the fire. It's a possibility. I do recall seeing something that looked like a ledger. Descendants might be tracked. It's certainly a possibility." He paused. "My haystack could be considerably reduced—I mean, to find that needle."

Emily jumped onboard his train of thought. "You might get your hands on a modern-day sample yet. Maybe we can find out if an alien race jumped into the mix to create this Basque family, because I tell you, it has to be a Basque family. I think people here are part alien or something. I've never seen a politer bunch of humans. They're so civil, it's like they're hiding something."

David laughed again. "I'm Basque, and I can tell you, I'm not covering up a thing."

"So you say."

"Can I tell you something?" David leaned over the table conspiratorially. "I wish I *were* hiding something. I wish I were hiding that gene so I could do tests on myself ..."

Emily nodded but said nothing. She knew he had, more than likely, tested himself repeatedly already.

"The code in this strand is an enhancer to brain functions, but it appears that only the race who shared it to begin with would have the full benefit of all the endowments it can give."

"Wait a sec. So what you're saying is that we're only looking at the offspring of the carrier? Like maybe the mom or the dad had the full set of genes but mated with a regular human and gave us what samples you have now?"

"That's exactly what I'm saying. This has to be interspecies breeding, although who or what the other species are, I don't know. But their brain functions are quicker, sharper, they could even direct their thoughts—you know, launch their ideas wordlessly at others. And their mass would be relative to the environment. They could take on different shapes and sizes, even fly." As he went on, he gradually became more excited. "Or maybe not even something as ordinary as flying. Rather, they could will themselves to move through space, maybe even through solid objects, like walls, or rocks, by dispersing their molecules. What is it?" David paused for Emily had taken a deep breath and was exhaling through lips pursed into a perfect O.

"May I?" Emily said, her hand already on David's glass of wine. He nodded.

"I just need a taste." She wasn't ready to share her speculations concerning what had been happening with Maité, although with each new declaration from David, Emily wondered if there were no superhuman aliens—what if there had only been, *and always had been*, faeries?

She tried to unflare her nostrils as the taste and vapors of the sip of wine seemed to fill her sinus cavities. How could people drink glass after glass of the stuff? She swallowed and smacked her lips, pondering what her mother would do if she saw her drinking in public.

She'd drag me out by my ponytail, Emily thought. She set the glass back on the table.

"So let's say you have this strand," David continued. "But because it's recessive, you may or may not see signs of it. You mentioned your father's weight-loss situation. That would mean that his ability to manipulate mass has been damaged in the recessive mode, but what if the strand was dominant? Your father could command his mass to tighten around his frame. Weight-loss issue gone," David said, clapping his hands.

"You know," Emily began tentatively, "Maité's been talking about some weird stuff."

"She has?" David raised an eyebrow. "Like what?"

"Like very real dreams, like hearing—sometimes even seeing things that are happening to other people." Emily felt like a traitor confiding this to him, so she quickly changed the subject; after all, this was Maité's secret.

"Speaking of her, how are we going to handle tonight?"

"I think we should call Soledad before we leave here," David said, glancing at his watch. "We need to get an idea of what Mr. Gonzaga is doing."

"Good thinking. Hopefully he won't be home when we get there, and we can just pretend she went straight to her room," Emily said. The uneasy feeling about Maité came back to her, but she squelched it. It was too late to reverse what had happened. The only option now was to stick to the plan.

"We were wrong to leave her," David admitted. "But I can't seem to get too worried about it."

"I know what you mean." Emily pursed her lips, a thought taking shape in her mind. "David?"

"Yes?"

"Before we go back to the house, can we stop at your lab?" Emily had her hand inside her bag. She again felt like a traitor, but her curiosity got the better of her. Besides, Maité had agreed to let David test her. Emily had decided Maité's "um, yeah" earlier in the car was as good as a signed release. "I want you to take a sample of my blood, and I want you to take a look at this too." She pulled the brush from the bag and held it out to him.

David stared at it doubtfully.

"It's Maité's." Emily explained. "I took it out of her bag to make more room for food." She felt unaccountably tense about this, as if she already knew what the results of the testing would be. If Maité had the protein strand and she could do the things David described, it would make her like one of the creatures described in Xiomara's book.

Although Emily didn't feel prepared to accept scientific proof of a magical dimension, because it would turn her structured, predetermined world of science upside down, she would go through with it.

David took Maité's brush with an expectant grin.

CHAPTER 37

"You cannot meet the council as you are," Amets told Maité.

For a moment, trapped in the embrace of his amber gaze, she didn't understand what he meant. Then she looked down at herself and wondered in shock how she could stand it. Her clothes had a dried crust of mud and sweat, her boots were caked with dirt, and when she ran her fingers through her hair, it felt exactly like the door to the cave—gnarled beyond recognition.

Seeming to detect her embarrassment, Amets clucked his tongue and said, "Come with me."

As if in a dream, Maité followed Amets along the narrow hint of a trail; his bare feet trod soundlessly over the irregular ground. He was smooth yet masculine, beautiful in an otherworldly sort of way. Unable to stop herself, she reached out and placed a trembling hand on his shoulder, half-expecting him to disappear in a swirl of golden mist. He did not.

"Am I walking too fast?" Amets rounded on her and gazed at her through amber eyes filled with a longing that made his whole face look sad.

"No," she said a little out of breath. *How can a living being be so perfect?*

"We're almost there," he told her and resumed walking with Maité close behind.

Xiomara's description of Etienne's first visit to the realm of faery swirled in Maité's mind—how he suffered the bewitching effects of the Moon Dancers, and later, of Nahia and Oihana—Etienne had been warned about lapsing into a stupor over their beauty, had it not been for … *What was it? A gel-type thing applied to his eyelids?* "Should I have had some sort of vaccination? After all, I'm not your kind," she asked.

"You *are* my kind," Amets said matter-of-factly.

Maité knew he was smiling, even though all she could see was his back— and what a spectacular sight it was. *One of his kind?* she mulled the idea over in silence. As Amets thought she was Celeste returned, Maité couldn't exactly rely on his accuracy. According to Xiomara, Celeste once told him she felt she was at least part faery after having lived among them all her life. *But Celeste wasn't a faery. So how can I be one of his kind?*

"Here we are," Amets announced.

Maité saw they were back at the small clearing with the ancient trees where she'd first seen him. She was struck again by how glum the place looked with long, mossy tangles draped over maples and sycamores. The tree of life from Xiomara's tale, though still a massive oak, appeared depressed—only a shadow of what it had once been. At its foot were Paloma's remains, Maité recalled, and closing her eyes, she allowed a moment's silence for the woman with whom it all began.

To the left of the oak she saw the huge willow with its long tendrils dragging on the ground. Between her and the willow, Paloma and Celeste's fabled pond sparkled, complete with a dam and water trickling on its way to deeper regions of the realm. There too was the Hall of Glamour, built more than two hundred years before by Celeste and Nahia, and by Amets, of course. Except there was nothing glamorous about the hall now; it stood forlorn and in moldy tatters.

"I painted you, Celeste," Amets said, "standing on the edge of this very pond ..."

Maité's mind flitted back to the portrait hanging over her bed in the manor. "You painted Cel—I mean, you painted me?"

"You were already gone from me," he said, and Maité could clearly see the *1844* at the bottom of the painting. Celeste had married Etienne by then. "But I remembered every detail of your person," he confessed.

The emotion she felt on discovering Amets was the artist made her shudder—to be painted by him *had* to be as pleasurable as hearing his voice inside your head.

"Welcome, Maitagarri."

A female voice made Maité turn abruptly. She brushed the dirt and leaves off her clothes before facing this new representative of the fair dimension but didn't feel her appearance improved much.

She perceived a bright ray of golden sunshine peeking through the trees, but then she realized her mistake. A luminous creature about a foot and a half tall and perfect from every angle hovered before Maité. *Holy cow! She's naked under there*, Maité thought, trying not to stare at the flimsy green tunic worn by the faery.

Spider silk, Maité thought, remembering Xiomara's book. The faery's legs were smooth and long, and the subtle shape of her muscles, dainty as they appeared, told Maité this creature was no stranger to physical exertion. No doubt she excelled at whatever activity gave her such muscle tone. The roundness of her bottom slimmed upward into a tiny waist, and around the front opened subtly into a voluptuous breast. Delicate shoulders, a slender neck, and a head full of auburn waves streaked with gold fell down her back and grazed her creamy face. Her eyes were a mesmerizing shade of brown and her red lips were a perfect heart above her dimpled chin.

"You may call me, Aintza," the faery said musically.

It took a moment for Maité to snap out of her mute observation of the faery and realize Aintza was speaking to her. Maité now sympathized wholeheartedly with Etienne and what he must have gone through on first meeting a faery.

"I have come a long way to meet you," Maité admitted, feeling she'd blown her chance to impress the faery.

Amets smirked as if he knew something Maité didn't.

"You will find you did not come here to meet *me* at all," Aintza replied solemnly. "And, incidentally, I *am* impressed by you."

Maité tensed at this—it seemed Aintza could read her thoughts. "What do you mean?"

"You will discover many things while you are here," the faery said calmly. "Amets too, for there is much he ignores as well."

Maité saw the knowing smirk vanish from Amets' face as he realized something had been withheld from him. The faery, Aintza, had kept a secret. *A secret that will be revealed only now that I'm here.*

Maité tried not to look too pleased over being singled out as the recipient of a revelation. And to think this revelation would more than likely confirm all the hopes she'd harbored since she first read Xiomara's book!

"What will I discover?" Maité blurted.

"In due time," Aintza hinted, gesturing toward the trees.

Maité became aware of other faeries. They had approached in silence and now hovered around the oak, their auras emitting a faint glow in the dwindling daylight. There were four male faeries in addition to Amets, and three other females besides Aintza. They all looked at Maité as if they'd been expecting her.

"Amets did well," Aintza told the others. "You see? She is here."

"*Maitagarri* ..." Their voices combined into a musical whisper that echoed both inside and outside Maité. She shivered as if their whispers physically caressed her.

"And you thought your voice would not travel over the great big sea!" Aintza taunted Amets. "You could summon demons from the center of the earth with your sweet voice."

"Maitagarri," Amets whispered dreamily, his fingers grazing Maité's cheek. She leaned her face into his touch; she could hear the mixture of pleasure and longing in his voice. "It is really you."

"If I had been Celeste, I too would have fought for you," Maité whispered back, recalling the part of Xiomara's book relating a contest between Celeste and Nahia for his affections.

Once again, the discordant note in the familiar tune jarred the air. Amets's brow creased, and he backed away from Maité toward the trees. She wished she'd kept her mouth shut—she meant to flatter him, but in her clumsiness she again disrupted the thin shell of rationality he seemed to live in.

"I'm sorry," she said to him, but he folded his arms over his chest and kept his distance from her. Maité turned a pleading eye toward Aintza but found no sympathy there, even though it seemed clear that Aintza wasn't mistaking Maité for Celeste.

"He will recover, I should think—it might help if we do something about your looks," Aintza said with the first hint of humor.

Maité looked at her thick-soled hiking boots, the rough denim shorts, and the coarse thermal shirt; she was as far from feminine as a person could get.

As if taking pity on her, Aintza said, "This way, please."

Amets and the males disappeared between the trees, and Maité stepped from rock to rock, following the female faeries as they leisurely propelled their foot-tall bodies over the boulders damming the pond.

Once on the other side, they prompted Maité to strip to her bare flesh and step into the cool water, her eyes darted this way and that to make sure all the males were gone as her soiled clothes were spirited away.

Probably to an ethereal trashcan, she thought. *Do faeries even do laundry?*

After a cool bath in the pond, she was taken into the tattered canopy of the Hall of Glamour where she saw a handful of dusty jars strewn about. The myriad of oils, ointments and items of clothing Xiomara described in her book were long gone.

Inside the hall, the faeries shifted to human height and covered Maité's naked body with a thin sheet of woven silk. It was so smooth she could hardly feel it against her skin, except for the luxurious weight attaching itself to every inch of her. Maité closed her eyes and surrendered to the delicate fingers pressing and massaging her face and neck, smoothing away Maité's stress.

The touch of their perfumed hands made all negativity evaporate from Maité as they massaged her body. The smell of Jasmine hung in the air, and Maité felt alive and brimming with new sensations. She saw herself as a brand-new flower: soft, supple, beautiful, and bursting with the desire to be pleasing to the eyes of everyone who encountered her.

Maité's limbs tingled as she began to wake from the delicious stupor. She opened her eyes, looking forward to whatever came next. She saw Aintza.

The faery held a dress out for her. Maité studied the garment and recognized it right away. It had belonged to Celeste. It was just as Xiomara described, made of silk the color of Celeste's skin, which made it seem she wore nothing.

Maité slipped into the dress unable to make out if the dress took on the color of her skin, or her skin absorbed the color of the dress. Maité puzzled over this while one of the faeries braided her hair down her back and fixed jasmine flowers throughout.

As they finished, Aintza announced the time had come for them to talk. "I have sent for the others, and they will be here presently," said the faery.

Amets, like those who had already shifted to the reduced height more comfortable to them, perched himself on a fallen tree trunk, but not before he brushed past Maité with a knowing whisper, "Not quite the scented showers I prepared for you ..."

Her eyes grew wide with surprise. *He's responsible for my showerhead at the manor!* Maité realized, but she couldn't voice her pleasure or even express her thanks; other pairs of eyes appeared in the clearing and followed her every move with endearing alertness.

Pleased, Maité noticed the effect her makeover had on all of them. They stared at her with almost reverent affection, and she imagined they might be struggling to accept, or maybe deny (she glanced at Amets) the span of almost two hundred years separated their Celeste from this descendant of hers.

"The resemblance is uncanny, save for the eyes of course," Aintza remarked.

Amets looked away.

Chapter 38

"I never had the gift of prattle," Aintza reflected, "so I cannot make this pretty, or more interesting than the facts actually are."

Maité nodded, though she couldn't imagine the facts being boring or uninteresting. From her seat at the foot of the ancient oak, Maité lent her ears to the faery—certain Aintza would launch into the missing piece of the story between the conclusion of Xiomara's narrative and the present day.

"The ties between your family and the faery realm had to be severed," Aintza announced, fixing Maité with an accusing glance.

Maité bristled. This wasn't at all what she expected. Had she been brought here to answer for her family's wrongdoings, whatever they might be? A dozen questions swirled in her mind, but the faery quelled them with what sounded like a reproach—even less helpful than the opening statement.

"The boundaries of our relation were violated."

"But why? How?" Maité stammered, again feeling accused, but Aintza's knitted brows said she would admit no interruptions. This gave Maité her first surge of frustration in the realm. Why would Aintza hold Maité responsible for boundaries being violated? And why could she not ask questions?

"Oihana warned Nahia, but Nahia ignored it all," Aintza went on.

"What was the warning?" Maité interrupted and then flinched before spluttering a hasty, "Sorry."

"Oihana foretold nothing good could come from a union such as the one Nahia proposed, no matter how amicable things were then, because in time, and with the essential element of *truth* being withheld, Nahia's selfish plan of uniting two worlds would crumble. The life she sought would eventually be taken over by hate, like weeds take over a garden if left unattended," the faery explained.

Maité felt that though the accusation had shifted to Nahia, Aintza was now clumping Maité with Nahia in this judgment.

"One lie would have to follow another. The very foundation of what Nahia proposed was a lie, but she could not accept that."

"What lies? Sorry ..." Maité felt the faery's speech was filled with gaps— one question piled after the other in her throat, making her anxious for clarity. "It's just that you went from having a tight relationship straight to severing what you had. How? Why?"

A spark of aggravation lit Aintza's eyes, and Maité bit her lip. She'd have to keep her questions to the end. *What did Nahia propose? What was the big lie?*

"Nahia did something forbidden. She betrayed her kind and *your* kind. Going against her mother's wishes, Nahia indulged in her own wants." Aintza spoke calmly, but Maité saw a condemning fire in the faery's eyes. Clearly Aintza disapproved of what Nahia had done.

What did Nahia do that was so terrible? Maité dared not interrupt again, besides something seemed to have shifted; she noticed the declining sunlight no longer reached them under the trees. Dusk settled with finality around the council.

The faeries paused as one in the gathering darkness. Aintza cast her glance upward, as if something had caught her attention in the cobalt sky beyond the canopy. A faint buzzing pressed upon them from above the treetops, easily mistaken for a swarm of flying insects, except that in the few seconds they listened, the buzzing became more distinct.

Amets shifted on his branch, his head cocked to one side.

Maité stared at the faery, waiting for her to continue, but Aintza let out a sharp gasp.

Maité saw a red blaze, like a javelin, slash through the trees and explode at Maité's feet, startling her. The violent gust of heat emanating from it knocked Maité on her side. She got to her knees and scrambled for cover; others did the same.

More spears sliced through the air. Maité heard branches breaking and felt pine needles flying all around; they pricked her perfumed skin like microscopic darts. She reached the nearest boulder at the edge of the pond and clung to it, gasping for breath and tasting the dust she'd stirred up as she scrambled to safety.

A flaming red lance struck Aintza across the shoulder, and the next instant the faery lay motionless on the ground.

The wailing of the other female faeries snapped Maité out of her shock. She heard Amets marshaling the males but couldn't see him. Splintered wood, fiery flashes, and tufts of withered grass like shrapnel whirled beneath the dome of trees in a raucous symphony of destruction.

"What the hell is going on?" Maité shouted through the screams of the faeries to Amets, who dashed past her. He'd spotted the position of the attacker and targeted it with his own ocher-tinged fiery blasts. A searing heat whistled past Maité's ear; she ducked to one side just in time.

The red projectile hit one of the male faeries square in the chest, destroying him. Maité swiveled, but her eyes seemed to be one second behind the assailant. Everywhere she looked, the blazing red spear struck helpless faeries. Maité crawled toward the crumpled heap that was Aintza, her milky skin gashed, her clothes smoldering. Maité knelt beside her, cradling the faery's head to shield her from flying debris.

"Find Nahia," Aintza pleaded, more with her eyes than with her voice, which came out in pained gasps. "She will know what to do about the Beautiful One!" Aintza's body gave a fatal convulsion, and her eyes became vacant, as if fixed on a distant point quite beyond this world. Then her muscles relaxed, and Maité was left holding nothing but Aintza's charred dress. Her body had disappeared.

Chilling peals of laughter filled the air around Maité like the cry of a Banshee straight out of a Gaelic nightmare. It prevailed over the screams of dying faeries and the whooshing sound of shattered branches whizzing within inches of her head.

Maité scuttled to her feet, looking wildly around, desperate to find anyone left standing, but the smoke and darkness made it difficult to see. She coughed and rubbed her watering eyes. She had an eerie conviction no one was left, and she was next.

The Beautiful One, Aintza had said. *Where have I heard that?* But she had no time to think about it.

From the center of a swirling mass of dirt and leaves, a blazing red spear hurtled through the air, straight toward Maité's chest.

Aintza's vacant expression flashed before Maité's eyes. *Soon I'll be skewered too!* She braced herself for the strike, but an unexpected force shoved her sideways a split second before the spear made contact.

Maité slammed into the trunk of the oak. Her neck creaked ominously as her ribs made contact with the tree. With the wind knocked out of her, she collapsed to the ground. She thought of Emily and David, far away in San Sebastián, not knowing what had happened to her—completely clueless as to her whereabouts and the fact she needed help.

Maybe if they charter a helicopter they will find me, she hoped feebly.

Something wrapped itself around Maité's waist, lifting her up. This something held tight to her, and she, powerless to even string two thoughts together, surrendered to its hold.

The heat from all the blasts and the smoke from the fires they set off were trapped under the canopy of trees, suffocating her. Maité knew she was covered in sweat and blood. She thought she couldn't possibly feel anything besides her aches, yet the oddest sensation came over her.

She felt an alien flutter above her navel, cradled in her rib cage.

That's your solar plexus, Emily said in her head. A plug of sorts seemed to have been pulled, making Maité feel like her body had turned into liquid—skin, bones, and all—as if she was being poured into a tiny bottle shaped like herself. She felt constrained, tied down, yet incredibly light.

Maité couldn't see through her tears, and she struggled in vain against the strong warmth coiled about her. Her head began to pound from the strain and from the bizarre sensation of rising swiftly. She stopped fighting.

A sudden gust of fresh air enveloped her like a soothing, cool blanket. Maité let out a groan of relief, but in the same moment a chilling realization came over her. *All is quiet!* She heard no snapping branches, no screams, no red lances crashing around her or being hurled at her. There was only a strange humming in her ears.

She managed to free one hand and wipe her eyes. She blinked repeatedly to clear her vision and found herself in Amets's arms. Everything around them seemed a blur of smoke.

But it doesn't smell like smoke, she thought, confused. *Is it clouds then? Is that the moon?*

It took her a few seconds to realize she was airborne, with Amets's arms tight around her waist. Warm. Safe.

The scene of the massacre smoldered far, far below.

CHAPTER 39

She drifted in and out of consciousness while Amets carried her. The air no longer smelled of charred pine or burnt silk. Instead, Maité picked up the scent of iodine—they were close to the ocean. Now she regained clarity, and with it came the shock and grief of the deaths she'd witnessed. Aintza and the other faeries she'd hoped to know were gone, out of her reach.

Destroyed.

She pressed herself to Amets, her arms tight about his torso and neck, and she placed an anguished kiss upon his sooty face. He was all she had left of the realm. But Amets cringed at the pressure of her touch, and his face twisted into a grimace at her kiss, which hurt her feelings as much as it frightened her. When he let out a grunt of pain, she realized he was badly injured.

"I can't keep it up much longer," he said hoarsely.

Again her body began to feel like liquid, except this time, she felt as if she were spilling out of a tiny bottle, being poured out fast, into a much larger one. In terror, she strained to see the ground below.

Good God!

They were so high up; she thought she was looking at a satellite image of the earth. She wanted to clamp her arms and legs around Amets but she feared hurting him.

"Please, please don't drop me!" she cried.

The shadow of a smile colored the pain on Amets's face. "You said that very thing during your first solstice celebration," he said in a faltering voice, "Did I drop you then?"

Maité searched his eyes wildly. He was again thinking of Celeste, who attended her first solstice celebration when she was fifteen. Amets had raced across the lake with Celeste in his arms and they won the faery game. And no, Amets hadn't dropped her.

But this was no solstice celebration or a game, and she certainly wasn't Celeste.

Maité's body expanded to its full height, and Amets, still a mere fifteen inches tall, could hold her no longer. They plummeted headlong toward the sparkling city lights and architecture below. Maité screamed. Her hand formed a tight fist around Amets's entire forearm; she dragged him with her to their death. A terrific howl spiraled endlessly out of Maité's throat as they dropped.

In a series of snapshots clicking at prodigious speed, Maité saw the dark outline of the mountain they'd fled, the lit-up skyline of San Sebastián, pedestrians on the streets below, the busy promenade, the darkened water of the Cantabrian, the fluorescent foamy crests of the waves.

I don't want to be conscious through this! But it seemed it would take much more than she'd already endured to knock her out cold. There was no escape. She would soon feel her body break when it hit the water.

On the palm of her hand, where their flesh touched, heat rose, as if Amets burned with a fever. She thought the speed of the fall slackened somewhat, and she understood Amets *must be* wielding the last of his strength to disperse her weight—to perhaps steer them to a safe landing.

"Help me," he begged in a strangled growl, and with all her heart, Maité wished to become as light as a feather. She thought she'd succeeded, but perhaps the brief halting she felt was no more than an air pocket or an upward current.

No time to think about it.

They came crashing down through thick brush, "Wha—" she yelped. She'd been expecting to plunge into the ocean like a cannonball, but instead she was getting a brand-new set of scrapes from the brambly bushes. She landed flat on her back on the lumpy ground of *God knows where!* Amets toppled over beside her.

Maité fumbled with trembling fingers over her neck, wondering if it was broken. It didn't seem to be. She touched something sticky and wet that didn't feel like sweat at all; a jagged rock or a branch must have made a gash right below her ear, and blood trickled from it. She sat up feeling disoriented.

Amets, too weak to shift to human size, writhed feebly on the hard dirt, looking a complete mess. A horrible cut stretched across his powerful chest, and one of his legs was bent at an angle that made Maité cringe. On her hands and knees now, she peered at him, at a complete loss for how to help him.

"Tell me what to do!" she cried.

"There is nothing to do, except say good-bye, Celeste."

Maité didn't have the heart to correct him. She pinched her eyes shut and bit her lip; she wanted him to say her name—her real name—only once, to hear him utter the syllables, to delight in the sound of his voice saying her name.

Two fat tears made clean streaks down her cheeks as Xiomara's words came back to her.

"There is nothing to do, except say good-bye, Celeste." Amets had said those words to Celeste the night before she'd left the realm of faery—the night Amets sacrificed his first kiss to her, a human. And since the death of Celeste, until this very night, he'd borne the curse of a life without love.

Who am I to deny him his dying illusion?

"Good-bye then, my splendid champion," she said in a voice broken with sobs.

In between clipped breaths, he confessed, "You were always the one."

Tears sprung from Maité's eyes. He meant Celeste—she'd always been the one.

"You saved my life," she moaned, realizing that back in the forest, he'd taken the deadly strike meant for her. He'd whisked her away from destruction and had just prevented her from falling out of the sky at full speed, which would have certainly killed her. He did all of that, expending the last of his energy and forsaking his own safety—for her. For Celeste.

"It is the least one can do—for the one he loves," he said through gritted teeth, his face disfigured with pain.

Maité shook her head miserably. She dared not touch him. His wounds were so raw, especially the one across his chest. "I love you too," she whispered, and lowering her face to his, she kissed him tenderly on the lips, careful not to hurt him further.

When she withdrew, his lips formed a contented smile, which Maité saw in a brief red glow, like the flash of a camera. Their eyes locked, and her heart raced with the satisfaction of having said the right words, of having done the right thing, at precisely the right moment. She'd made Amets happy, perhaps even allowed him a brief contact with the heart he'd lost to Celeste.

But this was a short-lived pleasure. Vicious flashes of red exploded around them. Chunks of dirt splattered everywhere, and the horrible cold laughter, like a curse, engulfed Maité's hearing.

"Over there!" Amets groaned anxiously, his eyes fixed on a spot covered in brush not five feet from where they were.

"What, Amets? What is it?" She followed his shaky finger and saw a clump of thick shrubs disintegrate into mist, revealing a trapdoor. A fraction of a second later, the effect he'd conjured vanished, but Maité had seen the door. She gave a start, torn between tending to him and racing over to discover what was hidden there.

"Go. *Now*," he commanded.

"You cannot get away from me!" a disembodied voice above and around them shrieked. "How could you have brought her *here*? You traitor!"

Amets dragged himself to a sitting position, and Maité instinctively reached for him.

"I didn't know it was you," he said, weeping. "But when I found you, I had to save you. I took you out of that flying machine."

Maité shook her head, horrified. Hideous recollections of the fateful night in which her parents died washed over her in cold waves. It was *he* who'd put his arms around her when her parents' plane was about to crash, not the pilot. She wanted to say something, maybe ask what he'd been doing there in the first place, maybe let him know she hadn't really been on the plane. But what did it matter now?

Amets continued his fragmented speech. The seconds left to him ticked away mercilessly. "I called you to me," he said. "Nahia told me you'd come. Nahia knew I'd been tricked."

"Nahia?" Maité fell back, electrified by this revelation.

A red beam, like a fiery sword, pierced the air, missing her shoulder by millimeters. But it struck Amets, leaving him sprawled on the ground. Dead.

A guttural snarl came out of Maité. This was a crime, a tragedy. Seething, she lunged ferociously toward the trapdoor Amets had shown her and ripped it open, thankful the hinges had already been blasted apart.

"I will not be next!" Maité flung herself into the gaping hole and fell some ten feet into total darkness. She landed on her hands and knees with a groan but rose at once in spite of the splintering pain in her leg. She kept her eyes wide open, as if doing so might help her penetrate the inky blackness, but besides the yawning mouth of the hole above, she could see nothing.

A fetid mist filled the chamber. Maité breathed fast and hard while she felt her way around. The earthen walls were covered in notches and markings she sensed with her groping fingers, but couldn't see in the gloom. She tripped over a massive chain on the ground. She felt along it. The iron shackles at the end of it were locked, as if a prisoner had simply vanished; the chamber was empty. Why had Amets brought her here?

Did he mean to imprison me? No. He was tricked, and Nahia knew it.

A wrathful howl made Maité cover her ears.

"She has escaped!" it shrieked. The mist around Maité swirled up and concentrated itself into the familiar spear shape that had persecuted her relentlessly.

But I haven't escaped. I've trapped myself! she thought in a frantic daze.

Maité watched the spear resolve into a sharp point. She closed her eyes and bellowed inwardly, *Not happening!* In her belly, the flailing sensation grew so vast and so overwhelming as to make her think of large bats furiously flapping their wings inside her rib cage.

"*Not happening.*" The words issued from her like a concrete wall rising against the deadly attack.

The smoldering spear struck the conjured wall, but even so, Maité was lifted off the ground and flung backward. She landed unconscious on the dirt.

CHAPTER 40

Maité dreamt. She knew the sleeping infant in the hospital nursery was her newborn self.

"Snug as a bug in a rug," she heard her father say in his Italian accent. She turned to look for him, but he wasn't there.

The appearance of a woman in a shabby blue cloak and hood made Maité back away a couple of paces. She watched the woman step stealthily into the room and rest an unsteady hand on the acrylic lip of the crib where the infant Maité slept. The woman eyed the baby as one might gaze at a stormy sky, anticipating the next bolt of lightning. Maité frowned, puzzled.

When at last the woman cast her glance on the grown-up Maité, it was through a pair of aquamarine points of light, seemingly afloat within the shadowy hood. The woman turned back to the baby and began speaking in a melodic whisper that made Maité's skin tingle with foreboding. "Beware of the *Beautiful One*."

Her head swimming in the sudden rush of memory, Maité said to the woman, "I knew I'd heard that before. It was in that dream, wasn't it? The dream I had on my fifteenth birthday!"

The woman nodded. "Come with me."

Maité followed her out of the hospital nursery. The door swung outward, and as soon as Maité passed through, she found herself on a windswept, irregular landscape.

Dreams are so weird, she mused, but didn't dwell on the thought further for fear of waking herself. Her ear tuned in to the deafening roar of waves crashing against an unseen rocky wall, which disoriented her for a moment. The woman glided on ahead, and Maité groped for a fistful of branches and began to scale the serrated ground in pursuit.

The woman waited for Maité at the top of the craggy slope; the wind played with her tattered cloak. Maité reached her at last, but without a word, without allowing her a respite, the woman floated over the

226

brittle vegetation covering the wretched place while Maité again traipsed haphazardly behind her.

Sweat broke out all over her. *Where the heck are we going?* She felt short of breath, and her leg muscles throbbed miserably.

"Isn't this where Amets brought me?" Maité asked, looking at a trapdoor on the sandy ground, but the misty gloom around them made it impossible to recognize anything else.

With a dismissive motion of her arms, the woman opened the trapdoor. Maité followed her down a flight of steps—which she was certain wasn't there before—and stepped into a marvelously lit room. The walls were carved in gold. Maité gasped as her eyes swept over every corner of the chamber. Each carving on the wall constituted an episode of a story she now knew by heart.

A woman bathed in a pond while small creatures floated around her, dropping petals into the water. A couple kissed on the sandy shore of a moonlit lake. Two young girls sat at a loom in deep conversation as they wove. A woman cradled an infant in her arms while creatures hovering above them spilled petals all around.

"It's our story." Maité smiled.

The woman in the cloak walked over to a specific plaque. Maité looked at the engraving of a woman stooped on a tree branch, looking over what appeared to be the city of San Sebastián.

The woman lifted the plaque off the wall to reveal a secret compartment, and then she removed an ancient chest hidden inside. She set it down on the floor and opened it. The woman withdrew a piteous-looking plant and handed it to Maité. "The survivor," the woman said.

Maité nodded, recognizing the little plant at once and wondering why such an insignificant thing should be hidden with such care. But the plant seemed to be the only reason the woman had come to this strange chamber. Maité followed her back up the stairs, into the wearing wind.

The sandy surface around the trapdoor was gone. Maité heard branches cracking and leaves crunching under her bare feet. Oddly, it didn't cause her any discomfort. She clutched the survivor safely in her hand until they arrived at a table set for two under the turbulent sky. The woman took one of the chairs and motioned for Maité to take the other.

Materializing from nowhere, Amets leaned close to Maité and said, pointing at the feeble little plant, "The island of Santa Clara is filled with these."

"Santa Clara," she echoed, her eyes riveted on him. Amets was so beautiful; she couldn't stop gawking at him. "He didn't die then?" Maité asked the woman, though still looking at him.

The woman ignored Maité's question. "The Beautiful One believes *you* are dead."

"I'm not?" Maité replied, with the eerie certainty that though she felt quite alive at the moment, somewhere very close to this scene was a reality quite opposite, where pain and death called.

The woman smiled. "Not remotely."

Amets receded into the darkness around them.

"You're Nahia! Please tell me you are." Maité gripped the edge of the table and leaned across it.

"I am," she returned, pulling off the hood, and Maité recognized the turquoise-streaked curls.

She leaned back in her chair, pleased and relieved. "Then you'll destroy the Beautiful One, won't you? Aintza said you could."

"Aintza said I would *know* what to do," Nahia clarified.

This was maddening. "So then you *can't* kill the Beautiful One?"

Nahia shook her head wearily. "She is my cousin, and I, being of royal blood, cannot bring about the death of one who shares my blood—even if it is only my uncle's blood," she said and then added as an afterthought, "She is also lower than I am in the royal legacy, which further secures her safety, for her station and ability are much humbler than mine."

Maité cocked her head to one side, scowling. "Humbler, my butt!" she fumed. "You didn't see what she did! Nahia, she destroyed everything up there like some kind of invisible Navy Seal team! There is nothing and no one left, but Aintza said you were the one to destroy her. Did she lie?"

Nahia's eyes bore on Maité, as if willing her to understand something, but that something eluded Maité—fresh in her mind were the shrieks of the faeries as the blazing lance vaporized them, one by one. *But not Amets.* She had flown in his arms away from there, yet she'd also seen him lying dead on the ground.

"Amets was just here, wasn't he?" She shook her head irritably, unable to separate reality from the dream.

"She's trying to destroy those who've sworn loyalty to me," Nahia said.

"Why?"

"Faeries are certainly not above greed." Nahia sighed patiently. "The Beautiful One has longed for power for centuries, and when she succeeded in my capture, she thought she would at long last achieve her goals."

"But you escaped."

"That I did, with Amets's help." Nahia looked off into the distance. Her eyes sparkled brighter for a moment. "But I am too far away now to be of any help to you, except in dreams. I cannot return until I have recovered, until I have succeeded in mending what I ..." Nahia paused and looked away giving Maité the impression she was hiding something.

Maité clicked her tongue impatiently. "Nahia, please! This isn't the time to keep secrets."

But Nahia would not look at her. Maité followed Nahia's gaze and noticed the glittering lights of the city.

It can't be more than ten or eleven at night, she thought, and San Sebastián, ensconced on the sloping hills across the intervening arm of water, thronged with crowds going in and out of restaurants and pubs, or ambling along the breezy promenade, in boisterous conversation.

"We're on Santa Clara Island!" Maité cried in surprise. The instant of waking loomed over her consciousness as a serious threat. She saw herself crumpled in a cave floor, blood dribbling from a wound on her neck, and feared she might wake from this dream without doing as Emily had said: *Get some answers for a change.* She turned her back on her crumpled self and ordered her dream-self to focus on Nahia.

"There is great power in a name," Nahia said, "especially in a faery's name."

"Isn't her name the Beautiful One?"

"You already know her *true* name," Nahia hinted.

Something quickened in Maité's mind, but no name revealed itself.

"And that gives you the power to call her down, or if you choose, to destroy her completely. You see, to defeat one's own kind, one must have the powerful matriarchal blood that will enable her to do so."

"Right, and you're Oihana's daughter, so you have that blood! Where are you that you can't finish off the Beautiful One?" Maité exclaimed.

Nahia shook her head. Her eyes closed for a moment, as if begging for patience. "I cannot finish her for the reasons I have already explained. But there is another who can. There is you." Nahia's eyes bore into Maité. "Not only do you have immeasurable force borne of the desire for revenge, but you—"

"What? What desire for revenge?"

Nahia leaned across the table, and Maité sat up straighter, instinctively bracing herself for whatever might come out of Nahia's mouth.

"Were you not ripped from your happy life and transplanted into a world you had no knowledge of? Was not the life of your mother and father an unreasonable price to pay for something you knew nothing about?"

Maité's entire frame shook; her hands flew to the sides of her head but flashes of the death of her parents came to her anyway. *Just like in the forest.* Again, the unaccountably strong arms gripped her from behind, seconds before the plane crashed. *Amets! God in heaven!* Alba's eyes were round with fear. Over the din of the struggling engine, Sósimo's anguished voice said he loved her.

"What are you saying?" Maité roared at Nahia, trying to silence the noise inside her head, but she already knew. Hadn't Maité survived the same attacker this very night? It became quite clear—the Beautiful One killed her parents. The Beautiful One was now after her.

Hadn't Maité already been struck by her? Hadn't she felt the blast of red heat stabbing her chest? *Yes.* She'd fallen into the underground chamber and made herself an easy target, and it was there, cornered like a rat, that she had been killed. But no! She wasn't dead. "Not remotely," Nahia had said.

Breaking away from the hellish dream became paramount to Maité. She wanted no more of this nightmare, no more of this hopeless business. Aintza said Nahia would know what to do. Amets had brought Maité here, to Santa Clara, where she should've found Nahia. But Nahia was no more than a dream, and even in the dream, Nahia confessed herself incapable of destroying the killer of her parents and an entire troop of faeries.

Wake up! Wake up! Wake up! Maité ordered herself, but Nahia spoke again, and the composure of her voice, as much as the light pressure of her hand on Maité's shoulder, soothed her and forced her to keep her wits about her.

"Her goal is to rule the realm of faery," Nahia said. "And to do that, I must be destroyed, as she believes she is next in line for the throne." Not a trace of fear or concern was discernible in her voice. "I am afraid I played right into her hands by showing her my weakness. You see, it was I who brought the Beautiful One to you in the hospital, when you were born."

Maité's tears flowed freely. Where were the happy endings? Where was the faery tale? This was nothing but a basic recitation of the follies committed by faeries; Maité thought them no better than the average pettiness of humans. Nahia's melodic words repulsed Maité as much as they fascinated her.

"After decades of keeping away, I decided to resurface, bringing a cradle gift to the newborn descendant of Celeste, so it was I, with my thoughtless behavior, who made her aware of Alba's existence and of yours.

"And so she set her trap for me. The Beautiful One deduced, correctly, that if I saw fit to bestow a gift on the child, then it followed that, should the mother be threatened, I would do my best to avert any danger coming to the child. And so I did and she captured me. With Alba and me out of the way, there was only you. And you, she told me, would be her leverage.

"Your safety was put into my shackled hands, Maité. Either I gave her what she sought, or you would be destroyed. Her plan was to get to you, to have you brought to the realm and be placed at her mercy so you would give up what had been handed down from mother to daughter since Celeste. But to make you do her will, she needed the type of help Amets could give—his particular gift being that of reaching across vast expanses with his voice. So she took him along on that fateful night, betting that his loyalty to Celeste would engage him in drawing you, her last descendant, back to the realm and to him."

Maité shook her head and then covered her face with her hands, feeling lost and toyed with.

"But she suffered an unexpected setback. Because of the cradle gift I gave you, you actually materialized in that airplane. Amets at once latched on to the sight of you, because you are almost a copy of Celeste. He would now do the Beautiful One's bidding without any qualms, because he wanted to have you back, but she could not trust him anymore; she'd seen his allegiance shift from herself to you.

"You see, my dear friend's mind had long been in a fog—since the death of his love, to be precise. To behold her again, even if it was only a replica, was like a breath of life to him." Nahia again looked away, as if granting a moment's reverie for those cherished ones who were no more.

Maité wiped tears from her face, and Nahia exhaled slowly before continuing. "She told Amets that Celeste, whom he had seen with his own eyes after all this time, would come back to him once the humans keeping her in exile were destroyed. Amets believed this." Nahia bowed her head.

The faery waned; a sense of urgency overwhelmed Maité. Only moments before she wanted this nightmare to end, but now, resignation, curiosity, and a morbid desire to kill every surviving bit of her own childish hopefulness took over her. Maité wanted it all—every single detail of this intrusion from the realm of faery—every last reason why her parents had to breathe their last.

Maité struck the table with her fists, her eyes intent on the fading cloak and diminishing form of the faery. "Don't you leave me, Nahia, not yet!" She had no clue how these things worked, but because she could now see through the faery, she understood the near impossibility of sustaining an image of oneself over unfathomable distance. "I need you here! Where are you that you can't stay by my side?" she cried, but Nahia made no reply. To Maité's mounting panic, Nahia became even more translucent; Maité could see through her to a small island, lost in an immense green ocean glinting in the dark sky.

The sight puzzled Maité; besides Santa Clara, she couldn't recall any other islands visible from La Concha. She thought she saw palm trees and immediately thought of her parents; she'd seen them in a place like that. *Warm and salty.* Maité shook her head irritably. "At least tell me the name of the Beautiful One! Tell me, Nahia!"

All too quickly, Nahia became one with the twinkling stars. Maité shut her eyes tight and gritted her teeth. "Tell me, please. I don't know her true name!"

Maité woke on the earthen floor of her prison. Her tears mingled with the dirt and blood smeared on her face. Her aching body shook with each sob. Then, when it seemed certain all hope was lost, a searing word slipped into her jumbled thoughts and branded itself on her brain.

Ederne.

Maité stopped crying and rolled on to her back, her eyes fixed on the square bit of sky visible above her. Fog sped across in windy wisps, giving Maité a hopeful hint of the stars sparkling far above.

Ederne. The name figured in Xiomara's account of the curse placed on Paloma.

"Of course her name is Ederne," Maité said to herself. "But how do I kill her? Or how am I supposed to *call down* a faery?"

Daunted, but far from despairing now, Maité gave a watery sniff, recalling all Nahia said and all Xiomara wrote in her book about the Beautiful One. All about Ederne.

Chapter 41

The chill and dampness of her prison settled in Maité's bones, numbing her yet punctuating every scrape and cut on her skin. Celeste's delicate dress hung threadbare on Maité's frame; it had been singed and shredded to ribbons through the recent brushes with death. But overnight, Maité had gained a peculiar clarity of mind. She deliberately recalled every detail of her dream along with every word Nahia had uttered.

Minutes ticked by while she mulled it over until, at length, the bit of sky visible through the opening became tinged with a telling bluish glow.

Time to rise, she thought. *Dawn approaches, and with it, the dispelling of evils born of the dark.* Had Sósimo read that to her? Probably. When? And what had the story been about? She couldn't remember.

Maité wiped the tears from her face and pulled herself to a sitting position. She hugged her knees as she squinted at the dirt walls around her. Even in the dark, she could tell they weren't carved in gold as they had been in her dream, but she felt certain the plaque Nahia had shown her would be there.

Maité stood up with a grunt of pain and limped over to where Nahia had indicated. The etchings on the dirt, which she had no hope of seeing in the dim light, felt crude to the tips of her fingers.

What I wouldn't give for a flashlight. But she remembered the dream well enough.

She walked the length of the wall like a blind person, counting her steps so she could place herself at the center. Eight feet, heel to toe. That was the length of the wall. She traced her way back four steps and, according to the dream, "Here should be the faery perched on a tree." She stroked the irregular surface. A square, perhaps meant to be a frame, had been carved into the dirt.

Maité dropped to her knees and fumbled blindly over the ground until she found a twig in the straw. Using it like a chisel, she picked around the frame-like fissure until she succeeded in dislodging a brick. When she tried to remove it, it fractured.

Letting the pieces drop to the ground, she brushed off whatever remained inside. Her fingers grazed something hard at the back of the cavity. She froze, her mind trying to account for it. *Whatever it is, it's not alive*, she told herself, and relaxed a little.

Maité prodded until she managed to hook two fingers into what felt like a thick handle. Thrilled, she pulled on it, and a heavy chest slid out and dropped to the ground with a dull thud. The rusty handle had come away in her hand.

She tossed the useless handle to the side and picked up the box. She took it to the spot under the opening, where there was more light. Feeling around all the carved sides of the shoe-box sized coffer, she found no lock. Maité simply undid the rough metal latch and opened the lid. She had become so used to the staleness of the cave that when her nostrils filled with the sweet scent of jasmine trapped in the box, a pleasurable sigh escaped her, and she momentarily longed for a bath, for her aromatic showerhead back at the manor.

Amets did that for me, she remembered, and blinked away tears.

Knowing it was pointless to dwell on her shower, she felt around for the contents inside—nothing but a single sheet of parchment.

How could the chest be so heavy with only one piece of paper inside? She pressed, prodded, and knocked against the box until she realized it had a false bottom. She tore the felt lining and lifted the second lid. The contents here were cold and hard to the touch. With her eyes keenly trained on these items, she detected a sparkle.

"It's jewelry," she whispered. Her voice had grown raspy. She dug her fingers through the small treasure crammed into the four compartments of the box. Inside were brooches with sharp pins to fasten them to clothing, and smaller trinkets she thought might be earrings. Also several rings and a large, flat sort of nugget with a hole through its middle; she fondled that one for a few moments, intrigued by the image it put in her mind.

Could it be?

Maité recalled Xiomara's description of a self-bored stone; the only device that could enable a human to see a faery, the very thing Arantxa had used to discover and trap the faery queen and which Celeste gave to Etienne's mother, Elise.

A flat, smooth stone with a hole through the middle. She brought it to her eye and looked through the hole, wondering if a world of light would materialize before her. It did not.

But I'll bet this is the one, she thought with a furtive smile. She resumed her rummaging.

In a compartment all by itself lay a particularly large pendant on a thick metal cord, perhaps made of gold. The pendant seemed to be made up of three large stones. Her mind readily conjured up a trio of gorgeously set diamonds big as walnuts, or rubies, or maybe emeralds!

On the hard-packed floor, Maité sat with her legs sprawled in the shape of a V, the jewelry box sat open in front of her. She leaned against the wall with an exhausted sigh and rolled her head side to side against the wall. She played with a fistful of gems, picking them up and then dreamily letting them slip through her fingers. The pendant on its thick cord seemed to place itself under her touch. She stopped rolling her head and held up the jewel. It was ludicrously large, but she put it around her neck anyway, and there it sat, cold and heavy against her breast.

An image of Emily popped into her head. "She's probably dead asleep in her bed, not worried about me." Maité sighed, dejected. "I wiped away her good sense, just like I did with David. What an idiot I was! This is no faery tale, I'm no faery princess, and years from now, someone will find my carcass down here. I might even make the news. They'll find all these pretty stones in the bones of my hand, and they'll say, 'The poor thing—all her riches couldn't save her.'"

A derisive chuckle rang in her head. *I can't believe Ederne's gonna win! She killed my parents, she killed Amets and Aintza and all the others. She thinks she's killed me. Actually, she has killed me! I don't see a way out of here. But she'll get the realm, and she'll live happily ever after—that is, until Eva plops down her ski lifts and runs. She might even put a lodge up there.*

The thought of Eva methodically developing the wilderness Ederne wanted at once amused and revolted Maité. *Eva and Ederne.* Something sour came up to the top of her throat as she recalled Xiomara's description of Ederne. *Yes. She had red hair too.* Maité shivered. *Could it be?*

Emily's voice taunted her. "What will you do about it, Maitagarri?"

"I don't know," Maité said sullenly, "I'm not a faery. Just a human sentenced to a slow death. Hell, I'm already in a grave." She curled up on the dirt. She had no Amets to encourage her or point her in the right direction. No Mom or Dad, no Emily, and no David.

He'll go to the mountains to get me, and when I don't show up, they'll do a pointless search. They'll never know I'm right across the beach from them …

Maité couldn't cry anymore; she felt spent and began to wonder how different her own death would be from that of her parents'.

From there, however, other thoughts came in rapid succession, colored with a logic she couldn't deny. She *had* physically been on that plane with her parents when they died. Before that, she'd shared dreams with her mother, father, and Finn, although she'd never discussed that with him. She'd communicated across the ocean with Amets, and that astral communication brought her to the mountains where she'd found the rest of the faery troop. And, just hours ago, she'd shared a dream with Nahia, which led to finding the coffer on the wall.

She sat up again smelling hope in the fetid air, but her inner critic was way ahead, seeming to know where her thoughts would go next.

Sure it's an exciting prospect, the critic said tersely, *but can you use that ability at will?*

"Yes!" Maité cried, "I *did* do something to David and Emily. I felt it coming out of me. And I did do something to Eva when she was trying to drown me—it was like energy becoming a physical something that could strike out!"

Maité closed the coffer, put it off to one side and then sat up straight, her legs twisted like a pretzel.

"I can do this," she said, closing her eyes. She stretched her neck from side to side several times to clear her thoughts and then made herself breathe as evenly as she could, bent on gathering her will and directing it toward David.

She wished she knew where he lived, but since she didn't have the smallest clue, she ignored it. This was a time to believe, not to doubt.

"Focus," she ordered herself, and without further preamble, she dived into thoughts of David: his eyes, his hands, that crease—like a big comma on his cheek—punctuating his smile and making her knees go weak. How he'd shuffled his feet that day on the sidewalk, half a block from the María Celeste. How he avoided her eyes when he confessed his feelings about the death of his mother.

David.

The giddy flapping in her belly began.

Focus.

She felt her temples pulsing to the rhythm of the wings in her belly.

It's working! She thought ecstatically, and the flapping slowed down as if on cue. "No, no. I'm *focusing*. Not bragging. *Focus.*"

David, David, she pleaded and there he was—David's lips lingering on her cheek as he wished her good night. The flapping flared up again. He seemed so close she could smell him, and the memory of his scent took her over the edge. The flapping burst from her solar plexus, no longer just inside her. It was all around her, or better yet, she seemed to have *become* the flapping wings.

Maité felt David's breath on her face, saw the stubble on his chin. He was a giant, towering above her. For a moment she thought she'd unwittingly shrunk herself to the size of a faery, but then she realized it wasn't the case.

Maité lay on her back on the hard, cool surface of a specimen slide. David looked at her through a microscope.

I'm in his dream. I made it.

She stood barefoot on the glass, free of aches and pains and dressed in a paper hospital gown. He held out his hand and she stepped daintily on to it. It felt warm.

"Do I have news for you," he said bringing her closer to his face. Maité wobbled and chose to sit instead.

"I have news for you too!" She grinned, bowled over by the fact she'd managed the feat while awake. "I need you to come find me," she said reaching out to touch him.

"You're in the mountains," he said, and then grew angry. "I shouldn't have left you. I should have gone with you! Crazy girl. You haven't died, have you?"

Maité grazed his stubbly cheek with her fingers, glad to discover that in a dream-state he was free of the spell she'd put him under. "I'm not dead, but I'm going to be if you don't come get me soon."

"Where are you?"

"On the island of Santa Clara," she said, focusing hard on an aerial view of her location.

"What?"

"Santa Clara! I'm trapped in an underground cave." She told him while arranging images for him of what she'd seen and feeling thrilled by her new means of communication.

Of course, the thought streaked across her mind, *it remains to be seen whether he'll remember the dream when he wakes up—and act on it.* An uncomfortable little flutter disturbed the rhythm of the flapping wings in Maité's belly, but she stifled it as quickly as she could. *This is no time for doubting.*

Right on cue, David said, "I know that spot."

Maité gave him a winning smile. "Now listen. When you wake up, you're going to doubt this ever happened, and you may want to go find me in the mountains. Don't! You can't because I'm not there anymore. You have to come to Santa Clara—do you hear me? *Don't go to the mountains.*"

His eyes twinkled and his cheek dimpled as he worked his jaw into that knee-buckling smile of his. "Your feet feel cold on my hand," he said, and she knew he believed all of it was a dream.

Maité closed her eyes—it was imperative to convey the urgency of the situation. She tried her hardest to produce an image of her true circumstances. No sooner had she wished it than a hologram-like figure of herself flickered into being.

David gasped, looking at the image on the palm of his hand. For the space of a blink, she no longer wore the hospital gown. She no longer stood straight. Instead, she was bruised and wounded, a dark mist enveloping her.

That did it! Maité thought.

He leaned close, his brow furrowed. "What is going on? What in God's name happened to you?"

Maité touched his cheek with her grungy fingers. "I'll tell you when you get here. Come get me already. Wake up!"

David woke, startled, Maité's words still echoing in his ears.

The clock on his bedside table read five fifteen. He'd overslept; he should be at the waterfall by now.

He scrambled out of bed, feeling frazzled. On the way to the bathroom, he froze as the dream came back to him in full force. A faint smell of jasmine hung in the air, and for a few seconds he stood there, arguing with his rational mind.

"Santa Clara?" He frowned, and his eyes swiveled suspiciously about the room looking for—he didn't know what.

Then he smiled and said, "She'll tell me when I get there."

CHAPTER 42

Maité couldn't believe she'd actually fallen asleep, but she must have, because she was startled awake by branches being disturbed as someone approached.

"David?" Maité croaked as she crawled to the spot beneath the opening, clearing her throat impatiently, "David, I'm here!"

"Maité—"

David's voice washed over her like liquid relief. She swallowed hard but couldn't dislodge the lump forming at the top of her throat. *He's here!*

It hit her now how much she had doubted herself, and the horrible night plagued with fear she'd spent because of it, but it was over now. David being here validated everything; Maité had managed to break into his dream to ask for help, and David—*he's so brilliant!*—had acted on that dream, he had believed her.

And he's saving my life—tears spilled down her cheeks as she looked up.

Dirt and pebbles slid down from the edge of the opening, onto her upturned face. Right before shutting her eyes to the falling debris, she got a glimpse of David.

"You found me," she sang, staggering as she stood on her numb legs.

"How did you do that?" David asked getting on his knees and squinting down at her. "I mean, about the dream."

"Oh boy," Maité said under her breath, but then it occurred to her the simple truth would set her free, *literally and figuratively*. "I have a gift," she replied, remembering Nahia's words to the baby in the nursery: "Your dreams will take you into the world of others." "It was given to me," she clarified.

David nodded mutely until Maité spoke up again. "Could you help me out, please?"

He sprung into action. "I'm lowering a rope!"

Maité fumbled in the semidarkness until she caught it.

"Coil it round your wrist and hold tight to it," he called.

"Give me a minute," she croaked, picking up the heavy chest. She latched it and knotted the rope firmly around it. "First I'm sending up this box."

David pulled it up and she watched him set it aside before lowering the rope again.

Maité grabbed hold of it and twisted it once around her wrist. "Ouch! This is gonna hurt!" she complained.

"You'll have to walk up the wall—maybe in a squatting position," David advised.

"Easy for you to say—but I guess it's only a few feet." Maité began climbing. This required the use of a whole new set of muscles, ones she hadn't used the night before—*I guess I'll be sore all around*, she thought grimly, convinced her eyelids were the only part of her that didn't hurt. With David pulling, however, she seemed to reach the top in no time at all.

No sooner had half her torso emerged from the gaping hole than David pulled her to him, though he lost his footing in the process and fell backward. Maité landed on top of him.

She rolled off him, exhaling hard, torn between feeling hideous and embarrassed and wanting to kiss him. Her eyes felt grainy from the dust. The gash below her ear no longer bled, but it throbbed dully.

"What happened?" he asked, turning his head to look at her. "How did you get here?"

She pulled herself up on her elbows, feeling the ache of the myriad of scrapes and bruises all over her body. "If I told you, you wouldn't believe me."

David eyed her, intrigued, his glance dropping below her neck. With a surge of alarm Maité remembered all she had on was what was left of Celeste's dress, which had been pretty flimsy to begin with. She drew her knees to her chest and put her arms around them, trying to cover as much of herself as she could.

David grabbed his jacket, which he'd left on the ground by the mouth of the cave. "Here, put this on," he offered.

Maité stuck her arms through the sleeves. "Thank you," she said, making a fist over the pendant she still had on. A swift glance told her the gems were not diamonds after all, but rather two large, multifaceted black stones, perhaps onyx. They were almond-shaped and looked like eyes. Between the black stones sat a beautifully cut ruby. The three gems were arranged vertically in a pewter setting with a silver cord to match.

"Try me," David said, helping Maité to her feet.

With Maité clinging to one side of him, and the coffer under his other arm, they started back for the boat, slowly because of her bare feet.

"Try you, what?" she asked, holding tight to him.

"You know, whether or not I believe your story."

David's eyes seemed focused on the uneven terrain, but she could feel his strength, the heat of his body so close to her, and the dashing, clean scent of his skin. Again she felt embarrassed by her condition. *I have perfectly good reason for looking like I do right now!* she thought, but still worried about what it would mean to tell David everything.

She stopped, teetering on her sore feet and gave a pathetic sniff. "You're going to think I'm crazy, but I know I'm not."

"Who said you were?" David steadied her by the shoulder until she found a flat spot on the ground. "Of course you do *look* the part," he teased.

"It's not funny!" Tears rolled down her face, and she promptly smudged them with her dirty hands.

David set the coffer down and put his arms around Maité—all her muscles relaxed and she melted in his embrace. Overwhelmed by a sense of safety and gratitude her eyes welled with tears again; nothing could harm her now.

"Tell me all of it, please." David whispered in her ear.

"I will—I'll tell you the whole story even if when I'm done, you'll wish you hadn't heard it."

David kissed her forehead tenderly. "Not a chance."

He picked up the coffer again and put his free arm around Maité's waist, almost lifting her off the ground, which made walking a whole lot easier for her.

By the time they came to the side of the island where the boat was docked, the whole tale had poured out of her in a frenzied flow while David kept his eyes on the ground, as if absorbed in finding the smoothest path for her.

When she finished, Maité stopped and glanced at him warily, waiting for his reaction. Behind him, the boat bobbed in the water, secured to a dilapidated dock only a few feet away.

"Were you in love with Amets?" he asked soberly, placing the coffer on the ground and gazing at the sleepy city across the water.

Maité stared at him. *After everything I dumped on him, he picks up on that? Oh my God!* Ripples of pleasure coursed through her and her mouth began to quiver until a smile formed. *He's jealous.* She wanted to kiss him and tell him how much she loved *him!* But the dirt, sweat, and blood caked on her face began to crack at the hint of a smile.

When David turned expectantly toward her, she remembered she hadn't answered his question. "No!" she cried. "I wasn't in love with Amets." She shifted on her sore feet, aware that she looked like a corpse in the beginning stages of decay, but she had to tell him, even if this wasn't at all how Maité had imagined this moment, she confessed, "I'm in love with *only* you."

David looked like he'd been granted clemency in a death trial. He scooped her up into his arms, but she grimaced, and he was forced to set her down again, "I'm so sorry, I …"

"It's okay, really. I'm just, um, sore." She looked down at herself. "And disgusting," she added.

"I didn't mean to hurt you," he stammered. "What I meant—I just meant to kiss you. May I?"

Maité smiled, trying to ignore the cracking feeling on her face, like a mud mask ready to be washed off. "If you can stomach it," she murmured hopefully.

David kissed her, setting Maité's insides into a flutter of happiness.

When they docked on the mainland it was close to seven in the morning.

"Uh-oh," Maité grunted, "I should've jumped in the water and rinsed off while I had the chance."

People in the harbor stared while David tied up the boat, but luckily it was too early for the full-blown crowd of sailors. David navigated them to the parking lot, doing his best to block Maité from prying eyes. She ducked into his car as soon as he opened the door. He put the coffer in the backseat and then came around to the driver's side.

"I hope you know this doesn't count as the sailing trip you promised me," Maité teased, feeling suddenly giddy. She knew a surge of exhilaration presaged the return of the powerful flapping in her belly and Maité wondered when it might start again—part of her hoped it wouldn't, at least until after she'd had a shower and a nap.

David grinned, but then a chiming noise came from his waist. He plucked his mobile out of his belt. "It's from the lab."

Maité nodded, thinking about what he'd said in the dream. *Boy, do I have news for you.* She looked at him, meaning to ask what he'd meant, but they were already entering the manor's private drive.

CHAPTER 43

Maité knew Emily expected her back no later than six in the morning, and here she was, more than an hour and half late. So it was no surprise that the instant David and Maité walked through the front door, Emily and Soledad pounced on them, one shaking her head in disapproval, the other howling in surprise and relief.

"Man, somebody needs to get hosed down," Emily declared, pursing her lips.

"*Ay, mi Dios!* Mi niña!" Soledad bounded over to fret over Maité's condition up close, "How you are looking—when Miss Emilia told me what you were doing"—she clucked her tongue examining Maité head to toe. "Are you hungry, mi niña?" Soledad asked, going straight to the coffee pot.

"I had a hard time getting back across the waterfall," Maité said to Soledad's retreating back, and to Emily, who stood with her hands on her hips waiting for an explanation, she gave an arch look; Maité didn't feel at all up to retelling the truth at this moment. She glanced sideways at David, and he nodded almost imperceptibly.

Soledad set some fresh coffee on the table along with a basket of bread.

"The lab pinged me, so I've got to run," David said, declining the coffee and excusing himself, but he promised to be back early that afternoon.

"I need to get cleaned up," Maité said, snatching a piece of bread on her way out of the kitchen, leaving Soledad and Emily to look at one another in silence.

Thirty minutes later, Maité returned, her skin emitting a vague scent of lotion, as her showerhead was no longer perfumed. The entire time she'd spent under the water, she'd cried for Amets, but now she looked relaxed in a clean pair of pants to cover her scrapes, and a long-sleeved T, for the same reason. The pendant lay safely tucked under her shirt—a heavy coolness against her skin. The gash beneath her ear felt painfully raw.

No sooner had Soledad spotted it than she fell to applying antiseptic and promising that before Maité knew it, there wouldn't even be a scar.

"Had it not been for Eva coming over last night, your grandfather would've had an aneurism," Emily was saying.

Maité stiffened at once, and Soledad apologized with kisses, thinking she'd rubbed a tender spot and caused her pain.

"He wanted to go in your room, but Miss Emilia and me, we didn't let him," Soledad chimed in.

Emily rolled her eyes. "Yeah, she came in here a giggling, bouncing mess of curly hair in lots and lots of pink chiffon. Yuk! Cooing away in her sappy, throaty little way, 'Ooh, tomorrow morning! I'm so excited!'" Emily mimicked Eva, but comical as it was, it didn't distract Maité from what was being said.

"Your grandfather totally forgot he was halfway up the stairs, ready to storm your bedroom to make you come out."

"Wait—today is the day for what?" Maité asked tensely.

"*Dile, dile!*" Soledad nudged Emily. "Tell her!"

"I'm *dile-ing,*" Emily retorted with a shake of her head. "They're signing the papers today."

"You gotta be kidding me!" Maité fumed and Emily quickly attempted to soften the news.

"Apparently it wasn't supposed to happen for another week, but I guess Eva got tired of waiting, so last night—"

"And Grandfather agreed?"

"I guess you can call it that. They disappeared into the south wing of the house in a lip-lock worthy of a porn award."

Maité grimaced as if Emily's words smelled rancid.

"Sorry," Emily said at once. "You know, I don't really think he knows what's going on, it's like whenever she's around, somebody slips him an *I'm-this-creature's-slave* pill, and he just goes blank. It's eerie to watch."

Eerie to watch, Maité thought, uneasy about the sinister suspicion that had begun to form in her mind back in the cave. *What if Eva ...* but the issue at hand was to stop the signing of the papers.

"So where are they now? Making out in the library?" Maité laughed humorlessly, wishing she could take a long nap before trying to avert the next catastrophe.

"I told you, she wanted to really get down to it," Emily said. "They've gone to sign the papers."

"When?"

"They came out of the library about twenty minutes ago and left."

"Why didn't you say so? You've let me sit here chatting away. We have to stop her. Soledad, where is the place? Please get us a cab—we have to go. Now!"

"They said they'd stop for coffee. Their appointment isn't until nine thirty," Emily said in a placating tone.

"That's in less than half an hour!" Maité cried.

Everyone scrambled from their seats. Soledad babbled into the phone, Emily raced upstairs to throw some clothes on, and Maité tapped her foot, waiting for Soledad to finish.

"I need to get hold of David," Maité said when Soledad hung up the phone. "I forgot a box in his car."

"Ah, mi niña," Soledad said, "David came back and left this when you were in the shower."

"I love him!" Maité lunged over and clamped her arms protectively around the chest. "Thank you, Sole!"

Maité ran to her room to examine the parchment, which she hadn't been able to read in the cave. She also found a separate paper folded in half, lining the compartment where the pendant had rested.

Maité read the first document; it was covered in fine calligraphy with legal-looking words. With her heart knocking in her chest, she read the contents, which clearly stated the rights to the María Celeste and the land at the foot of the western Pyrenees were the sole possession of the chosen female descendant of Celeste Santillán. It took her a few seconds to realize that what she held in her hand was the holographic will signed by Anahí Santillán and witnessed by her husband, Calisto. This appeared to be the original bequest to the properties her grandfather wanted to give away to Eva, the will David said had been lost for decades.

Maité's heart was a beating lump in her throat as she read on.

Henceforth, the designee shall be chosen from the female offspring of Zorione, daughter of Anahí and Calisto, and from her daughters thereafter. Said designee shall take possession of the estate known as the María Celeste in this city of San Sebastián...

The land occupying the foothills of the western Pyrenees, including its waterfall...

Said designee shall not dispose of the land, nor of the estate, for monetary reasons or for gain, nor will she fail to care for and nourish...

On it went, affirming that only a female heir was entitled to the land and to the María Celeste, only a female of the line of Celeste Santillán.

Maité saw the family tree in her mind as clearly as if she were holding it in her hands. Her name was at the very bottom of that tree—she, Maité, was the last living descendant of Celeste Santillán—but as a minor, her grandfather being her legal guardian and only living relative, could manage her affairs however he saw fit.

Thinking Emily would be ready soon, Maité unfolded the second, smaller piece of paper, which had lined the pendant's compartment. She noticed right away the handwriting on this document was different than that of the holographic will. Maité made a fist around the three jewels as she read.

Here lies Basajaun.

The pendant had a name. Maité squeezed it a little tighter and read out loud, "His return will signify the realm may flourish. Look upon us with your favor once again, O Basajaun. May the beating of your heart infuse renewed life to that which has been dormant for years past. O Basajaun."

Maité closed her eyes and folded the paper. *Basajaun*, she repeated inwardly as Emily came into her room.

"What's up?"

"This is the box that Nahia—"

"The good faery," Emily interjected, straightening the twisted sleeves of her shirt as she listened.

"Right. She told me where to find this." Maité handed Emily the bizarre little poem about Basajaun, which Emily examined carefully.

"*Ya llegó el taxi!*" Soledad called from the bottom of the stairs.

"What is this about?" Emily asked, rereading the lines while hurriedly zipping her shorts. "And what is a Basajaun, what's up with that?"

Maité raised one brow significantly while she pulled the pendant from under her shirt.

"Niñas!" Soledad called again, and the two darted out of the room.

"Are those real?" Emily asked breathlessly.

Maité nodded as they hurried down the steps. "I'm sure they are."

"Who names their jewelry?" Emily asked and then answered herself. "Rich people, that's who."

Maité shrugged noncommittally. Basajaun was a riddle; maybe it was no more than an old wedding gift from Calisto to Anahí. But why *did* it have a name? And what about the strange poem? To Maité, the lines seemed more like instructions than anything else.

Soledad told the cab driver where to take them while they climbed into the backseat. Maité and Emily waved to Soledad as they drove off, watching her make the sign of the cross after them.

Emily squeezed Maité's hand, murmuring darkly, "She's blessing us, M, like we're heading into battle or something. Level with me. Is this gonna be dangerous? Was a blessing necessary? I tell you right now, I'm anticipating harsh words, maybe even a tantrum on Eva's part, but that's it."

"That's what I'm expecting too. I might even pitch a tantrum myself if I can't get Mr. Córdoba to side with me. I'm hoping he might be able to at least delay this thing," Maité said, pulling the folded holographic will from the pocket of her cargo pants. She had placed it there before leaving the house and now handed it to Emily.

"OMG!" Emily exclaimed after scanning it from beginning to end.

"What?" Maité jumped.

"I can't believe I forgot to tell you this! Holy sh—"

"Emily!"

"Sorry, M. It's just that I can't believe I forgot."

"Spit it out!"

"My mom sent me an e-mail today—I always check first thing in the morning—actually, she sent it to you and copied me ..."

Maité stiffened with worry. "And?"

"Yesterday she got a call from an attorney—your mom and dad's attorney."

Maité reeled. What could possibly come out of Emily's mouth now? "And?" Maité prompted again.

"Your mom and dad left a last will and testament and besides the normal *will* stuff, there was a section that said my mom has legal custody of you."

Maité gave Emily a startled look as comprehension dawned; her gaze drifted, unseeing, to the scenery outside the car window. "So ..."

"That means you can come home with me. Not that you'd want to at this point, but do you realize what that means? Your grandpa is signing over all this stuff thinking because you're a minor he—"

"But he can't!" Maité interrupted—the unexpected shift in her dilemma gleamed in her gray eyes, "because Aunt V's my legal guardian, and she'll have to approve everything having to do with me." Maité clapped her hands ecstatically. "This is the best news *ever*—and bonus! We're like sisters now!"

Emily grinned as they reached for each other's hand at the same time and held tight to one another—but Maité felt the cool weight of the pendant under her shirt and wondered about it again.

> *His return will signify the realm may flourish.*
> *Look upon us with your favor once again.*
> *O Basajaun.*
> *May the beating of your heart infuse renewed life*
> *To that which has been dormant for years past.*
> *O Basajaun.*

In less than fifteen minutes the driver stopped at the edge of a grand courtyard spreading from the sidewalk to the town hall—a majestic old structure consisting of two towers and a central nave.

Since Soledad had prepaid the fare, the girls hurried out of the car, murmuring a polite gracias and hastening to the main entrance of the building. To reach it, they traversed grassy patches and flowerbeds, rounded an enormous fountain, and sidestepped wooden benches and sculptures. They walked beneath the mammoth portico with iron gates, which stood open for business, and found themselves inside the darkened hull of the building.

They looked down one side and up the other—nothing but pillars and closed doors, presumably leading to various offices housed inside. Lots of artwork graced the walls, elegant sequences done in oils of the progress of San Sebastián over the centuries, each painting illuminated from the top by its own lamp.

"Which way?" Maité asked helplessly, and Emily shrugged.

In no time, however, a man in military uniform approached and asked how he might be of service. The fluttering began in Maité's belly, and, no, it wasn't just the excitement of good news; it was the wings, the bizarre flapping that made things happen. She knew her eyes and her voice were working together to beguile him. She introduced herself as Maité Santillán—the better to liken herself to the heiress described in the document in her pocket—and proceeded to lay out what she needed.

A sort of blissful if not altogether foolish expression spread over the man's face as he gawked at her face, her hair, and the line of her neck. He showed no signs of concern or even curiosity over the numerous nicks on her face or the bulbous bandage Soledad had stuck under her ear.

Emily watched him and gave Maité a triumphant thump on the shoulder when the man offered to walk them to the very office where Mr. Gonzaga's private party was gathered.

"You go, M," Emily whispered, and Maité's fluttering belly gave a joyful leap.

The man rapped twice on the door and opened it without waiting for an answer, and then in his most agreeable voice, while Emily elbowed Maité, he said, "*Perdón por la interrupción—la señorita Maité Santillán y la señorita Emilia—*"

"It's *Emily* Allen!" Maité interrupted, finishing the introduction for him.

Mr. Gonzaga looked stupefied.

Mr. Córdoba appeared hopeful, and the other man, whom Maité assumed was Eva's lawyer, didn't even bother to hide his confusion. But Eva, much to Maité's glee, looked on the verge of bursting blood vessels, or at least cracking a few teeth from grinding her jaw so hard. Eva's eyes seemed intent on stabbing Maité, but Maité did not flinch.

"How did she survive?" Eva muttered, and then, "No matter. She is too late."

Eva's wrathful thoughts, Maité realized, were coming straight into her own brain. But Eva didn't seem to know it.

The thrill Maité felt on account of this discovery popped like a bubble when she took stock of what she'd heard. *She wants to know how I survived last night.* Maité's eyes grew wide with the jolt of the unexpected confirmation. *Eva knows my life was threatened. She knows I survived last night. Because she is—*

The horrible certainty overtook her.

Eva had invaded Maité's dream a couple of nights ago and tried to kill her in her sleep. Her ankle was still bruised from the attack, but that injury no longer stood out thanks to all the other cuts and scrapes.

Nahia's voice came back to her. *You already know her name.*

Although shaken, Maité's gray eyes fixed on Eva's dark ones. She saw the spark of a red flame ignite in them. *God in heaven*, Maité thought. *Eva is Ederne.* The final piece fell into place at last.

The Beautiful One is Eva; Eva is Ederne. The thought circled in her head for a few stunned moments. The swift sense of Eva's thoughts, and the fear Eva might realize at any moment Maité had seen inside her—or worse yet, that Eva might claw at Maité's mind—almost knocked her off balance. Without wasting another second, Maité imagined a stainless-steel, airtight door slam shut in her mind. She glared defiantly at Eva, whose countenance had already recovered from the disappointment of Maité being alive.

Eva went straight to Mr. Gonzaga, her tantalizing smile already in place and aimed at Mr. Gonzaga's common sense.

"Look, darling, your granddaughter has come to congratulate us on the signing." Her voice dripped with hypocrisy, and a look of intense hatred sparked in her eyes as they fell like an anvil on Maité.

The pendant felt warm against Maité's skin; she didn't know if it heated up of its own accord or if it absorbed her warmth, whatever Basajaun did, she held down her mental fort so not a single nonverbal word would penetrate it. She would keep Eva out even if it meant losing the advantage of the woman's incoming secret communications.

Maité turned to Mr. Gonzaga. "Grandfather, this woman is not who she says she is—"

"You will not start your disrespectful nonsense again," he said, as if responding to Eva's nudge at his elbow.

"All her identifying documents are in order," Eva's lawyer offered solicitously, rifling through the neat set of papers in his briefcase.

"I'm sure whatever you prepared for her is in order, but that doesn't mean it's true," Maité said. "Did you know her name isn't even Eva?"

"That is not possible," the self-important little lawyer said. "I have several copies of identifying documents on file. They are all quite legitimate, I assure you."

Mr. Gonzaga grabbed Maité by the elbow and dragged her toward the door. "I have had enough of your disrespect."

"You have to listen to me! I have information that will change everything. It was my—"

Here Maité hesitated. She noticed Emily staring at Eva as if she couldn't help herself, and she caught a glimpse of the faery, and for a moment, she saw something that struck terror in her heart. The rim of Ederne's pupils blazed red again, giving a touch of madness to the satisfied smirk on her face. She was drawing from Emily what she couldn't get out of Maité. "It was my—"

"Fernando," Mr. Córdoba said as his eyes swiveled between Mr. Gonzaga and Maité. "I beg you—"

"There is no need for you to be here," Mr. Gonzaga said to Maité.

"Grandfather, please …"

"There is no use in listening to this child," Eva said in a lofty voice. The flicker of red had left her eyes and Maité thought she must be through picking on Emily. "It is all done now, and it is time for us to celebrate," she cooed, gliding to the other side of Mr. Gonzaga and cleaving to his arm. She motioned to her lawyer, and he at once approached Mr. Córdoba's desk to retrieve the newly signed contract.

"You cannot sign over anything without my consent," Maité declared, and Mr. Córdoba snatched the papers a second before the lawyer could get to them. "I am the rightful heiress, and you have no right to deed away my land."

"You are also a minor," Mr. Gonzaga replied succinctly.

Eva nodded with a smug grin.

"I'm afraid that as a minor, your grandfather can handle your affairs as he sees fit," Mr. Córdoba explained with a note of apology, though he still didn't put the papers in the outstretched hand of Eva's attorney.

"That's not true," Emily piped up. "My mom is Maité's legal guardian."

"What?" Mr. Gonzaga and Mr. Córdoba exclaimed at the same time.

"That's right." Maité raised her chin defiantly as she tried to wriggle free from her grandfather's grip. "My parents, Alba and Sósimo, left a will in which Verónica Allen was awarded legal custody of me."

"This means nothing," Eva said to Mr. Córdoba. "The papers are already signed. And we have no proof that what they say is true." Her hand motioned jerkily toward Maité and Emily. "Where is this will? They don't have it, I am sure, because it does not exist."

"But what *does* exist is a reasonable doubt," Mr. Córdoba remarked coldly. Maité wanted to hug him. "I'm afraid we'll have to put this transaction on hold until we can contact Ms. Allen."

Maité's strength suddenly faltered. A strange phenomenon took place—a quivering of the air, like a transparent sheet someone shakes before laying it over a bed.

Mr. Gonzaga's grasp on Maité hardened, and the look in his eyes froze on her. He seemed to have turned to stone. She looked wildly around and saw the same had happened to Mr. Córdoba, Emily, and the lawyer. They all stood frozen in whatever attitude they were in at the moment the air throbbed. Their eyes glazed in an unblinking stare, and their skin appeared waxen and hard. The entire room clouded over with a red mist emanating from the faery.

This is Ederne's way of getting a little privacy, Maité realized.

Again she struggled to free herself from her grandfather's clawlike grip but found his fingers wouldn't budge.

Her eyes turned turbulently on Ederne's. "I know your name!" Maité shouted, but that was all she could get out. She felt as if she'd tried to swallow a whole apple, and it wedged at the top of her throat.

"You are finished, little girl," the faery hissed, her beautiful face twisting into an unsightly mask of rage.

Maité flared her nostrils, trying to suck in as much air as she could to squelch the terror erupting inside her. *I need to chill*, Maité tried to think reasonably, *can't panic! Would be stupid to panic—just breathe.*

The beating of her heart slowed to a less dangerous rate and the flapping of the enormous wings in her belly seemed to fall into that rhythm. Then came the bizarre power, up from the depths of her solar plexus; it bypassed the apple choking her and shot a message straight into Ederne's head. *I know you can hear me!*

The faery's eyes narrowed, perhaps wondering if she'd heard something or imagined it. "You are no match for me." She shrugged.

Having stifled her panic attack, a sudden clarity struck Maité; she could defeat the faery from the inside out. She had reached David this way, and she'd already broken through with a first message into Ederne's mind. Maité went to work immediately. She imagined the airtight doors to her own mind cracking open and sent forth a declaration of war, hoping the faery would catch the image of Nahia somewhere in there.

I have been given power to command you, Ederne.

Ederne's face registered shock, and her pupils again smoldered as she fixed Maité with a look of pure loathing. The moment's distraction cost the faery, for the lump began to disintegrate in Maité's throat giving her instant relief and the satisfaction of knowing that, however inexperienced or ignorant of faery warfare she might be, she was on the right track.

"That you know my name is nothing!" Ederne spat, and Maité's courage blinked.

Refusing to doubt herself or Nahia, Maité repeated what she had been told in her dream. "I have the power to call you down, faery."

Ederne's triumphant smile said she didn't believe what Maité said. "You are going to suffer a malfunction of some sort," the faery continued, her voice arctic as she rounded on Maité with a measured turn of her shoulder. "Something simple, an internal injury, perhaps. And you're going to collapse."

Maité's eyes narrowed as the faery drew back, her eyes positively ablaze, and Maité knew what came next.

The red mist trapped in the room would gather into itself, commanded by Ederne's silent voice, until the energy spear was fully conjured. Maité could already feel the faery's initial probes like microscopic electric tentacles rummaging through the molecules making up her body. Ederne meant to tamper with her blood vessels, perhaps manipulate them until they clogged.

Everything around Maité seemed to come to a point.

Maité screwed up her courage to face the attack; she knew how it would be—she'd collapse at the point of a spear, as the faery had predicted, and the people in the room would wake from their paralysis to find her dead. Ederne would explain it away as yet another tragic loss and Maité felt certain even an autopsy would show "death by natural causes." Yet the flapping inside her belly made her feel as if she'd soon be airborne, if only her grandfather's fist wasn't holding her on the spot.

The spear hurtled through the air toward Maité; there seemed no escaping the strike.

The blazing spear struck the pendant over her heart and bounced off as if it had hit a granite wall. Maité staggered backward, dazed by the blow but unharmed.

Ederne looked outraged at her own failure. The red haze exploded back into the room and then dissipated into nothing. The others began to come out of their paralyzed state, unaware that several minutes had been stolen from them.

Emily put her arm protectively around Maité's shoulders, "M?" she said, sounding worried. "You're vibrating," she whispered.

Maité nodded. A deep tremor continued to rattle inside her along with her beating heart and the flapping wings in her belly, but Maité couldn't take her eyes off Ederne; she couldn't stop cursing her through the silent link between them.

I'm not like you, you miserable, greedy creature, Maité said. *So I wouldn't dream of killing you, but you will give up your immortality and live out the rest of your life like a human, starting today. No more faery glamour for you. You will stay away from those I love, and I don't ever,* ever *want to see your face again. Your energies will be spent in making up for the lives you took, do you understand me?*

But you are just a human, came Ederne's disbelieving rebuttal. The faery now looked like a wide-eyed bug pinned to a wall. Her head shook jerkily, seeming to negate whatever the voice in her head said.

As the seconds ticked by, the others looked from Eva to Maité, unable to hear the exchange between them but sensing something was amiss.

"Eva? Are you all right?" Mr. Gonzaga said, looking alarmed. "You've gone pale."

You are bound to do my bidding, Maité went on relentlessly. *Nahia, daughter of Oihana, has given the power to me.*

"No!" Eva blurted, but quickly corrected her reply. "I mean, yes, I am fine, darling."

"Are you quite sure?" Mr. Gonzaga insisted, though still not letting go of his granddaughter's wrist.

"Yes, quite," Eva snapped.

It was Maité's turn to probe. She had felt Ederne doing it to her, and she would exercise what she had learned. Maité breathed in and looked inside herself; she picked the strongest of her emotions: pain over the death of her parents, loathing over the senseless death of the faeries and Amets, love for those who stood beside her. Maité now had a sense these feelings were raw energy to be directed, and she intended to do just that.

Pain, loathing, and love streamed into a single current, which Maité visualized coursing through Ederne's body, like a blast of adrenaline. Although she didn't quite formulate it, Maité's underlying desire, the solution to her predicament, was to destroy the collection of brilliant faery cells, which stood out like beacons in Ederne's genetic makeup.

Aided by the power of the flapping wings, Maité pumped destruction into the faery, the words, *You have been caught. You will stop,* were repeated every time a sparkling cell fractured into nonexistence until Ederne sagged, looking broken and incomplete at a cellular level.

Maité stared at her, staggered by what she had caused. Eva had been a faery, passing herself as a human super model in her twenties, and now here stood Ederne, stripped of her faeryness in the space of three minutes, looking like a woman well into her forties.

Maité's knees quaked beneath her. Thankfully, Emily was there to catch her as Mr. Gonzaga released her wrist.

Chapter 44

The bizarre flapping of large wings in Maité's belly settled into a confident glide. She rubbed her sore wrist while surreptitiously scanning the room; very soon they would notice the changes in Eva.

As if directed to do so, Eva coughed and dramatically cleared her throat, like she'd been the one who nearly choked on an apple. All eyes turned to her, and Maité bit her lip to avoid grinning. *She's in for it now*, she thought.

"Oh, this is all nonsense," Eva declared, fluffing her skirt with a series of contrived motions. Maité watched her pause, splay her fingers, and stare at them looking startled.

She knew what had shocked Eva; her skin wasn't as tight as it had been moments before, veins had popped up like cords over the tops of her hands, and Maité wouldn't be surprised if a few age spots had surfaced as well.

Eva folded her fingers into fists and thrusting her chin forward she started clickety-clacking on her high heels back to Mr. Gonzaga's side. "We have a signed transfer, and in a few days, I am sure that custody statement will be proven false."

Maité's eyes flickered to Mr. Córdoba, who stuck the signed papers in a drawer, turned the lock, and pocketed the key, holding Eva's glare. The lawyer a few paces away swallowed hard, as if his mouth had been watering over the papers now locked away.

"This delay is of little consequence," Eva returned, sounding unconcerned. "Fernando, my darling, it is time we left here and we celebrate as we planned."

Maité observed with pleasure how others in the room greeted these words. Eva's lawyer, who still hovered near Mr. Córdoba's desk, eyeballed his client with a wary expression. Mr. Córdoba seemed to have dropped pretenses, and Maité thought it intimidating the way he now examined Eva with open suspicion, as if trying to pinpoint what was wrong with the picture.

Beside Maité, Emily also seemed to be cataloging everyone's attitudes. She longed to explain what had happened, but now was not the time.

Most gratifying of all was her grandfather's reaction—she could almost hear him wondering where Eva's flirtatious, enticing voice had gone. The bewildered frown on Mr. Gonzaga's face told Maité he had noticed the lost musicality and the sudden flatness in the once-throaty voice.

Eva cleared her throat again and fixed an awkward glance on Mr. Gonzaga; she compounded it with an even more awkward smirk, which was nowhere near the seductive pout she was famous for.

"Er, yes, celebrate." Mr. Gonzaga rubbed his chin, looking doubtful. Maité tried to catch his eye but Eva rejoined at once.

"Then please, my darling, let's go. It is so tedious here." Eva giggled, making a show of playfully pulling Mr. Gonzaga toward the door. But either because of his reluctance to be led or because her high heels became too much for her, Eva twisted her ankle and slumped gracelessly to the floor.

"Eva, are you all right?" Mr. Gonzaga asked, at once pulling Eva to her feet.

Emily gave Maité's arm a squeeze. Again she wanted to spill all the details but could do no more than flash a wink at Emily before turning her attention to Eva, whose struggle with the loss of her faery nature and the unexpected weight of her human condition was evident in her flustered demeanor.

"Oh, thank you, darling," Eva said, flashing her most coquettish smile as she sappily looked up at Mr. Gonzaga.

Maité noted her grandfather's unfavorable reaction to Eva's lack of radiance and she experienced a surge of sympathy for his predicament. He was probably questioning how in the world he'd been leashed to this woman for as long as he had. His expression seemed to confirm this, yet Maité knew he was an honorable man and must be steeling himself to keep his word to Eva.

"Yes, well. Emilio ..." Mr. Gonzaga stammered as he addressed Mr. Córdoba, who hadn't moved a muscle to assist Eva but continued to examine her.

Eva fastened herself to Mr. Gonzaga's arm while looking daggers at Maité.

"If there is nothing else for us to do here, I believe we'll be on our way," Mr. Gonzaga announced, looking uneasily at the clumsy woman at his side.

"To celebrate!" Eva declared tunelessly looking around the room as if they should all join in her excitement.

Eva received no such approval, not even from her lawyer.

When their eyes briefly met, Maité shot out with, *You enrapture no one anymore*, and was pleased to see the defeated faery squirm.

Bells seemed to clang inside Maité over Ederne's transformation and the certainty that somehow she, Maité, had caused it. She had stripped the Beautiful One of her powers. The reality of it was clear on everyone's face.

Maité gave Ederne a cold smile and continued to read her body language, for it seemed Ederne could no longer project her thoughts.

Eva's humiliation and frustration seemed to peak; she untangled her arm from Mr. Gonzaga's and with evident rage in her eyes, went straight for Maité, hands like claws, to strangle her.

"You can't do this to me!" Eva screeched.

Maité caught Eva's hands in hers. They struggled, but Eva twisted away from Maité's grasp and managed to land a stinging slap on her cheek, and then several things happened at once.

"Oh, no you don't, lady!" Maité heard Emily say, but was so infuriated herself she didn't wait to see what Emily meant to do.

Mr. Córdoba lifted the receiver on his desk and firmly said, "Send security."

Maité grabbed the lapels of Eva's tailored overcoat, drew her close, and brought her knee forcefully to Eva's abdomen.

Eva doubled over with a breathless groan but recovered almost at once. "You will pay for this, you miserable—" Eva growled, going for Maité's neck once again.

The little lawyer piled his belongings inside his briefcase, apparently seeing the case as closed.

Seeming to come out of his initial shock, Mr. Gonzaga demanded, "Contain yourself, madam!" He reached Eva in two strides and yanked her off Maité.

"Thank you, sir," Emily said. "I was just about to do that."

Breathing fast, Maité watched her grandfather, in a towering temper, almost shake Eva.

The guards burst into the room in answer to Mr. Córdoba's call.

"The papers are signed!" Eva raged, struggling to rid herself from Mr. Gonzaga's iron grip.

"Quit your yelling, lady, or I'll hogtie you in under nine seconds," Emily spat.

"It all belongs to the Santillán family, and that's where everything will stay," Maité said firmly.

Eva's attorney dismissed himself with a quick nod toward Mr. Córdoba and Mr. Gonzaga. He avoided his client's glare as he rushed past her and out the door.

Eva suddenly stopped struggling, and with a disturbing change of tactic, said, "Fernando, darling, you and I need to discuss this calmly. Why don't we go to that little place we love, you know, in Monaco? We can talk this over. After all, we still have our wedding to discuss."

Maité gaped open-mouthed at Eva. Beside her, Emily let out a derisive snort.

Mr. Gonzaga didn't appear to be moved by Eva's plea. "I thought you said we would marry *after* the transfer was effected," he reminded her, and Maité found his sarcastic tone indicative of him seeing right through Eva.

Eva laughed a mirthless laugh, which made her face ghastly to behold. "Darling! I only said that because I was so excited to start work on the resort. And I *so* wanted to refurbish the María Celeste. But that is hardly important now. You know I am insane with love for you. Nothing can come between us, is that not so?" she simpered, trying in vain to inject her voice with the spellbinding timbre she no longer commanded.

Mr. Gonzaga's lips pressed into a thin line. He took a step back from Eva, establishing a proverbial distance between them, "Eva," he said coolly, "I believe your only interest in me had to do with the contract that is now suspended, if not cancelled entirely. I say it is highly improbable we shall have any discussions about marriage."

"Oh, you cannot mean that, darling!"

Maité stepped closer to her grandfather and looked triumphantly at Eva.

"I'm afraid I do," Mr. Gonzaga said, eluding Eva's attempt to clutch his arm. "And now, if you'll excuse me, I need to take my granddaughter home. She and I need to talk about how she came to be hurt like this," he said, casting an anxious glance toward Maité, which caused a shudder of emotion to sweep over her.

"But, Fernando—"

"Enough, Eva," Mr. Gonzaga halted her, though not taking his eyes off Maité.

That's right, Maité thought, *talk to the hand*.

Under her grandfather's caring gaze, Maité felt the loss of a family's love and protection wash over her anew. How she'd missed that bond since the death of her parents. How hopeless it had seemed to ever recover it, yet in a mere three seconds, this stranger—this man she'd despised for various reasons—had become the embodiment of the home she'd lost. She could see her mother's eyes in his. His voice had Alba's flavor. And his blood called out to her.

I am your family, it seemed to say. And she knew it was true; she could feel it. Ederne had no hold on him anymore.

"Beat it, lady!" Emily spat at Eva.

The ex-faery flinched involuntarily. Mr. Gonzaga directed a dismissive glare toward Eva, echoing Emily's request.

Eva drew in her breath and surveyed the room with an air of superiority. Even in the sour face of defeat, she glared disdainfully at all of them and then strode toward the door, wobbling atop her high heels.

"Stay off my property and away from those I love," Maité whispered as Eva passed.

Eva halted for a moment, seeming to consider a response, but in the end resumed her unsteady exit without looking at Maité.

"I recommend sandals," Emily called after her with a snort. "There'll be no more runways for you!"

It was not quite noon when Eva stepped into the sunshine of the square. The press, having acted on what Gio let slip, waited for the goddess of fashion, the epitome of beauty, the sexiest thing to have posed on a Lamborghini to emerge triumphant from the town hall on the arm of her distinguished beau, after having received the gift she named as the price for her hand.

No sooner were the abundantly photographed red tresses glimpsed than the cacophony of reporters jabbering into microphones and the fast clicking of cameras redoubled.

Eva was alone. She looked unsteady.

She waved at her fans, but instead of them rushing toward her, crews lowered microphones, cameramen looked on her with their own eyes rather than through their lenses, and the furious clicking of cameras faded away.

Eva's waving hand froze midmotion.

Gio, who'd been elbowing his way to the front of the crowd, came to a sudden stop. He gasped theatrically and covered his mouth, adopting the general mood of the crowd.

Eva couldn't make out whether it was disbelief or confusion she saw in their faces. It was not rapture; *that* she knew for sure.

She wanted to disappear, or better yet, to show them who she really was. "I am Ederne!" she declared recklessly to the disenchanted crowd. She had meant to shrink to faery-size at the same instant and hover long enough to see their repentant faces—how dare they humiliate her so! But nothing more than a tremor went through Ederne; she had failed to execute even the most basic shape-shift.

A wave of murmuring rose from the paparazzi, and Ederne hissed at them—with a snarl on her face she watched them leave. Her world shook. She felt naked, empty.

You enrapture no one anymore! Maité's words came back to her, and Ederne recalled the sense of ruin she experienced at the wretched girl's hands.

"But she's only a human," Ederne muttered, "she couldn't have!"

Gio was the only one left. With a wild surge of hope, Ederne started toward him, but he turned his back on her and she stopped in her tracks. She watched him go, forced at last to accept the destruction of all that had made her a faery.

Ederne's shoulders sagged in spite of the anger that should've been strong enough to hold her upright.

It was over.

CHAPTER 45

By the time Maité, Emily, and Mr. Gonzaga walked to the sunny courtyard of town hall, Eva had disappeared, as had the media.

Considering all that happened, they were a quiet trio, and Maité reasoned her grandfather and Emily, like her, were mulling over the strange circumstances they had caused, witnessed, and survived.

As Mr. Gonzaga drove, Maité took advantage of the weighty silence in the car to decide what she would say when he asked about her condition. As they passed the manor's main gate, Maité settled on telling a portion of the truth—she felt certain he was nowhere near ready to hear of her discoveries regarding the realm of faery.

Soledad's initial surprise at seeing the girls back in the company of Mr. Gonzaga was replaced with satisfaction when he answered her inquiry with, "No, Eva will not be joining us anytime soon."

Maité gave Soledad a meaningful look as they passed into the dining hall, hinting with a squeeze of her hand that details would come later.

They sat at the table in silence until Soledad finished ladling their soup and left them to their meal.

"It happened on the island of Santa Clara," Maité said to her grandfather. Emily started but Maité quelled her surprise with a swift glance and went on. "We went exploring and I fell into a hole in the ground that turned out to be a deep cave."

"Good Lord, child!" exclaimed Mr. Gonzaga, giving Emily a questioning look.

Emily nodded and quickly took a spoonful of soup.

"It was tough getting out—that's how I got all these nicks and cuts," Maité said, gesturing to the abrasions on her face and neck. "But I didn't break anything."

"Well, it is fortunate David and Emily were there to help you," Mr. Gonzaga said, observing her with an anxious look on his face.

Soledad bustled in with the main course, and Maité and Emily were quick to praise her superb vegetable soup as she set covered platters on the table. Beaming, Soledad headed back to the kitchen with their empty dishes.

When they had helped themselves to the next part of the meal, Maité addressed her grandfather again.

"There's something else." Maité hesitated when Mr. Gonzaga set down his fork and gave her his undivided attention. "Er—I found a compartment in a wall in the attic, here at the house," she stammered.

"Pardon me?"

"Behind a portrait in the attic—Soledad let me go up there to look through the things my mother collected from the María Celeste," Maité explained hastily, "Those things meant a lot to my mom, and Soledad thought I would like to see them." She watched his tension ease into acceptance and the fondness she'd started feeling for him at town hall deepened. Now that he'd been released from the tentacles of the faery, his emotions seemed to surface readily through his facial expressions.

"I wanted to see if there were dates or names behind the paintings on the wall, you know, to identify my ancestors, so I took down a portrait and found a secret compartment. I opened it and there was a box hidden inside. I don't think my mother even knew the compartment was there ..." As the incomplete truth came out of her mouth, sounding too much like a lie, Maité told herself this edited version of the facts was only temporary, that in a few weeks at most, she would be telling him the whole thing.

"Anyway, that's where the will was," she concluded, giving Emily a sharp don't-you-dare-contradict-me look.

Emily's hazel eyes darted to the lump under Maité's shirt where Basajaun rested, she knew it was a hint to tell about the piece of jewelry, but Maité ignored it. She wanted that little riddle for herself, for now.

"That's how I found out that I am the designated heiress, and when I mentioned this to Emily, she told me about my parents' will, and well ..." Maité trailed off, not wanting to remind him that she, through Verónica, had the final word concerning the family's property.

Mr. Gonzaga nodded thoughtfully, and after a moment's pause he said, "I want to apologize to you."

Maité felt an unexpected tightening of her throat. Perhaps it was because of the repentant tone in which he said it, or maybe it was the regretful look she saw in his eyes. Whatever the case, tears welled in her eyes as she gazed with anticipation at her handsome grandfather.

"You arrived here—a complete stranger in this country and this house—a stranger, because I was too proud to make peace with my daughter, even though I knew I was cutting myself off from both your lives. Oh, yes, I knew of your existence through Soledad," he explained when Maité questioned him with her eyes. "But I was too angry to forgive my Alba for going against my wishes, and then when things turned out well for her, I was too proud to accept she had found happiness on her own, and that I did not have a hand in it."

Maité thought he spoke with the air of someone confessing an ugly sin, she could hear the remorse in his voice. Beside her, Emily shifted in her chair and Maité squeezed her hand, understanding how tense this had to be for Emily.

Maité also reflected on her own emotions, which had been pressing on her since Eva's clumsy departure, but now, another realization overtook her; Maité discovered she had a grandfather only eleven days before, and being told she'd have to live with a complete stranger had sickened her. When they met, his preference for Eva and his cold reception only enhanced her dislike. But the bottom line was Maité only had eleven days of turmoil over it, whereas *his* unrest had gone on for almost twenty years—since the day Alba left.

A profound tenderness crept into Maité's heart as she looked at him, his new attitude agreed with her idea of how a grandfather should be.

"I did not ask Alba to forgive me," he said. "And now she is dead; gone from me. I shall never have the opportunity to tell her that I wasted all those years we were apart. I cannot tell her what a beautiful child she had!" His eyes shined with feeling when he looked at Maité, and she briskly wiped away her own tears. Beside her, Emily sniffed loudly.

"I did not ask for her forgiveness," he continued. "I did not even seek the opportunity, but I must beg yours. My behavior before and upon your arrival was unpardonable. I've mistreated you so."

"It wasn't your fault," Maité said, in spite of him shaking his head. An overwhelming desire to embrace him came over her. She leapt from her chair, and he rose from his to receive her.

"Oh, *abuelo*, what happened to my parents wasn't your fault, and I do love you, even though I don't know you very well yet, I *do* love you," she sobbed into his shoulder. Someday she might tell him exactly whose fault it had been, but not today.

Mr. Gonzaga accepted her embrace and held her close. "There, there," he said, smoothing down her hair. "I want to spend the rest of my life getting to know you."

Maité could hear the smile in his voice, which made her hug him tighter in response.

"*Perdón, Sr. Gonzaga, los señores Córdoba están en la biblioteca,*" Soledad said, smiling broadly at them.

David's in the library! Maité's insides did a flip.

"*Gracias* Soledad—please tell Mr. Córdoba and his son I will be right with them."

"Sí, Señor."

Mr. Gonzaga caressed Maité's cheek and said, "I'm sure David is here to see *you*. Why don't we all go into the library?"

"We're right behind you," Maité replied, turning to Emily, who was already tucking in her chair.

"That was intense," Emily whispered as they followed Mr. Gonzaga out of the dining room.

"Isn't he handsome and wonderful?" Maité asked, smiling radiantly.

"I particularly like the fact he's lost that permanent redheaded attachment. Who knew it would be just an outpatient procedure." With a wicked grin, Emily added, "I was hoping for a more prolonged, way bloodier amputation-type thing."

Maité stifled a laugh as her grandfather greeted his guests.

"Emilio," Mr. Gonzaga said, holding out his hand to Mr. Córdoba.

"Buenas tardes, Fernando."

"Señor Gonzaga." David shook hands while looking at Maité. He kissed Emily briskly, and then with his hand on the small of Maité's back, he drew her to him and kissed both her cheeks. "Hello," he whispered.

"I missed you," Maité whispered back.

"Let's go out to the garden and let them talk business," David suggested to the girls.

Maité and Emily hooked their arms in his and they headed outside.

"Don't go too far, Maité," Mr. Córdoba called after her. "I have some papers for you to look at."

"Okay," she said cheerfully.

The three of them walked into the courtyard outside the library. The day's heat rose from the wide pavers in peaceful contrast to the cool afternoon breeze. They sat on cushioned chairs around the wrought-iron table, under the thick foliage of a magnolia tree. David placed a portfolio before them, bulging with papers; he had a most peculiar look on his face.

Soledad set a tray with drinks on the table then clamped Maité's face in her hands. She planted a loud kiss on Maité's forehead before returning to the house. No sooner had the door closed behind Soledad than David jumped straight into what he was obviously dying to share with them.

"So, I'm fairly confident that after today my name will be engraved in the hall of fame of genetic research," he said, tapping his fingers on the portfolio he'd set on the table.

Emily grunted, "Feel free to start over—from the beginning though."

"I'm sorry, I'm just continuing yesterday's conversation, remember? In the car."

Emily nodded. "Yeah, but remember, she wasn't there," she said, jerking her thumb in Maité's direction. "And there's a big chunk of what happened today that I don't know about."

"So what are all those papers?" Maité asked, thrusting her chin toward the portfolio.

"Test results, among other things," he said.

Emily sat up straighter. "You mean from the samples I gave you yesterday?"

"Precisely!"

"So am I an alien?" Emily gushed.

"I'm sorry to disappoint you, but it looks like the only alien here is Maité."

Emily pouted. "Why does all the weird stuff happen to her?"

"What?" Maité asked, startled.

"Do I have news for you!" David grinned.

"What do you mean?"

"Emily gave me DNA samples yesterday—hers ... and yours."

"How? What did you give him?" Maité demanded, suddenly horrified that Emily may have given David her sweaty clothes or something more hideously embarrassing.

"Just your hairbrush," Emily replied innocently.

"Oh," Maité said, relieved. "So what happened?"

"I had them analyzed at my lab of course, and Maité, you have it! You have the dominant gene that disappeared from Monte Perdido," David announced.

"You make it sound like I won the lottery," Maité teased, setting down her frosty glass half-filled with lemonade while he went on excitedly.

"It's a momentous find. This is the gene that has been missing for centuries! I'm positive we'll be able to track down Maité's ancestors to a survivor from the site."

"So now what? Emily shifted in her seat and smirked. "Will you have to do something like a live autopsy? Remove entire limbs for testing? Graft square yards of skin in the name of science?"

"I don't know about yards of skin, maybe just feet. And there will be at least a local anesthetic for the live autopsy," he replied matter-of-factly.

Emily grinned appreciatively, but David cleared his throat seeming to notice Maité hadn't joined in their clinical banter. "We'll have to do a second test to confirm what we've already found. It'll take no more than a prick of the finger, I assure you."

"And if it's confirmed, then what?" Maité asked.

"Then we will go through your family tree and backtrack this thing."

"So does this mean Maité can change her body mass at will and become invisible and all that?" Emily asked, giving Maité an awed look.

"Theoretically, yes. But—" David paused for a moment, looking troubled.

"But what?" Maité urged, imagining herself sprawled under the microscope.

He shook his head. "I just mean—we'll have to do a lot more testing to figure out what it all means. Some of it may not even have to happen in the lab."

"Do you promise to keep it a secret if it turns out my ancestors *were* aliens from other galaxies?" Maité laughed uneasily, not sure how she should react to these developments.

"You have my word," David assured her. "We'll come up with the best way to protect your family from whatever ancestry horrors we discover."

"Unless, of course, it's a really good race of aliens. If that's the case, you'll want to claim the relation," Emily remarked helpfully.

"What are you thinking about?" David asked, catching the distant look on Maité's face.

"I'm thinking about the testing that won't take place in a lab—do you mean some of it can be done right here?" Maité closed her eyes not waiting for a response, but willing every note of her mental voice to reach Emily and David in private—as she had done with Ederne. She knew that the pleasurable flapping in her stomach would come to her aid.

She made it happen; she spoke to them without words, directing her thoughts straight into their minds. Ignoring Emily's paranoid look, she poured out the entire story for them, her dream conversation with Nahia, how Maité failed to find Nahia in Santa Clara. She told them how Ederne had caused the death of her parents and plotted Maité's own death to get the land of the faeries for herself. That Amets gave his life to save Maité. And how she wished she could find Nahia, because she had the answers to all the remaining questions but she was somewhere far away, doing God knew what.

Maité finished showing them her tale and then opened her eyes to the dappled sunlight under the magnolia tree.

David gave a sort of shudder and beamed at her.

Emily's creased brow said she was trying to process the information she'd just received, but rather than one of the many questions Maité expected, Emily jumped up from her chair and said only, "Nahia!," and then raced into the house before Maité could figure out what had gotten into her.

Three minutes later, Emily returned at a trot, clutching a stitch in her side and Xiomara's book against her chest.

"This is the story of Maité's great-great-great grandmother Celeste," Emily said to David between breaths.

"Nahia is one of the main characters in this story," Maité clarified, though she had no idea where Emily was going with this. "Nahia is the daughter of the faery queen."

Emily flipped helpfully through the pages of the manuscript, showing David the few illustrations along with a broad stroke summary of the story Maité had read to her only two nights before.

"It's nothing but scribbles," David said, laying a hand on one of the pages Emily fanned before him.

"Not to Maité," she said significantly.

"What do you mean?"

Emily showed him the warning page, how it acted as a sample taker and scanner. Of course David felt compelled to check it out, but the scribbles didn't turn into words for him, not even after a sixth drop of blood had been absorbed by the parchment. The magnitude of the science-defying discovery passed over his face like a brief shadow. He stared at Maité wide-eyed.

She nodded but couldn't think of a thing to say except, through a poorly concealed smile and a shrug. "Magic." Then, extracting a page from the book she offered it to David and added, "Here's my family tree."

"I remember that," David remarked. "We found it in the attic."

Maité nodded.

David scanned the entries on the page. "I suppose I can read these because they were never part of the book?"

Maité shrugged again; she didn't know the answer.

"And you say that to kill an evil faery, a faery has to have the strong matriarchal blood that only comes from the Queen, and that Nahia has it?"

"That's what she told me, yes," Maité said. "She also said she couldn't kill Ederne herself because they shared blood from the male line. They're cousins."

"So you didn't kill Ederne, but you could have," Emily said, picking up the thread. "You had the power to do it because Nahia told you her name, and because she transferred some of her power to you?"

"But I chose not to," Maité clarified. "Can you picture me killing anybody?"

Emily shook her head. "But you sure put her out of commission; imagine that, all her faery charms gone, just cuz you knew her name."

"From what I heard," David interjected, "Maité also showed a great deal of courage in confronting her."

Maité smiled bashfully at him. "I don't know how courageous I felt—honestly, I think I felt mostly angry so I kept picturing strings of brilliant faery cells exploding, until there were none left."

"Out of commission," Emily repeated and Maité laughed.

"Okay—out of commission."

"Hmmm." David looked up from the family tree he'd been studying.

"What are you *hmm-ing* about?" Emily frowned.

"I'm just wondering about what you told us," he said to Maité. "And I think there's a lot more to it than just knowing the faery's true name. Follow me on this one, because I think there are two possibilities here. It sounds like faeries can communicate telepathically, they can change their size at will, and they can fly. They can also transfer some of those abilities to a chosen human through something called 'cradle gifts.' And thank God for Maité's cradle gift. Otherwise how would I have known to find you in Santa Clara?"

Maité kissed him swiftly but turned to Emily, who seemed to be puzzling over something. "What are *you* hmm-ing about?" Maité asked her, but it was David who answered.

"I don't believe Nahia had the ability to transfer any of her powers to you …"

Maité sat back, affronted. "How else then …"

"Nahia gave you a cradle gift and confirmed Ederne's true name, but she could do no more."

Maité shook her head. "But David, she had to have given me something, because there is no way I could've done what I did without some sort of a transfer of—"

"Maybe what she gave you was something much more valuable than powers for one mission. Maybe what she gave you was a more permanent gift."

She felt the nervous flutter begin again in her belly. Emily looked from Maité to David but didn't say anything.

"I'm lost—what do you mean?" Maité asked.

David spread the parchment on the table and tapped a particular entry with his index finger, "Haven't you noticed?" Maité and Emily leaned over the paper as he explained. "Look at your relative here—Anahí."

"Yes, but what about her?" Maité asked, distracted by Emily's eyes flying over the words and to her irritation, Emily seemed to understand what David pointed out before Maité could even focus on the name.

"OMG!" Emily gasped. "And here I brought this book down just to show off the blood sample thing—"

"I'm not 100 percent sure how you'd spell *Nahia* in the faery world," David took out a pen from his shirt pocket, "But here in the Basque country, we spell it like this." He clicked the pen and wrote a word on a piece of paper from the portfolio: NAHIA. He showed it to Maité and Emily.

Maité stared hard.

"The two names have the same letters," David said helpfully.

"They're just rearranged!" Maité's eyes darted from Anahí on the parchment to Nahia on the paper. "You don't think ..."

"I *do* think," David said, sounding excited. Emily nodded eagerly. "But let me go on—you said one must be inoculated, or something like it, to enter and survive an encounter with a faery. One must be granted faery sight, but you have no recollection of either thing being given to you, correct?"

"That's right," Maité said with a distant nod.

"Yet from what you told us, you weren't in a trance while in the company of faeries. Maybe a little dizzy and overwhelmed, but not out of your mind, like the rest of us would be if exposed to them." Maité nodded again. "You said you asked to be inoculated, but Amets refused you and told you *you were his kind*?"

"Yes, but I told you his mind wasn't quite right—he thought I was Celeste." Things clicked into place suddenly. "You think *Anahí* and *Nahia* are the same person?"

Emily's eyes swiveled from David to Maité. "So that *would* make you one of their kind then?"

"Makes sense to me," David answered cheerfully. "And it would certainly explain a lot of things." He put his hand over Maité's, and giving her an earnest look, he added, "I think Amets was able to take you out of the mountain without transferring any of his ability to you, because your genetic platform allows you to do the shape-shifting yourself, maybe with a little help, or training on the job, as it were." He grinned.

Maité's mind raced with excitement.

"I think what you did to Ederne was not thanks to Nahia letting you borrow her powers or because of the cradle gift she gave you. I think it was because, as Nahia said, you have the matriarchal blood it required," he concluded, raising Maité's hand to his lips and kissing it.

Maité felt dizzy. *Yes. Nahia and Anahí are one in the same. Aintza said Nahia betrayed them all—faeries and humans. Nahia had proposed a union based on a lie. The lie must have been Nahia passing herself off as a human. Why not? Ederne did it! It does make perfect sense. Holy cow! I am related to a faery. And that's probably what Nahia didn't finish telling me in the dream. She also thought I knew about Ederne having killed my parents. She probably expected me to read her mind ... but how was I supposed to know?*

In the midst of trying to sort her scrambled thoughts, Maité caught a glimpse of David and Emily, both apparently in pain. They had their hands clamped over their ears and were staring, horror-struck at Maité.

"What's wrong? Are you okay?" Maité cried, stopping the loud voice of her thoughts.

"You *do* realize you're screaming in our heads!" Emily reproached angrily. "You're gonna have to really fine-tune your ability!"

Looking bewildered, David brought his hands down from his ears.

"It's true, isn't it?" Maité murmured more to herself than to them.

"It looks like a genetic certainty to me," David said, patting the portfolio with his hand and holding up Maité's family tree with other. "Around 1914, the Santillán family became part faery," he declared, raising his glass to Maité.

"You know what this means?" Emily chimed in, her index finger in the air. "Didn't you say your samples from Monte Perdido are way older than 1914?"

"They're from the 1500s," David said vaguely.

"So that means faeries were bathing in the human genetic soup way back then," Emily said with a satisfied nod.

David looked stunned. The words washed over him in visible waves of realization, and Maité had no trouble reading him. She could almost hear his conclusions: the origin of the anomaly that had captured his imagination might be linked to the act of willful faeries that broke their own rules to mix with the human race, altering the genetic makeup of almost an entire town.

David looked from Maité to Emily. "I don't know what to say. We need to do more tests," he said and added almost defensively, "and that's all I'm committing to at this time."

Maité leaned toward him. "This is another reason why I need to find Nahia—all we're doing is speculating. You're assuming I have faery genes because I have the protein strand. But the truth is, you've never looked at faery DNA under your microscope, so there's really nothing to go by or to compare against. And an anagram is not enough evidence." Maité waved the sheet of paper David had written on.

"Yeah, but you have to admit," Emily piped up, "it's an interesting coincidence for a faery and a relative of yours to have the same letters in their names. Besides, the protein strands David's been studying told him enough about what a person could do if she was made up of the stuff, and it's pretty much all the things your faeries can do."

"Yes. So, Maité, while you're using your cradle gift to find Nahia, I'll be running comparison tests between your DNA and the samples we found in Monte Perdido." David seemed eager now. "That will confirm whether your

DNA is a match with those ancient samples. Do you still have the clothes you were wearing during the attacks and flights and all that?"

"Good thinking, David." Emily clapped.

"I do," Maité said. Amets's blood, even Aintza's, might be on Celeste's dress, the one she'd been wearing through the entire ordeal.

David started counting off a to-do list. "I have to map out a strategy to go forward. And I need to apply for funding, and—"

"I can probably help a little with the funding," Maité said, remembering the jewels. "In exchange for absolute secrecy," she added, not knowing where such practical thinking came from, but feeling confident that helping out was crucial right now.

"Absolute secrecy?" David paused for a moment, and then said gravely, "I give you my word, my faery princess."

CHAPTER 46

In the last forty-eight hours, Maité's attempts to locate Nahia through her cradle gift had been fruitless. They only succeeded in transporting her to the place she'd started referring to as "heaven," the place where her parents were.

Maité had a handful of clandestine visions of her parents sleeping peacefully in the shade of a palm grove, and in addition to those, twice she'd had full-length dreams with them. Holding their hands, Maité had strolled on a beautiful beach, telling them about David. Her father seemed to be gradually accepting the idea of his daughter with a serious boyfriend. She told them about the bizarre things that happened to her since their deaths. Twice she opened her eyes in the morning with Alba's joyful laughter ringing in her ears and Sósimo's voice reminding her she would be, first and forever, *his own faery princess*, no matter what David claimed.

Maité wondered how bad it would be to die if it meant joining her parents in the Caribbean paradise they seemed to perpetually roam.

Not too bad, she thought. But the idea of being separated from David prevented her from wishing it wholeheartedly.

Maité and David returned to the manor at sunset after sailing to and around Santa Clara the entire day.

As soon as they opened the double doors, Emily, who had stayed behind to entertain herself with some of David's research papers, raced into the hall shrieking, "M, you are *so* not going to believe this!"

"What happened?" Maité paled.

"Gasp, M, I've been eating my nails, cuticles and all, waiting for you. You don't even know." She wriggled her fingers in Maité's face; her nails were indeed gnawed off.

"Emily, please," David interjected, becoming a little alarmed himself.

"Ay, mi niña, mi niña!" Soledad howled, her words shaking to the rhythm of her bouncing bosom as she too raced over to greet them.

"What is it?" Maité demanded, her heart fluttering with dread.

"Oh, M, we got a telegram," Emily announced, her voice quivering with excitement.

"What? From where?" Maité cried, her mind racing to America and the safety of the Allens.

"From the Virgin Islands!" Emily declared.

Maité's knees trembled, "What?"

David stared at Emily seemingly as bewildered and as much at a loss for words as Maité. "The Virgin Islands?"

Emily nodded frantically, "It arrived about three hours ago. Oh, M, it's the best news!"

Maité visibly sagged with relief at the reassurance of no new tragedy. *But the Virgin Islands?* She couldn't bring herself to even imagine. "Please, Em, tell me what it said." Maité had never seen Emily like this, her hazel eyes sparkled with tears prompting Maité to hope. *Oh, can it be?* "Please, Em, speak!"

"Your parents!" Emily squealed, jumping up and down in place and then spilled the rest of the news with breathless glee. "Three days ago, a deep-sea fishing boat filled with tourists got blown off course and landed on a speck of sand in the Caribbean. They planned to make repairs and leave in the morning. But, oh! M, your parents had seen them arrive and met them on the beach to offer their help and be helped in return—oh, and some dude named Ollie was with them," she added.

This was more than Maité could handle; her legs turned to Jell-O. She slid down the wall and sat on the floor. David and Emily joined her on the tiles. Soledad cried into her apron, leaning against the open door, too overcome to participate in retelling the miraculous news that had thrown them all into a euphoric flurry of activity in Maité and David's absence.

"Your grandfather went to the airport, in person, to arrange their flight directly to San Sebastián," Emily rushed on. "But anyway, they fixed the boat, and of course, the captain took your parents with him to the Virgin Islands, the nearest port. Mr. Gonzaga is also arranging for Gabriel and my parents to fly in. They should all be here for lunch tomorrow!" Emily gushed. "Can you believe it? And oh! M, I actually talked to your mom!"

Maité was speechless, her heart fit to burst. This seemed almost as incomprehensible as their deaths had been. *They've been in a Caribbean island—not heaven,* she could do no more than plead with her eyes for Emily to continue.

Continue Emily did, though the things she said hadn't a hope of anchoring in Maité's whirling mind. The details would have to be repeated over and over again.

The very next day, Alba and Sósimo called Maité from Madrid, and although she'd been unable to say more than several tearful, highly emotional, if not hysterical I-love-yous, she heard their voices—not in a dream, not just in her head, but through a landline. They really were in the same dimension.

As she waited for her parents' flight to land, with her hands and nose pressed against the glass window at the small airport in Fuenterrabía, she began to truly believe. Her grandfather, Emily, Soledad, David, Mr. Córdoba, and even Plinio, all of them waited as one for the miracle to materialize.

The plane landed. The portable flight of stairs was attached to the door of the craft. David put his arm around her waist, and only then did Maité realize that, overcome with emotion as she was, she might have collapsed if he hadn't supported her. "Thank you," she said.

Two, eight, ten passengers deplaned, and then ...

He pointed and whispered, "Is that them?"

Maité's hand sought David's and she squeezed it viselike. "Yes." She couldn't keep her eyes off her parents.

Hand in hand on the tarmac, Alba and Sósimo approached the terminal.

Maité would never remember exactly what they wore, only that for some bizarre reason, she'd expected to see them in a wedding gown and tuxedo. But she shook her head and drank in the sight of them, delighting in it.

Not caring that she wasn't allowed out of the terminal building, Maité hiked her leg over the ropes dividing the waiting area and the arrivals zone and ran out.

Alba and Sósimo paused for only a second as if to make sure it really was their daughter and then they raced to meet her.

Maité lost herself in her parents' embrace.

That night in her bed at the manor, with her parents on either side of her, Maité asked them about their experiences, the things she'd been too frazzled to understand the day before.

Alba went into more detail about what happened. "Captain Spencer, of the damaged fishing boat, told us a light guided them through the storm, a sort of greenish glow he took to be an intermittent safety signal from a rocky point on land. Had it not been for that hopeful glimmer, they would've certainly foundered. Once they got ashore, the fact there was no such safety signal anywhere on the deserted island puzzled them, so that night, while we feasted on crabs, your dad and I told them about our miracle."

Here, Sósimo took up the narrative. Maité snuggled into his brawny arms to listen, her fingers still laced with her mother's.

"A sea-angel guided us." He smiled down at Maité's upturned face. "A beautiful angel with blonde curls streaked with turquoise, inside a sea-green bubble. She stayed with us for hours in the dark water while the storm blew itself out. She made us hold on, ordered us to live, and we could not refuse her." He winked at Maité. "She was very bossy; she made me think of your mother!"

Maité grinned, wondering if he had any idea how accurate his observation was. The sea-angel sounded like none other than Nahia, and if that was the case, and if David's theory was correct, of course Alba might have inherited a little of the faery's temperament, like Maité had.

"When at last the angry sea calmed down, she guided us to the island, and once there, to fresh water and to a less windy part of the island so we could recover." Alba said.

"And she stayed with you the whole time?" Maité asked, bewildered.

"She wasn't always in sight," her mother replied. "But we knew she was around."

That's where you were, Nahia. That's why you couldn't be with me ... Maité looked from her mother to her father, who, for all practical purposes, had returned from the dead. Whatever resentment she may have felt over Nahia not being there when Maité most needed her was forgiven.

"Good night, sweet girl." Alba kissed her cheek. Sósimo had already given her a hearty scrunch and stood at the door, waiting for his wife.

"I love you both so much," Maité said.

"We love you more," her parents replied as they always had in years past.

The door closed behind them, and Maité smiled.

Now this is a proper faery tale. She sighed.

CHAPTER 47

Seven years later

The festivities at the spectacularly refurbished María Celeste died down.

All the improvements and repairs, which Maité envisioned the afternoon when she first arrived in the Basque country, had been brought to magnificent fulfillment by the newly established firm of Bottini & Santillán, of which Sósimo and Mr. Gonzaga were the main shareholders. Maité had gotten her architectural degree, and after a one-year internship with the firm, became a junior partner and took on the massive remodeling of the María Celeste as her first professional project.

The inaugural feast, for the christening of Maité's and David's baby, was a smashing success. San Sebastián's morning papers would undoubtedly say so, as several guests were high-profile editors of the local media.

But all was quiet now within the mansion.

Her parents, who had arrived the week before, were out with Verónica and Michael as the ladies wanted to showcase their hometown to their husbands.

Mr. Gonzaga, accompanied by Mr. Córdoba, had returned to Santillán manor, where Soledad, having relinquished her hold on the baby she doted over like a grandmother, left earlier to fix a nightcap for the two bachelors.

Emily and her husband of one year, Finn Hayes, chatted pleasantly with David around the pool table on the second floor, waiting for Maité, who had taken the baby to bed.

Outside, the heat of the day lingered in the air, cooled by the breeze of the lazy flowing Urumea River across the avenue.

On the third floor of the María Celeste, in the nursery, Maité gazed fondly upon her three-month-old daughter, Aintza, sleeping soundly in her crib. The sea-green chiffon panels on their heavy curtain rod ballooned in the breeze and the song of the river wafted about the room soothingly. Aintza slept now, exhausted from all the attention and activity of the day.

Maité kissed her baby's forehead once more and turned to leave, but as she reached the door, something caught her eye.

A shimmering movement—a twinkle of light—perhaps a fleeting reflection from a car below caught in the mirror above the armoire. Maité looked at the baby again to make sure all was well.

A hooded figure hovered near the crib—an intruder? But Maité's instincts told her no danger had come into her home.

Not from this world, anyway, she thought. Maité didn't call for help; instead she braced herself to receive the visitor she'd been waiting for.

A strange sort of singsong echo filled the air while something like white confetti floated about her baby. Maité didn't dare blink. From within the folds of the hood drifted a series of whispered words in the Basque language Maité partially understood by now. She reminded herself to breathe, not wanting to miss an instant. A cradle gift was being bestowed.

I knew you'd come back! The thought issued out of Maité, and she hoped with all her might it would reach the intended target: Nahia.

It did. Through her luminous aquamarine eyes, the faery peered at her, pulling back the hood of her cloak, which released the turquoise-streaked curls Maité knew would be there.

"Maité?" David startled her, coming from behind. His arms encircled her waist, and he kissed her neck. In her ear he whispered, "Is she asleep?"

"She is," Maité replied, tempted to turn and kiss his lips.

"Then are we ready?" He nuzzled her below the ear, unable to see the foot-tall faery hovering above the crib.

"I'll be down in just a minute," she said and then kissed him back and watched him longingly as he tiptoed out of the room. He hadn't noticed a thing.

Faery sight is a gift, Maité thought—or was reminded by Nahia; she couldn't be sure.

David had been in her life for seven years now—two of which they'd been husband and wife. Even now she felt the same palpitations she experienced on the day she first set eyes on him.

"Celeste was no different," the melodic voice said. "If Etienne was anywhere near, she had eyes for no one else. Of course, it might be just a human condition ..." the faery mused. "But no. I too loved like this—once."

One moment Nahia hovered over the crib, and in the next she shifted to human height and stood only inches from Maité.

They were so close Maité could feel the faery's flowery breath on her face.

"Nahia!" Maité sighed. "Where have you been all this time?" She tried to whisper so as to not wake the baby, but her words still came out reproachful. "It's been years, and I haven't heard from you, or seen so much as a—"

The faery gave Maité a knowing smile glancing toward the door through which David had left. Then, looking at Maité's expectant face, Nahia said, "Let's you and I talk."

Maité had long been waiting for this; the thrill of anticipation felt excruciating, but she managed to catch her breath and stammered, "Now?"

"Yes," Nahia replied simply. "Let's go back to the woods where it all began."

Maité's heart raced. *Surely you can't schedule a later appointment or a conference call with a faery. But what about David and Emily?* For a fleeting moment, she felt remorse. David waited downstairs with Emily and Finn. They'd arrived two days before for Aintza's christening, and with all the last minute details before the party, Maité hardly had time to be a hostess.

Em's my baby's godmother, for crying out loud!

Having caught Maité's thought, Nahia gave her an impish grin as she said, "But *I* am her faery godmother."

Nahia's eyes flicked down to Basajaun, which rested in plain view over Maité's breast. But the gesture was brief as lightning and lost on Maité, as her indecision between staying and leaving dissolved into silent laughter. The flapping of wings in her belly had begun. The thrilling sensation of her body turning into liquid took over, and she welcomed the feeling of being poured into a tiny bottle, a reduced version of herself.

Unable to resist, she let out a long whoop then cringed, knowing it would wake up the baby and alert David and Emily downstairs through the baby monitor.

Nahia clasped Maité's hand and they shot out the open window into the starlit sky.

Aintza cried; David raced back up the stairs with Emily and Finn close behind.

Maité laughed out loud, incapable of containing her excitement. Looking back to the open window, she called out, "I won't be long." She knew her voice would dissipate in the breeze before a note of it reached them. Her exhilaration was such she couldn't bring herself to worry or regret.

David stood at the open window, and Maité locked eyes with him. *I'll explain later, in a dream,* she told him using the silent voice of her mind. *Take care of our baby girl,* she added as she turned away.

Nahia's hand held tight to Maité as they made a revolution around Santa Clara Island and then shot eastward toward the mountains.

The sweet, crisp alpine scent soon replaced the humid, salty air.

Presently, all answers would be hers.

Basajaun felt cool against Maité's skin; Nahia's hand felt warm and reassuring, palm to palm.

FIN—AZKEN

THE END ... More to come with, Nahia.

www.ingramcontent.com/pod-product-compliance
Lightning Source LLC
Chambersburg PA
CBHW020959120726
47905CB00009B/2767